THE
SUMMER
QUEEN

THE BURIED AND THE BOUND TRILOGY

THE
SUMMER
QUEEN

ROCHELLE HASSAN

ROARING BROOK PRESS

NEW YORK

Published by Roaring Brook Press
Roaring Brook Press is a division of Holtzbrinck Publishing Holdings
Limited Partnership
120 Broadway, New York, NY 10271 • fiercereads.com

Our books may be purchased in bulk for promotional, educational, or
business use. Please contact your local bookseller or the Macmillan Corporate
and Premium Sales Department at (800) 221-7945 ext. 5442 or by email at
MacmillanSpecialMarkets@macmillan.com.

Library of Congress Cataloging-in-Publication Data is available.

First edition, 2024
Book design by Samira Iravani
Printed in the United States of America

ISBN 978-1-250-82225-3 (hardcover)
1   3   5   7   9   10   8   6   4   2

ISBN 978-1-250-35834-9 (OwlCrate edition)
1   3   5   7   9   10   8   6   4   2

For those of you walking a dark and thorny path,
either by choice or by chance.

May good fortune be your companion.

CHAPTER 1

HAZEL USUALLY LEFT after midnight.

She snuck out the back door or through her bedroom window, even though she hadn't figured out how to free her wings from the glamour on purpose yet. She just climbed down the side of the house like a frizzy-haired, pajama-clad Catwoman. In her backpack she carried a thermos of chai, because the wind sprites liked the smell, and empty mason jars to catch the lesser fairies. She always let them go before she came back home; she just wanted to talk to them. Not very many of the borderland fae were willing to talk back. Most of them were afraid of Hazel and her kind.

His flashlight excavated a path through the forest. The thought of Hazel alone out here chilled him all the way to the core.

"You still there?" Leo whispered, knowing the answer but needing to hear it anyway.

"Right behind you," Tristan said. When he wasn't speaking, he was a ghost. He made no sound. Not his breathing, not his footsteps. It could've just been Leo and the moths staggering in and out of his light.

In June, the woods smelled of berries, smoke, and impending rain.

The bangs and pops of not-too-distant fireworks resounded through the night; someone was setting them off in St. Sithney's Park, so they went off almost right above their heads, bathing the forest in flashes of blue and red. Typical Blackthorn; Christmas fairs lasted weeks, Halloween was two months long, and Fourth of July fireworks began on the first day of summer.

"You could've sent the hound with me and gone back to bed," Leo said guiltily. "You have an early shift."

It was Tristan's blækhounds that alerted them whenever Hazel slipped away. They were supernatural wolflike creatures, and about as similar to actual dogs as a grizzly was to a Care Bear. The hound scouted ahead of them now, tracking her by scent and relaying what it learned to Tristan through their magical link.

"Are you saying you prefer the hound's company to mine?" Tristan said. "I'm insulted."

Leo laughed under his breath. "I'm saying it would be nice if one of us got to sleep through the night every now and then. Might as well be you."

"We'll take turns and exchange notes later. Between the two of us we'll have one whole functional human being." A sharp intake of breath punctuated the words. "I think we're close."

Leo glanced at him. He looked desaturated and blurry outside the reach of Leo's flashlight, like a smudged charcoal drawing, and his eyes had gone dreamy as he lost himself briefly in the hound's consciousness.

"You found her?" Leo asked.

"No, but her scent got stronger. Do you hear that?"

It took another minute before he picked up what Tristan had: music, voices, the crackle of a fire. They'd reached the campgrounds. A small crowd had gathered there—most likely students from the community college nearby. And he'd bet their friends were the ones responsible for the fireworks. They had tents set up and a bonfire that had grown higher than was probably safe, its flames leaping up seven or eight feet tall. Top 40 music blared out of someone's speakers, and a couple of coolers were open, raided of their contents so that only soupy, half-melted ice remained.

"She's *here*?" Leo said, dismayed.

"Here, or close," Tristan said.

Jesus. Was this the next phase of Hazel's identity crisis? Crashing college parties at the advanced age of thirteen? A few months ago, he'd have laughed at the idea. Hazel still had a bedtime. Her friends were Girl Scouts and honor roll kids. She wouldn't so much as sneak into an R-rated movie, let alone crash a party. But everything was different for her now. Normally, she would be spending the summer away at camp or having sleepovers. But ever since the hag had torn the glamour off her, it was . . . glitching. It kept slipping, showing glimpses of her fairy features. So there wouldn't be any overnight trips for her this summer. And based on what little she said when he managed to get her to talk about it, her friends didn't get why she didn't want to hang out with them anymore, so they'd just. Stopped texting her.

They split up to search, since Tristan still didn't trust the hounds near a crowd. Tristan would make a loop around the perimeter of the campgrounds, where, if she'd struck out in a different direction, the hound might pick up her scent again. Meanwhile, Leo wove past drunkenly dancing couples and a group of frat guys playing beer pong using a fallen, half-rotted tree in place of a table. The bonfire was so bright that the sky was black, except for when the fireworks went off. The air was thick with about ten different types of smoke: the spicy-sweetness of the bonfire, the acrid tang coming off the sparklers someone had lit, the bitter haze of cigarettes and weed. Hazel wasn't by the speakers; she wasn't by the fire; she wasn't among the small huddles of people trying to talk over the music, arms slung over each other's shoulders and elbows bumping together.

He'd almost reached the edge of the crowd and was steadily losing hope when a girl wandered past him, and his hand caught her shoulder instinctively.

"Shit, sorry," he said, letting go. "I thought you were someone else."

In the play of firelight, something in the girl's features had reminded him of Hazel. But it wasn't her. She was old enough to drink, for one thing. Her skin was dusted with specks of brown and white, like vitiligo spots mixed in with freckles, under curls that might have been blond—it was hard to tell in this light. She wore an oversized denim jacket and a beanie pulled low over her ears, which struck him as a little odd; he could feel the warmth of the fire all the way from here.

"I don't know you," she observed, tilting her head. Another round of fireworks went off with a bang; her eyes reflected their colors, shining liquid-like until the sparks fizzled away.

"Yeah, no, I don't know anyone here. I'm just looking for my sister." He'd shoved his hands in his pockets so that he'd take a second to think next time before he went around grabbing innocent strangers. "You haven't seen a little kid running around, have you?"

"I'm afraid not," she said. "But I could help you look for her."

He shook his head. He didn't know what state Hazel's glamour was in right now, if it was a good night or not. If a stranger saw her with pointy ears—even a drunk stranger who'd probably tell themselves they'd imagined it—Hazel would flip. Less because she was

LEO

worried about being identified as something other than human, and more because she was embarrassed about the way she looked as a fairy. *Weird*, she said. *Like an alien.*

"It's all right. I don't wanna keep you," he told her.

"If you're sure." She held out a red Solo cup. "Here. You might as well have a drink."

"No, thanks. I'm driving."

"Are you quite certain?" Her voice was sweet, almost childishly innocent, and he was tempted to take the drink just to humor her.

"Maybe another time," he said. "You all go to BCC?"

Blackthorn Community College. That was the closest one, and where Leo was most likely headed. He used to have vague thoughts about going out of state, but he'd nuked his own grades a couple of years back and probably couldn't swing a scholarship anymore.

"No, we're from out of town." She scratched idly at a pinkish scar above the collar of her jacket, her slim fingers tipped with black nail polish. "North of here."

"What, like Boston?"

The wind must have changed, because the fire gave a gusty roar, coughing out ash and sparks. They swept through the campground, little swirling specks of red and gold that mirrored the fireworks overhead. The smoke made his eyes water; the crowd was a raucous blur, and the girl a luminous, grinning, dark-eyed shape that bore only a passing resemblance to a person. He blinked until his vision cleared, and she was just a pretty girl again.

"Not quite," she was saying. "Where we're from doesn't have a name. It's in the countryside. You'd be welcome to visit, if you ever wanted."

"Thanks," he said distractedly. "Anyway, I'd better . . ."

"Of course. Go find that wayward sister of yours." She lifted her cup in a mock toast. "If you change your mind about that drink, you know where to find me."

He hadn't gone very far before Tristan caught up with him.

"I don't think she's here anymore. We just missed her," Tristan said, his face flushed from the heat of the fire and his white-blond hair in disarray, as if he'd run his fingers through it in frustration. "Come on."

Leo glanced over his shoulder as they left the bonfire party behind. Mostly their departure went as unnoticed as their arrival had, but a handful of people watched them go, shadowed faces turned toward them and eyes glinting over sparklers that burned slowly down to charcoal nubs. He rubbed the back of his neck to ward off the inexplicable shivers.

Soon, the party disappeared behind them as if it had never been. Leo pulled out his flashlight again. But they hadn't gotten far before Hazel's high, trembling voice reached them:

"Just leave me alone," she was saying. "I'm a fairy, and if you try to hurt me, I'll—I'll—I'll curse you!"

"Yes, I can see you quite clearly through that fading glamour of yours," someone said. His words had a drone to them like the hum of an AC unit, a disquieting buzz in the back of Leo's mind. "Falling asleep in a place like this, you should count yourself lucky it was only I who found you."

"I wasn't asleep. I j-just sat down to rest."

"Fairy dreams," said the stranger, "are potent. Or was it only a daydream that I sensed?"

Leo raced ahead and broke into a small clearing, leaving Tristan to catch up a moment later. Instantly, Hazel crashed into his side. Sure, *now* she was happy to see him. He wrapped an arm around her shoulders, looking for the stranger, but there was—no one?

Then it came again, mechanical and low, the vocal equivalent of white noise: "I wondered when I'd meet the famed hag-slayers."

Leo tried to find the speaker, and couldn't. His eyes slid away. His mind wandered. He fixed his gaze instead on a spot slightly to the figure's left and watched him through his peripheral vision. The stranger was humanoid, but not human—too thin and too tall, with black eyes pierced by white, needlepoint pupils.

A sandman. The slow-building dread that had festered inside him all night hardened into something hooklike, piercing him and sinking deep.

"How do you know about that?" Leo asked, to buy time.

They'd caught a sandman once at Towne High. It had imprisoned a group of missing kids in an enchanted sleep, feeding off them, like a vampire that drank dreams. They'd gotten rid of it, but it was a close call, even though they'd come prepared and had the element of surprise on their side. Neither of those things was true now.

"Who doesn't?" the sandman asked. "Three humans went into a hag's den, and by night's end, they were alive and the hag was dead."

Leo didn't like having a *reputation* in Elphame.

"If you know that," Tristan said, "then you know you're better off leaving us alone."

The hound that had been tracking Hazel unsheathed itself from the shadows. It was big enough to carry two people on its back, and had a thick coat of black fur that was hot to the touch, like coal freshly pulled from a fire. It moved so lightly and fluidly it might have been a cinder construct, but as it circled the stranger, its growl resonated in Leo's chest.

He saw the sandman's smile from the corner of his eye, and the wave of a long-fingered hand. The hound's snarls cut away as abruptly as a television being switched off. It wobbled on its over-sized paws, panted through its bared teeth, and collapsed. If it hadn't snuffled softly, Leo would've worried it was dead—but the hounds couldn't die, and this one was only asleep, already deep into a dream.

Hazel shrank behind him. Tristan shook his head once, sharply, a hand rising to rub at his eyes. He felt what the hounds did. Leo's mouth went dry at the thought that Tristan might fall asleep, too. That he could somehow catch drowsiness from the hound like an infectious disease. Telepathic rabies. And then Hazel would only have Leo to protect her.

"Tris," he breathed. "You good?"

"I didn't even know they could sleep," Tristan murmured. "I can't wake it up."

"Should I put you to sleep, too?" asked the sandman, in his slow, ponderous drawl. "There are those who would reward me hand-somely for the little fairy's return."

Leo pictured the sandman spiriting Hazel away and offering her to the Fair Folk, who existed in his mind only as mythic, faceless figures that presided over some faraway land. The borderland fae talked about them like they were gods—mercurial and unspeakably powerful.

"Let me, uh—let me make a bargain with you," he said.

The sandman's teeth, when he smiled, were as black as his eyes. "What kind of bargain?"

There were certain rules of engagement by which you had to abide if you wanted to walk away unscathed from an encounter with the borderland fae. Some of those rules were more like commandments, divinely ordained:

Trespass is forbidden.

Retaliation is justice.

Thieves and oath breakers must be punished.

And everything—absolutely everything—has a price.

That was where things got complicated. There was no common currency he could trade with. He couldn't walk into a bank and exchange dollars for solid gold coins or bills inscribed with hermetic runes, a fixed quantity of which any being—from a sprite to a siren— would accept as payment for Hazel's life. Many of the borderland fae could be paid in shiny trinkets, but he'd only embarrass himself—or, worse, cause offense—if he offered a pixie's token to a sandman.

"What do you want?" Leo asked.

"Allow me to take a dream from your mind." The hum of the sand-man's voice should have been terrible, but it was soothing, like a lullaby. "A favored dream. A recurring one, or a memory you revisit often in your sleep. Call it to your mind, and I will siphon it away."

Of all the things he could've asked for. Of all the times he could've asked for it.

The hook in Leo's gut gave a yank; he felt cut open.

"Take one of my dreams," Tristan said quickly, and, not for the first time, Leo was both shamed and bolstered by his steadfast bravery.

"No," Leo told him under his breath. "I've got this one."

"My collection is not lacking in nightmares," the sandman said, dismissing Tristan before he could argue.

Leo opened his mouth to accept the sandman's terms—

A second flashlight cut across the clearing.

"Then make your deal with me instead."

Aziza had caught up with them. The summer humidity had made her untameable curls double in size. She wore a pair of torn denim shorts, and her legs were covered in scratches, old and new, from shoving through brambles. Her backpack was slung over her

shoulder, her lit-up phone in her left hand; the right hung motionless at her side.

She didn't know this about herself—it wasn't the sort of thing you
could know unless you saw it from the outside—but when Aziza
was calling on her abilities as a hedgewitch, there was this gravity
to her. Like she could pull moons out of orbit with a single, pointed
glare.

She was his best friend in the world, and the last person he wanted
to intervene on his behalf.

"Zee, no—I can—" he protested.

"Make your offer, then, gatewalker." The sandman sounded
pleased to see her.

"A dream of my mother," she said firmly. "In exchange for the
fairy's safety. You will not harm her, mislead her, steal from her, or
enlist another to do the same in your place. Now and forever."

Leo never would've thought to add all of that. He felt a surge of
gratitude for Aziza's help—gratitude, and guilt. He was supposed
to be Aziza's friend. Her covenmate. Not another hapless human
she had to rescue from fae mischief. And while she'd never been
sentimental about her parents, he couldn't help but think even a single dream of someone you were never going to see again was a steep
price to pay.

The sandman lapsed into a crocodilian silence: predatory and
motionless, except for a slow blink.

"One dream is hardly a fair price for an eternal promise," he countered. "I will take every dream of your mother. Now and forever."

"Wait—" Leo said, Hazel's grip on his shirt falling away as he
took a few faltering steps forward. He couldn't let Aziza do this.

But Aziza didn't miss a beat. "Deal," she responded, and she was
across the clearing before Leo could say another word to stop her.

The sandman touched a finger to her forehead and hummed thoughtfully, as if he'd come across a witty line in a book. Leo didn't know exactly what the sandman did, how a dream—how past and future dreams were extracted from a person's mind. But something happened. It was like he nodded off and then jerked awake again. He felt groggy and light-headed; when the fog cleared, the sandman was gone, and so, too, was the memory of what he had looked like.

THEY'D JUST PULLED up to Aziza's place when Hazel broke the silence by bursting into tears. Loud tears. Snotty, full-on, face-screwed-up weeping.

"It's going to be okay," he began, at the same time that Hazel choked out:

"My friends—"

"Huh?" he said, intelligently.

"All my friends got their periods already except me!" she sobbed.

Aziza's eyes met Leo's in the rearview mirror, wide with alarm. Tristan studied the dashboard unblinkingly.

"I thought mine—was just late—but it's not—is it?" Hazel said, through hitching gasps. She pulled up her knees and buried her face in her arms. "It's because I'm a fairy. I'm never getting my period."

"No, that doesn't make sense, not unless they—" He stopped himself, barely, before he could say *lay eggs* and make this night even more excruciating for everyone than it already was. "Zee? Do fairies get periods?"

Aziza shot him a look that said, *how the fuck am I supposed to know that?*

Not the sort of information she'd ever deemed necessary for her bestiary, then. Or thought to ask one of her informants about. For the past few months, Aziza had been bribing the pixies with the usual—Jolly Ranchers, rhinestones, polished seashells—for information that might help Hazel. What she'd learned so far hadn't been promising. Fairies lived in secluded communities hidden deep in Elphame, usually led by a monarch. But a fairy raised in the human world would be an outsider. Maybe even worth tormenting with the sort of mind-bending illusions, compulsions, and curses they used—as either sick entertainment or vengeance for obscure slights—on any human unlucky enough to stray into their paths.

Hazel somehow found it within herself to cry even harder.

"Sometimes my wings pop out at night and I can't sleep on my back. I have to wear a hat all the time in case my ears get pointy. The last time I saw her, Leah Kim asked if I was sick because she thought I looked *green!*" The tips of Hazel's ears were, in fact, starting to poke through her hair. He willed her not to notice. "What am I supposed to do?"

"I know," Tristan said, softly. "It's hard to find out you're not the person you thought you were."

Leo's heart constricted in his chest. The car was quiet except for the sound of Hazel's wet, broken breathing. She rested her cheek against her knee and stared out the window, the picture of desolation. Aziza slipped out of the car with a quiet *good night* and a glance at Leo—eyebrows raised, a slight twist to her mouth, a look that said, *you're okay.* Not *are you okay?* But an assurance, a belief, and an insistence that he was. He exhaled, slow, and nodded.

As she opened her gate and crossed into the safety of her grandfather's wards, he dashed off a text:

thanks. you didn't have to do that.

Eventually Aziza would get sick of bailing him out of trouble. If not this time, then maybe next time.

She checked her phone as she got to the door and paused there; he read the exasperated humor in the tilt of her head as she sent back:

no apologies and no thank yous. it's in the coven blackthorn code of conduct.

Not this time, then.

The knot in his chest loosened. He pulled away from the curb and headed home.

Hazel went straight to her room. Spot—their dad's poltergeist—rattled the picture frames by the staircase, but she didn't say hello to him, even though she must have known he'd open her bedroom window during a downpour later in retribution.

Leo locked the front door and leaned against it. He could've passed out right there. Tristan tugged his boots off and lined them up by the wall, giving Leo a moment to collect himself.

"Going to bed?" Leo asked.

"No point."

He was right; it would be light out soon. They ended up on the couch, sharing Leo's headphones and watching music videos while the sun rose. Tristan's shoulder was a warm pressure against his. It wasn't the first time they'd kept each other company like this. Sometimes Leo would wander downstairs when he couldn't sleep and find Tristan there already. Leo hadn't known Tristan all that well when he'd moved him into his house; he'd just figured that once you'd almost died fighting monsters with someone, living with them should be a breeze. And it was. Behind his guarded exterior, Tristan was, secretly, deeply empathetic and kind. He was incredibly good with Hazel; sometimes, even when she didn't want to talk to anyone else, she would still talk to Tristan. He was a talented artist, which Leo hadn't expected from the boy he'd once seen respond to a nip from his hound by biting it back. And Leo had slowly come to realize that, for someone who had been hurt and let down by so many people he should have been able to trust, Tristan seemed all too willing to trust Leo without reservation.

Leo couldn't stop himself from sneaking glances at him now. He'd dozed off, chin almost touching his collar and tousled hair brushing into his face. His hands—graceful, clever hands—were curled in his lap. His breathing was slow and even, lulling Leo into a state of half sleep, too. The music jangled in Leo's ear, a song he'd heard a million times, but if you'd asked him just then, he couldn't have named it. He probably couldn't have named any song he'd heard ever.

Okay. So he had kind of a crush.

It was nice. Harmless. Easy like nothing else was easy, lately. He wasn't planning to do anything about it. He couldn't, even if he'd wanted to. Firstly because Tristan lived with him now, and he wasn't going to risk making things awkward when Tristan had nowhere else to go.

And secondly, because Leo already had someone.

Technically.

He just didn't know who.

Hazel was a changeling; her mother, an enchantress, had kidnapped a human baby from Leo's family and left Hazel disguised in her place. But Leo's parents had caught on. When the enchantress returned to take her changeling daughter back—and returned empty-handed, as human children taken to Elphame usually died there—Leo's mom

LEO

had killed her. With her dying breath, the enchantress had cursed his whole family. Leo's curse was this: He would meet his true love young, but forget who they were—losing all his memories of them, including any knowledge of their identity—the day he turned sixteen. His true love would be *lost to him*, according to the words of the curse, and *taken from his reach*. That word, *taken*, it scared him. Fairytales were full of humans who got spirited away to Elphame and met with horrifying fates. Had he, just by loving someone, doomed them to be turned into sea-foam or waste away in the dungeon of a glass castle?

Sounded ridiculous when he thought about it like that. But so did his parents' curses—Mom vomiting toads whenever she tried to speak and Dad being haunted by a disembodied force of chaos— and those were undeniably real.

A selkie had once told him that the victim of a curse had the power to break it. He just had to find the loophole.

But there was one place he was guaranteed to see his true love, and that was every single night in his dreams. He could never remember the dreams, but he knew he'd dreamed of his true love because of how he felt after. The helpless grief of missing someone who should've been there, but wasn't. The knots of frustration that twisted inside him whenever the curse held a memory just barely out of his reach, like a lyric from a song he'd heard once a long time ago. An unbalanced, disoriented sensation, like his hand had reached out to grasp the rung of a ladder and closed on empty air. A lingering warmth in his chest, like he'd just spent a long time being held tightly by someone who cared for him. It was the worst way to wake up, but he'd found a kind of triumph in it, too, because the dreams left impressions. Left tiny snatches of images and feelings like a breadcrumb trail. They used to sneak out to see each other, he thought.

Late-night texts and someone zipping up his hoodie for him because he'd run out the door without bothering. Hands riffling through blank pages, a notebook maybe, passing it to him, and he'd fit his palms over where the cover was still warm from their touch. The smell of sunscreen, and they'd wandered away from their group so they could be alone and let the crashing of the waves cover their voices. A knee bumping into his under the table and every muscle in his body tightened as he suppressed the reflex to lean closer.

He didn't know anything about the person in his dreams. What they looked like, what they sounded like, how old they were. But he knew they had loved him back—he *felt* it, with such certainty it filled every part of his dreams and clung to him after they faded, like fingerprints smudging the inside of a glass. They had looked out for him, worried about him, laughed with him, walked side by side with him, confided in him. And they were gone, and part of Leo was gone, too.

These were the dreams that had leapt to the front of his mind when the sandman had made his demand—and the ones he would have lost if he'd managed to go through with the bargain. He was sure of it.

And maybe it wouldn't have mattered. These were dreams, not memories, or else the curse would've wiped them away, too. But they were so vivid. Not true memories, but maybe something close: a composite of real moments, a tracing made by his imagination, a fiction wrapped around a seed of truth.

He had the power to break the curse. Maybe this was how. By being patient. By being devoted. By being *true*.

But devotion hurt. In comparison, his silly crush on Tristan was a relief. It was nice to just like someone and not have it mean anything more than that. His true love wouldn't begrudge him this brief respite from missing them.

A sound upstairs made Tristan flinch, and then he was awake.

"What was that?" he said, voice hoarse.

"Just my dad, I think," Leo whispered soothingly, trying to let him sleep a little longer.

Tristan sat up and tugged the earbud out. "I should go get ready for work."

He wasn't as jumpy as he had been a few months ago, but he always made himself scarce when Leo's parents were around. Leo figured he needed time to get used to new people. So he didn't try to stop him as he got up, shot Leo a small smile, and vanished upstairs.

CHAPTER 2

AZIZA

IN THE LAST dream Aziza would ever have about her mother, Leila's skin was transparent, like an X-ray image. Aziza could see through the Leila she knew from old photographs to the skeleton she'd been at the cemetery, her finger bones crusted with dirt from when she'd climbed out of her grave.

"We didn't leave you alone," Leila told her.

I know that, Aziza tried to say, but in the dream, she couldn't speak. *I know that Jiddo has always been there for me.*

"We made sure you would be taken care of," Leila said.

Why won't you get out of my head? Aziza wanted to snap at her. *You're dead. Stay dead.*

She'd had that dream at least a dozen times over the last few months, always returning in her sleep to the graveyard. Thanks to the sandman, though, she'd never have to go back again.

She slipped into the house unnoticed, but her grandfather came downstairs maybe an hour later and found her in the kitchen nodding off into a mug of instant coffee. Even on his days off, Khaled El-Amin still dressed like a history professor, in his button-up, slacks, and reading glasses. Like Aziza, he was a witch—one with the ability to build magical wards, which he used mostly to protect their home from unwanted supernatural visitors. He was her only parent, and though he could be gruff and taciturn, she had never doubted that he loved her. It was part of why her dreams of Leila had been so confusing—she didn't need a ghost to tell her that.

He paused in the doorway, taking her in—the coffee, the backpack discarded at her feet. She could practically see him swallow the rebuke he wanted to give.

"Where were you?" he asked instead, pulling down a kettle from the cabinet.

"We had to go and get Leo's sister. She keeps running away to Elphame."

He filled the kettle with water and put it on the stove. His hands no longer shook these days, and he stood a little taller, as if he'd aged in reverse. "She's a fairy. Elphame is where she belongs."

"That doesn't mean it's safe for her."

"You still haven't learned to mind your own business," he grumbled. "Even after your meddling cost you a hand."

The hand in question had healed as much as it was going to. It had lost all mobility and sensation, and it was knotted with ugly scars. Usually, it didn't hurt—but there were days when it sent pain shooting up her arm all the way to the shoulder, sometimes bad enough to make the whole limb seize up.

Being bitten by a blækhound was, it turned out, no fucking joke.

She was slowly learning to write left-handed, but even with special permission to take extra time on her finals, she'd barely finished. Washing her hair took forever now. So did doing the dishes. Tea bags were an ordeal. She kept trying to rip the little paper packets open with her teeth, but half the time, she tore through the bag inside, spilling powdered leaves everywhere. It was a silly thing to be annoyed about, but god, it was *so* annoying. These countless inconveniences—some trivial and others significant—were worse than the pain.

"Like you can talk," she said, as he stretched an arm up to take a mug down from the cabinet, a motion that used to be slow and cautious but now looked effortless.

"What do you mean?" He turned the burner down, fingers resting lightly on the dial.

She forced herself to finish what was left of her lukewarm coffee, stalling. She'd been meaning to bring this up before, but there hadn't been a good time. Last winter, Aziza, Leo, and Tristan had stumbled into a conflict with a hag: a malevolent, magic-devouring entity that had lurked in the woods outside Blackthorn for many years—even centuries—going through cycles of dormancy, where it slept, and wakefulness, where it preyed on innocent people. The three of them had managed to kill it for good, which Aziza felt was a net positive and merited at least a moment of grudging approval. Maybe a *"you were right, Aziza, and I never should have doubted you."* But Jiddo had been angry with Aziza for being reckless and disobeying him, and *she* had been angry because he hadn't been honest with her. She hadn't wanted to risk their tentative truce on another difficult conversation.

"I know you were with my parents when they fought the hag." She set her mug down with a soft *clack*. Her parents had sealed the hag away when Aziza was a baby, dying in the process. Jiddo had always lied to Aziza about what had happened to them. Worse, he had never bothered to mention that he had been there the night her parents had died. She only figured it out because she'd felt his magic, his wards, at the entrance to the hag's prison.

It was hard to wrap her mind around it. Her skinny, bookish grandfather, who taught ancient history and fed the stray cats that sometimes found their way into the garden—locked in battle with a fiery monster. Part of her was still convinced he would deny it.

"I had to be," Jiddo said, his back to her. "My daughter was there."

"I thought the house wards were draining you. But all that time, it was the ward you put on the hag. You kept that up nonstop for *years*," she said indignantly, warming to her argument, "but you want to talk to *me* about meddling?"

He sighed. "Don't start. I'm not drained."

"Not *anymore*."

"Worrying about you takes far more out of me than any spell could."

We didn't leave you alone, Leila had said, but Aziza had felt alone when the one person she should have been able to trust had kept secrets and shut her out. Now that she knew what she knew, she understood why he'd acted that way. He had been there when her parents were killed. He had taken their bodies out of the woods, had buried them, and had come home to a baby granddaughter he had to raise by himself. She didn't know if he had ever truly worked through his trauma and grief. But understanding hadn't undone the hurt.

We didn't leave you alone.

The words returned to her, insistent, as she watched Jiddo. His bald head was bent slightly over the infuser he was filling with tea leaves from a tin on the counter. The water in the kettle bubbled comfortingly as it came to a boil.

It was only then that she saw what should have been obvious: Her parents *and* Jiddo had fought the hag. Aziza had been a baby.

"Who did you leave me with?" she asked, the words spilling out of her almost as soon as the thought formed. "That night. If all three of you were there, then . . ."

Jiddo's shoulders went stiff. He took the kettle and mug to the table and sat down. "Why does that matter?" he said. "It was so long ago. Let it stay in the past."

"I promise to stop keeping secrets if you promise the same."

"Do I look like one of your pixies? There is no bargaining with me," Jiddo said severely. "I'm your grandfather. I get to keep my secrets. *You* are still a child."

"If it doesn't matter, there's no reason not to tell me."

He glared at her over the rim of his glasses. She suspected he was thinking about the fact that the last time he had ignored her questions, she'd gotten Tristan to reanimate her parents' corpses so she could interrogate them instead. When he'd found out, he'd been angrier than she'd ever seen him in her entire life.

"If I tell you this, you drop the subject," he said gruffly. "Understood?"

She nodded.

He folded his hands together atop the table and looked down at them, frowning in thought. Then, abruptly, he heaved himself to his feet. "Wait here."

His footsteps traveled up the stairs and down the hall. When he returned, it was with a photograph that he placed in front of her. It was old, overexposed, and a little blurry around the edges—a candid shot taken in their living room, with the kitchen in the background. But she only recognized one of the three people in it.

"Your father took this," Jiddo said. "I got rid of the rest, but—"

But he had saved this one. Maybe part of him had known the day would come when he'd finally want to tell Aziza about it.

"Is this . . ."

"Their coven. Yes."

Jiddo had mentioned this coven only once before, and all he'd said was that they had let her parents face the hag alone; that they'd had no loyalty, and her parents' trust in them had been misplaced. Curiously, Aziza examined the photo. Closest to the edge of the frame was Leila, who must have been sitting next to Aziza's father. She had an arm wrapped around her knee, her other hand blurry with motion as she carried on what looked like a spirited discussion with two men in the chairs across from her. The first was politician-handsome, but his tousled blond curls and unbuttoned cuffs took the sharpness out of his looks; he wore a faint smile as he leaned forward, responding animatedly to Leila. The other man, farthest from the camera, was a burly redhead who leaned against the arm of the seat with an air of fond amusement as he listened to the other two.

Jiddo tapped the redhead in the photo. "This cowardly excuse for a witch refused to fight, so he stayed with you. If I hadn't come back, he would have taken you in."

Aziza felt her eyebrows go up. "I've never even met him."

"I told him I never wanted to see his face again," Jiddo said unrepentantly.

"And him?" She pointed at the other man.

"Castor wasn't in town, and he didn't pick up when Leila called," Jiddo said. "He had started to grow distant from the others. The coven was unraveling even before the hag appeared."

She couldn't fault Jiddo for his uncharitable feelings toward them, but would Leila have blamed her friends for being afraid? Somehow, Aziza didn't think so.

But she kept these thoughts to herself. This was already a greater concession than he'd made in a long time when it came to talking about her parents. She could let it go for now and learn more another day.

When the sun was a little higher in the sky, she got up to leave again, kissing him on the cheek and pocketing the photo on her way out.

THE MORNING AFTER they battled the hag and won, Aziza had paid a visit to Bridget Bishop Memorial Library. Tristan was asleep on her couch, and she and Leo were texting back and forth. They had made plans to meet at a coffee shop later, because neither of them wanted to be at home, and because no one but the three of them understood, would ever understand, what they'd all been through the night before.

But, before that, Aziza wanted to talk to Meryl, the librarian. The last Meryl had heard, Aziza and her coven were going to run an errand with Meryl's father—an errand that involved a tiny boat, a big storm, and an emotionally compromised kraken—in exchange for a token infused with enough selkie magic to drown the hag. But Meryl didn't know how things had escalated, or that they'd ended up confronting the hag much sooner than they had meant to.

The library was open when she arrived. But the person sitting behind the circulation desk was *not* Meryl.

Aziza slammed her palm on top of its surface, making the stranger jump.

"Who are you?" she said. "And where's Meryl?"

In all the years she had been visiting this library, Aziza had never seen anyone else working there. Meryl had never taken a sick day or a vacation. In retrospect, it was sad; what had always been a safe place for her was a prison for Meryl—a selkie whose sealskin had been stolen and who had been forbidden from returning to the sea. But that didn't change the fact that her absence now could only mean something was terribly wrong.

The boy peered up at her with polite confusion. "I'm sorry?"

"Meryl. The librarian. This is *her* library and that's *her* desk."

"Libraries are public institutions." He had the gall to smile, a perfectly pleasant customer-service smile. "They belong to their communities. I'm the new librarian, and I'm happy to help you find whatever you're looking for."

"You're not a fucking librarian," Aziza snarled. "Where is she?"

The boy couldn't have been much older than Aziza. At a distance, his clothes had aged him—dress pants and a collared shirt—but he was a senior in high school or *maybe* a college freshman at most. His black hair was neatly combed, his expression bland and neutral. He looked at her hand, still resting with borderline possessiveness on the desk; at her other hand in bandages and a sling; at the raw, ugly welts on her neck where she had almost been strangled; and at last, her face. Whatever he saw there made his gray eyes narrow.

"Why would I be here if I wasn't a librarian?" he said placidly. "I see that you're upset. Would you like me to call someone for you?"

"I'd like you to stay the hell out of my way." She leaned over the desk—taking vindictive pleasure from the way he flinched back, as if he thought she was going to smack him, but she was only opening a compartment in the desktop organizer and grabbing a small key out of it. He protested; she ignored him, shoving away from the desk and striding down the hall while he trailed after her.

The key unlocked Meryl's office. There, she found:

Absolutely nothing.

The office had been gutted. The dented filing cabinets, the desk that smelled like the tea tree oil Meryl used in her homemade all-purpose cleaner, the couch with the saggy middle that Tristan had slept on for several days—it was all gone. Even the entrance to the underground tunnel had been boarded up.

Defeating the hag was supposed to mean that Aziza could focus on helping Meryl find her sealskin and win her freedom back. Instead, while Aziza had been fighting for her life, someone had taken Meryl away. Aziza had defended everyone in Blackthorn last night, except for her oldest friend.

She had expected to wake up that day with a sense of victory. But the only thing she'd felt so far was exhaustion. Now, confronted with this empty office, any glimmer of triumph or relief that might have grown inside her was supplanted by a horrible, crushing defeat.

"What are you looking for?" the boy said, sounding mildly concerned. "This is just a storage room."

"Who are you?" she demanded again. She didn't want him to see how shaken she was.

"My name is Dion Legrand," he said, which was high on the list of the most ridiculous things she had ever heard.

"I didn't mean your name," she said. "I mean, who sent you? Who . . . put you here?"

"You mean, who . . . hired me?" Dion said, eyebrows lifting in mild confusion.

"This is not a normal library," she said. "I know you know that. You weren't hired. You're not a librarian. Who the fuck *are* you?"

He leaned forward, as if to confide in her, and she caught the faint, incongruous scent of smoke. Not like cigarettes; more like woodsmoke, bitter, sharp, and cleansing. His gaze on hers was piercing.

"I'm the new librarian," he said again, very patiently, "and I have a lot of work to do today. If you're finished?"

Their relationship had only gone downhill from there. Aziza returned to Bishop Library whenever she could, but she never got anything useful out of Dion. She didn't even know why she kept going. Maybe she just wanted to feel close to Meryl.

Maybe she wanted Dion to admit the truth about who—*what*—he was. She had a pretty good idea. But she wanted to hear it from him.

No one was at the circulation desk when she got there that morning. She rifled through it half-heartedly, finding only a stack of incomplete paperwork and a spent match.

"Can I help you?"

She jumped, which made her quietly seethe. The day Dion stopped being able to sneak up on her couldn't come soon enough. She spun the chair around to face him.

"No, I'm good," she said.

He crossed his arms and looked witheringly unimpressed.

"Why are you behind the desk, Aziza?" he asked, with the long-suffering air of someone who interacted with the public on a regular basis, which cheered her up a little. Not as perky as he'd been back on day one, that was for sure. Maybe, she thought hopefully, the customer service part of this job would break his spirit and he'd give up the whole charade. He didn't have what it took to be Meryl. Sometimes when she needed a mood-booster, she imagined Dion finding spoiled food or syringes still half-filled with unidentifiable liquids in the book drop bin, or opening a DVD case to check it hadn't been returned without the disc only for fingernail clippings to pour out into his lap.

"Since anyone can sit here these days, I figured I'd take a turn," she said.

"A Saturday morning in the middle of summer, and you have nowhere better to be than here?" he asked her, with just a faint, maddening touch of pity. "You could have slept in. It would do wonders for your temperament."

"You're here, too," she pointed out. "Doing fake work at your fake job. Are you even being paid?" She glanced down, pointedly, at his expensive watch and his expensive leather shoes and then back up again at his arrogant smile with the perfect white teeth that must have cost a fortune. He had money, but it wasn't from being a librarian.

"Your concern is appreciated, but I can assure you that I'm being compensated fairly for my time," he said smoothly. "Which reminds me—I have something for you."

He leaned around her to open the drawer at her elbow and rummage through it. She glared at the side of his head, the photo she'd gotten from Jiddo burning in her pocket. After what had happened to her parents, Jiddo had wanted nothing to do with other witches. If the rest of them were anything like Dion, maybe he was right.

She was sure Dion was a witch. Even though she had never gotten him to admit it. Dion was unquestionably the most magical person she'd ever met, in a literal sense. Magic was a quality he possessed as obviously as the color of his hair or the shape of his eyes; it seemed impossible that anyone could walk past him on the street and not see it. Impossible to be in his space and not feel it, something different than what she felt from Elphame's boundary—not an arcane, wild magic, but a clear and ringing energy like the toll of a bell.

She burned with envy.

When Dion straightened, he held a slip of paper, which he offered to her. She took it reluctantly. It was an application for a library card.

"Since you're here all the time, I thought you might want to check out a book every now and then," he said brightly. "Get something useful out of your visits. Other than the pleasure of my company, of course."

"I already have a library card," she said, because she did. In theory. She had lost the physical card a long time ago, but she'd never had trouble checking anything out, so she had always assumed that Meryl had a way of pulling it up on the computer. Or something.

"About that," he said, leaning over her to tap something into the keyboard. "I double-checked, and it turns out your library card expired five years ago. I imagined you would want to remedy that."

She looked at him, and then at the screen.

"Sure," she said. "Why don't I fill this out right now?"

Aziza took a Sharpie from the pen holder, yanked the cap off with her knees, and wrote in big, block letters: *FUCK YOU.*

She presented it to him calmly, picked up her bag, and stood.

"Good talk, Dion. Till next time."

"Bored already?" he asked, with what appeared to be genuine curiosity. "Are you feeling all right?"

She smiled, which visibly alarmed him. That was understandable, as Aziza had never looked at him with anything but unmasked scorn.

"Don't worry," she said. "I'll be back before you have a chance to miss me."

He smiled back, a false, patronizing smile. "Till next time, Aziza."

CHAPTER 3
TRISTAN

Most nights, he couldn't sleep. He either read the books he borrowed from Leo or skimmed through the hound's thoughts, which by now he knew like his first language. It rested in the preserve behind Leo's house during the day, hunted raccoons and foxes at dusk, and kept vigil all night in case Hazel slipped out. When she did, it followed her; it changed the shape of her shadow, lending it the bristle of fur and the curve of claws, as it tailed her through Blackthorn's darknesses.

Fairies smelled like when you dug your snout into a hollow spot under a rock or a tree root after it rained, and the soil there was half-dry, half-wet, and many small wriggling things had just begun to poke at the surface to share the sweet-stale air with you. On the morning after their narrow escape from the sandman, the hound was still agitated enough that this scent made it sit up with a spike of alarm that yanked Tristan into its mind. His—*its* muscles stiffened. It rose into a crouch even before its eyes fully opened. Twigs caught in its fur, stinging like a dozen tiny insect bites. A screen of honeysuckle leaves shielded it from view as the hound peered through the gaps in the wire fence.

Summer to the hound was a million shades of green and a film of gold sunlight sticking to everything, and many rain-scented shadows to swim in. Hazel—whose broken glamour could not fool the hound, and whose wings were visible to it and thus to Tristan under a fire-spark layer of magic—sat in the shade of a tree while Maria tended her garden. The tomato and pepper plants were heavy with unripe fruit, yellows just beginning to deepen into orange. Maria knelt there, armed with gloves and shears, her hair pinned back and sweat beading on her brow.

Assured that all was well and its charge was secure, the hound settled in to watch them. Tristan was about to pull away from its mind when Hazel said, "I ran away last night."

Maria sat on her heels, wiped her forehead with the back of her glove, and signed clumsily, "It's okay. You came back."

"No," Hazel said, with a resolute viciousness. "Leo *made* me come back. But if you tell him you don't want me here, he'll let me go."

A twist of incredulous humor spun from Tristan's thoughts into the hound's. It huffed in response, its hot breath fogging up the wires on the fence. That was an impressive logical leap on Hazel's part. To think that Leo would stop caring about her if their parents told him to.

Maria whipped off her gloves and dropped them on the ground.

"I want you here," she signed.

"If you could trade me for your real daughter—"

"You *are* my real daughter."

That wasn't exactly what she said—*to be* verbs didn't really exist in ASL—but the emphasis was there in the look on her face and the snap of her wrists.

The hound wanted to know if it should jump over the fence and take the small fairy by the scruff of her neck and put her back inside. Tristan forbade it.

"But isn't it weird?" Hazel insisted. "Me, pretending to be her. It's like I stole her face. And her family. And her life."

"No," Maria said, aloud this time, but it came out as more of a sputter as a tiny brown frog squirmed from her mouth. It gave her a kick on the chin as it fell into the grass, where it hopped away. She switched back to signing. "You're not pretending. You are yourself."

"Don't you miss her?"

The hound's eyes followed the frog's progress through the grass. Its sharp ears picked up its tiny chirps. Not worth the effort of catching that. It would be slimy and its bones would get stuck in his teeth, and his summoner would be angry with him for leaving his—for leaving *its* post—

Tristan remembered himself then. He was standing over the bathroom sink with the water running—it had been running for several minutes now—and his toothbrush in his hand.

Damn, he thought, meeting his own eyes guiltily in the mirror.

Sometimes he got a little lost in the hounds. They experienced the world so vividly. Compared to that, when he was just himself, he felt like a ghost. Tethered to the land of the living, but not inhabiting it. Not really.

He hurried, wanting to get dressed and out the door before Maria came back inside. He'd found a part-time job at an art supply shop, where he worked up to twenty-nine hours a week selling fake flowers for amateur photoshoots, miles and miles of yarn, and birthday decorations patterned with cartoon dogs.

Not long after Tristan had come to stay at the Merritt household, Greg had asked him whether he planned on enrolling in Leo and Aziza's school next year so they could get the paperwork. Tristan had told him no. He wasn't going back to school. A few days later, a GED prep book had appeared on his bed. It was nice of Greg to think of it, but Tristan wasn't taking the GED, either. He didn't have the time or money for college. He just wanted to work, and save up, and not be homeless again. Ever.

He'd thanked Greg for the book the next time they saw each other, but kept it stashed under his bed and never opened it. Greg didn't mention it again.

A few months ago, Leo had told his parents he would be bringing someone to stay over for a while. Tristan had seen the white shock on their faces when he'd walked through the door, and then he'd looked away, unable to meet their eyes. Leo introduced them as if they were all strangers, and his parents went along with it, so Tristan did, too. They had no choice; part of how the curse worked was that it didn't only suppress memories from before Leo's sixteenth birthday, but also prevented him from retaining *new* memories that would help him uncover his true love's identity. Tell him, and the knowledge would pass through his mind and out again. Write it in a letter, and he'd be unable to read the words. Show him a photograph, and his mind would blot out the faces. If Greg and Maria hinted to Leo that they already knew Tristan, and if Leo correctly guessed *how* they knew each other—or even *suspected*—the curse would wipe the interaction from his mind. So it was easier, kinder, to pretend, at least when Leo was around.

At first, Tristan had tried to avoid being alone with them, hoping to stave off the conversation he didn't want to have. That didn't last long; inevitably, the time came when Tristan walked into the room and Maria was already there and he couldn't turn back around because she'd already seen him.

But there was no conversation. She gave him a quick wave and went back to what she was doing. Greg never confronted him, either. It was like they really were the strangers they'd pretended to be. Like they'd forgotten who he was, too. Except sometimes Maria's smile was a little subdued when she looked at him, like she was holding something back. But the GED book meant Greg probably didn't hate him, which meant Maria probably didn't hate him, either.

It should have been a relief. It wasn't . . . *not* a relief. He'd been afraid to talk to them. It turned out he didn't have to.

AFTER WORK USUALLY found him helping Leo with the grocery shopping or unloading the dishwasher while deftly sidestepping Spot's attempts to participate by yanking the silverware from his hands and lobbing them at his head. Most days, Aziza came over to chip away at summer homework with Leo while Tristan kept them company with a book in hand. Sometimes he added sketches to Aziza's bestiary after they encountered a rare-to-Blackthorn weeping-willow nymph or black-tailed sea serpent, since she could no longer do it herself. Or they'd put on action movies with lots of mesmerizing explosions and talk through the whole thing. Or they went out, usually wandering around the park or the coast just so that they wouldn't have to be cooped up. With the hag gone, the boundary to Elphame didn't need round-the-clock supervision from Aziza, and they hardly ever had to deal with bitey shades finding their way into people's recycling bins anymore, but they did their leisurely patrols anyway.

Through all of this, the hound watched him. When he had not given it a specific order, it stalked him in the shadows, observing him from under the fridge while he and Leo did the washing up after dinner or behind a stack of canvases as he swept the aisles at work.

"It's like it wants something," Aziza said, when they returned to the car one evening to find its eyes, aglow with the fading sunlight, peering out at him from between the tires. It shouldn't have fit under a car, but it was a shadow-flesh creature and could fit anywhere it wanted, as long as that place was dark enough.

The three of them were grimy and pleasantly tired, having driven to just outside Blackthorn to spend the afternoon by the river, running from the summer heat. (The beach was crowded, and Leo had never looked at the ocean the same way after the thing with the kraken.)

"What could it possibly want?" Tristan said, exasperated.

"Maybe it just likes you," Leo said.

"It doesn't," Tristan said. "It's not capable of *liking* things, it doesn't think that way."

None of the other hounds behaved like this; it was just the one, the hound with the scars on its belly—long, pale slash marks around which the pattern of its fur was all in disarray—from where Tristan had once cut it open to retrieve the selkies' clamshell token. Blækhounds healed almost instantaneously even from things that should kill them, and they usually bore no marks from such injuries, but he thought these wounds had scarred because the blade he'd used was silver. Maybe Aziza was right, and the hound did want something from him. Maybe the thing it wanted was revenge.

Regardless, it was the first to respond to his call when he needed something. And it obeyed his every command without any sign of reluctance. He didn't get it. At first, he'd dismissed it in favor of calling another, but eventually he'd decided he was being ridiculous. The hounds were all alike. This one wasn't any more dangerous than the others. Even if it was the hound that had bitten Aziza and destroyed her right hand.

He'd asked Aziza whether she wanted him to try and banish it for good. She had refused, determined not to be afraid of the hounds—any of the hounds, but especially this one. She had even taken to feeding it when it joined them on patrol, placing a Tupperware of leftovers before it with such affectionate remarks as, "You did good today, you goddamn terror. Here's your prize."

He usually tried to stop it from eating the empty Tupperware when it was done. He succeeded maybe 40 percent of the time.

"I think it likes chicken," she observed.

"The hounds don't *like* things," he kept saying, in vain.

"They like food," she said.

"They *need* food. It's not the same."

"They like *me*. I think," Leo said smugly, and Tristan was too mortified to tell him that the hounds accepted head pats from Leo not because they liked him, but because Tristan did.

His connection to the hounds felt like a natural extension of himself. The other bond, the one between him and Aziza, was nothing like that. It stemmed from a magical contract he'd entered with the hag, a ten-year spell intended to bind him to her as her servant. When the hag had died, the contract would have killed Tristan, too, had Aziza not slotted herself into the hag's place and taken it over. But Aziza had turned the bond from one of master and servant into one of equals—and the two of them were equally clueless about how to control such a bond. It was a direct link between their two magics, and a conduit for their emotions. The hag had been able to push feelings, intuitions, and abstract concepts into his mind when she'd wanted to communicate her orders and her moods. In its new form, the bond was still a conduit for all of those things, only he and Aziza couldn't always decide what they shared with each other.

The first few weeks with the bond had been fraught. Aziza hated feeling exposed, hated that he sometimes knew how she felt before she did. And she hated knowing the minutiae of his emotional ups and downs. She didn't mean to let him know that she hated it. She never complained to him aloud. But he could feel it, and the prickly sting of her frustration, the bone-grinding stress, and the heavy crush of her instinctive resistance to the bond had put his already shattered nerves even more on edge.

Slowly, they had gotten better at blocking out each other's emotions. Aziza had started putting up mental walls—that was how she visualized it, she said, as a literal wall—and he was learning to do the same. That had given them both a measure of privacy. Sometimes, though, a powerful enough emotion could slip past their barriers.

This meant that she knew, frankly, far more than he had ever wanted her to know about his feelings for Leo.

But when Aziza went home, when Hazel was in her room, when they were done with their share of the housework—there always came a point in the day when it was just Leo and Tristan, slowly building a friendship that for Leo was brand-new and for Tristan was a second chance, one that he lived in terror of ruining. The first time he and Leo had met, their friendship had fallen into place so naturally that Tristan hardly had to think about it. This time, he was keenly aware of every word he said, wondering where he'd make the misstep that would push Leo away for good, or whether—if he did everything right—he could somehow create a perfect facsimile of what they had before.

MOST NIGHTS, HE couldn't sleep.

Last year, he'd fought for scraps of rest wherever he could get it—in the woods, in abandoned buildings, in overcrowded shelters. Now he had a room to himself. And not just any room, but *this* one. There had been a time in his life when he'd spent more nights in the Merritts' guest room than in his own house. It should've been easy to fall asleep here.

He squinted through the darkness at the digits on the clock. It was a little over an hour past midnight. He squeezed his eyelids shut.

If he were fifteen again, Leo's door would be opening around now. Tristan could usually hear him moving on the other side of the wall. The creak of his bedsprings as he got up. His footsteps in the hall, closing the distance between them. The rasp of the doorknob turning, slowly, as if he was worried about waking him—as if he didn't know that Tristan was waiting up for him.

Go to sleep, he told himself furiously. *He's not coming.*

He turned on his side and pulled the blanket up.

It had always been Leo who came to him. Before. Or let him in through the back door when he snuck out of his parents' house to be with him. Leo had kissed Tristan first, too. Leo with the curse hanging over his head ready to split it open if he dared fall in love. All Tristan ever had to do was wait for him to make a move. And when it had been his turn, when *he* had been the one who should've been there for Leo—he'd walked away.

He'd promised himself that was never going to happen again. But *this* wasn't right, either. Wallowing in the memories. Missing him and doing nothing about it. It wasn't good enough to just not run away. Maybe he had to be the one to go to Leo, this time. *He* had to close the distance. Until Leo forgot there had ever been space between them. Until the only thing Leo couldn't remember was a time when Tristan wasn't his.

Before he could talk himself out of it, he was getting up and dragging a shirt over his head. He crossed the room, slipped into the hall, and stopped in front of Leo's door. Light spilled out from underneath it. He knocked. Quietly.

When the insomnia was at its worst, he sometimes showed up at Leo's door just like this, if he saw a light on and could gather the courage. They were friends, he told himself; he and Leo could stay up all night talking, as friends. And they did, and these quiet hours they spent together were swiftly becoming the most cherished part of his week. Or he went downstairs the moment the first rays of light leavened the night sky, when he could pretend it was morning, and chances were Leo would end up there soon, too. But this time felt different.

In the subsequent moments, the last of his drowsiness left him. The floor was cold under his bare feet. It occurred to him, much too late, that he probably shouldn't be making important decisions at one in the morning when he had slept maybe five of the past forty-eight hours.

The door swung open.

Leo was in a T-shirt so old the logo on the front had worn away, his hair in such disarray Tristan had to shove his hands into his pockets to keep from reaching out and fixing it. He'd taken his contacts out and put on his glasses; his fringe had gotten long enough to catch against the frame. Behind the lenses, his brown eyes were tired and warm.

"Tris," he said, unsurprised to see him. "After last night, I thought you'd be out cold."

"No such luck. But I could say the same to you."

"Yeah," Leo said. "I thought about coming over to bug you, but I didn't want to keep you awake if you were trying to sleep."

"You should have," Tristan said softly. Of all the things that kept him up at night, Leo had always been his favorite.

His lips parted slightly, as if Tristan had said something surprising, but the look was gone again so quickly Tristan dismissed it as his imagination.

"Something on your mind?" Leo asked, in that coaxing tone of voice that made Tristan feel like he could tell him anything, even though of course that wasn't true now.

"Just the hound. It's . . . digesting something," Tristan said, hating how easily he lied. Leo wrinkled his nose in distaste. "Why can't *you* sleep?"

He leaned heavily against the door frame, arms crossed. "I keep having these dreams."

"Nightmares?" Tristan asked. He managed to sound sympathetic and not like someone who was trying very hard not to look at his ex-boyfriend's biceps.

"Not this time. Just . . . the kind of dream you can't stop thinking about." The corner of his mouth dimpled in a weary half smile that just about stopped Tristan's heart. "You wanna watch a movie or something? If we both can't sleep, we might as well not-sleep together." He stopped; Tristan could practically see the gears in his head turn as he replayed what he'd just said. "I mean—I just meant—"

"No need to elaborate," Tristan told him, deadpan. "I think that was pretty clear."

"Shut up," Leo said, through a laugh. "Are you coming in, or would you rather go back to—I don't know, watching the hound pick bits of raccoon out of its teeth?"

"I think it was a fox."

For a second, as they both tried to stifle their laughter, it was like nothing had changed at all. Leo moved back to let Tristan in, but Tristan caught his wrist impulsively to stop him. Leo's pulse thrummed against his fingertips until Tristan snatched his hand away, releasing him.

"What was the dream about?" he asked softly.

Leo's fingers touched the spot on his wrist where Tristan had held him. He started to say something but reconsidered, and instead shrugged with forced nonchalance. "I can't remember. Typical for me, right?" After a momentary silence, he added, "What's wrong?"

Tristan hadn't realized he was staring. He swallowed dryly.

In the fairytales, there was one surefire way to break a curse.

"Nothing's wrong," he answered, much too late.

Carefully, he tugged Leo's glasses off. Leo only blinked at him with mild confusion.

"I think I need those more than you do," he said lightly. And then Tristan shuffled in close, his free hand rising to brush Leo's jaw in a barely there touch. "Tris?"

That time, he breathed more than spoke Tristan's name, and Tristan felt more than heard it, warm against his own lips. He was near enough to soak in the heat radiating from Leo's body; he smelled like toothpaste and soap, and very faintly of sweat. There were no nerves anymore. It was the easiest thing in the world to lean in that final fraction, to use his gentle grip on Leo's chin to tilt him closer and kiss him.

If Tristan had been a ghost before, now he was mortal again. Every place his skin touched Leo's burned as if it was discovering sensation for the first time. When Leo kissed him back, muscle memory took over. He walked them backward into Leo's room, kicking the door shut behind them, his hand sliding under his shirt—the glasses still dangled from the other one, he really hadn't thought this through. But Leo's hands were on his shoulders, gripping tight enough to bunch up the collar of Tristan's shirt, his fingers slipping higher so that they brushed Tristan's neck. He was making a helpless, stunned noise in his throat that Tristan would be playing on loop in his head for the foreseeable future. He was melting into Tristan's arms where he belonged.

He was—

Pushing Tristan away.

Hands against Tristan's chest, careful but firm. The tip of his nose brushing against Tristan's cheek as he nodded out of the kiss, chin dipping, lips dragging apart. Tristan drew in a breath, and another, eyes blinking back open, his mouth feeling swollen and sensitive and his entire body slowly going cold.

Leo was breathless, chest heaving, and flushed all the way down his neck and up to the tops of his ears. He'd never looked more perfect. But even that was little consolation for Tristan as he processed what had just happened.

"Sorry," Tristan croaked, jerking back so quickly he almost banged into the door. He held out the glasses, as awkwardly as anyone had ever done anything, and prayed for death.

Leo took them, looking everywhere but at Tristan. "It's okay! I just—"

"You don't have to—"

They both stopped talking.

So much for true love's kiss, Tristan thought, with the blackest humor.

"Don't be sorry," Leo said, replacing his glasses. He rubbed his forehead, briefly hiding his expression. "If things were different, I would've—but—you know."

Tristan clearly didn't know a single goddamn thing. "W-what?"

Leo finally met his eyes.

"I have someone," he said, with a sort of quiet, desperate fierceness. "And I'm faithful. Even if I don't remember, I can't—not until I know—" He cut himself off. "You were right before, when you said the curse took something of value. I can't give up."

A hysterical laugh bubbled up in Tristan's chest. This, too, he suppressed.

"Right, I—I wasn't thinking," he said.

"Um, so." Leo fiddled with his glasses as if he couldn't get them to sit right. He crossed his arms, changed his mind, and hid his hands in his pockets instead. "Still up for that movie?"

"Maybe I'd better—" He gestured vaguely for the door, inching away. "Good night."

Leo's relief was poorly hidden. "Night."

Tristan fled. The embarrassment was wearing off already. His chest felt hollow and heavy at the same time.

He couldn't be with Leo because Leo was faithful to a version of Tristan that no longer existed.

When he got back to his room, his phone was lit up with a text from Aziza:

are you okay

Then, a minute later:

tristan. answer now

That one had just arrived. His fingers tapped out a shaky response.

yes. why, he sent back.

feels like you got shot

The laughter he'd held back before came out now, scratchy and harsh, a scarecrow's laugh.

can confirm I'm not bleeding to death in an alley somewhere, he assured her, and collapsed on the bed.

He didn't have the right to be upset. How could he be mad that Leo didn't want to cheat on him? Did he want Leo to be *less* virtuous? No.

Yes.

Maybe a little.

No, he didn't. What he wanted was to take back the last ten minutes. He had probably just sabotaged their tentative new friendship by throwing himself at Leo, who *barely knew him now*—

His phone gave a happy chirp. He peeled his face off his pillow and squinted at the screen.

you're spiraling, Aziza had written.

stop spying on my emotions, he replied.

then stop being so loud. Another text quickly followed: *I take that back. just go to sleep already.*

This elicited more unhinged laughter. If Aziza was this worried, then whatever she was getting from the bond must have been pretty dire. The scarred hound, which he had assigned to Hazel, was in the corner of his room now—he knew without having to see it—as if it, too, thought he'd been attacked. If he turned over, its eyes would be hovering somewhere in the vicinity of the digital clock that had tormented him before, but he was not in the mood to be judged by something that had to be told not to eat plastic, so he didn't.

Whether she knew it or not, Aziza had managed to distract him. His exhaustion won out at last. He fell asleep.

CHAPTER 4

LEO

HE WAS STILL awake a couple of hours after Tristan had left, sitting at his desk with next week's homework spread haphazardly in front of him. But it was no use; he was distracted. To say the least.

For probably the tenth time in the last half hour, his mind drifted back to the flushed, hazy-eyed look on Tristan's face in the instant after Leo had pulled away. Heat flooded his body. He pressed the heels of his palms into his eyes as if he could block out the images, with little success. It would be so much simpler if Tristan was just some unattainably gorgeous guy in his class that he saw for a few minutes every day and never spoke to. But Tristan was one of his best friends. They'd been through so much together already. He'd known he had a crush, but he hadn't anticipated how strong a crush could feel when it had grown on a foundation of real trust and affection. It was like a crush on hard mode. Which just seemed unfair.

He almost laughed at himself. Was this his *first* crush? His first kiss?

His first that he could remember.

All at once, his eyes stung. He pressed a hand to his chest, as if pressure would alleviate the ache. It hurt like something had been cut out of him, but his heart still thumped comfortingly against his palm. He knew this pang of emptiness was mostly his imagination. Memories didn't live in the heart, and love didn't either.

He closed his eyes, letting the scraps of sense-memory from his dreams wash over him again, comforting and painful in equal measures. Despite everything, the phantom of that warm presence still filled him with light.

How are you so good at making me feel better even when you're not here? he thought, a weak smile tugging at his mouth.

He would give Tristan some space for a day or two. Leo could use some space himself, honestly, to make himself forget how good Tristan had felt in his arms. And then he'd apologize. He had totally led Tristan on, hadn't he? He must not have hidden his *harmless crush* as well as he'd thought he had. He just needed to make sure he hadn't hurt Tristan too badly. Or blown up a friendship that meant everything to him.

A sound outside his door made him pause.

Footsteps whispered down the hall. It could only be Hazel—she was so light on her feet now that they made no more noise than the patter of a cat's paws. Anyone else would've ignored it. But he knew what to listen for. He left his door open as he followed, taking the stairs two at a time. Hazel froze in the entryway, hand on the door-knob, as he swung around the corner.

"Really?" he said in a harsh whisper. "Two days in a row?"

She gave a sulky little shrug. "I couldn't sleep."

"Me neither," he admitted. "Come on."

Her shoulders slumped, and she let her hand fall away from the door. She dragged her feet on her way back, making him wait, arms crossed in exasperation.

"Wanna put on the *Elementary* pilot?" he said, as she trudged upstairs before him. They'd seen that episode so many times he knew the dialogue by heart. "I'll watch with you, if you want."

"You're only saying that because you think it'll put me to sleep," she said, indignant.

"I bet it will."

"Bet it won't."

"You're on," he said. Hazel's room was dark, like she'd been asleep right up until the moment she'd decided to sneak away. She slipped inside without bothering to turn on the light, so he felt around for the switch automatically as he followed her in, only—Hazel had stopped short. He looked up and into the darkness.

There was someone in the room already.

"Oh dear," the girl said, in a down-feather voice that glided into the dark as if on wings. "You weren't supposed to come back here."

She was about Hazel's age, if he had to guess, but there was really nothing quite like the feeling of finding a strange child in your house in the middle of the night. She had tempest blue skin and wings that curved like the blade of a scythe, and she sat crisscross on Hazel's bed, sniffing curiously at a tube of sunscreen she'd taken from Hazel's nightstand. Her eyes reminded him of what Hazel's looked like under the glamour, silvery and prismatic.

Leo tugged at Hazel's arm and backed away, but the girl gave a flick of her hand—a quick, thoughtless gesture, as if shaking off a drop of water—and a breeze nudged the door shut.

"Excuse *me*," the girl said, eyes narrowed. "I was speaking with you. It's terribly rude to ignore people."

It was a bad idea to offend the fae.

Even if she *had* been rude first, by *breaking into his house.*

"How did you get in here?" he said evenly.

"How? Is there meant to be a trick to it?" she said, puzzled.

Another wave of her hand, and the glitter on her dress dispersed to hover in midair, illuminating the room like stars she'd caught out of the sky and pulled indoors. She tossed the tube of sunscreen aside and darted into the air. Leo stepped in front of Hazel, shielding her from view, but the girl just ducked around him, as casual as if she were sidestepping a poorly behaved dog. She threw her arms around Hazel's shoulders.

"I just *had* to see you in person!" she trilled. "That's why I volunteered."

"Volunteered?" Leo repeated. She ignored him.

Hazel pulled away to stare back at her in what was either fear or awe. "You're like me," she said, in a small voice.

Leo wanted to tell her that just because the girl was a fairy didn't mean she was like Hazel. But he didn't dare. His next thought was to make enough noise to wake up Tristan and his parents—but he didn't want to know what the girl could do to silence him. In the false starlight she'd made, her skin was the faded blue of shadows on ice; her fluttering wings caught the illumination and threw it back in his face.

"I'm Ephira," the girl said. "The Summer Court sent me to make sure you stopped resisting the call."

"I . . . don't understand," Hazel said.

"The *call*," Ephira said impatiently. "It's our magic—it calls us home. To the Summer Court. We thought perhaps your glamour was interfering with it. But it wasn't the glamour at all, was it?"

She glanced over at Leo, and now her smile was just slightly off— uncanny as the frozen, painted expression on a porcelain figurine.

"What's the Summer Court?" Hazel said quickly, drawing Ephira's attention back to her.

"You'll see soon enough. Oh, but you can't show up in that!" She took Hazel's face in her hands and kissed her on each cheek. At once, Hazel's glamour burned away like fireworks dissolving into the air, a slow un-becoming, as if the magic was eating itself up. Her dragonfly wings peeled open on her back. Her skin flushed green. Her ears grew into points, and her hair turned black with the faintest emerald sheen and so silky that the scrunchie slipped off the end of her braid. She looked down at it, and then at her hands with her inhumanly long fingers, and gasped.

"That filthy old thing was really clinging to you," Ephira said. "And look! You're so pretty."

"I need the glamour," Hazel said desperately. "Put it back. Please!"

"But you *don't* need it, not anymore," she said. "Come on."

She took Hazel's hand and tried to tow her toward the window, but before Leo could intervene, Hazel planted her feet.

"I'm not going anywhere," she said.

Ephira gave a huge, dramatic sigh, as if thoroughly put out. "But if you don't come with me, they'll send the Gallowglass to retrieve you."

"The who?"

"Our knights. Prince Talarix might come for you personally—he's Captain, so it's only right. Or maybe you'd prefer it that way?" Ephira grinned. "I'd cause a bit of trouble, too, for an escort from the prince." She released Hazel's hand and drifted away, twirling once in the air and perching on the edge of the open window. "Don't worry. I won't tell them that—it'll be our secret."

"Wait! Where are you going?" Hazel said. "The glamour—"

Ephira was halfway out already. Over her shoulder, she said, "I'll see you soon."

And she was gone, launching herself away and vanishing instantly into the night. The glitter in the air followed her out in a stream, the light dimming to nothing, and the room was plunged into darkness. Hazel lunged at the window like she meant to jump out after her, but Leo caught her around the waist and hauled her back.

"Hold on! What do you think you're doing?"

"I have to—she—my glamour—"

"I'll go," Leo said. "She's got to be headed for the boundary at St. Sithney's. She can't fly faster than I can drive, and you don't have the stamina to keep up with her in the air. Just stay put."

Hazel was breathing fast, tears welling up in her silver eyes. "She said they're going to come after me."

"No one else is coming tonight. Maybe if I catch her, I can convince her not to say anything to the . . . the rest of them. But I need you to stay here," he said again. "Anything happens, wake up Mom and Dad."

"I can't let them see me like this!" she said, the tears spilling over.

"Then wake Tris up. It'll be okay—I'll be back soon."

He grabbed one of the tea light candles on her desk—he'd use it to pay the wind sprites, who would point him in the right direction once he got to St. Sithney's—and practically flew out of the room himself as he hastened to catch up with Ephira.

He made the trip to St. Sithney's in record time, ignoring every speed limit and racing past every stop sign. Luck was on his side. He didn't see another soul on the road.

His phone rang. Steering one-handed, he tugged it out of his pocket, glanced at the name on the screen without surprise, and answered.

"Tris," he said sheepishly. "Did Hazel—"

"She told me everything," Tristan said. "Are you okay?"

"Fine. I know I should've talked to you—everything happened so fast, I couldn't waste any time—"

"I'm on my way now."

"No," Leo said. "I need you to stay with Hazel in case more of them show up."

He had assured Hazel that no one else would come for her tonight, and while he believed that, he wasn't certain enough to risk leaving her by herself.

"I don't like this," Tristan said fretfully. "I'm sorry. The hound should've been watching, but it got . . . sidetracked."

To think that Leo had worried, even for an instant, about whether their friendship would survive that brief, disastrous foray into romance. And here Tristan was, apologizing for not doing enough to help Leo, when he had already done so much more than Leo would have dared ask of anyone.

"It's not your fault," he said roughly. "Look, I'm almost there. I have to go."

He was pulling into the parking lot. A glow hovered over the woods, where it looked like another bonfire party was taking place. The bang of fireworks sounded overhead.

"I'll call Aziza," Tristan said.

"She won't get here in time."

"And I'll send a hound with you."

"Okay. Okay, yeah. Thanks, Tris," he said, and now he could hear it in his own voice, how poorly he'd concealed his feelings for Tristan. Where did he get off speaking to Tristan so softly? What had he been thinking, saying his name so easily and all the time, like he had a right to it? Now would be a good time to start setting some boundaries for himself.

But maybe, as long as Tristan couldn't see the look on his face, it was okay if he said Tristan's name too softly. And he'd work on those boundaries later, when he'd slept off the feeling of Tristan pressed against him. When Hazel could feel safe at home again.

As THE WIND sprites led him in the direction of the campgrounds, he grew uneasy. Had Ephira seen the party and gotten curious?

"Stay in the shadows unless I call for help," he told the hound.

The trees blocked out the firelight, and he only glimpsed the sky through gaps in the canopy. So he heard the party before he saw it. He didn't recognize the music they were playing this time. It was an intricate and restless melody, airy like laughter one moment, lingering and mournful the next. Some indie song. When he listened too hard, it muddled his thoughts—the way it rose and fell, sounding by turns closer and farther than it should have. He had to tune it out to focus on where he was going, plodding through the woods with his usual lack of stealth.

A whistle and a pop, and fireworks burst overhead in a shower of blue sparks. The glow of firelight lapped at the trees. He hesitated.

"That way? Are you sure?" he asked the sprites, as they tugged invisibly on his sleeves.

In response, they filled the air with the sound of wingbeats and chiming laughter.

He blew out the candle and dropped it in his pocket. With the sprites gone and the hound hidden, he felt very much alone. He should've slowed down and given his tired eyes time to adjust, but he didn't, and when he broke into the campgrounds, the fire was so bright it hurt. He threw an arm over his face, peeking gingerly underneath it at the people lounging by the tents or dancing to the music that was still—so strange and slow, so not the kind of thing you'd play at a party. He breathed in a lungful of smoke and coughed, his eyes stinging. Whatever they were burning had a ferny, floral scent, thick and sweet as clouds of perfume.

He must have looked like a mess, stumbling out of the woods in his ratty old T-shirt and sweatpants, because people moved away as he passed, almost as if the crowd was parting for him. Faceless silhouettes milled around the fire. They'd let it grow bigger than yesterday, maybe ten feet high now.

And the sprites had been right: Ephira was there, her winged outline dwarfed by the tall, slender figures on either side of her. She wasn't even hiding; she wasn't glamoured. Her wings caught the firelight, phoenixlike. She turned and beamed at the sight of him.

"There he is," she said to the others—who he was starting to suspect were *maybe* not college kids from out of town after all, go figure. "He's the one who keeps stopping her."

And whatever magic had fooled him into mistaking all of *this* for an ordinary human gathering was . . . slipping, one sense at a time. The music first, and then the springtime scent of the fire, and now he could see it, too, bits and pieces of impossible realities. Lesser fairies ventured out of hiding places in the woods, more than he'd ever seen in one place—dozens, hundreds of them, flung like nets of light over the trees. The music came from a shadowy place beyond the fire where the light glinted off gossamer strings on instruments he didn't recognize, played by hands with proportions that would've been unsuitable for a guitar. The girls holding the sparklers giggled to each other behind curtains of raven feathers that grew straight out of their heads in place of hair. What he'd thought was a game of beer pong involved crystals, cards, and something that squirmed in the hands holding it. The dancing was no drunken swaying like he remembered from yesterday, but a graceful, spinning dance, done alone or in pairs, with intention to it, like a wordless chant.

The Summer Court was already here.

They all had pointed ears, like Hazel's. Their wings were leathery and claw-tipped, or slick and iridescent, or patterned in colors as bright as paint streaks. Others had no wings but bore antlers instead. Their skin was every shade of blue, purple, green, or it was close to a human color, light tan to dark brown, sometimes dotted with freckles that were less blemishes and more adornment, like gold dust.

He backed away one step, another, and almost collided with a pair of dancers whirling by. He'd have to weave around a lot of people to return the way he'd come, and from the sly, sidelong gazes of those nearest, he didn't think walking out was going to be as easy as walking in had been.

The two figures on either side of Ephira broke away from the fire.

"Don't run," one of them said softly. It was the girl who'd offered him a drink yesterday. He could see now that she had round, long-lashed, cervine eyes, and what he'd taken for vitiligo spots on her face were more like the markings on a fallow deer. What he'd thought was a denim jacket, he saw now in the play of light across its shoulders, was a richly embroidered mantle of deep, smoky red. With the next gasp and flicker of the flames, the light changed and hid the truth of her again. For a few seconds and a handful of shadows at a time, if he hadn't known better, he could've sworn she was human.

"How . . . how did you get through the boundary?" he said, reeling.

She hid a smile behind her hand. "Such things are no concern for our kind."

"You are not the visitor we were expecting tonight," the man beside her said, in a voice like pure ice. He bore a clear resemblance to the girl—the same eyes, the same wavy golden hair. He was dressed in armor that looked as if it were made of scales, or maybe ripples of water overlapping each other; an impressive set of antlers rose from his brow.

"Now, there's no need to frighten the boy," she said. Her finger ran across the scar on her throat as if tracing a necklace. It was more obvious now than it had been yesterday, a straight-across slash as if from a rope or a knife. "He may yet be of use."

His heart pounded. Adrenaline surged through him in a dizzying rush. The hound was still with him, in his shadow, but he didn't dare call for it. They were so badly outnumbered he couldn't count on the hound to get him out unscathed, and even if it did—the Folk could follow him. They knew where he lived.

They wanted Hazel.

"My name is Princess Narra, the Summer King's heir and regent," the girl said. "This is my brother, Prince Talarix, Captain of the Gallowglass."

When she spoke their names, something in the air shifted, as if the night had slid a few degrees closer to dawn.

"And you are?" she prompted him, politely.

Does it matter? he wanted to ask, but of course he couldn't.

"Leo Merritt," he said. "I came here because . . ."

He couldn't finish. It was one thing to ask Ephira to return the glamour; it felt like an altogether different matter to make requests of a prince and princess of Elphame.

"You came here because Ephira led you here," Princess Narra said. "Quite unintentionally. She was sent for the girl you call Hazel, our lost changeling."

"What do you want with her?" Leo said. The music was in his head like smoke, choking out his thoughts.

"Want?" the princess said. "We want her to come home, of course."

"Elphame's not her home. Not anymore," he said, refusing to be cowed, though he knew arguing was dangerous. "She was abandoned."

"Her mother was *killed*," Prince Talarix cut in. "If the borderland fae speak true."

"No one else came for her."

"No one knew she existed," Princess Narra said. "But the borderland fae saw the hag tear her glamour off, and the borderland fae told the wild fae deep in Elphame, and the wild fae talked, and eventually the Summer Court heard. From what they told us, Hazel bears a striking resemblance to her mother. And a glamour that resilient can be none other than Lady Thula's work. She was our best enchantress."

"Enough of this," Prince Talarix said. "The boy interfered with something he had no right to. He will have to pay the price."

In the corner of Leo's eye, someone moved—several someones in leather jackets. Or maybe it wasn't leather; maybe they had bony plates and misshapen appendages. Armor, like the prince's, but not like it exactly. The firelight flickered. He didn't look at their eyes; he looked at their hands, their long fingers with the extra joint. The hound might be his only option after all.

But Princess Narra said, "It's all right. The other night, you were so quick to leave when we were hoping you'd stay a little while. You need not be in such a hurry. We are not inhospitable. You might have a drink, dance with us, and see how well we take care of our own. It might give you comfort when it's time to say goodbye."

"Goodbye?" Leo echoed. "And I'm supposed to be okay with you taking her and—and never seeing her again?"

He noticed distantly that the voices were dying away—that, around them in a growing circle, the silence spread like a stain, the revelers halting their conversations to watch and listen, their surreptitious glances turning into overt gawking.

"Why would you need to see her again?" she asked, with innocent confusion.

"Because she's my sister," he said, baffled himself. "That's why *you* want her back, right? She's someone's daughter."

"We want her because she belongs with us."

"She belongs with her family," Leo said. "That's *me*."

"Fairies are no kin with humans," Princess Narra said, gentle but unyielding.

"Let me make a bargain with you," he said, desperately. "I'll do anything."

Prince Talarix's eyes flashed. "If you bound yourself and five generations of your descendants in lifelong servitude to the Summer Court, it would not amount to even a fraction of what one fairy is worth."

The princess shook her head. "I'm afraid my brother is right. You don't know what you're saying. Go now, and send the changeling girl back to us by sundown. You must."

"And if I don't," he said, remembering what Ephira had told them, "then you'll take her by force? Is that what you're saying?"

"We had hoped she would choose to return," she said. "But if we must compel her, we will."

"The boy's insolence cannot be forgiven," Prince Talarix said. "You would allow him to leave and disregard the insult he has dealt us?"

It was like being caught between twin deities of the sun and moon— the princess aglow with firelight, her red mantle pooling in the grass; the prince a head taller, his armor carved as if from blackest night.

There were murmurs of approval from the watching Folk. They were on the prince's side.

"I said nothing of forgiveness," Princess Narra said. "I had something else in mind. A game, perhaps."

"Let's have him play High King of Finches," someone in the crowd said.

"Or Yellow Dwarf," another voice chimed.

But Prince Talarix shook his head.

"Those are games of skill. The outcome is a foregone conclusion; there's no fun in that," Prince Talarix said, with a cutting smile. "If we're going to play, it needs to be something he has a hope of winning."

"I suppose that leaves games of chance," Princess Narra said. Her eyes gleamed with mischief as she turned back to Leo. "There is nothing fairer than fortune. No friend more capricious, and no judge more impartial. What do you think? Will you play?"

He swallowed hard, willing his voice not to shake. "So, if I win, I get to leave? Unharmed?"

"Very well," the prince said. "We'll cast lots."

There was a flurry of motion around them, and then Ephira appeared again, shyly passing something to Prince Talarix. She turned to Leo next and offered him the same—a handful of shiny stones with symbols carved into the sides. Dice, he thought, upon closer inspection. Ten-sided crystal dice.

"You'll pick a number between ten and one hundred," Princess Narra said. "When the numbers are tallied, the one with the closer guess is the victor."

"Well?" the prince said, sounding bored. Evidently, Leo was supposed to go first.

The dice could have been tampered with. But if so, then what could he do about it?

Nothing at all.

"Fifty-five," he said.

Distantly, he thought: *Will I ever see you again?*

The prince laughed. "Fifty-six, then."

They threw the dice, which landed glittering in the dirt. Ephira knelt to read out the numbers.

"Ten," she said. "Seven, three, one, seven, seven, eight, one, four. And one."

Leo was doing the math in his head, and his breath escaped him in a gust. Nervously, he looked up at Prince Talarix.

"Fate has fallen in your favor tonight," he said. "Go, then. Only remember, the next time you think to cross the Summer Court, that fortune turns as inevitably as do the seasons."

The prince stood aside, giving Leo the dismissal he had been desperately waiting for. He went away from the fire, past the Folk as they turned their backs and continued their revel as if nothing of interest had happened, and into the safe, blissful darkness of the forest.

CHAPTER 5

AZIZA

THE FIRST TIME Aziza ever saw a fairy, she was eight years old and lost in Elphame.

None of the fae had ever made her feel threatened before. Most of her encounters thus far had been with easily appeased sprites, grass pixies, and lesser fairies, who approached her with the same inno- cent curiosity she felt toward them. So when the wills-o'-the-wisp appeared, she followed them not because they had tricked her, but because she wanted to and had no reason to fear they would hurt her. They led her to a circle of lemon-yellow mushrooms with soft, fleshy caps that were ribbed underneath and waxy on the top. She bent down to touch one, and the wills-o'-the-wisp waited patiently for her to straighten and wander another few steps forward, into the circle, which was, of course, a fairy ring.

A fairy door was an opening between the human world and Elphame; a fairy ring was something different, much less passive than a door, and to step inside one was giving permission for Elphame's magic to spirit you away and deposit you wherever it pleased. The world twisted, and Aziza was someplace else. She stumbled out of the fairy ring and into a forest of graceful birches, all slender and white. Moss grew so thickly on the ground that her shoes sank into it. Lesser fairies plucked inquisitively at her hair, their glow making her squint. The forest was an old place, quiet, and likely did not exist in the human world. Close to boundaries between the human world and Elphame, there was overlap; the woods at St. Sithney's existed in both realms. Here, in the birch wood, there was no overlap at all. It was too deep in Elphame.

She'd headed toward where she hoped the edge of the forest lay. A tree line might mean a boundary she could use to cross back over into the human realm. Soon, a valley opened up ahead of her. A dirt path crossed in front of the birch forest, and a stranger traveled along it.

It was a man in armor atop a copper-colored steed, just like a knight out of a fairytale—though even then she had known well the difference between *real* fairytales and false ones. His mount clopped along at an easy walk. He had golden hair that fell in waves around the long tips of his ears, and antlers that branched into a forest of deadly points. His armor fitted to him in overlapping layers, like black scales. His head lifted as if he had somehow heard her, though she hadn't moved an inch since catching sight of him, hadn't even breathed. His eyes met hers. They were dark as creek water—deceptively still and solemn, but teeming in their depths with things unseen.

This, she would later learn, was a fairy.

He smiled and tugged on the reins to draw his mount to a stop. It whickered softly, a horselike creature whose mane shed pollen with every movement, whose flesh was intermittently translucent, like a pane of glass turned briefly opaque by sunbeams, and which left no hoofprints in the earth.

"Hello there," the knight said, and his voice was as smooth as a stone in a riverbank. "You've wandered far from home, gatewalker.

Have you been led astray?" He released one of the reins and held out a hand gallantly, as if she were a noblewoman and not a scruffy eight-year-old witch with dirt under her fingernails. In the sun, with his yellow hair and black armor, he resembled nothing so much as an overgrown hornet. "Come with me, and you need never be lost again."

The words were steeped in what she would later identify as fairy charm: His magic lent them a silkiness, a sincerity that harmonized with some truth-seeking instinct within her. In the same way that a kelpie could persuade an otherwise rational human being to climb onto its back, the hornet knight made it so that taking his hand would have been the simplest, most logical, most natural thing in the world.

But hedgewitches could not be snared in this way. The sound of the hornet knight's voice filled her only with an overpowering dread. When she didn't move—frozen with fear—he urged his sunlight-and-pollen steed off the path, its unshod hooves nudging through the wild grasses. It was the gentlest chase a predator had ever given. But a chase was what it was.

This, at last, jolted her into action. She ran the way she'd come, back into the birch wood. She ran until her ribs burned and the cramps were a knife in her stomach. She didn't know where she was going, other than away. And when she couldn't go any farther, she stopped and stumbled to a tree and hid behind it, ears straining for the sound of hoofbeats. But she couldn't hear anything except the pounding of her heart. Her lungs gasped for air, and she clamped her sweaty hands over her mouth in a vain effort to muffle the noise.

There was a tug on the hem of Aziza's shirt.

"Come away from there, gatewalker," said a high, thin voice from somewhere about level with Aziza's waist. It belonged to something that *looked* like the pixies she sometimes encountered in Blackthorn—a little like a giant praying mantis—only it was larger than they were, maybe two feet tall, and its wings were like flower petals, pastel pink and white with sunny yellow markings.

Aziza obeyed without question. Her rescuer took her to a tunnel made of twigs, leaves, and sap. She crawled inside. Small shining treasures were woven into the walls, and she was surrounded by tiny bodies all chittering and whispering to each other. The tunnel was warm and smelled sweet, and was drenched in pixie magic that tickled the back of her throat, so that she had to hold back a sneeze.

She crouched there in the dark, feeling her protectors' wings and antennae brush against her, hearing more of them skittering about deeper in the tunnel. Soon, the fear ebbed away. The light outside changed with the approach of sunset. And she was somehow certain the hornet knight was long gone.

"You saved me," she whispered finally.

In response came a feather-soft touch to her cheek.

"Be an ally to pixies," said her rescuer, "and your debt to us is repaid."

That day, in hiding, she began her true education as a hedgewitch. After that, anytime she had a question about magic or Elphame that Jiddo couldn't answer, it was the pixies she turned to. They helped her find her way back into the human world. The fairy ring had taken her far from Blackthorn's boundary; she ended up in Vermont, on a dirt road that passed by a lone cottage, and was lucky enough to run into an older boy who helped her catch a bus into the nearest city. Jiddo, who was frantic with worry by then, had to come and pick her up from a police station. They had CPS on them for months after that because they couldn't explain how she got there. But it could have been so much worse.

After what Leo had seen last night, what he'd told her, she couldn't stop thinking about that day. About the hornet knight and the visceral fear she'd felt. About how, when Leo had described Prince Talarix, a shiver had swept over her. He sounded uncomfortably familiar.

A coincidence. It had to be. Maybe there were many fairy men with black armor and golden hair. But how should she know? The Fair Folk were not borderland fae. She'd never met any other than the knight and Hazel. And she had always hoped that the next time she encountered a fairy—a grown one, a fairy of Elphame and not a changeling girl who thought and acted like a human most of the time—Aziza had hoped she wouldn't need to run away again. But the Summer Court had blown through Blackthorn's boundary, *her* boundary, like it was nothing. Was it that they were strong, or that she was weak?

That her craft was weak?

Why hadn't she thought it strange that she didn't remember seeing the glow of firelight or hearing music from the bonfire party Leo and Tristan had come across the other night? She'd thought her route through the woods had just taken her far enough away from the campgrounds, and that she'd been so focused on finding Hazel, that she hadn't noticed. Careless of her. Had her narrow victory against the hag made her so cocky that she thought nothing could get past her anymore? Maybe this was the wake-up call she'd needed.

Last she'd heard, Hazel was locked in her room, refusing to speak to anyone. They hadn't told Leo's parents what was going on. Leo was keeping them away from Hazel's room so that they wouldn't see her without her glamour—how, Aziza had no idea, being no expert on parents herself. Meanwhile, Tristan thought the blækhounds could defend them all. Aziza's gut instinct said that one untrained necromancer's blækhounds didn't stand a chance against the number of fairies Leo had seen last night.

So, first thing in the morning, Aziza paid a visit to Marinus—Meryl's father and chief of the local selkie pod. He had a small fishing vessel that he used mainly to keep an eye on the boundary to Elphame that followed the jagged coastline. He also fished for real; he sold his catch to a few sushi places, using the money to maintain the boat and—he had once confided—occasionally take the children in his pod on outings into Blackthorn. Selkie pups liked movie theaters and Swedish Fish.

It was still dark when she found him on the docks, in yellow waders and a wide-brimmed hat, prepping his skiff to set sail. Out here, Blackthorn felt a world away. There was only the salt wind snagging at her hair, the low waves churning under her feet, and the squawking of the gulls as they woke.

Marinus straightened up from checking his navigation lights. "All week, the storms off the western winds brought bad tidings. I wondered when I'd hear from you."

"It's definitely bad," she admitted, and told him about the Fair Folk. Marinus worked while she spoke—checking battery levels, uncovering the gauges. When she was finished, it was several long moments before he turned back to her.

"You mean to keep their daughter from them," Marinus said gravely. His tangled mane of gray hair was specked with sea-foam. "Do you think that's right?"

"It's not like Meryl," she argued. "Hazel isn't being kept away by force. She's being taken *back* by force."

He regarded her over his hooked nose. "We can't fight the Fair Folk. You can't, either."

"So we should give up?" Aziza said helplessly.

"It's not giving up. It's accepting the inevitable. Just as I have accepted the inevitable."

The platform rocked beneath her; her stomach lurched, seasick and dismayed in equal measures. "What have you accepted?"

"That my daughter is not coming back," he said, and in his voice she heard both the pain those words caused him and the calm determination of one who'd charted a course and intended to see it through to the end.

"It's—it's only been a few months. I know we don't have any leads yet, but—"

"It hasn't been a few months. It's been almost twenty years," he said, not harshly. "Selkies are meant to migrate, and we haven't for a long time. At summer's end, we are leaving. It is time for us to reclaim our old routes and our old homes."

"But what changed?" Aziza said, reeling. "Do you . . . know something?"

To her relief, he shook his head.

"This is the longest my daughter has ever gone without contacting us. She used to send us signals to assure us of her safety. Seagull feathers dipped in ink. Rings carved from coral or pearl. Freshwater she had cleansed in moonlight, adding to it a single tear. These talismans she would deliver to us in the mouths of eels and marlins. And now, nothing? If she is not dead, then she is urging us to move on by giving us no more reason to stay."

"Or she's under orders not to contact you and can't find a loophole anymore," Aziza said.

He dug something out of his pocket and handed it to her. It was the note that Aziza had given to him from Meryl a few months back, which Meryl had sent with a lock of her hair to convince her father to hear Aziza out. She opened it with a sinking feeling of dread. Her eyes scanned the words, the sight of Meryl's tidy handwriting making her throat go tight with how much she missed her.

It was a farewell note. What Meryl couldn't say with the talismans she'd sent before, she'd taken the opportunity to put down in the letter Aziza had volunteered to deliver. She had told her father to stop waiting for her.

"I think she has always wanted us to move on," Marinus said quietly. "The signals she sent us, to let us know she was well, were meant to give us the freedom to keep going. Part of me always knew that. I tethered us here, and now that the messages have ceased, leaving is harder than ever. But I must. I believe it is time."

Aziza said, fiercely, "Meryl is not dead."

"Are you saying that because you believe it to be true, or because you wish it to be true?"

Both.

Meryl *couldn't* be dead. Aziza had not spent all those years rescuing fae and humans from each other just to fail to save someone as important to her as Meryl was.

She left him in a grim mood, more worried about Meryl than ever and still no closer to finding a way to help Hazel. And since that was the immediate problem, that was what Aziza would have to focus on, despite the guilt she felt at putting Meryl out of her mind . . . again. There was always something or someone else taking precedence over Meryl's suffering.

The sidewalk was starting to fill up with people. Early morning joggers and bikers, mostly. Dodging them, she headed briskly toward the train station. She was so preoccupied that the light tug on her shoelace almost went unnoticed. Then it came again, insistent enough to almost trip her.

She looked down. Her shoe was untied. Sand was sprayed across the pavement, as if it had been kicked up from the beach, but there was no one nearby.

"Is someone trying to get my attention?" she asked nobody in particular.

The sand stirred, though there was no breeze.

She crossed the narrow strip of grass between the sidewalk and the beach. A little whirlwind of sand, barely visible in the sunlight, swished around her calves and grazed the fingers of her good hand.

"*I know a secret,*" said the sand sprite, its voice a scratchy whisper.

"A secret?" Aziza watched mounds of sea-foam fling themselves upon the shore and recede, leaving frothy white trails behind. "Something that would interest me?"

"*Yes, yes, a good secret for the gatewalker.*" Three pits opened in the sand, like the burrows made by ghost crabs, the bottommost one curved in a toothless smile. Her shoelace fell into it, so that the sprite seemed to chew on it as it added, pointedly, "*Time sensitive.*"

"All right, fine." She dug a Hershey's Kiss out of her bag, unwrapped it clumsily, and dropped it into the sand, where the sprite gnawed at it until it melted. Creatures of salt liked to be paid with things that were sweet. They also liked stealing. Sandals, bottle caps, scrunchies—anything dropped on the beach that might provide some entertainment and could be deposited on the surface again once the sprites got bored.

"*Someone,*" said the sprite, "*is following you.*"

And despite the simmering June heat, a chill washed over her.

To her shame, her first thought was of the hornet knight, and she felt a rush of the old, childish fear. Before she could ask the sand sprite anything else, it was gone, along with the last traces of chocolate and the plastic tip of her shoelace. She cursed under her breath and hurried onward to the train station, eager to get out of the open.

CHAPTER 6

TRISTAN

NOTHING GREW WHERE the gateway tree had once stood.

The opening to the underground chamber had collapsed in on itself, scorched and sealed over by the elements. Around it, though, the clearing had burst into renewed life. The hag's magic had been a gray sickness; since it had dissipated, even the songbirds had no fear of this place. Moss had grown over the remnants of her cabin, over the broken and blackened pieces of the nymph-enchanted trees that had shielded Aziza from the worst of the hag's flames, turning the glade into a haunting of bulbous green ghosts.

He was alone, but not for long.

The hounds kept to the woods and to the pockets of emptiness within Blackthorn, the small shadowed nooks that existed in all cities. One lifted its dripping maw from the belly of a freshly killed alley cat, ears pricking at his silent call. Another, lying flat under a car and watching things walk, crawl, skitter by, pressed its chin to the hot, acrid-smelling asphalt and listened. Yet another rested with its front paws dangling in a brook, the water steaming where the hound touched it, observing the flash of light on tiny fish scales, the flick of a squirrel's tail, the shiny beetles puttering over cracks in the stony bank; it yawned with wide-open jaws but rose to its feet obediently. The scarred hound heard him, too, but Tristan bade it stay put in its usual post under Hazel's window.

Soon, they were there in the clearing with him; though his eyes were shut, he felt grass under the sensitive pads of his paws, and he smelled the new growth slowly eclipsing the rot and misery baked into the earth here, and he was hollow with hunger—the hounds were always hungry, no matter how much they ate. He saw himself a dozen times over, through their eyes, their strange summoner who was white and rangy as a hare, but who was not afraid to bite and snarl and cut with the silver claw he kept hidden in his boot.

"Your last summoner died here," he told them. "And I need you to find them. *Go.*"

They went.

A few weeks after the hag's death, Tristan had gathered up the nerve to talk to Aziza's grandfather. He had been anxious; Khaled had never said an unkind word to him, but he knew that Tristan was the necromancer who had helped Aziza dig up her parents' graves. He was also aware that Tristan had been the hag's bondservant, that his blækhounds had been the ones terrorizing Blackthorn, though Aziza had told him that Tristan had never meant for any of that to happen.

But there was a lot that Aziza had kept from him. Khaled didn't know that Tristan wasn't a trueborn witch. The story they'd come up with was that Tristan had been born into a nonmagical family with a distant witch ancestor, and that his parents had forced him to suppress his powers until he couldn't any longer. They hadn't mentioned the bond to him, either. Aziza didn't dare tell him that she had taken up a magical contract the hag had created. Even if the hag wasn't part of it anymore, it had been hers first—and Aziza had willingly claimed it. He was already upset about the risks she'd taken; knowing about *this* would only cause him more pain. And Tristan, for his part, always preferred to keep his secrets.

Still, Khaled was the only adult witch he knew, and Tristan had gone to him in the hopes of learning something—anything—about his craft. But Khaled couldn't teach him spells; he was a rook, a witch with an affinity for protective magic, in his case ward-crafting. He had been acquainted with a necromancer once, but had gotten no response when he'd tried reaching out to his old contact after the blækhounds had appeared in Blackthorn. When Tristan had fallen silent, having run out of questions to ask because even knowing *what* to ask required a basic level of knowledge he lacked, Khaled had taken pity on him.

"Where did you get your grimoire?" Khaled had said, the way tech support might say, *have you tried turning your computer off and on again?* Just prompting him with something easy.

"My . . . grimoire?" Tristan had repeated blankly.

"You couldn't have made the hounds without one," he'd said. "There are things you can do with clear intent, sheer stubbornness, and a little magic, but the creation of blækhounds isn't one of them."

Made the hounds, he had said.

There were ten blækhounds in Blackthorn, magically connected to Tristan; they were the same hounds the hag had called on the night when she'd turned him into a necromancer. He'd always thought of the hounds as creatures that were born in the shadow plane and came to the mortal realm as visitors. It had never occurred to him that hounds weren't born, but *made*. The hag hadn't called them, but created them—or, more likely, they'd been created by the necromancer whose power the hag had stolen. She couldn't use the necromancy gift; that was why she'd forced it on Tristan.

So he had taken not only a witch's magic . . . but that witch's familiars, too.

"I . . . found the grimoire," he had said, struggling to make the lie sound plausible while his mind was running in about twenty different directions at once. "With some old things that belonged to a relative who passed."

"I see. So it could have been in your family for ages," Khaled had said thoughtfully. "A grimoire is a book of spells that can be charged with an offering *before* the spells are cast. A necromancer's grimoire is made from animal remains, usually, and that creature's death becomes the offering for the spells in the book. The one in your possession must be powerful if it contains blækhound spells. My advice is to leave it alone." He had paused, his eyes softening. "I know that's not the answer you wanted."

Unfortunately, *leaving it alone* wasn't what Tristan had in mind.

He should have searched for the other necromancer's remains before, but he hadn't felt ready to come back here. Now there was no choice. If he wanted to get his hands on a grimoire, this was his best chance. With it, maybe he could create more hounds. An army of them. Enough to protect Hazel and everyone who mattered to her— everyone who mattered to *him*—from anything that would harm them.

Some of the hounds searched the clearing, and others dispersed into the surrounding woods. Whenever one of them smelled something promising, he took the shovel he'd brought and dug a shallow hole under its impassive gaze.

There were a lot of human remains in this place. Enough to call it a paupers' grave.

"Well? Do you recognize this one?" he asked the nearest hound, fighting the urge to be sick as he used the shovel to nudge at what he thought was someone's wristbone. If this person wasn't the necromancer, then they were one of the hag's other victims, dead because Tristan had marked their home with his blood.

How could he communicate the abstract concept of recognition or familiarity to a creature he wasn't even certain had the capacity for such things? The hounds recognized *him*, but was it only because they were bound to him? If he was gone, would they remember him?

The hound sniffed at the wristbone once and sat back, unimpressed.

"Okay," he said, filling in the hole. "I'll take your word for it."

The hours wore on. He only paused when his phone vibrated in his pocket.

Aziza had said: *no luck yet.*

With a grimace, he replied: *same.*

Leo had said nothing all day.

That morning, before Tristan had left, they'd stood side by side in the kitchen, Tristan stirring sugar into a mug of coffee and Leo picking half-heartedly at a piece of toast. There was a kind of mutual understanding between them—that there were too many more important things happening in their lives to worry about one unfortunate kiss. Leo leaned heavily on the counter, head low, like if one more thing went wrong, it would break him. Tristan wanted so badly to make him feel better. But he didn't have the power to do that anymore. He drank his coffee and kept his eyes on his own hands, feeling useless and out of place.

"Can we skip the part where things are awkward?" Leo said abruptly, glancing over with a tired smile. "And talk later?"

"We can skip the awkward part if you can skip the part where you let me down easy," Tristan said without thinking. The second it was out of his mouth, he cursed himself. He didn't mean to sound like a petulant brat because Leo had turned him down. Even though he *did* feel kind of petulant and kind of bratty about it.

But Leo just laughed. "As opposed to, what, letting you down hard? Can I have a demonstration?" That earned Leo a sidelong look, and he reddened. "I didn't mean . . ."

"*That*," Tristan said, emphatically. "I don't want you to start censoring yourself because you're afraid I'll take something the wrong way. And you don't owe me any explanations."

"So you don't wanna hear 'it's not you, it's me'?"

Tristan made a face. "I'd almost prefer it if you just told me it was a terrible kiss."

"It wasn't," Leo said, and then buried his face in his hands, the flush on his neck rising to his ears. "Just don't listen to anything I say from now on, how about that?"

Tristan's smile hurt. Of course Leo had liked kissing him. Tristan had had practice, *with* him. But Leo didn't know that. If Leo hadn't pushed him away last night, what then? Would Tristan have been okay with Leo liking him back because of subconscious feelings brought on by a shared history Leo couldn't remember? If that was the only reason, then was it even real? Or was anything that grew between them now only a hollow echo of what they had before?

In the present, his despondent thoughts were interrupted when his phone vibrated.

Aziza said: *i doubt any number of hounds will save us from a fairy siege. if we stay and they get through the hounds, we're trapped.*

running is risky too, he argued. *where could we even go? if we stay put, we have more control over the situation.*

Leo broke his silence at last: *i don't think control of the situation is on the table either way.*

Tristan hesitated. *what does hazel want to do?* he asked, because if they didn't have a plan, then they might as well give Hazel the deciding vote.

what she wants to do isn't happening, Leo said, and Tristan felt his eyebrows go up.

what's not happening? he replied.

she thinks we should hand her over.

He and Aziza must have stayed silent for too long, because a flurry of messages came through from Leo:

she doesnt want them to come after the rest of us

she wants to leave without saying anything to mom and dad

how am i supposed to tell them

Tristan's heart felt like it was being throttled. He'd known Hazel almost as long as he'd known Leo. After they'd killed the hag and he'd gone to stay over at Leo's place, it had taken a few days for Hazel to catch him alone and talk to him. When she finally did, she had about a thousand questions, each one more blunt than the last. Why had he left? Did he still love Leo? Was he sad Leo couldn't remember him? Did it hurt to use magic? Had he missed them, had he missed *her,* did he think she was weird now?

He tapped the screen with his thumb to start another message.

if someone gets hurt she'll blame herself. but we won't let that happen.

Leo didn't respond.

Tristan put his phone away, returning his attention to the hounds.

CLOSE TO SUNDOWN, Aziza texted them one last time.

i'm coming back. we're on our own

He had scoured every inch of the clearing, and there was still no sign of any grimoire. Defeated, he replied, *me too.*

A beat, and then Leo's response: *i just checked hazel's room. she's gone.*

CHAPTER 7

LEO

THEY WASTED NO time getting to St. Sithney's; he was petrified that the moment Hazel was in their grasp, the Summer Court would disappear without a trace. But the bonfire still burned. The music still played; when he listened closely, he could hear the unearthly notes of the fairy instruments he'd glimpsed yesterday buried inside the illusion of guitar chords and pop melodies, like its skeleton.

Hazel hadn't been taken. She'd left a note. She had gone willingly, not wanting Leo or their parents to get hurt protecting her. Leo just wanted to know why the hell Hazel thought protecting *them* was her job, and not the other way around.

"Leo," Aziza said. "You already know they won't bargain with you."

"I know. I just need to talk to Hazel." Improbably, he felt calmer now than he had all day. They were here, and whatever was going to happen next would happen. He gave her and Tristan what he hoped was a reassuring smile. "Will you stay here and watch my back?"

Tristan did not look reassured. "Why can't we come with you?"

"I'll need you to get me out if something goes wrong," Leo said, willing them not to press further.

Aziza met his eyes with a weighted look. His subterfuge was useless against her; she didn't need a psychic bond with him to read his mind.

"You're right," she said at last. "We'll be in a better position to help you if we don't get caught ourselves. Just be careful."

He left before they had a chance to change their minds, emerging into the clearing and letting the revel sweep him away again.

A boy tugged on his arm, trying to pull him into a dance; Leo didn't make eye contact as he said, *No, thank you*, because as long as he didn't look too hard at anyone, they *just* managed to pass for human. But as he slipped away, the firelight glistened over eyes that were far too bright, and the shape of the boy's smile was broken somehow, and he didn't look, he didn't need to look. The fire both lent the illusions some cover—so easy to write off a flicker of strangeness as *a trick of the light*—and created opportunities to see through gaps in the enchantments.

He wasn't surprised when he didn't see Hazel anywhere. They weren't going to make it that easy for him. Besides, Hazel wasn't the one he was really looking for.

He had to circle around a group of people who struck him as imposingly tall and broad, in dark clothing his eyes still interpreted as leather, even though he knew, after yesterday, what it really was. The trick was to watch from his peripheral vision. Like he had with the sandman. It was easier to see past the illusions that way. These were the Gallowglass. Up close, their armor looked *alive*, as if it had grown around them—something organic that would wither and die if the person within were extracted. Many of them wore boots and gauntlets studded with thorns. Some had more distinctive pieces—carved opal-colored chest plates like iridescent carapaces or horned helmets like Atlas beetles.

"Caught a thief," one of them was saying, with cold amusement. She tossed something to one of her companions, whose helmet had protrusions in the front like a spider's fangs. "I found it sneaking around, getting into the food."

The spider-fang knight lifted the squirming creature to eye level. It was a snake—until it morphed into a bat and attempted to fly away. A pooka. They were shapeshifters who drifted into Blackthorn sometimes—harmless, curious beings that were easily shooed away. Its captor had a firm grip around its middle, and something gleamed on its throat: a silver collar.

Silver burned and repelled fae beings. They were torturing it.

It started to transform again, but the man's gloved fingers squeezed hard around it. It let out of a cry of pain and subsided, settling back into bat form, quivering with fear.

"What shall its punishment be?" the spider-fang knight said, sneering.

"Perhaps we can convince it to change into a grouse, and then we can cook it," someone else volunteered.

The others laughed while the pooka turned into a snake again and tried to slither out of the spider-fang knight's hand. It became a squirrel, tiny claws scrabbling at his gauntlet; it was a songbird for an instant, its fearful cries shrill as its wings got crushed, and then it was a mouse, and then a snake again—the silver collar wasn't letting it get any bigger, and its smaller forms were restrained with little effort by the knight's unforgiving grip.

Leo had seen enough. Hands in his pockets, head down, he shouldered past the Gallowglass, knocking into the spider-fang knight, who stumbled forward a step and dropped the pooka. It was gone in an instant, disappearing into the grass and through the crowd. And Leo was gone, too, not slowing long enough for anyone to realize what he'd done. He hoped. But when he glanced back once, to make sure he wasn't being followed, he met a pair of eyes—black eyes behind a fanged helmet.

He averted his gaze. He'd come around to the other side of the bonfire. As he hesitated, one of the women with raven-feather hair tapped on his shoulder.

"That way," she said, pointing through the trees. "The princess is expecting you."

"Thanks," he said, and went on.

He found Princess Narra in a moonlit glade, where the forest canopy split apart along a dry creek bed. She had allowed her illusions to fall. Tonight, there was no mistaking her magnificent red cloak for something a sorority girl would have thrown on. Little spots of brightness fluttered around her, like oversized fireflies, or maybe lesser fairies; then one of them perched on her shoulder, and he realized it was a bird. She tilted her head, as if listening.

He stepped cautiously forward. "Hello?"

A sharp intake of breath, and then she was turning to him. "Ah, you're here. I suspected we'd see you again."

Another one of the light-birds landed in her cupped palms. She closed her hands over it, and it vanished, as if she'd extinguished a flame. The others disappeared one by one.

"What were those things?" Leo asked. It was easier than saying what he'd planned. Nervous energy buzzed inside him. His nails pressed into his palms, but he didn't uncurl his fists. He'd just fidget like an anxious kid.

"They bring me messages," she said. "From distant friends. I rarely leave the Summer Court, as you can imagine."

"I can't," he said honestly. He imagined the Fair Folk did exactly as they pleased. "Why?"

"I am the heir. Father needs me to stay close, where I'll be safe, especially since my brother is away so often." At his blank look, she elaborated: "He has treated with other courts and warred with them; he has met with witch ambassadors and traveled to give counsel to our cousins across the sea. These are among his responsibilities, as Captain of the Gallowglass."

"Is your brother going to kill me if he finds me here?" Leo asked.

Her fingers tugged at the edges of her cloak, drawing it close around her neck. "You must think him so fearsome. It's only that the subject of the changeling girl is rather sensitive for him."

"Sensitive," Leo echoed in disbelief. "Sorry, but I find that hard to believe."

"Let me explain. I think it will help you understand," she said. "Prince Tal's mother was an enchantress called Lady Cirrine. She was my father's consort, while my mother was the Summer Queen."

"So he's your half brother," Leo said.

"Yes. Lady Cirrine wished to rule, and for Tal to be heir. She conspired to have me and my mother killed." Her voice was measured and calm, as if telling a bedtime story. "She succeeded in eliminating the queen. But my father learned what she'd done before she could get to me. He had her executed. After that, Cirrine's sister was all but cast out. They were very close—it was assumed she had known Cirrine's plans, and had kept her sister's secrets, though she always denied it."

It was all so bloody and sordid.

"I'm sorry about your mom," he said.

"It was a long time ago," she deflected. "I tell you this because I believe it explains Lady Thula's secrecy. Even years later, she had few friends here. Perhaps that was why she told no one about her child."

"Lady Thula . . . ?" he repeated slowly. He'd heard that name yesterday, but it was a few seconds before his memory caught up with him. His eyes widened in horror. "Thula. That's Hazel's mom. She was Lady Cirrine's sister?"

"Yes," Narra said. "And so, her daughter . . ."

"Hazel is Prince Tal's cousin," he said. The realization gave him a sick jolt. Hazel had family here. A living blood relative. It somehow made his own familial claim on Hazel feel frighteningly tenuous.

"Tal loved his Aunt Thula," she said. "And he values family very highly."

"So do I," Leo said, steeling himself. "I know that Hazel's here. I came to get her back."

"It will be easier for you and for her if you can make peace with this," she said. "Let her go. For both your sakes."

All he wanted to do, in response to that soft voice, was nod along and tell her whatever would make her happiest. This, he figured, was how a feeble human brain typically responded to gentle pleas from a princess of Elphame: with fawning, dazzled obedience. He had to bite his tongue until the urge had passed.

"You're the one in charge here," he said. "If you said Hazel could leave, the others would listen to you. Right?"

"It's not that simple," she said. "The Summer King rests in an enchanted sleep, but in one week's time, at the solstice, he will awaken. My power is temporary and limited. There is little I can do without the support of my brother and the Gallowglass."

"And what if I gave you a way to convince them?"

She shot him an assessing look from under her lashes, the way she had when he'd refused to accept a drink from her that first night. "What did you have in mind?"

Although it was only the two of them there, he felt watched, as if eyes had opened in the dark spaces between the trees, or ears had bloomed out of spirals of moss.

Since meeting Aziza, he had helped her rescue a lot of people from fae mischief. He'd never judged any of them. Not the ones who followed the wills-o'-the-wisp out of plain curiosity even before their hypnotic magic set in, or the ones who blamed increasingly frequent bouts of sleepiness on stress and exhaustion rather than checking in their attics or under their beds for sandmen. Even the ones who willingly sought out magic, thinking themselves clever enough to make deals with the supernatural, he couldn't blame them. The woman they found under the pier with a flute in hand, enticing sirens with melancholy songs because she'd heard seawomen could grant wishes, hoping they would cure her unrequited love and almost getting her heart literally ripped out for her trouble. Or the man who'd asked the voice in the hollow under the oak tree in his backyard to bring back his dead son, not realizing the voice belonged to a doppelganger, and that when his child returned, it wouldn't really *be* his child. Even Tristan had been fooled into signing a hag's contract, and Tristan was—levelheaded, perceptive, brilliant in every possible way. The very best people still had moments of vulnerability, and magic was good at wriggling into your vulnerable places and breaking you open.

Still, it was one thing to think, *That could've happened to anyone*, and another for it to happen to *him*. In the blink of an eye, Leo sold his fate to the Fair Folk.

This was how it went:

"You said fairies and humans aren't kin. Let me prove we're more alike than you think," he said. "Your people like games. Put me up against anyone you want. If I win, Hazel comes home with me. If I lose, then—I forfeit my life. And Hazel will stay with the Summer Court."

It was a reckless gamble, with the highest stakes. Which was what made it interesting.

That was what he was counting on, anyway.

Princess Narra watched him so intently he worried, for a moment, that he'd made a mistake—he'd pushed the limits of her patience too far.

"In the old days," she said musingly, "humans would voyage through Elphame, slaying our monsters, sharing their art and music, marrying into our families, earning titles of nobility in our courts. But as your cities grew, the borders that allowed passage between our two realms began to disappear. We don't mingle so much with your kind now. But we do miss those days. Few of us are old enough to remember, but there is a pull, you know, between our folk."

Leo didn't know what to say to that, so he didn't say anything.

"Allow me to suggest a slightly different set of terms," she said, her eyes alight with an almost childlike excitement. "You'll join the Wild Hunt. If you succeed, Hazel may go home with you. If you fail, Hazel stays. And so do you. As a servant to the Summer Court."

"What's the Wild Hunt?" Leo asked.

"A sacred journey across Elphame, to retrieve something very precious—something we will need to complete the summer solstice ceremony," she said. "It used to be a competition; the successful Huntsman would prove their valor and earn a place of honor in the Summer Court. It fell out of favor, after a time, for being too barbaric. Now the Huntsman is appointed by the king or queen. But . . . it could be a competition again, perhaps. Just this once."

"I'll do it," he said.

This was a choice he'd already made. No matter what she had asked of him, the answer was always going to be yes.

"I am not the only one you'll need to persuade," she warned him.

"Then who?" he said grimly. "Prince Tal?"

"Not exactly. Come with me."

CHAPTER 8

AZIZA

"I DON'T LIKE this," Tristan muttered, the moment Leo had left. "We shouldn't have let him go alone."

"We'll make things worse if we barge in there."

If he offended them, the Folk could trap Leo in a life of indentured servitude in a castle so deep in Elphame he could never find the way back home. Or magic him into dancing until he passed out from exhaustion. Or force-feed him lily wine until he was pliant, suggestible, and unable to stop himself from blurting out all his deepest secrets. Or they'd saddle him with another curse just to see how many he could carry before his mind broke, or they'd beguile him into spending the night with some fairy maiden who wanted to try for a half-human child, or—

If fairies were merely violent, they would have been less frightening. But fairies dealt in illusions and compulsions. They'd turn you against yourself before they ever lifted a hand to harm you.

"I can't see him anymore," Tristan said, and at his side, his fingers curled into a beckoning gesture that might have been unconscious. The shadows around him twitched oddly, like membranes about to be torn open by something strange and squirming that lived inside.

"It's too soon to bring the hounds in," Aziza told him sharply. "I'll get closer to the fire—that's probably where he's headed. See if you can find Hazel in the meantime."

She left him behind and made a circuit around the campgrounds, staying under cover.

Earlier today, as she'd sought information about what they were dealing with, she'd found a colony of orchid pixies that had followed the Summer Court to Blackthorn. Orchid pixies resided mostly in the deeper parts of Elphame, so they knew much more about the Fair Folk than their borderland kin did. It was an orchid pixie that had saved her from the hornet knight, all those years ago.

They had told her that the Summer Court was one half of the Court of the Seasons, the highest law in Elphame, at least on this side of the ocean. They were counterparts—one nomadic, the other fixed in place; one making their home in the woods, the other deep in the mountains—and while they ruled together, they were also rivals, forever competing with each other for territory and sovereignty over smaller clans, such as the Autumn Court, the Cattail Court, the Buried Court. Any minor court could ascend to power and become the new Summer or Winter Court, if they had the means to overthrow the existing monarchy. But such a move posed great risks, and entire courts had been obliterated after failed coups.

All fairies were magical; fairies of the Summer and Winter Courts were the most magical of all, but their formidable power came at a cost. It flowed from a binding connection to the land, which conferred upon them the authority to rule, as well as the duty to watch over Elphame and all that lived and grew there. To maintain that connection, every seven years, for seven months, one of the two reigning monarchs of the Court of the Seasons retreated into an enchanted sleep that ended with a solstice ceremony. This year, King Illanthus slept. In another seven years, it would be the Winter Queen's turn. Without the ritual, their power would collapse, their connection to Elphame severed. In its absence, they would fall victim to the jade rot—a wasting sickness of some kind, which the pixies spoke of with fearful, almost superstitious reluctance.

This was a seventh year, the end of a cycle and start of a new one. In one week, the Summer King would wake and complete the ceremony that would cement their rule for another seven years.

But when she'd asked, *How can we make the Folk leave?* the pixies' only response had been to laugh riotously.

Something shot out of the campgrounds, fleeing, and almost collided with her shoe. It was a pooka. It transformed into a sparrow and attempted to take flight, but there was something wrong with one of its wings, and it fell to the ground again, turned into a hedgehog, and curled up into a tight ball. Something glinted on its neck—a collar?

She reached out to the pooka with her magic, and its own magic prodded back tentatively. The little ball on the ground began to uncurl, slowly and distrustfully. She plucked a leaf off a nearby tree, set it on the ground near the pooka—not so close it would feel threatened, but not too far, either—and poured some water from her bottle into it, using it as a makeshift bowl. The pooka turned its beady black eyes on her before shifting into a dormouse and approaching. While it drank, she took a closer look at it, and winced when she realized the collar on its neck was silver. When it had had its fill, it looked up at her with a spark of the curiosity that she had come to view as the defining trait of its kind. This pooka was young, and had never met a human before, not even a hedgewitch.

"You tried to steal from them, didn't you?" she whispered, and reached out to it, gently. "I'm going to get that thing off you. It will hurt less once it's gone."

She kept murmuring to it, soothing things, while her fingers found a clasp and unlatched the tiny silver collar—ring-sized, really. If it had turned into an insect, it probably could have slipped out of it, but insect forms were harder for pookas; this one might not have learned any yet. Pookas took best to shapes that were made for roaming, and could move quickly. It froze with fear, not moving a muscle even after she withdrew; but then it saw the collar on the ground and felt that it was free. Calmer now, it looked up again at Aziza. Evidently feeling that it could not conduct a thorough enough investigation in its present form, it turned into a possum, with large eyes and a twitching nose, which inched toward Aziza's fingers with the same lack of caution that had probably gotten it into the mess Aziza had just rescued it from.

"Yes, you're welcome," she said under her breath, allowing it to sniff at her hand. "But if you're smart, you'll get out of here before you wind up in even more trouble."

As if on cue, footsteps came up behind her, crunching through the detritus. The pooka flinched violently, its whole body shaking, before shrinking back into dormouse form and fleeing into the woods.

Aziza looked up.

A man stood over her, yellow-haired and clad in black armor. Antlers rose from his brow like a crown. The firelight from the campgrounds shone off his eyes, reminding her of streetlights seen from inside Leo's car: eyes that were thin glass panes between her and the dark.

It was the hornet knight.

He tilted his head and regarded her with a look she could not read. She held her breath. Had he recognized her? It was possible. Fairies lived for centuries; less than a decade had passed since he had first met Aziza, which must have seemed to him like no more than a few beats of a hummingbird's wings.

She was a better witch now, and no child. But the cold fog of that same old fear threatened to come down and swallow her.

"Hello there. You've wandered far from home, gatewalker. Have you been led astray?" He smiled with wicked amusement and held out his hand. "Come with me, and you need never be lost again."

His words carried the same magical charm and allure that they'd had before, even though he had to be aware that it wouldn't work on her.

He just wanted to see if she would refuse him again.

She accepted his hand and allowed him to pull her to her feet. His armored gauntlet was smooth and cool to the touch, and not as rigid as she'd expected. Taking her hand back, she dipped into a bow. The pixies had told her what to do should she ever meet a fairy she couldn't run from.

"Forgive me," she said. "I've come to escort a lost human home."

"It's in poor taste to leave a revel before midnight," the hornet knight said, with another dazzling smile. "I'll forgive your ignorance. It is your first time."

"It's also in poor taste to attend a party I wasn't invited to," she countered.

"But of course you're invited. Gatewalkers always are, although too rarely do they accept our invitations." He leaned in and dropped his voice conspiratorially. "You can be my personal guest."

"If I stay until midnight," she asked, "will I be permitted safe passage back home, with the human I came here for?"

"I see," he said. "You're with the boy. The borderland fae called him hag-slayer. But I suppose that was mostly you."

She thought of Leo following her into the darkest place she'd ever been.

"It was all of us," she said, more sharply than she'd intended. And then, as the full implications of what he'd said dawned on her: "You already know he's here."

"Yes. I thought he wouldn't dare return. My sister was certain he would." He gave an unhurried shrug. "She always did understand human nature better than I. But what she does with him is of no consequence to me, now that our changeling is back where she belongs."

"You must be Prince Talarix," she ventured.

"And you are Aziza."

She inclined her head in a tense nod, wondering just how much she'd have to pay the borderland fae to keep them from telling stories about her to anyone who asked.

"Tell me something, Aziza," he said. "Why did you run?"

A heavy silence. Her mind went blank.

"Why did you chase me?" she said, forcing a smile, as if they were only kidding around.

"You wouldn't be the first human child lost in Elphame who found a home in the Summer Court," he said, softly, beseechingly. "I only meant to help."

"I didn't see any humans at the revel."

"They don't travel with us. The journey would be too difficult for them," the prince said. "They wait in the castle for our return."

The borderland fae had told her that humans taken by the Fair Folk were kept as servants or playthings. To the Folk, humans held value only insomuch as they could be of use or provide entertainment;

they lived a fraction as long as the Folk did, bred at alarming rates, exhibited terminal levels of foolishness, and—as if they weren't already unfortunate enough—usually had not even a drop of magic in the blood. The rare human who matched a fairy in wit or bravery might earn their favor, but those humans were few and far between. Witches, though, were more intriguing; they had unique magical gifts that could sometimes be successfully introduced into fairy bloodlines. A witch vulnerable enough to be caught and powerful enough to contribute worthwhile magic to the Folk was a prize they did not often come across. He would have bound Aziza into a contract she was too young to know how to refuse. Losing her the first time would have been frustrating, a blow to his pride. He didn't intend to let her go again.

"Is that where you're going next?" she asked. "Back to the castle?"

"Yes. We might never see each other again, you and I," he said. His mournful tone didn't fool her. She could spot fae mischief a mile away, and Prince Talarix was undoubtedly enjoying himself. "Before that happens, I must insist on accompanying you to your first Midsummer Revel."

He offered his arm for her to take. There was no getting out of this without making everything worse, for herself and for Leo.

Only, before she could accept, the prince stiffened and looked back into the revel, as if someone had called his name, though she hadn't heard anything over the music.

"Excuse me," he said. "We will have to continue our conversation later."

He turned on his heel and stalked away. At the same time, her bond to Tristan shuddered with a sudden wave of anger.

What were the chances those two things were unrelated?

Little to none, if she had to bet.

She'd gotten a reprieve. Unbelievably, miraculously. This time, the hornet knight had been the one to walk away from her. And this time, she had to be the one to chase him.

She followed Prince Talarix into the firelight.

CHAPTER 9

TRISTAN

FIND HAZEL. THAT was easier said than done.

In the revel, the crowd was backlit by the fire. He called the scarred hound to him, but, for once, its sharp senses were worse than his—all those distracting colors and shapes. Scents were even harder to tune out than sights. The sweetness of wine, perfume, wildflowers, and magic filled his head.

Find Hazel? He didn't even know where to start.

Something moved in the woods; the hound noticed it before he did, bristling, and he whirled around to face whatever was coming. The hound's killing instinct rose up sharply inside of Tristan; he felt it in his lungs, in his throat, like a cough.

But it was just a cat—a stray with a welt on its throat where the fur had been chafed off, as if by a too-tight collar. He flung an arm up in front of the hound to stop it from lunging. The cat froze at the sight of them, its yellow eyes watching them out of the darkness, and then it turned and fled in the direction of St. Sithney's. The hound chuffed, disgruntled.

This was getting him nowhere. He looked back into the revel with a mounting sense of futility, his gaze drifting to the far side of the campgrounds. And, for an instant, he could've sworn he saw a pair of eyes watching him.

He jerked back, retreating into the dark. He hadn't hidden well enough. He'd been seen.

But nothing happened. No one sounded an alarm. No one came for him. The hound sat on its haunches, watching him. He saw himself through its eyes for a flash—and saw, too, the figure standing over his shoulder.

"We meet again, summoner."

You weren't supposed to look at the Ash Witch. Or speak to her, either. She was a spirit of truth and of vengeance, and to acknowledge her was to allow her magic to take hold of you, to pull your secrets out from inside you, to give her what she needed to judge your wrongdoings and dole out punishment. But as the Ash Witch had already judged him once, and found him guilty, he supposed there was no harm in answering her freely now. He'd committed no new sins. As far as he knew.

"It worked," he said, as she drifted closer. She wore a ragged dress over soot-streaked skin, and her eyes burned as if with reflected firelight. A few months ago, thanks to the hag, the Ash Witch had absorbed a piece of Aziza's magic, and it had overpowered her to a dangerous degree. In suppressing her, he, Aziza, and Leo had all but destroyed the Ash Witch. Tristan had found what was left of her later; he'd given her some of his own magic in the hopes that it would revive her.

It had seemed like a good idea at the time. Like justice. But he didn't really know if he'd done the right thing in bringing her back. She wasn't a monster like the hag, but she wasn't harmless, either.

"It did indeed," the Ash Witch said. "And I do not like being in a summoner's debt. You find yourself in a predicament, do you not? Perhaps I can help."

"Help how?"

"You've lost someone," she observed. "Come with me."

The Ash Witch could be dangerous, but she was also no liar, so he followed her without hesitation. He kept glancing toward the bonfire uncertainly, but when they stopped, she pointed at something not far from where they stood on the edge of the forest. It took a second for him to see what she did—like his eyes didn't want to focus on that spot. It was Hazel, mostly concealed in a group of other children. She was safe.

Now he just had to figure out how to get to her. He turned to the Ash Witch, but she was already gone. Tristan was on his own.

Once he'd seen them, he had no clue how he'd missed them in the first place. Unlike the other fairies, the children didn't bother with illusions to make them look human. One was a blue-skinned girl with silky black hair. Another, a boy with stubby antlers and sable curls. The last had black wings with red veining folded neatly against her back.

The hound's sensitive ears picked up their conversation, even from this distance.

"I heard," the antlered boy was saying, "that after a few decades, human skin shakes loose like a wyrm in molt."

"Oh?" The blue fairy's wings gave a dainty little shiver of disgust. "That can't be true. Is it, Hazel?"

"Um," Hazel said. "That's true. I guess."

"I heard they fly around in gigantic, stinking metal tubes," said the other girl, the one with box-elder wings, in a deep, ponderous voice.

The boy dropped his hand from his stubby antlers—he kept prodding them self-consciously, as if they were new—and wrinkled his nose. "That's impossible. Humans can't fly."

"They can fly in their machines," the box-elder girl insisted.

"Hazel, tell her that's impossible," the boy demanded, in imperious tones.

"Um," Hazel said again. "Glora's right."

The boy narrowed his eyes—a fathomless dark brown rimmed with amber—and said, "You're lying."

"Oh, *hush*, Vetiver," the blue fairy girl said, waving a hand to dismiss the boy's accusation as if it were an unpleasant odor. "I'm sure she only lies around humans. It's part of their customs. She wouldn't lie to *us*."

"Why not? If I could lie, I'd do it all the time," Vetiver said.

A tense moment passed as Tristan wondered what he'd do if these strange, terrifying children turned on Hazel.

Then the box-elder girl said, "I heard they smell."

Hazel's wings gave a nervous flick, a gesture not unlike the fidgeting of the blue fairy; she was picking up on their body language already. "Only sometimes," she said, looking around distractedly. "How come—" she began, and then hesitated, as if she wasn't sure she was allowed to ask questions.

"What is it?" The blue fairy was so excited that she lifted a couple of inches off the ground, her iridescent wings fluttering. The box-elder girl clasped her by the wrist before she could float away.

"How come everyone else looks human . . . mostly . . . except for us? And the other kids?" Hazel asked in a rush. A tremulous, painful note of hope threaded through her voice.

"We won't learn how to do costume illusions until our twentieth year," Ephira said, cutting Vetiver off before he could answer. "All we have are look-away charms."

Tristan's mind hooked on that phrase, pulled it in to examine and absorb it. *Look-away charm.* That explained why it had taken him so long to find Hazel and her new friends.

"And we only use them when we're close enough to human territory for some of them to stumble into us," Vetiver added, not to be outdone.

"Or if we've invited them," Glora said. "That's how we find the ones we want to keep. They make the best servants, even if they are short-lived."

Ephira appeared to have grown bored of this discussion, because she took Hazel's hand and began to lead her away. "Come, Hazel, let's find something else to do. You've hardly seen anything."

Hazel couldn't seem to stop looking around, taking everything in. At last, her gaze landed on Tristan where he was mostly concealed in the woods. Doubtless she'd caught sight of the hound's reflective eyes, and from there picked out his own pallid face through the darkness. She froze.

He held out a hand. If she wanted out of this, he was on her side, no matter the consequences.

But Hazel shook her head. She turned away, gripping Ephira's hand and following the other children into the crowd. It broke his heart a little, but it didn't surprise him; she was as stubbornly brave as her brother.

The hound gave a warning growl. Tristan turned to it reluctantly, saying, "If you make me lose her because of another stray cat, I swear—"

But there was no cat this time. The eyes he'd seen from across the campgrounds watched him from the woods now, startlingly near.

He turned tail and ran. But he only got a few steps away before a hand caught him by the back of the shirt, yanked him backward with impossible strength, and slammed him against a tree. Tristan groaned as pain radiated through his back and skull.

The hound gave a ragged snarl that cut off into a sharp yelp—Tristan's hands rose to his neck and clawed at it, at the phantom grip he felt there. A massive hand was clamped on the hound's neck, squeezing down hard in warning. The hound writhed and snapped its jaws to no effect.

It was a dizzying shock. He hadn't known it was possible for something to be stronger than a blækhound; he'd seen his hounds chew through metal, snap deer bones like they were twigs. And now it was being held by the neck while it thrashed with all its strength, as though it were no more than a puppy.

The man looked at the hound for a moment longer, as if evaluating it, before turning his attention to Tristan. Although he had the telltale pointed ears, barely visible between strands of lank brown hair, he had to be the ugliest fairy in the Summer Court. Possibly the *only* ugly fairy. He had a thin, broad mouth; lined, weather-worn skin; and a large nose with a crease at the top where it met his brow. Three jagged scars tore from his cheekbone to his jaw—claw marks. He wore layers of leather armor and furs, and a gloved hand rested on the hilt of a sheathed sword. His deep-set eyes burned like a pyre, a swirl of red, black, and gold.

"I sensed a summoner here," the man said, in a rough baritone, "but you're only a whelp. Haven't the faintest clue what you're doing with this, do you?"

He gave the hound a shake. It swiped at him with its claws, and missed. Its growling was a ceaseless, unbroken rumble; its lip curled, showing a hint of fang, and Tristan felt waves of dislike emanating from it through their bond.

"I should put you out of your misery," the man continued. "Feral summoners do no one any good."

"Who are you?" Tristan said, his voice ragged as the pain in his throat refused to let up. As he spoke, three more hounds crawled out of the shadows behind the man. But Tristan's weak attempt at distraction failed, because the hounds were still half-disembodied when the man glanced over his shoulder as if he'd somehow heard them coming, bared his teeth in a disgusted grimace, and rounded on Tristan.

The hand he wasn't using to hold the hound captive flew up and slammed into Tristan's chest, knocking the wind out of him and pinning him to the tree.

"Send them back," the man ordered. "Or I dig out your spine and use it as a leash."

Tristan's ribs felt like they were buckling under the strength of that hand. He had no doubt the man meant every word. He banished the hounds with a thought; only the scarred one remained, still writhing in the man's grip. Its back legs kicked up as it tried again to claw at his belly, but only succeeded in nicking the outer layers of his leather garments. Its tail swept the ground. Tristan pushed at the hound's thoughts with his own, ordering it to leave him and go with the others, but it only tilted its head toward him with what limited movement it had and shot him a doleful look.

"No, this one stays with me," the man said, with a wolfish grin. He took Tristan by the arm, twisted around, and flung him to the ground. Tristan landed hard on his side. He threw himself forward, away from his attacker—cornered, because the only way out was into the revel—and scrabbled to his feet as he was backed into the firelight. The hound was making a terrible yowling noise, almost like a scream, and Tristan looked into the glittering revel, looked back at the man, and felt a searing, incomprehensible rage flare inside him. He couldn't even tell if it was his or the hound's.

"Let go of it," Tristan said. It came out like a snarl, hardly sounding like himself, hardly even sounding human.

"If you want it back, then take it from me," the man said, and he shoved Tristan forcefully into the light.

"Let *go!*" Tristan said again.

"You don't give me orders," the man responded. He drew a silver sword from a scabbard attached to his belt.

It wasn't a conscious decision to call another hound—at this point it was instinct, his hand flinging itself outward and curling as if to grasp a rope, four hounds springing from the flickering shadows and leaping forward.

And then a flash of motion. It was a man in black armor who could only be Prince Talarix, accompanied by a knight with a helmet like a spider's head, both of them moving with a swiftness even sprites would envy. The prince caught one hound by a fistful of fur on its flank, used its own momentum to toss it to the ground, and— Tristan braced himself for the pain—ran a blade like a crystal spike straight through its side, pinning it momentarily before it melted into the shadows. Without missing a beat, Prince Tal was spinning to face the next one as it lunged at him, throwing an arm up so that its bite caught him on the gauntlet. He didn't flinch, but Tristan did, teeth aching as the hound clamped down, unable to pierce the armor. Before it could release him and draw back for another strike, his blade was sinking into its gut. The spider-fang knight was just as fast, catching the remaining two hounds and slicing their throats with a glass dagger that shone in the firelight like a fragment chipped off the sun.

The hounds were already healing, but Tristan banished them. He felt pathetically naïve; Aziza had warned him the hounds wouldn't be enough to fend off the Summer Court's warriors, and while he'd taken her seriously, he hadn't *truly* believed it. He got it now. Even the army of hounds he'd hoped for might not have been enough.

"I could have handled that myself," said the man who'd caught Tristan in the woods, still holding the scarred hound and the silver sword.

"Better to save your energy, Beor. You'll need it later," Prince Talarix said, sheathing his own weapon.

"Perhaps," the swordsman—Beor—said, in a low, dangerous voice. He hadn't taken his eyes off Tristan. "But I found a pair of mongrels that needed to be put down."

"Wait!" Aziza said breathlessly, like she'd sprinted there—he didn't even know where she'd come from. She planted herself at Tristan's side. "Prince Talarix, this is my companion. I told you about him."

"You told me about a lost human; you neglected to mention another witch," the prince said mildly. "It appears that your companion has caused something of a disturbance."

"A misunderstanding, I'm sure," she said, and bowed. A yank on Tristan's sleeve, and he followed suit.

"There is no misunderstanding. You saw what he is," Beor said.

"Could we not keep him?" the spider-fang knight suggested. "We know how useful his gift can be."

"An untrained summoner his age is too dangerous to be left alive," Beor said. "Give me leave to kill him, sir."

"Very well," the prince said indifferently.

"Prince Tal—" Aziza began.

"His decision is made," the spider-fang knight hissed, yanking Aziza away from Tristan. "How dare you defy him?"

Aziza sent a warning through the bond, something that translated roughly to, *What are you waiting for? Run!*

But how could he run? Aziza was caught. And so was his hound.

He could only watch with helpless wrath, frozen in place, as Beor advanced on him.

CHAPTER 10

LEO

THE WARMTH FROM the bonfire was beginning to skim across their faces when Narra paused, as if something had startled her, and then took off running. Leo followed on her heels. Through the trees, the silhouettes of the Folk were restless with the rhythm of their fluid, mesmerizing dances. A commotion on the far side of the clearing sent ripples of disruption through the crowd—people knocking into each other; drinks being spilled; a game board with ivory pieces carved into exquisitely detailed birds tumbling to the ground; a tussle breaking out between two men in coats like liquid copper and shimmering emerald scales down their necks. Narra cleared a path with no more effort than a light touch to a shoulder, here and there. Leo wasn't certain if the Folk even knew they were in the presence of their princess, or if some force of beguilement like a magnetic field made them fall instinctively away.

At the edge of the clearing, the revelers gave a wide berth to a giant of a man. A hound—*Tristan's* hound—writhed in his grip, its legs dangling. In front of him, getting to his feet as if he'd been knocked down, was Tristan. A fight ensued; it lasted only moments, as Tristan summoned more hounds, Prince Tal and the spider-fang knight put them in check with minimal effort, and Aziza intervened unsuccessfully. By the time he and Narra were close enough to hear what was being said, Leo's heart had come to a standstill.

"They're with me," he told Narra urgently.

"You have such interesting friends." She drew herself up, raising her voice as they broke through the final ring of spectators. "Stand down. All of you."

At a nod from Prince Tal, the spider-fang knight released Aziza. The man they'd called Beor uncurled his fingers, letting the hound drop unceremoniously to the ground. It whirled on him, but Tristan crooked his fingers at it, and it skulked over to him and Aziza, teeth bared, ears flat to its skull.

Leo moved to join them, but Narra held up a hand to stop him. He caught Tristan's eye over her shoulder and raised a hand to sign—pointing at him once, and then a gesture with his index and middle fingers apart—*You OK?*

Tristan nodded. He still looked rattled, but Leo couldn't see any injuries on him.

"Revels are for dancing," she said, sounding cross. "Couldn't you have saved the brawling for some other time?"

"It's under control now," Prince Tal said.

"Actually," Narra said, "I have plans for those two. But it all depends on Beor." She turned to the giant, whose sword was still unsheathed. "I've brought you a challenger; this boy wishes to compete in the Wild Hunt."

Some of the fairies who had turned away, as if bored with the proceedings now that the violence had ceased, were beginning to pay attention again. A few of them looked to Beor—but many more of them were watching Prince Tal.

"The Hunt begins tomorrow," Prince Tal said coldly. "The boy is unprepared. He has no hunting party."

"They're my hunting party," Leo said, with a glance at Aziza and Tristan. Then it hit him, with a stab of regret, what he'd just done. He'd volunteered them for what was shaping up to be a perilous and difficult task, with no prior discussion. Was it too late to take it back? He had meant to challenge the Summer Court for Hazel's freedom by himself. But Aziza gave him a minuscule nod, her expression reassuring, and Tristan showed no surprise at what Leo had said.

They wouldn't let him take it back even if he tried, he realized. He didn't know if he was more guilty or relieved, or maybe guilty *because* he was relieved.

Prince Tal glared for a long moment at his sister, who met his gaze evenly. In the end, he was the first to look away, with a short, sharp laugh. "Very well. That's one way to dispose of him. By all means, Beor, do rid us of this nuisance."

Beor was stone-faced and unreadable. Leo's heart sank. One word from him, and all of this could be for nothing.

"There is no honor in battling an unworthy opponent," Beor growled. "But I cannot rightly bar him from competing. He shows resolve, and he has managed to assemble such allies as to give him what might generously be called a fighting chance. If this is the manner of death he has chosen for himself, I can only oblige him."

It wasn't exactly a ringing endorsement, and it took Leo a moment to understand that his challenge had been accepted. A clamor of approval rose from the watching Folk—Leo had all but forgotten they were there—and then he was being swept away, herded toward the towering bonfire in a flurry of motion.

"We haven't had a real opening ceremony in ages," Narra said to him under her breath, gliding along beside him. "We'll have to improvise."

He tried to look back for Aziza and Tristan. He was painfully aware that if they hadn't been here, Leo wouldn't have even been allowed to compete. It was *their* strength, not Leo's, that Beor had deemed worthy. But all he could see were the Folk calling off their musicians and pulling each other away from their dances, pouring fresh glasses of wine and letting the lesser fairies perch in their hair or on their antlers—and before he knew it, he was alone except for Narra and Beor, in a space that had been hastily cleared in the middle of the gathering.

Narra raised her voice to be heard over the roar of the fire.

"There are seven nights left until the solstice," she said. "Beor will depart on the Wild Hunt tomorrow, as he does at the close of every second seven-year. This time, a challenger will embark on the journey, too. They will travel across Elphame to the domain of the springtide lord. Only the most skilled and daring of huntsmen can conquer it, for it is a beast which cannot be caught or killed, which cannot bleed and never tires, and which can be neither outwitted nor overpowered."

Leo frowned—that sounded almost like a riddle. What exactly were they hunting?

"When they depart, we will return to the castle, where the Summer King rests," she went on. "The successful Huntsman will meet us there before the solstice, with the heart of the springtide lord, and wake the king from his enchanted sleep. Our Huntsmen do us a great service, and we honor them."

Murmurs of agreement swept through the crowd. There was always a strange quality to the voices of the fae—the rasp of autumn leaves in a nymph's words, the hush of the wind in a sprite's—but to hear the Fair Folk speak was even stranger. A fairy never stumbled over their words; their voices never caught or broke, and never wandered with their thoughts. They sounded human, except that they were perfect, which meant they didn't sound human at all.

"You may take any route you please, and subdue the springtide lord using any means necessary," Narra told them both. "Complete the hunt before your competitor does, or you fail. Those are the *only* rules. Do any other challengers wish to come forward?"

No one did.

"Doesn't he get a hunting party, too?" Leo asked warily.

Beor's mouth twisted in a grim smile. "Yes, but I daresay their presence here would ruin the festivities. You'll meet them soon enough."

"I will deposit in your mind a map to guide you," Narra said, approaching Leo first. He closed his eyes automatically as a pair of cool fingertips brushed over his eyelids. A soft, mistlike magic poured into him, and when the clouds had dissipated, images bobbed in and out of his consciousness: fields into forests into mountains, a quicksilver river carving a path through a canyon, a place where the sky had fallen on the ground—no, a lake, a vast mirrorlike lake tucked away in a gorge. Leo's eyes flew open as her cold touch withdrew.

"How did you do that?"

"It's a kind of illusion that only you can see," she said. "Like a dream."

She repeated the process with Beor; he bowed slightly so that she could reach. When she was done, she stepped back.

Voices called out, some encouraging and some mocking; the music started up again with more fervor, and there was laughter, drunken and delighted. After that, it was like time sped up, or maybe like the past few minutes had existed outside of time. Before he could move, Beor's hand landed on Leo's shoulder, holding him in place with a bruising grip.

"Traditionally," he said, "the Huntsman only rides at night. You are not beholden to tradition. You may travel by day, and if you're wise, you'll be well out of my way by sundown. If I see you on the road, you won't live to see the solstice. This is the only warning I'll give you."

And then he was gone, walking away into the dark.

"Speaking of tradition," Narra said, startling him. He hadn't realized how close she still was. She'd overheard everything. "Normally, the night before the Hunt, anyone competing would stay and celebrate with us, and we would see you off in the morning. But since Beor is no fan of revels, and always slips away when no one's looking, I don't see any reason to hold you to that custom."

"So we can go?" Leo said hopefully.

"You and your friends can go. Hazel stays with us." She held up a hand before he could object. "The deal was that she can go back with you *if* you win. Now, listen. The Hunt begins at dawn, and no sooner. Once the first rays of sunlight touch the sky, you can set off, and I suggest you waste no time. Your gatewalker friend can help you leave the borderlands and reach the wilds of Elphame. That's where you'll find the springtide lord. Do you understand?"

"I—think so," Leo said.

"Good fortune follow you, young Huntsman," she said, withdrawing. "You will need it."

CHAPTER 11

AZIZA

LEO DROPPED HER off at home, but she was too restless to sleep, knowing how soon they would be departing. She went out again, shutting the door soundlessly, and walked three blocks away to the twenty-four-hour corner store.

Since her injury, Jiddo had taken over most of the cooking; he had the energy now, and the arthritis wasn't so bad anymore. She had jokingly commented that they barely had one pair of working hands between them, but it turned out he was a better cook than she ever was, and enjoyed it more. It rankled a bit—this was one of the few things she'd always been able to do for him, and now she couldn't, not until she got better at using her left hand.

But she could still get the groceries, at least. It would be one less thing for Jiddo to have to remember to do. If she didn't come back.

As she passed a row of darkened shops across from an empty lot, it dawned on her—from the prickle of heightened awareness at the edge of her senses—that she was being watched. She carried on at the same pace as before. Her hand closed around the pocketknife in her jacket, and her ears strained for the sound of footsteps shadowing her own. But there was nothing.

Before she'd made up her mind to take off running, someone spoke.

"I'm sorry for turning up unannounced," he said. "You've been a difficult person to keep track of today."

She made a conscious decision to let go of the knife, as she would no longer be able to claim self-defense as an excuse if she stabbed him with it.

"Are you kidding?" she said. "Why are you following me?"

Dion didn't even have the decency to look abashed. Hands in his pockets, dark hair uncharacteristically tousled and gray eyes slightly pinched at the corners, he looked weary but otherwise perfectly at ease.

"I have an urgent matter to discuss with—what are you d—?"

She was still walking—toward him now. By then she was close enough to grab his wrist, yanking his hand from his pocket; he was so startled it took no effort to pry his fingers open and reveal the match in his palm.

"What is it with you and these matches?" she said, and then answered her own question. "It's your offering, isn't it? Fire. It's how you cast your spells."

There were three parts to a spell: the language, the offering, and the magic. The magic was innate, something a witch was born with, but the language and offering were what gave the spell its form. Jiddo built his wards on incantations written in Arabic script and herbs burned by candlelight or wrapped in linen and tucked under the floorboards.

"You're right," he said, and did not elaborate.

There it was. The admission she had been waiting for almost since she'd met him, handed over to her with complete nonchalance. It was as if they'd been pulling on two ends of a rope and he'd suddenly let go, or like a game he'd let her win—there was no triumph in it.

She flicked the match away and turned on her heel. "Okay. See you."

The corner store was at the end of the block, close enough for her to see the crooked fluorescent sign over the door. Dion's footsteps picked up after a beat, following.

"Is that it?" he said. "Normally I can't shake you off no matter what I do. Now you don't have anything to say?"

"You're the one who wants something." She pushed the shop door open, the bell at the top giving a half-hearted *ding*. Another moment of hesitation before Dion caught the door as it swung closed and followed her inside. He offered to carry the basket for her. She refused.

A middle-aged man in a football jersey smoked behind the register as he scrolled through his phone; a scruffy gray cat slept on the shelf next to the tomato sauce. Pristine, polished Dion Legrand could not have looked more out of place here. The library had a grandeur to it, a stateliness that suited him. And then she was annoyed at herself for thinking that, because the library was Meryl's, and it didn't suit anyone *but* Meryl.

"I want the same thing you want," he said in an undertone. "To talk."

"Why now?"

"Why not now?" he countered.

She regarded him flatly over a box of pasta. "I'll trade you a question for a question."

"You hedgewitches and your bargains," he said. "Fine. Deal."

She led them down the aisle, away from the register.

"You use some kind of . . . silencing spell," she guessed. "So that you can move without making noise. And that's how you keep sneaking up on me. Right?"

"No," he said, with an irritating note of amusement in his voice.

She dropped a few cans of broth into the basket she'd hooked over her arm, more carelessly than she'd meant to, and they clanked together.

"Invisibility?"

"If I could have simply disappeared whenever you came in to argue with me, I would have." Until this moment, she hadn't known that you could *hear* a smirk. "But I believe it's my turn."

"All right," she said. "Tell me what was so important that you needed to hassle me about it in the middle of the night."

They continued down the aisle, Dion dropping his voice and walking close enough that she could feel his body heat through her jacket. "A few months ago, Blackthorn had a problem with a pack of wolves, which were unusually large and impossible to catch, by all accounts," he said. "There were attacks, deaths, disappearances—until, one day, they just stopped. But there are still rumors of sightings, here and there. Do you know anything about that?"

"Sure," she said, carefully neutral. "Everyone heard about the wolves."

"But you're aware they weren't really wolves," he pressed.

"Is that a question?" she asked, in feigned confusion. "But it's not your turn anymore, remember?"

She glanced up from inspecting the sell-by label on a loaf of bread.

"Of course," he said, unfazed. "Go on."

"What do you know about Meryl? The librarian who was there before you. *Don't* pretend you don't know what I'm talking about."

"I'm not pretending," he said, cautiously, as if he had surmised—correctly—that his response to this question was going to determine how much longer this conversation lasted. "I don't know anything about her. I've never lied about that, I swear."

"How can you not know who you're replacing and why?" she snapped.

Something in his cool expression faltered, and she felt a rush of triumph—she'd caught him out in a lie. She waited, dimly noticing the faulty light panel flickering overhead, the crackly noises of some video the cashier was playing on his phone, that stale grocery-store smell that was some combination of freezer air, produce, and hours-old cleaning product, and all of it just—not touching Dion, like even in the most mundane place imaginable, he was somehow above it all. On the contrary, he gave the rest of it a brush of the strange, as if he turned the world into a more magical place just by existing in it.

"It wasn't supposed to be me." His tone had taken on the hush of a confession. "I . . . paid off the person who was being moved to this post. To be honest, almost no one knows I'm here."

"Paid off? What are you, a crime lord?"

"I'm searching for someone that I believe is here in Blackthorn. His name is Emil Wulfsige," Dion said, digging out his phone. She repeated it under her breath in disbelief—*Emil Wulfsige*. That was a name, all right. Dion showed her the picture he'd pulled up, a professional headshot, and her heart gave a queasy jolt.

Emil Wulfsige was a middle-aged gentleman with red hair going white at the temples, piercing blue eyes, a square jaw, and a neatly trimmed beard. Broad-shouldered and muscular for someone who looked so refined—a roughness under all the polish. And, other than the fact that he was about two decades older, he bore an undeniable resemblance to the man in the photo Jiddo had shown her. The one she had in her backpack at that very moment.

"Do you know this person?" Dion was saying as he held it up, but he must have seen the recognition cross her face, because he answered his own question: "You do."

"I don't."

"But?" he prompted.

She had already given herself away, and she couldn't think of a good reason not to tell him, anyway. "I think he was friends with my parents."

"Your parents? What are their names? How do you know—?"

"Why are you asking?"

They watched each other like duelists in a standoff.

"Maybe we should continue this outside," he said, with a glance toward the register, out of sight but certainly not out of earshot, no matter how quietly they spoke.

She nodded. He left to wait for her on the street, and she finished the grocery shopping at record speed—by the end, she was only half paying attention to what she was throwing in her basket. When she emerged, she had two bags clutched in her left hand and the other hooked over her right arm. Dion offered again to take them from her; again, she refused.

It was a warm night and they walked slowly, lingering on the block with the corner store by silent, mutual agreement.

"Tell me about Emil," she said.

"He is . . . a high-ranking witch who vanished a few months ago. And my . . . mentor," Dion began, haltingly. "He's known to drop off the map sometimes, but never for this long. And he's never been completely unreachable. The last anyone heard from him was a little while before the first wolf sighting here in Blackthorn—and you and I both know that those weren't wolves, but blækhounds."

He paused. Grudgingly, she nodded.

"Emil didn't tell anyone where he was going," Dion said. "An oracle pointed me here."

"Really?" Aziza said, interested despite herself. Jiddo had told her about a clairvoyant cousin who knew when it was going to rain and could prevent minor mishaps like burned food or shattered dishes. Other oracles told prophecies about events that would change the world.

"Her tracking spells can predict where a person is likely to be in the future—that's how I kept finding you today. And she can see places of significance to her subject, past and present," Dion explained. "When she tried to find Emil, she saw Blackthorn. Over and over again."

"You could have told me that before."

"I didn't want to drag you into this. Or anyone else. But you were so persistent about this missing librarian of yours, and I got curious. Nelle—the oracle—casts her spells using a libation of water, or . . . whatever she has on hand . . . and her subject's handwriting in ink. And then—"

She groaned. "The application form I wrote on."

He didn't laugh, but his sidelong glance said he wanted to.

"One of your places of significance was a house she saw briefly in her visions about Emil. That's how I realized there could be a connection between you."

She would've been more put off by this invasion of privacy if she wasn't so impressed. They'd gotten to a crosswalk; the light was green, and there weren't any cars coming by at this hour anyway, but neither of them took another step.

"Then you and I are both looking for someone who disappeared," she said.

"That does seem to be the case. It only makes sense that we should help each other, then."

"Maybe."

They'd abandoned any pretense of exchanging questions at an even rate; she had lost the motivation for bargains, anyway. It had struck her, with this talk of oracles that he could apparently ring up anytime he pleased, that Dion came with a wider context—a wider community of witches, something she knew so little about that it might as well have been another world.

"If Emil knew your parents, is it possible that he came here to see them?" he asked.

"No," she said. "They're dead."

"I'm sorry to hear that," he said, sounding sincere. "That might not have deterred him, though."

"What?" she said, and then a sick, sinking feeling of dread set in as she recalled their earlier conversation. "You mentioned the blæk-hounds. Twice. What does that have to do with anything?"

"Emil is a necromancer," Dion said, like it was a minor detail that had slipped his mind. "Some of the hounds have been caught on camera—nothing very clear, usually just a few blurry frames here and there—but I *know* what Emil's hounds look like. I'm as sure as I can be, without seeing them in person, that they're his. Emil would never harm anyone, but I think . . . if something happened to him, if he was hurt and couldn't control his magic . . . it's possible that the hounds lashed out in a panicked response to his condition. The attacks have stopped, so something is keeping the hounds in check, but Emil still hasn't reappeared."

She barely heard him; inside, she was numb. She knew exactly who Emil Wulfsige was now. Not just an old friend of her parents, but the necromancer whose magic had been stolen by the hag—and given to Tristan. Jiddo said Emil had refused to fight the hag the first time. Almost twenty years later, when the hag woke, he must have known somehow. He must have come back to Blackthorn to stop her—the thing he hadn't dared to do before. Only he'd failed.

Emil was dead, and she couldn't tell Dion.

Dion came with a wider context. A community. He had money to throw around, if he could pay someone not to work for three months and counting, and the luxury of being able to leave behind his usual responsibilities to go undercover as a librarian. He had described Emil as *high-ranking*, and *rank* suggested some kind of hierarchy. Some sort of . . . government or ruling class. And a magical government implied law and order. Someone important was dead, and a force of evil had taken his magic and given it to Tristan. Would whatever higher power Dion answered to believe that Tristan had been the hag's victim, too? Would it matter to them? And when the hag had died, Aziza had caught the necromancy gift in the bond and returned it to Tristan. She had no right to do that, but she hadn't cared then, and she couldn't say she regretted it. So she and Tristan were equally guilty, maybe her more than him.

"I tried to steer clear of the blækhounds," she said, her mind on autopilot producing this partial truth. "I needed to keep the local fae from adding to the chaos."

"Why would he come here and not reach out to you?" Dion said, more to himself than her.

She shrugged. "What'll you do if he doesn't turn up?"

"He has to," Dion said. "I can't leave without finding him, or . . . finding out what happened to him."

They crossed the street; her block was the next one over. It had to be past midnight by now. Felt like it. Midnight was a witching hour. At Blackthorn's boundaries with Elphame, fairy doors might be forming even now, temporary whirlpools in the sea or archways in the woods. And if Dion had seemed unusually magical against the backdrop of the corner store, now he was faelike, seen at his clearest when the veil between worlds thinned. She could hardly stand to look at him; she was afraid she'd tell him everything, as if his company had made her faelike, too, and unable to lie.

"If that's the case, you might be stuck here for a while," she said.

"You're the first and only lead I've found in the last three months. Please." And he didn't say it in that perfunctory, well-mannered way that made her scoff. He said it like he was *this* close to begging. Smug, arrogant, self-assured Dion Legrand, begging for her help. And she couldn't even enjoy it.

It was risky to keep associating with Dion, but he was the only person who could help her get information on Meryl's whereabouts. Aziza was done letting everything else take priority over her; she had kept her waiting long enough.

"If you can help me find Meryl . . ." she began.

"I can try, but it will be difficult, since no one is supposed to know I'm here."

She heard his unspoken question: Could she make it worth his while?

"I can ask the fae what they know," she said. "They noticed the blækhounds. Maybe they saw Emil, too. And I can see if my grandfather heard from him recently. But I can't guarantee I'll come up with anything useful. What's that worth to you?"

He let out a slow breath. "Even the smallest chance I'll find him is worth everything. *Thank you.*"

Aziza's stomach felt like it was made of ice. It was laughable that she'd ever thought Dion cold when she had it in her to speak such cruel lies of omission. The fae would be impressed. Jiddo would be disappointed. Dion would—

He would never forgive her, if he found out.

If she was in his place, she certainly wouldn't forgive herself.

"You'll have to wait a week," she said, averting her eyes. "I'm leaving Blackthorn tomorrow morning."

"Leaving?"

"Something I have to do out of town."

His eyebrows lifted. "In Elphame?"

She hesitated, thinking again about the laws of witch society, of which she had no knowledge. All this time she'd been doing what she wanted, living by her own rules, and now, meddling in the affairs of the Summer Court. What would Dion and his people think about that?

But she was quiet a beat too long, because Dion said, "Are you in trouble?"

"No." He made a skeptical noise, and she scowled. "How did you know I'm a hedgewitch? Did your oracle friend tell you that, too?"

"I happened to walk by when you were getting swindled by a sand sprite," he said, clearly amused.

"That's what I get for paying in cheap chocolate," she said, less amused. "Mind your own business. And don't follow me around anymore."

"If you get killed before you can hold up your end of our deal, it is my business." His tone was light, but his eyes betrayed him, grave and shadowed by strands of dark hair. "Maybe I can help you. Whatever it is, you don't have to do it alone."

"I won't be alone. I've got my coven."

"Fine. If you're sure." They had just about reached her house by then. He gave it a long look, his expression opaque. Doubtless thinking of Emil, and wondering what this place had meant to him.

She wondered, too.

"I'm sure," she said.

He accepted that with a rueful, unsurprised smile. "Good night, then. And good luck."

She was relieved to get inside and away from his uncomfortably sharp eyes. And it was only much later that it occurred to her that he had neatly sidestepped her questions about his craft. She was *certain* it wasn't an accident; he just wanted her to have to ask again. Nettled, she decided, then and there, that she would not give him the satisfaction.

ON HER WAY back out the door in the dark hours of earliest morning, she found a paper parcel just inside her gate. Scrawled across it were the words:

For protection.

When she tore it open, a silver cloak spilled out. True cloth-of-silver, from the weight and look of it, made of silver beaten into thread and woven with—she rubbed the hem between her fingers—silk. Draped over her arms, it was so supple it melted off her. It had a warmth to it, and a sheen, that made her suspect it was layered with enchantments, though what sort, she couldn't have said.

She glared down at it. Did Dion have rare magical artifacts just . . . lying around?

Show-off, she thought, but the guilt from before settled heavily in her stomach. They'd made a deal, and now he was treating her like an ally, using his apparently extensive resources to help her. But she had no intention of telling him what she knew. She'd gone back on her word before their alliance had even started.

Impulsively, she caught a wind sprite as it passed on the breeze. It blew some other city's cold air into her palm, tugged at her hair and the hem of her shirt as if it had something it wanted to show her on the other side of the horizon. She doubled back to grab some rosemary from the window box, crushing the leaves in her palm so that the sprite could catch the scent.

"Can you send a message to the person who left this package here?" She lifted the paper that the cloak had been wrapped in. That was all the sprite would need to find Dion, for there was little in the world wiser than the wind. "The message is this: I don't need protection, but thank you for the cloak."

The sprite took its rosemary-scented air and Aziza's voice and swept over her gate, kicking up the paper litter in the streets as it went.

CHAPTER 12

LEO

His ac was broken again.

He didn't even notice until they'd been on the road about an hour. As the sun rose, his trusty old Chevy turned into a swamp on wheels. He kept the windows cracked, the wind blustering noisily inside to pester at the corners of Aziza's map.

"Got it yesterday," she said, catching his glance in the rearview mirror as she'd unfolded it. Tristan was next to him in front, Aziza in the back, spreading the map out on the seat beside her. She'd brought a Sharpie to keep track of their progress. "We're going to be in and out of Elphame's borderlands for a while. The GPS won't be able to keep up. We need another way to stay oriented."

She meant the GPS on their phones; his car didn't have one. In Elphame, their phones couldn't make calls or tell the time, either, so they wouldn't be much help on this trip. Anyway, they needed to conserve their batteries.

"Let me see," Tristan murmured, and she leaned forward between their seats so they could share the map, Aziza holding the left side and Tristan taking the right. Rays of sunlight streaked into the car, scorching their edges away. "What are those markings?"

"Places we're likely to find boundaries. Forests, rivers, cemeteries . . ."

Elphame's borderlands were a patchwork realm, found in the crevices between ever-expanding human territory. A person could stumble across a boundary and slip into Elphame by mistake; the world didn't look all that different on the other side, until you had the misfortune to run into the fae. The landscape of the borderlands didn't match the human world perfectly, but it synchronized. Anything that existed in Elphame's borderlands existed in the human world, too. Forests, lakes, skies. The two worlds shared things; they overlapped. But some places were strictly human territory—and if you ventured deep enough into Elphame, you could eventually reach the places that *only* existed in Elphame. Bodies of water that changed location when disturbed. Hollow hills that sheltered fairy royalty. Magical woods.

"The lake I keep . . . picturing," Leo said. "I don't think that exists in our world."

The lake he kept *remembering*, he'd wanted to say. But you couldn't technically remember a place you'd never been. Or could you? After all, the things that counted as remembering, to Leo, included the impression left by a name he used to know, and the scant remnants of dreams that came close enough to reality to serve as an acceptable stand-in. So who was to say he couldn't remember a lake he'd never visited?

"It probably doesn't," she agreed. "But we can't get that deep into Elphame just by crossing a boundary. In most places, the borderlands end sooner rather than later. You'll hit another boundary and slip back out, or get stuck wandering around lost until you starve or something catches you."

"What about St. Sithney's?" Tristan asked.

"That would be a decent entry point. The woods go on long enough. But there aren't any trails wide enough for the car, and I don't think we can hike the whole way." She looked at Leo. "Right?"

"Yeah, no. I think we're going to end up somewhere on the West Coast," he said absently, not even really knowing how he knew that.

"So we drive," she said. "It's almost the solstice, so the veil is thinner. That will make it easier to slip in and out of the two realms. Eventually, Elphame's magic will catch hold of us, and we'll be able to slide past the borderlands and into true wilderness."

Leo's fingers drummed against the steering wheel. "It's like a Venn diagram."

Aziza gave him a mystified look. "What? No."

"Two separate things that overlap," Tristan supplied. "A part that's shared, and parts that aren't shared, all part of one greater . . . thing."

"See? He gets it," Leo told Aziza.

"Okay, sure," Aziza said. "But the Venn diagram isn't a diagram. It's more like a spring in the woods."

"A spring," Tristan repeated, in dubious tones.

The water in this spring bubbled up from a deep, illogical gap in the earth, Aziza explained. If you went through that gap, you'd wind up in a secret ocean. The ocean below represented Elphame; the woods above were the human world; and the water in the spring, linking the woods with the ocean, was a borderland, a shared place belonging to both realms.

"So the spring is the middle of the Venn diagram," Leo said, warming to this analogy.

"Yes, but then it gets complicated," Aziza said. "Because now we're wading into the spring. And although it's a shared place, we're on Elphame's side of the boundary."

"I see. This is where the Venn diagram falls apart," Tristan said.

"Wait, why?" Leo said, betrayed.

"The borderland exists in both realms," Tristan said. "But *we* only exist in one of them."

If you jumped into the spring from the forest, you crossed a boundary and entered the borderlands. You could return to the human world by crossing the boundary again. In Aziza's analogy, it was like climbing back onto the shore. But the banks were steep and slippery, so that wasn't always easy.

To get to the ocean—to the depths of Elphame—there was no boundary. You had to dive into the water until it got so black you couldn't even see your hand in front of you. Down there, the earth narrowed, pinching shut and growing treacherous with sharp rocks and tangles of aquatic plants. The gap that led to the ocean was the tiniest crevice hidden in the deepest and hardest-to-reach place at the bottom of the spring. If you wanted to get through, you had to feel your way in the dark until you found the gap, grasped the edges, and squeezed inside, all while fighting against the currents. Most likely, you'd slip or run out of air or get tired of swimming, and never find the gap. You'd just bob back up to the surface of the spring. But it wasn't impossible. And sometimes, if you were lucky—or unlucky, depending on how you looked at it—the currents changed direction, and the water sucked you *down* and before you even knew what had happened, you were floating in a wide-open sea. Most of the time, though, you'd get stuck in the spring, probably in the company of strange water-dwelling creatures you'd have preferred to avoid.

A hedgewitch could get you to the water, and she could get you back out. She couldn't take you to the ocean, but she could get you close, guiding you to the general vicinity of the gap, and when the currents stopped pushing you away, you'd be in the right place to slide downward and swim into that ocean.

"If we have to be in the borderlands to get to the wild parts of Elphame, why cross back over to the human world at all?" Leo asked. "Can't we just drive around in the borderlands until the magic lets us through?"

"We could, but we'd wind up driving in circles for hours," she said. "I don't know if we can afford to lose that kind of time. If you know we're headed west, that's where we should go—even if it means making the journey partly in the human world. When we finally get through, we'll still be closer than where we started."

Heading down the interstate in pursuit of magic was nothing new for him; how many times had he taken off in his car, following the faintest leads all over the East Coast in the hopes he'd find someone who could help him break his curse? He'd spent last summer that way, not returning to Blackthorn for months. Those trips had always ended in failure. Looking back, he hadn't been chasing viable leads so much as he'd been running from the reminders of his true love that surrounded him at home, triggering the curse's magic, which swept in and obliterated his memories over and over again.

But at the end of this road was an invitation to the Summer Court, where he'd find not only Hazel . . . but maybe his true love, too. The words of the curse said his true love would be taken from him. But taken where? For a long time, that had been the missing piece of the puzzle. Knowing the identity of the enchantress who'd cursed his family—knowing where she came from—changed everything.

This time, he wasn't running from something, but *toward* it.

LAST NIGHT, BEFORE he went to bed, he detoured to Tristan's room. It wasn't until he'd knocked that Leo remembered he'd resolved to be careful and put some space between them. Showing up at his door in the middle of the night was definitely not careful. But it was too late to second-guess himself. Light flooded into the darkened hall as Tristan opened the door.

Tristan had the kind of silky-fine hair that always looked nice without him having to try, even when it was disheveled and falling into his eyes. He'd filled out a bit since moving in; he still had a lean, spare build, but his clothes didn't hang off him the way they used to, and his face had lost its gauntness. The Tristan he'd met a few months ago had been all hard edges, fearful and closed off. *This* Tristan looked tired and soft and like he'd fold right into Leo's arms at the slightest touch. Abruptly and with painful clarity, he was thinking of how Tristan's hand had felt on his skin, smooth and warm and crisscrossed with scars that his own fingertips itched to trace.

"Leo?" Tristan said, delicately, like the silence was made of china, something to be set aside with care.

"I just wanted to make sure you were all right," he managed. "I saw the Huntsman corner you. Did he hurt you?"

Tristan shook his head, not quite meeting Leo's eyes, less like a denial and more like he wanted to banish an unwelcome thought. "I'm fine. Are you?"

Briefly, Leo was distracted by another scar on Tristan's shoulder, the edge showing where the collar of his shirt sagged on his skinny frame—an arc of raised puncture marks from a hound's teeth. He tore his eyes away.

"I'm going to be. Am I completely delusional for thinking we can pull this off?"

"Not completely," Tristan said, with a faint smile.

"I . . . thought we should talk. Could be now or never." It took saying it out loud to realize that was why he'd walked over here. "If we're doing this, I need us to be okay."

"What happened to winning?"

"Just in case."

"All right." Tristan breathed out slowly. "I was worried you'd be upset with me."

"Why?" Leo said, bewildered. The conversation had barely started, and already he felt thrown off balance, the half-formed thoughts he'd had about how this would go and the apologies he'd wanted to make slipping away from him.

The line of Tristan's throat moved as he swallowed. It was the first sign of nerves Leo had picked up from him.

"I did pretty much attack you," he said.

Leo laughed, incredulous. "*Attack* me? Come on."

"I should've asked."

"Look, I—you were probably picking up on—I must've made it so obvious."

"What?"

Tristan blinked at him, like he genuinely had no idea.

"I mean," Leo said weakly, unable to take it back now. "If things were different—if I wasn't already—I wouldn't have stopped you."

His face burned. He was supposed to be fixing things, clearing the air, not making it *worse*.

Without missing a beat, Tristan said, "It doesn't have to be serious."

In the silence that followed, Leo had the impression that both of them were equally surprised, as if even Tristan didn't know where those words had come from.

"You mean—uh—"

"No one would blame you for having some fun," Tristan said,

looking away. Maybe Leo had imagined that moment of uncertainty, because he sounded perfectly composed now. "You can't be unfaithful to someone you don't remember."

When he glanced up again, the look in his eyes stopped Leo dead in his tracks. Tristan didn't ask for things; he didn't let on that he wanted things, like he thought he wasn't allowed, and here he was unabashedly wanting Leo. It made Leo a little delirious, how bad he wanted to give Tristan what he wanted, and then sick, because he knew he couldn't.

"Part of me remembers," he said. "I remember, *here*."

His hand rose of its own accord to rest over his heart, which was racing, and even that felt like a betrayal, that his body would respond with such urgency to a few suggestive words from Tristan when his true love was still out there.

"Oh," Tristan said, his expression unreadable.

"So I . . . can't."

It was easy to want Tristan when he was right in front of him, and hard to put his faith in someone he dreamed of each night just to have them slip through his grasp each morning. But even though they weren't here, his true love felt as real as Tristan did. Felt like Leo could walk downstairs and open the door, and they'd be standing on the other side.

Maybe he couldn't be faithful to someone he didn't remember. But he was faithful to the person he thought of when he ran his fingertips down a sheet of paper he'd written on and felt the indentations his pen had left; when he caught the scent of smoke or salt; when he saw jack-o'-lanterns and string lights, and any other bright thing. Almost everything that had ever made him happy also made him a little wistful now, because he'd shared it all with his true love. Last year, it had hurt to be surrounded by all those reminders and feel like the curse had tainted every part of his life; with time, though, he'd started to feel grateful for it. His true love was in all of those things. In the pain that knocked him back when he least expected it and in the laugh that bubbled up when he didn't even know why, as if someone had leaned in to whisper a joke only he could hear.

"I can't," he told Tristan.

"I understand," Tristan said. "I shouldn't have pushed. Sorry."

"You don't need to apologize."

"All right." He shot Leo a tiny smile that threatened to make Leo's knees buckle. "If you ever change your mind . . ."

"Yeah. Okay," he said hoarsely. "I should go."

"Right," Tristan said. "Good night."

"Night."

By sheer force of will, he left without looking back at Tristan, standing there in a halo of lamplight. Because, if he looked back, there was a greater-than-zero chance he would not leave.

He hadn't told Mom and Dad he was going. It had been bad enough telling them where Hazel was, when he and Tristan had come home without her. He had been upset that Hazel had left without telling them goodbye, and he was a hypocrite, doing the same thing now.

But he tried not to think about that. Instead, he thought about where they were going, riffling through the map in his head.

When Narra had said she was giving him a map, he'd pictured something clear-cut, something he could have copied down onto a sheet of paper and held in his hands. A pretend piece of yellowed parchment etched with caret forests and mountain ranges in imaginary ink.

But Narra's map wasn't like that at all. In the way of old dreams, it was hard to hold all of it in his mind at once. He sifted through images one at a time, piece by piece, turning them over like cloudy shards of glass, each new angle revealing a different pattern of light. Hills that lay like sleeping bodies, motionless but alive. Miles of forest over treacherous, rocky ground. A canyon through parallel cliffs like the imprint of a knife blade in a stick of butter, the edges melting—was that ice? And beyond that, glassy water. He could feel the contours of the images in his head more clearly than he could picture them. He couldn't even articulate where they were going, other than which direction was right and which was wrong. Narra hadn't given him a map; she'd given him an intuition.

As he drove, he did his best to reconcile Aziza's directions with where his mental map wanted him to go. There was no reaching the endgame without getting past the borderlands, but he didn't want them to get too off course, either. One moment they'd be surrounded by typical human sights—a farmer's market, a UPS truck, a strip mall—and then they'd drive through a wooded area or cross a bridge over a ravine, Aziza opening the boundary before them, and wills-o'-the-wisp would be bobbing faintly in the shadows where the afternoon light didn't reach, or towering maples would be bending like new saplings as the nymphs inside stretched in their sleep. He got used to the warm, anticipatory prickle of magic braided into the blur of vacant American countryside, like an arcane pattern.

The map was soon covered in Tristan's and Aziza's notes. They kept track of landmarks and road signs they passed in the human world; that was how they stayed oriented after a stint in Elphame. Leo was the only one with a license, but they drove in shifts. After they'd been on the road for a bit, they caught each other up on what they'd each learned last night, piecing the events together. It was a relief to hear that Tristan had seen Hazel at the party, but frightening to think that they would be gone for days and *anything* could be happening to her. He wished he could've seen her for himself before he'd left. Told her he was sorry she'd felt like she had to leave to protect him and their parents. Told her that wasn't her job. Promised her that he was coming back for her.

She knew that, right? She had to.

"I didn't expect Prince Tal to be okay with me competing," Leo said. Narra had gotten her way, but he had a feeling that it had mainly turned out like that because Tal had allowed it to. "And if *I'm* supposed to be Beor's competition, why did he have such a big problem with *you*?" he asked Tristan.

"He could tell that I was a necromancer and untrained. Didn't like it," Tristan said, straight-faced, as if that wasn't understating the matter to the point of absurdity. "Other than that, he didn't say anything useful. And I was too busy running away to ask questions."

"Didn't look like you were running away from where I was standing."

"I tried, but he had the hound."

"The clingy one?" Aziza asked.

"It's not clingy, it just doesn't leave me alone," Tristan said waspishly.

"Think the word you're looking for is *loyal*," Leo suggested.

Both Aziza and Tristan scoffed.

They speculated about the creature they were meant to be hunting, which Narra had called "the springtide lord"—*a beast which cannot be caught or killed, which cannot bleed and never tires, and which can be neither outwitted nor overpowered.* Aziza and Tristan suspected it wasn't a living thing at all, that *beast* was a metaphor for something like an enchantment, and the *heart* was a magical artifact of some kind. Privately, he was just relieved he wouldn't need to kill anything.

Heading down the interstate in pursuit of magic was nothing new. But it was different with Aziza and Tristan there. Comfortable silences were interspersed with talk, with sharing the food they'd packed, with quiet observations about the things they saw outside. Later, he'd remember little of the scenery itself. The map memories, too, used themselves up the nearer they got to their destination.

But he'd remember Aziza tilting her head when they crossed over a boundary, an attentive and faraway look in her eyes, as if having a conversation that no one else was privy to. And Tristan holding one side of the map as he and Aziza studied it, and how he'd distractedly push the hair out of his eyes, the sides of his fingers black with ink. And when they passed a field in upstate New York awash in white flowers, and Aziza said, "Those aren't blooming yet in our world," and he didn't bother asking how she knew that. And when it was time to switch drivers again and Leo said, teasingly, "Tris, are you sure you wanna take over? You nearly ran us off the road last time." Tristan blamed it on the hound, which had poked its head out from the shadows under the steering wheel to watch him drive. Aziza had stifled a laugh, and Leo hadn't pointed out that if they'd been in a less sturdy vehicle, those hairpin turns of hers would've flipped them over.

He would remember taking turns flipping through radio stations and despairing when half the time the only clear channels were country music and conservative talk shows. He'd remember wondering, when he let his mind wander, if he didn't find his true love at the Summer Court and had to keep looking, whether he'd do this all over again—venture into Elphame and visit the other fairy courts until he found someone, somewhere, with information that could get him closer to dismantling the curse. Maybe he'd ask Aziza and Tristan to come with him again. He didn't know if they'd say yes, if it would be unfair of him to even ask, but asking them would be less hard than giving them up. He'd remember when they stopped in the middle of nowhere to stretch their legs and wound up leaning on the hood side by side, watching the horizon. And he'd remember, despite everything, feeling very, very lucky.

CHAPTER 13

AZIZA

A BRIDGE OVER a creek carried them out of Elphame and back into the human world; they stopped there to change drivers. Leo had the hood of the car open because it was making "a really weird noise, oh my god, please don't do this to me right now." She wandered to the bridge and looked down at the murky waters. They were somewhere in northeast Pennsylvania, heading west toward a long stretch of protected forest, where she thought they had a chance of making the final shift into deep Elphame. Not a guarantee, but a chance. Each time they crossed back and forth over the boundary, the magic held on to them a little longer; she felt its faint resistance before the boundary released them into the human world again. Sooner or later, they would make it past the borderlands. It was only a matter of time.

The wind picked up, purposeful and hard, as if to herald a storm. She looked up, frowning. The trees shuddered, their leaves shaking percussively, startling a couple of blue jays into flight. It was a wind sprite, but a very unhappy one.

She caught a snatch of Dion's voice, distorted by the sprite's agitation but still clear enough for her to make out the words: *"You're welcome, but why did your invisible friend just throw a book at me?"*

The sprite yanked at her hair.

"I know," she said. "I'm sorry. I should have expected that he wouldn't know what to do. Let's set him straight, okay?"

She crossed to the other side of the bridge—"Where are you going?" Tristan called. Leo was shutting the hood of the car, wiping his hands off on his shirt.

"Just over there. I'll be right back."

Irises grew high up on the banks of the creek. She knelt to pluck a few of their petals, crushing them, and as she let them drop, the sprite caught them eagerly. The petals gusted in spirals around her. The gale in the trees gentled in increments as the sprite accepted her token. "Please tell him this: The wind sprites expect payment in scents. Make peace with them. If you need to reach me, they can help."

The sprite blew away toward Blackthorn. That was the last she expected to hear from Dion, but the wind sprites caught up with her whenever they stopped the car, or they'd whistle inside through the cracked windows as they coasted down the freeway, carrying new messages.

"How do I find one of these if you don't send them to me?" Dion asked.

This problem had not occurred to her. When she admitted with some chagrin that she didn't know, he'd responded: *"Then we'll have to keep them busy enough to stick around."*

He took her advice and paid the sprites by prying open an old cedarwood box that smelled of dust and spice, and by riffling through the pages of a book to release the smell of ink and paper, and by brewing a bitter black tea. The sprites were fascinated by the takeout he ordered but alarmed by the cologne.

"They didn't like that one," she informed him. "If you use it again, they're going to throw a tantrum and start knocking things over."

She didn't know where he was getting half of this stuff; she had never seen any wooden chests or bottles of cologne in the desk at the library, and he didn't use the former office or the upstairs apartment Meryl had occupied.

"*Noted*," he replied, a couple of hours later. They were getting farther away from the East Coast, and the sprites were taking longer to reach her. "*That wasn't mine, anyway. It's Emil's.*"

"Stealing from your teacher?" she'd asked, surprised.

"*He won't mind. I said that he's my mentor, but he's more than that. He raised me.*"

The sprites caught most of the story and relayed it to her, and by extension to Leo and Tristan. Dion's family had died in a house fire when he was nine. But Dion's magic—the volatile magic of a powerful but untrained child—or, possibly, a protective enchantment cast by his parents had kicked in as he slept and carried him to safety. He'd woken up disoriented in a field miles away.

(That was a clue about his craft. Aziza *almost* asked about it, but it didn't seem like the right time, not after that story.)

By the time anyone found him, it was all over. The Legrand family was an old, well-known magical line; the entire community of American witches quickly learned what had happened to them, the news passed along in whispers. Plans would have been made for a witch to adopt him so that he wouldn't go into the foster care system, where he would've likely ended up with a nonmagical family—but Emil volunteered on the spot, not an hour after Dion was rescued.

"*He rearranged his life for me,*" Dion said. "*He never hesitated, or if he did, he didn't let me see it. I'm lucky.*"

Aziza's guilt had reached such an intensity that it rendered her mental blockades all but useless, and Tristan must not have been able to ignore it anymore, because he said, "We should tell him the truth. He needs to know what happened to Emil."

"What if they send you to witch jail?" Leo said. "Also, does Dion know he's on speaker?"

When she was driving—and she was the worst driver of the three of them, no question—it took all her concentration to focus on the road. If the sprites returned when she was at the wheel, Leo was in charge of bribing them with scents, usually by unwrapping one of the candies Aziza kept in her bag for the pixies or uncapping the Sharpie. He and Tristan heard most of what Dion said to her.

"No one is going to witch jail," Aziza said. "Knowing what happened to Emil won't bring him back. And Dion knows I'm not alone. If he wants to tell a wind sprite his entire life story, that's his business."

"I should be held accountable for my actions," Tristan said, with the serenity of one who had been in worse places than witch jail. Leo kept glancing up at him in the rearview mirror with the biggest, saddest eyes, torn between supporting Tristan's right to make his own choices—no matter how self-destructive—and the desire to save him from himself.

"When did you become such a saint?" Aziza said, confident Leo agreed with the sentiment if not the delivery.

"Doesn't it bother you that he's spent months looking for someone who's *nowhere*? Don't answer that. I know it bothers you." He gave a tug at his end of the bond, as if he thought she'd somehow forgotten about it.

"Yes, I sympathize with him. A *little*. So what?" she said, as if she could force her own guilty conscience into submission. "He'll figure out Emil's dead eventually. He doesn't need to know how he died. And then he and I can start a club for sad little orphaned witches and cry about our feelings, I guess. But we're not throwing you under the bus."

"So I don't get a say in the matter?"

"*No,*" she snapped.

"Can I put in my vote in favor of lying to keep you out of trouble?" Leo said softly. "I don't want anything to happen to you, Tris."

Instantly, predictably, Tristan folded. Aziza shot him a smug look that he sullenly pretended not to see. That was the end of the discussion.

She considered telling Dion that there had been a hag in Blackthorn, and that it was possible Emil had run into her and perished. But she could just imagine how the conversation would unfold then, how quickly they would wind up in dangerous territory. Dion would say, *There was a hag? What on earth happened? Is she still there now?*

And she would say, *No, the hag is gone.*

And he would say, *Gone? How?*

And she would say, *My coven and I took care of it.*

And he would say, *How?*

And she would say, *We were almost burned and buried alive. We had to drag each other out of there. We climbed out of the ground like we were rising from a grave. We still have nightmares about it; I know because we talk about it sometimes, only late at night when we're in the car and so tired that the words won't feel real in the morning.*

But that wouldn't be enough for Dion, the only nineteen-year-old she knew who spent his lunch hour cleaning the computer keyboard with a Q-tip and scrubbing the baseboards, and who kept a travel-sized garment steamer in his desk. She had once argued with him for a week straight when he'd decided to redo the entire library's shelving system because *I can't make heads or tails of the last librarian's setup, and Dewey Decimal is the most commonly used worldwide, Aziza, I'm sure she would thank me for this if she was here.* Dion was meticulous and inflexible, and he would want to know every detail of the *how*. He would ask about Leo and Tristan and what sort of craft they'd used against the hag. What was she supposed to say to that? That Leo wasn't a witch at all, just a really good person with no regard for his own safety and a talent for making people love him. That Tristan was a necromancer, but not to worry, it was just a coincidence, nothing to do with the hag's ability to hoard magic and deal it back out like a set of cards.

Through Dion, she learned that American witchcraft mostly happened in people's living rooms and basements. It happened in abandoned theaters, hospitals, amusement parks; in empty factories and mills; in ghost towns out in the Midwest. It was a relatively small community, and Emil—and by extension Dion—knew just about everyone. And Aziza knew no one. It was her, Jiddo, and her tiny coven, and they had to protect themselves because no one else would. Tristan thought it was a witch who'd woken the hag in the first place. Maybe even Emil himself. This was an argument both in favor of telling Dion and against it.

"Any word on Meryl?" she asked Dion.

"Nothing. For now. You're getting pretty far away. Any chance you'll reconsider your stance on what is and isn't my business, and who can or can't be involved in this mysterious road trip of yours, and how you definitely don't need any help?"

"How did you know it was a road trip?" she asked.

"The sprites smell like motor oil, asphalt, and roadkill. Are you afraid I'll tell someone else? In case you've forgotten, you know enough of my secrets to keep me in line."

In the end, she figured that giving him one truth would make it easier to withhold another. If she kept being cagey, he'd get suspicious and wonder what she was hiding, and possibly seek out his own answers. Would he ask his oracle friend to conjure up more visions from Aziza's *fuck you* note? Would he turn up on Greg and Maria's doorstep, or try to get past Jiddo's wards?

"We're doing something called the Wild Hunt," she said, and shared the broad strokes of what that meant, after consulting with Leo and Tristan.

When Dion responded next, they were parked by a rest stop somewhere outside Pittsburgh, where a narrow two-lane highway cut through scrubby grassland. She'd beaten the boys back to the car and leaned against it to wait for them, enjoying the fresh air while she could. That was when the sprite returned. She shielded her eyes against the sun; they were well into the afternoon now, and it hung dead center in the western sky. Cargo trucks rumbled past. A handful of people trickled in and out of the building. Inside had been jarring—linoleum and crowds and the smell of greasy fast food, but alongside all of that, the charged feeling that came with boundaries. A place like this, where everyone was just passing through and nothing stayed put, it was easy for magic to slip inside unnoticed. It wasn't a true boundary, but it was the sort of place where the supernatural was a little closer than usual.

"*Aziza,*" Dion said tensely, waking her from the fugue state those hours of driving had lulled her into. She'd never heard this kind of urgency in his voice before. "*You can't compete in the Hunt. It's suicide.*"

Then the sound of movement, like Dion was pacing.

Then: "*Wait! Don't go yet, I'm not done—*" and movement again, more frantic this time, as Dion searched for a new scent to keep the wind sprites from abandoning him.

And then, at last: "*Forfeit before sundown. If the Huntsman catches up with you—it's over.*"

Her hands rested in front of her, the good hand wrapped lightly around the wrist of the bad one—a new habit. Anytime it ached, which was often, she squeezed at her wrist. She didn't know if the pressure actually helped or if she was just imagining it did. Outside under the summer sun, it was warm as an exhale; the sprite circled her lazily, its touch a cool breeze against her cheeks. She dug in the backseat for some of the food they'd brought and produced a packet of chips, which she tore open awkwardly with her good hand. The sprite dove in and scooped out the smell of salt and vinegar.

"I can't do that," she said into the air.

Later, Dion would respond: *"One of Emil's close friends is a hedge-witch, so I grew up on her stories. Fairies have been entrancing humans since the dawn of time, and you're playing right into their hands. I know you're immune to their—compulsions, their charm. That doesn't mean you can't be tricked."*

And she would say: "Thanks for explaining my own craft to me, Dion."

And he would come back with: *"That's not what I meant. I'm worried about you."*

And she would say, "Two things that aren't your job: being a librarian, and worrying about me."

And he would reply, in tones of diminishing hope: *"It would be such a waste if you died. You have so much magical potential. Anne—the hedgewitch I mentioned, Anne Sterling—she would've wanted you for an apprentice. She'll be furious I never brought you to her—"*

She lost the last bit of what he said because she was choking down laughter. Her death would be *a waste of magical potential*? This was his last-ditch, life-saving argument? Pure comedy.

She again refused to return. Dion's final response before sundown was a terse *"Fine! Do what you like."* A pause as the sprite retrieved words that had been delivered softly and after a silence. *"Be careful."*

The sprite made it known that it would not be back until morning. It couldn't communicate why, exactly—only that nighttime would be dangerous. Because as soon as night fell, their head start was over. Beor the Huntsman would be setting off on his own journey, and if he caught up with them, it could very well be the end of the road. The Folk had been afraid of him; Dion thought Aziza should be afraid of him. And the sprite, too, was afraid. When the Huntsman rode out, it seemed, not even the wind dared get in his way.

CHAPTER 14

LEO

THEY CAME UP on a gas station maybe twenty minutes before sunset. There were no other buildings nearby—just the tiny, two-pump station alone on the side of the road like an abandoned toy, something discarded. Overhead, the sun slumped toward the horizon. But the LED lights above the pumps were on, and so was the lone streetlamp by the turnoff to the main road, struggling against the onset of dusk. Clouds of mosquitoes flitted around it.

He pulled up next to the pump. "Who's first?"

"I'll go." Aziza unbuckled her seat belt. She'd said they were close to making it past the borderlands. She could feel Elphame's wildest magic tugging at them; one or two more crossings, and Elphame would decide to keep them, would let them into its heart instead of trying to trap them in its outskirts where it lay along the seams of the human world. When they were this close to Elphame—close in magical terms, even though they were technically in the human realm—trouble was more likely to find them. So they couldn't risk leaving anyone outside by themselves. They would go into the station one by one to top up their supplies, splitting up what they needed to buy so that if something happened and they had to take off before they were done, they'd have a little of everything.

She slid out of the car and crossed the empty lot to the convenience store. Through the streaky glass, he could just make out the aisles and the man slouched over the checkout counter. Leo got out, filled the tank, got back in. Tristan had claimed the passenger seat during one of their shift changes earlier and was poring over the map, which he'd spread out on the dashboard.

Being alone with Tristan felt different now; all Leo could think about was the other night. His eyes darted over all the places where he carried tension—his pensive frown, his shoulders, his jaw, the corners of his eyes. And then, before he could help it, he was picturing his hands tracing the route his eyes had mapped, there, and there, and there. His thoughts went like a train pitching off a severed track and into a gorge—a slow slide into an uncontrollable free fall. Was there actually something alluring about the way Tristan's fingers held the marker, or had Leo fully gone off his hinges?

Tristan chose that moment to look up, and—despite the dwindling sunlight—it wasn't yet too dark to pick out the suggestion of green in his eyes. He bent closer, and Leo was certain for a wild moment that he was going to kiss him again—

"Here, right?" he said. "What do you think?"

Leo didn't have the faintest idea of what he was talking about. What was the mortal peril of a magical hunt compared to the shape of Tristan's lips around words that Leo barely comprehended? He might as well have been speaking in prophetic verse.

The map. He was pointing at the map, at a mark he'd made there.

"Looks right," Leo said, though he couldn't have read a map at that moment if the fate of the world had depended on it.

Tristan nodded and put the map aside with a soft sigh.

"I keep thinking it can't be a hunt if we're not actually . . . hunting anything," he said. "Maybe we're wrong that the *beast* is an enchantment. What if it's a lake monster? Some kind of freshwater siren?"

"Maybe it's more like a . . . scavenger hunt," Leo said hopefully. He had been mulling over what Narra had said about the springtide lord on and off all day. It couldn't be killed, so it must not be alive in the first place—because how could you take a living thing's heart without killing it?

He thought uncomfortably of his own hollow heart then. But he shook off the uneasy feelings.

Tristan propped his elbow on the console between their seats and rested his head on his hand, and he wasn't *technically* in Leo's space, or touching him at all, but even the potential for physical contact was agony. He couldn't decide if he wanted to catch Tristan by the collar and drag him closer, or push him away.

Maybe this was some sort of karmic payback for the time he'd thought having a crush was *nice*. He was being punished for his hubris. This wasn't nice. This was *torment*.

"Sounds a little too easy," Tristan mused. He looked up at Leo without lifting his head, his gaze half-concealed behind a screen of invisible-fine lashes.

It took a long time for Leo to respond, and then all he could come up with was, "Yeah. Probably."

Aziza returned, and Tristan volunteered to go next. Leo sat there in mortified silence after he had gone, grateful that the distance gave him a chance to clear his head and yet unable to stop himself from glancing across the lot at the store every couple of minutes.

"He's fine," Aziza said, having caught him following Tristan with his eyes. "He'll be back any second."

"How do you—oh, right. The bond." He went quiet, mulling that over. "So the other night, when he, um—and I—did you know?"

She looked over at him with an expression of complete bewilderment.

"Leo," she said slowly. "I knew about that because you called me five minutes after it happened and told me everything."

He took this in stride. "Well, yeah. Who else am I going to call?"

"What, did you kiss him again?" Her face in the rearview mirror was amused and unsympathetic. "Should I have taken my time coming back?"

The fact that she'd come to that conclusion just by *looking* at him brought his misery to new heights.

He let his head fall against the steering wheel. "Am I a shitty person?"

"For . . . not kissing him?"

"For not kissing him but thinking really hard about it."

"I'm going to say no, but don't take my word for it. Our combined romantic experience is—"

"Zero?" he finished. "Less than zero. Missing memories probably count as a negative value."

"A question mark isn't a zero."

"I never told you this, but I found a box of condoms in my room once that I don't remember buying. It wasn't opened. I guess I was either sleeping with someone or planning on it, but I just . . . have no idea. How fucked up is that?"

She contemplated this for a long moment. "Or maybe you were just really optimistic."

"Thanks. I'm like Schrödinger's virgin." He glared half-heartedly at the rearview mirror when she snickered, but his spirits lifted a little. Better to find the humor in his mess of a life than keep wallowing.

"This means it's your job to save us from being complete romantic failures, since I'm no help. You're our only hope."

"Oh, then we're doomed."

"Have you ever kissed anyone?"

"Yes."

"Wait, for real?" He twisted around in his seat to look at her. "Who?"

"A tadken. To make it leave Blackthorn."

"A . . . what?"

"They excrete toxins from their skin—"

"Oh my god."

"Like a salamander? They have this delusion that a kiss from a maiden will turn them human. So we made a deal—"

"Please. Tell me you didn't."

"My lips burned for a solid twenty-four hours after. Jiddo wanted to know why I kept putting on so much Chapstick."

He hid his face against his seat, shaking with laughter, while she grinned back at him.

Soon, Tristan was back, and Leo was the last one up. Despite the stops they'd made along the way, he felt hazy and stiff when he climbed out of the car. He stretched his arms over his head; something cracked. Wincing, he pulled the door to the shop open and blinked into its too-bright light.

The man by the checkout counter was gone; a BACK IN 5 MINUTES sign hung on the register. Leo went around gathering everything on his list. Gallon of water. Armful of snacks. He'd pay for the gas in here, too, since the card reader outside was broken. The low drone of the freezers in the back kept him company. A spinner rack of postcards extolled Ohio's virtues—they'd just crossed the state border. He made three cups of coffee at a self-service machine. They would be driving through the night, sleeping in shifts.

He set his things on the counter. The cashier hadn't come back yet. He bent down to grab a few energy shots from the rack underneath, for later. When he stood up, he jerked back, dropping the bottles. The counter wasn't empty anymore.

"Sorry," the man said, with a thin smile, as he put away the sign. "Didn't mean to startle you."

"Don't worry about it," Leo said. He picked up the energy shots and added them to the pile. The man . . . Leo had *thought* the man had short, dirty blond hair, but now it was dark and curly. Maybe Leo was more tired than he'd realized. He counted cash out of his wallet, started to hand it over, and hesitated. The man was younger now. So much younger that it couldn't have been merely a trick of the light. And his eyes weren't blue anymore. They were brown. Actually, the man was starting to look more and more . . . like Leo.

"You know what?" Leo said faintly. "I . . . forgot something in the car."

"No, you didn't," the man said, the tenor of his voice wavering like a radio station tuning in and out. His smile was growing wider, so wide his face distended horribly around it. His jaw dropped open, like an ambitious snake with designs on an ostrich egg, and he lunged over the counter. Leo dodged, swiping up one of the coffee cups; the man landed on the floor in a crouch, and Leo tossed the boiling hot coffee in his face. He—*It* screamed, blinded, as blistering red burns popped up over a face that still looked far too much like his own. Leo didn't wait for it to recover; he crashed through the entrance, raced to the car—Aziza must have seen him coming, because she was throwing open the door while Tristan jumped into the driver's seat and started the engine. Leo dove inside as Tristan slammed on the pedal, and they were lurching away before Leo even got the door all the way closed after him.

LEO

"What just happened?" Tristan asked breathlessly, but then his eyes flicked to the rearview mirror and widened. The burned thing, only barely human at that point but still wearing one of Leo's eyes, had appeared in the door of the convenience store.

"Come back!" it howled, in that radio-interference voice. "I wasn't finished!"

The gas station shrank behind them. He didn't relax until it was out of sight.

"You okay?" Tristan said at last.

"Mostly just upset I lost the coffee." He breathed out, releasing the last lingering traces of alarm. Beside him, Aziza was making a note on the map. "What's that for?"

"Gotta come back here later and deal with that," she muttered.

"It's already taken care of," Tristan said, with a kind of cold triumph. One of the hounds was probably dragging the doppelganger back to Elphame at that moment. Leo wondered briefly what had happened to the human cashier—the one that must have been there when Aziza and Tristan had been in the shop.

It hadn't escaped Leo's notice that he'd been targeted. Like a starved lion picking out the runtiest antelope in the herd, the sickly one with a limp, the doppelganger had let Aziza and Tristan go, and waited for Leo. For the vulnerable, unmagical human. That was what the hag had done, too—used Leo as bait to get Aziza and Tristan back where she wanted them.

He didn't want to be anyone's weakness. Not ever again.

CHAPTER 15
TRISTAN

As THEIR FIRST night on the road began, they were besieged by hauntings.

It began when they passed a stretch of marshland alive with echoes—the aural cousins of the wills-o'-the-wisp—which called to them in voices they recognized, bent on leading them astray. Into lakes, where they'd drown. Or ravines where they'd break their necks. But Aziza was at the wheel, and when Leo straightened and said, "Wait, stop—that's Hazel," she only shook her head and kept her eyes on the road, where their headlights burned a path through the night.

"It's not," she told Leo.

"But . . ."

"I don't hear Hazel. Just my mother," Tristan said flatly. "And she wouldn't be caught dead in a swamp."

Outside, the thing mimicking the woman he hadn't spoken to in almost two years said, *"You can come back whenever you want."* The voice was so clear she might have been sitting next to him, speaking into his ear. *"If you're sorry, we'll forgive you. If you promise to be good . . ."*

"I hear Jiddo," Aziza said, after a tense pause. "And . . . Meryl."

"So it's. People you love?" Leo's voice was shaky, and Tristan wondered, with a pang, what his imaginary Hazel had to say to him.

"Maybe it's just whoever's got the best chance of convincing you to run without looking where you're going," Tristan said.

For hours, the echoes stalked them. The voices were pleading, demanding, mournful in turns. It was maybe midnight when the world outside went quiet again; they hadn't passed another car in ages. The streetlamps were few and far between, and soon there was only their headlights and the moon. They'd crossed the state line into Indiana at some point, but that didn't seem to be relevant anymore. When Aziza told them, in a hush, that they wouldn't be returning to the human realm this time—that they had made it past the borderlands and reached the part of the world that was only Elphame—he wasn't surprised. He'd felt it.

Solitary trees dotted the countryside for a while; after that, small groves flickered past, distantly and then nearer, closing in on the road. Soon they were in a forest that skirted the base of a mountain range. The ground was all moss-covered stone bubbling out of the earth; the trees pushed crookedly through it, gnarled and bowed, their trunks forked like tongues. The road cut a furrow of flat land through the rugged slopes, sunken like a tunnel with earthen walls, so the trees loomed over them. Through a haze of mist, wills-o'-the-wisp vied for their attention.

Two hounds ran alongside them, sometimes in the shadows and sometimes not, depending on their mood. The scarred hound, in particular, liked it best when Tristan drove. It felt like they were running together, like a pack—and it had never occurred to him before that the hounds might have pack instincts. He'd always viewed them as solitary creatures. Its observations trickled into his head as he drove. The fog made dampness bead up on his fur, and the woods had a fungal, earthy smell, moss and stone and rot and rain. His claws clicked against a rocky ledge as he scaled the tunnel wall with the car just below, and his hands gripped the steering wheel. Inside, it was stuffy and warm; outside, the temperature dropped in tiny increments as the night deepened.

None of them had said a word for a while. They didn't acknowledge it, not out loud, but they were all waiting for the first sign that the Huntsman was close.

When Aziza replaced him at the wheel, he took the passenger seat and the map, and Leo climbed into the back. Tristan turned in his seat and looked him over, taking stock of the tension in his jaw and the slump of his shoulders. He wasn't fooled—or distracted, despite the way his heart tripped over itself—by the tired, fond smile Leo gave him.

"Try to sleep, in case we run into the echoes again later," Tristan said.

"'Kay," Leo said. "Wake me up at the next crossroads."

Tristan listened to the stream of information the hounds shared with him as Leo's breathing went soft and slow in the backseat. Aziza held the steering wheel stiffly with her left hand, but he felt certain she was thinking of something other than just the road.

"How will we find our way back out?" he asked her, quietly, after Leo had fallen asleep and some time had passed. "From Elphame, I mean. If there are no boundaries here."

"We'll retrace our steps." She lapsed into the kind of silence that meant she was trying to translate something she understood instinctively, in the private language of her own craft, into words that would make sense to other people. "There are boundaries, they'll just be farther away. Not . . . where we found them before. But I'll be able to sense them."

Aziza didn't seem worried, and that was good enough for him. Anyway, he wasn't actually all that interested in the mechanics of their return trip. He was just stalling.

"I've been thinking about Emil Wulfsige," he admitted, deciding to just come out with it. She glanced over at him warily but didn't speak, waiting for him to go on. "If you're right, and he didn't wake the hag . . . If he went to the hag to fight her, because of what happened to your parents . . . then he must have known who *did* wake her. And Dion might be able to help us find out what Emil knew."

She was quiet for a long moment. "I have a feeling that if we keep following this thread, it's not going to lead us anywhere good."

"You say that like we have a choice."

"I think we do."

"Like you could let it go. Just be okay with not knowing, when we have a chance to—"

"I *could* let it go."

He snorted. Aziza didn't let *anything* go. She held grudges and kept promises. She'd jumped into a nine-year magical bond with him, a near stranger she barely liked at the time, rather than break her word to Leo. She pursued the mystery of Meryl's disappearance without tiring, even after months with no progress. And she claimed she could *let go* of finding out who had woken the hag that had killed her parents and almost killed the three of them?

"All right, fine, you have a point," she grumbled, doubtless having felt his skepticism through the bond. "I just don't see how we can bring it up without making Dion suspicious."

Before he could think better of it, he said, "Did I mess things up with you and him?"

The car swerved underneath them, and she jerked at the steering wheel to steady it.

"There's nothing to mess up," she snapped.

"You do get attached to your librarians."

"He's not a librarian."

He watched the road. The beam of the headlights climbed the earthen walls and merged with tendrils of fog.

"You had to lie to him, to cover for me."

"For both of us."

"For a situation I put us all in. And it put *you* in a position where you had to . . . make a choice you shouldn't have had to make."

"Do you have a compulsive need to take the blame for everything?"

"Shut up, I'm trying to—"

"Trying to take responsibility for my choices."

"Acknowledging that you made the choice you made because you're stuck with me."

She shot him a narrow-eyed look of disbelief. "If it wasn't for you, I'd be *dead*. Leo and Hazel, too. The hag would still be out there. You were willing to die to take her down—don't you think that matters to me?" she said. "You even saved the Ash Witch—yeah, I know about that. I saw her a couple of months ago."

"Can't really save something that's already dead."

"Can't you, though? And you're stuck with me, too. Did you ever think of that?"

"That's different."

"How the hell is it different?"

Before he even knew what he was about to say, it was out of him: "I don't have anything but the two of you."

Pathetic, when he said it out loud like that. But he didn't know how else to put it. *Stuck* wasn't the right word for the three of them. You weren't *stuck* with the only people who made it so that you weren't totally alone in this awful world. Stuck was what he'd been without them.

"Me too," she said, so quietly he almost missed it. For a moment, there was no sound but their breathing; even the hounds' input was briefly muzzled.

Leo muttered in his sleep, shifted, and woke.

"'S it my turn?" he mumbled.

Tristan checked the time. "It can be," he said, and they pulled over to shuffle around. He returned to the backseat, Aziza took over the map, and Leo reclaimed his place behind the wheel. A misty rain wafted downward; its droplets seemed to levitate and dissolve before they hit the ground. It sprayed the windows lightly, smudging them. He lay down, thinking of witchcraft and hags and hounds. The seat was still warm from Leo's body, and the silver cloak he'd been using as a pillow smelled like him. It was almost enough for Tristan to forget where they were, almost enough to lull him to sleep.

He drifted . . .

Then the hounds' senses pricked with alarm. He didn't know how much time had passed, but he was wide awake at once, sitting up. His eyes caught on something in the rearview mirror. A blurry, moving shape in the rain and fog.

Aziza noticed something was wrong at the same time he did. Their shared apprehension bounced back and forth across the bond, but unlike an echo that faded with each reverberation, this unease only grew stronger.

One of the hounds started barking, over and over, like a tornado siren.

"What's up?" Leo said.

"Wait." Tristan tuned out his own senses and became a passenger in the hound's mind. The rain steamed off his—its fur. The ground under its paws had gone thick and gluey, and its throat ached from calling to its summoner. On the opposite side of the road was the other hound, the one with the strange markings on its belly, and it was quiet, howling no warnings, even though the enemy pack was gaining on them so quickly—

Tristan urged the first hound to climb to a higher elevation and face whatever was coming for them, while allowing the scarred hound to run on alongside the car. The one he'd ordered to stop fought him like no hound had fought for months. But it obeyed, in the end. His human eyes would have struggled to see through the night fog; the hound saw perfectly. A gray stallion carried a behemoth of a rider who wore heavy coverings of fur and hide, a scabbard at his hip containing the sword he'd drawn on Tristan once already, and a helmet with antlers that reminded him of Prince Tal. It wasn't clear where the mount ended and the Huntsman began, so it was as if a double-headed beast galloped toward him. Under the helmet, the Huntsman's eyes burned like sparks off a fire. He had a hunting party of his own, a host of riders on steeds that seemed made of gossamer, wispy and translucent and blurred at the profile. Was that the distortion of the night and the rain, or had Beor brought a company of ghosts? And that wasn't all. Bounding alongside him, and trailing after him, and still more keeping pace through the forest—were blækhounds. An army of them—a pack.

It was a hunting party led by a Huntsman who was also a summoner.

Tristan should have known—from the authoritative way Beor had subdued his hound at the revel, and how he'd seemed to take Tristan's inexperience as a summoner so *personally*. He should have known. The foreboding he'd felt then was magnified tenfold now, seeing the man for what he truly was, what he was truly capable of.

As they galloped nearer, the air grew staticky and warped, like a plastic film that melted when exposed to heat. The hounds were of no realm and all realms; they were not fae and not animal, were neither living nor dead. The Huntsman and his riders and his pack transcended every boundary. Where they trod, it was as though the night came untethered from the earth, mist spilling across the land as if from a tear in the world. Some of it was a cold mist that clung to the ghostly horsemen; some of it was steam, coming off the hounds where the rain struck their hot fur. Across the shrinking distance, Tristan could smell the exhilaration of the other pack. It ran through his body like a pulse, a pulse the hound did not have—

The car was long gone. The hound was alone, watching in the woods, frozen by Tristan's rising terror and its own fight-or-flight instinct. And then the Hunt was there, and Beor's fire-fleck gaze landed on the hound, and—when Tristan thought it would be torn to shreds, and ordered it to retreat, and ordered it again when it did not move—the hound ran. But it didn't run *away*. It leapt down from its perch and fell into step with the other pack. It was swept up into it. Infected by it. It forgot it had a summoner. Tristan pulled on the bond, and the hound pulled back with the power of its new pack behind it, and Tristan was slipping—

The hunting party moved as one being, one beast. The car and its passengers were small, slow prey before it. And there were two of him: the Tristan who was in the car, and the Tristan who was in the Hunt, slipping, slipping, slipping—

Something bit him, hard.

He was in the car, and it was pandemonium. The scarred hound had him pinned and his wrist between its teeth, biting hard enough to make him bleed but not to crush his bones, which for the hound was the equivalent of a gentle nip. Aziza had reached back between the front seats to take his other hand in a tight grip, yanking hard on their bond as she did—and being knocked around telepathically from three different directions had left Tristan with a splitting headache, which was not helped by Leo swearing colorfully as he floored the pedal.

"Tristan!" Aziza was saying; she must have called his name several times already. He tried to say, *I'm here, I'm fine*, but only managed to produce an unintelligible noise, so he squeezed her hand back instead.

He shoved the scarred hound off him—it was too big to actually fit in the backseat, so it was half-shadow, solid where it had pinned his chest and arms and then boneless, literally, where it melted over his legs and into the darkness under the seat, like a putrid fur blanket. And the other hound, the one he'd left behind—tentatively, he reached for it, but there was nothing where it should have been in the bond. His connection to it had been severed. It wasn't his hound anymore, wasn't even Emil's. The Hunt had taken it, like it would take the three of them, too.

CHAPTER 16

LEO

WHILE TRISTAN STRUGGLED to translate hound knowledge into human speech, the figure in the rearview mirror gained on them. His hounds bayed wildly—*dozens* of them, it sounded like—and the din made Leo's head pound. Usually, blækhounds were quiet when they hunted. Beor wanted them to know he was coming.

And Tristan was ashen and trembling, as if coming out of hypothermic shock. Aziza had climbed into the backseat with him and the remaining hound—which, at Tristan's behest, vanished to make room for her—and she'd dug the first aid kit out of their supplies, nudging Tristan to help her bandage the wound from the hound's bite. Between her only having one usable hand and his full-body shaking, they just about managed it, but it was a messy job, blood everywhere, and Leo's grip on the steering wheel was so tight it hurt as he listened to Tristan's stuttering explanation of what he'd just experienced.

I am going to get us out of this, he thought.

The ground rose, lifting them out of the ravine that had cradled the road for the past few miles. He yanked at the steering wheel, veering to the side, and sent them careening into the forest. He went to turn the headlights off, reconsidered—if he couldn't see where he was going, they'd wind up wrapped around a tree. They bounced and crashed through the woods, Aziza and Tristan just hanging on for dear life. The baying of the hounds followed them like the moon, impossible to outrun.

"Tris," he said. "How close is he?"

"I've summoned more hounds as a diversion," Tristan said. "I think I can lead him in another direction."

"But what if he—" He met Tristan's eyes in the mirror. The resolve he saw there put an end to his protests before he could voice them.

They reached a crest in the land and then they were tipping forward, rolling too fast down a steep slope. Gravity momentarily abandoned them. If he hadn't been strapped in, he would've banged his head on the ceiling. Aziza, still in the back with Tristan, clung to her seat belt with one hand and used her other wrist to shield her face from banging into the window. They hit level ground with a painful recoil, but he didn't slow down.

"Get ready," he told them. "We're going to have to get out soon."

"What's your plan?" Aziza asked tightly.

"*Hide.* Tris, is he . . ."

"He's taking the bait," Tristan said. "I don't know how long it'll fool him, but we have some time. Maybe."

"Okay. We're stopping," he warned them, and pressed down gingerly on the brakes. The car sputtered and coughed as he persuaded it to a reluctant, gradual halt. "Everyone out!"

They took almost nothing with them as they fled into the woods, leaving his car behind with all their supplies and the headlights still on, though it kind of broke his heart to do it. Something streaked past them, an animal spooked by the Hunt, he thought—but for some reason it made Aziza stop dead.

"That's the—" she said, and Leo didn't have the faintest idea how she would've ended that sentence because she cut herself off and went tearing after it without another word.

"Zee!" he called after her. "What the hell—"

But she was gone.

"*Shit*," he said. "Okay . . . Tris?"

Tristan clutched his backpack and the silver cloak. His eyes were unfocused, seeing something Leo couldn't. At the sound of his name, though, his gaze sharpened on Leo.

He held out the cloak. "Put it on."

Leo would've felt better if Tristan wore it instead, but there wasn't time to argue about it. He threw the cloak on, fixing the clasp with one hand. "All right. Stay close."

Clouds drifted past the moon. The craggy ground had produced hunched, misshapen trees, their branches so twisted it looked as if the forest had frozen mid-tempest. He hadn't seen which way Aziza had gone, and he didn't want to break Tristan's concentration to ask him to find her through the bond, so Leo picked a direction at random and started walking.

It didn't matter which way they went. They were in the woods, in the wilds of Elphame, and where there was a magical wood . . .

The clouds moved, allowing the full force of moonlight to shine down on them; the shadows shifted, too, as the trees peeled themselves apart, whispering to each other. Their voices creaked and rustled and sighed, so that he had to work to distinguish the words from the ambient noise of the forest.

"A pair of humans off the path?"

"On a Hunting night?"

"Strange."

"And one of them not even a witch."

"That one is the contender. My cousin saw him at the Midsummer Revels."

"How amusing."

"The Huntsman approaches. We must stay out of Beor's way."

Leo searched his bag and came out with a handful of pins. Three pins for the three of them, assuming Aziza was on her way back— and he had to believe she was, that she knew what she was doing and wouldn't be so careless as to let herself get caught.

"Hide us, please," he begged the nymphs. "I can give you a token in exchange for a safe place—"

"A token?" one of them said.

"Three tokens," he corrected himself. "For the two of us, and the gatewalker nearby."

In the dark, he couldn't see their faces; the movement of their shadowed figures was as the swaying of the woods in the wind. He wasn't even sure they had emerged into their humanoid shapes, or if their voices came from their home trees, out of fissures in the bark and the place where the branches split from the trunk.

"Oh? Is that all your lives are worth?" someone said. "You will have to sweeten the deal if you want salvation from the Huntsman."

Leo faltered. They'd left everything behind.

"This cloak—" he tried, but the nymphs murmured angrily amongst themselves.

"We cannot touch it," one of them said. "Do you mean to cheat us?"

"No!" he said, cursing himself for the careless mistake. It was silver; of course they couldn't touch it. "Then . . . what do you want?"

"Leo, I don't like this," Tristan whispered hoarsely, huddling closer. "We should turn back. We can run—all night if we have to—"

But Tristan was in such bad shape after just one indirect encounter with the Huntsman. Leo was terrified he wouldn't make it through another.

"We can't," he said.

"Come closer, then, contender," said one of the nymphs.

"Make your bargain with both of us," Tristan said.

"*You're* not the contender. We have no interest in you."

"It's fine, Tris," he said. "I'll be right here."

Tristan gripped the edge of the cloak, a protest on his lips, but Leo was pulling away already. He walked into the tangle of nymphs, and it was like the forest itself closing around him, the smell of sap and spice, the shiver of wooden limbs and their shadows lashing into his. Close up, he could make out vague impressions. One nymph that was tall and bowed like a willow. One with curling patches of lichen like wrought-iron flourishes. One with a pungent scent and a crown of toadstools. One with the upright pride of an oak. Something snagged his collar, a twig or a fingertip, and he leaned in. The nymph whispered her terms in his ear. As he understood what it was they wanted, dread crawled into his chest and curled up there.

A glance over his shoulder. Tristan stood where he'd left him, pale as winter, watching Leo's back and the hounds at the same time. He could shadow-travel away, but he wouldn't. And Aziza had gone alone into the wilderness in the dead of night. No hesitation or fear. He didn't know why, but he knew she had a good reason for it, because she always did; because he'd always been able to count on her, since the day they'd met.

There was nothing in the world he wouldn't do for the two of them.

I am going to get us out of this, he thought again. He turned back to the nymph and whispered a counteroffer.

Footsteps, and the puff of rapid breathing. Aziza had returned, arms wrapped around a fox with a welt on its neck like a collar had rubbed away the fur there. She saw Leo. Saw the nymphs. Her eyes went wide with panic.

"No," she said, storming past Tristan, but one of the nymphs intercepted her.

"Do we have a deal?" said the voice in Leo's ear.

"On the condition that you collect after the Hunt," Leo said. "If you do it now, I won't win."

"Why should we care if you win?" said the voice, with a tinge of wicked humor.

Behind him, Aziza was arguing furiously. "Make your deals with *me*. There's nothing he can offer that I can't—"

"What power does a gatewalker have in a place with no gates, no borders?" the nymph asked her. "If you want us to hide you from a Huntsman, then a Huntsman is whom we'll bargain with."

The words he needed materialized on his lips.

Why should we care if you win?

"Because a victor is worth more than a contender," he said. "And, for the record, I *will* win."

The voice in Leo's ear laughed, raspy as kindling and warm as the first day of summer. "Very well. But know that we will collect when the time comes. You can't run. Don't try."

"I'll keep my word," Leo said.

A sharp inhale from Tristan. "He's coming back this way."

His diversion had failed, then. Leo hoped it was because Beor had stopped following the hounds, and not because more of them had been ripped from Tristan. A coarse touch startled him—wooden fingers curling around his. Aziza and Tristan were being led forward, too. The nymphs took them deeper into the woods, until the clouds obscured the moon again, and he couldn't see a thing. He strained his ears for the sounds of pursuit, but the Huntsman's pack had gone silent, as if he no longer wished to be heard.

Soon, they were being guided into a small space, stepping up and in, the three of them shoved together shoulder to shoulder. The opening closed after them, or was covered—no, something was *growing* over it. Bark. They were being sealed into the trunk of a tree.

"Stay quiet," said one of the nymphs, voice muffled. "You must remain here until dawn, when the Hunt rests."

And then it was pitch-black, and silent except for their breathing and the fox's panicked snuffling. Someone's hand slipped into his— Tristan. He knew those scars. He held on tight.

In the woods, each snap of a twig was as loud as a firecracker, each rustle so close it could have been coming from over his shoulder. There was a howl in the distance, and then another, much nearer. Low laughter, too, unless his tired, terrified mind was playing a cruel trick on him . . .

And it was a long, long, long night.

IN THE MORNING, the nymphs unzipped the hollow trunk. Sunlight drove into the pocket of darkness within, an ambush, and then the three of them were tumbling free. Half-asleep, it felt like he fell much farther than he did. The forest floor leapt to meet him like an overeager Labrador, only one that was made of concrete. And then he was sprawled on his side, muscles screaming in agony at moving after all those cramped, stationary hours. Aziza and Tristan landed in a heap next to him.

Groaning, he covered his face with an arm. The fox squirmed out of Aziza's grip, nosed at her hair, and then made a popping noise like an engine backfiring, which nearly gave him a heart attack on top of everything else.

"You're confused," she told the fox, pushing herself up on her elbows.

"That makes two of us," Leo said, squinting at them through stinging eyes.

Tristan made a noise that might have been a whimper. "Oh my god."

"At least we made it through the night," Leo said.

"Are you sure?" Tristan had buried his face in his arms as if to hide. "I think I'm dead."

"I guess you'd know," Aziza said. "If anyone here is the expert, it's you."

"No, really, what's going on with . . . that," Leo said, making a vague gesture at the fox, which now emitted a rumbling noise—not a growl, like an animal, but a drone like a motor.

"It's a pooka. I found it outside the Midsummer Revels wearing a silver collar that the fairies must have put on it. I got it free, and then I guess it started following us." She shot it a disapproving look that was wasted on the pooka, as it was busy sniffing at a passing centipede. "When I saw it yesterday, I couldn't leave it to fend for itself. The Hunt would've caught it."

"I think I remember a pooka in a silver collar," Leo said. "Hey, little guy. Have we met?"

It made the popping noise again, which Leo took as an affirmative.

The tree they'd spent the night in had closed seamlessly after ejecting them. He'd never have been able to tell it apart from the rest.

"Thank you?" he said, tentatively.

"If the nymphs are listening, they don't need to be thanked," Aziza said, getting to her feet and brushing herself off. "Only paid."

And then, at the exact same time, it seemed they both remembered what Leo had done. Tristan lifted his head; Aziza turned. In unison, they pinned their expectant stares on him.

"What did you offer them?" she demanded.

"Nothing, for now. They're not collecting till after the Hunt." He scanned the area, trying to reorient himself. "Think we can find where we left the car?"

"Collecting what?" Tristan asked.

The pooka leapt into Aziza's arms, and they hiked uphill, toward the road.

"Does it matter? I mean, we got away!" he said, upbeat. "No one got skewered on a magical sword! It's a win! Let's just enjoy it while we can."

"You're not telling us." Tristan's voice was devoid of emotion, which was worse than if he'd been angry.

"I just . . . think we have bigger things to worry about right now," Leo said, diplomatically.

Turned out he didn't know the half of it. He almost cried at the state they found his car in. Windows broken. Tires shredded. Doors ripped off. Dents and scratches all over the carriage. All their supplies— food, water, first aid kit, the spare can of gasoline—had been strewn on the forest floor. An opportunistic squirrel was waist-deep in a bag of pretzels.

Leo must have looked pretty pathetic, because Aziza—who wasn't usually a touchy person—wrapped a comforting arm around him, and Tristan—who wasn't usually a liar—said, "This is . . . fixable. It's not like it's totaled."

"There's no fixing this unless we can get it back home, and that's not happening." He gave the banged-up hood a loving pat. "Thanks for everything. You can rest now."

"How are we supposed to finish the Hunt without it?" Tristan asked, cautiously.

"Well," Aziza began, but was cut off by the fox, which wriggled out of her grasp and landed on the ground. It spun around, as if showing off, and then transformed—in a smooth, liquid motion, as natural as a yawn—into a magnificent chestnut horse. After a beat of stunned silence from the two of them, Aziza finished: "We do have a magical steed."

"Is this why you went after it yesterday?" Tristan said. The pooka did a little prance like a pampered show horse and tossed its head, shaking out its silky mane.

"Sure," she said.

Leo gave her a pointed look.

"All right, fine. No, I honestly wasn't thinking that far ahead," she admitted. "But it did cross my mind last night when none of us were sleeping that it could come in handy, *if* it wanted to help us. And I think it does. Since we helped it first."

"So," Leo said, "not to be a downer, but do any of us know how to ride a horse?"

They'd all grown up in suburban Massachusetts. He was pretty sure none of them had even seen a horse in real life before.

"But I bet we could figure it out," Aziza said. She wasn't an optimist; she just didn't back down from anything—not jumping into freezing cold rivers, not sailing into kraken territory, and definitely not the prospect of learning to ride a shapeshifting horse while on the run from a ruthless magical huntsman. Almost nothing could have made this plan less appealing to Leo, but before he could either make peace with it or rack his brain for a less terrifying alternative, their majestic steed opened its muzzle and emitted a *vroom*—the unmistakable sound of an engine revving up. Leo jumped.

Then the pooka transformed again, and this time the transformation was . . . grotesque. Maybe because it wasn't a form the pooka was used to, so it had to take its time feeling it out. Its face stretched wide, and its eyes and snout disappeared like they'd been eaten from the inside, and—then Leo had to look away.

When it sounded like it was over, he looked back. Instead of a horse, there was—well, it wasn't exactly a car. The pooka had a good idea of what a car was supposed to look like on the outside, but the inside was—lacking. There was a steering wheel and the right number of seats, but no ignition and no pedals. No brake. No seat belts. No glass in the windows. It still had patches of fur here and there.

"I didn't know that pookas could turn into inanimate objects," Tristan said.

"They can't," Aziza said, uncertainly. "I don't think it realizes that cars aren't . . . actually alive."

"So it's hiding organs somewhere in there?"

"If I say no, will it make you feel better?"

"*No.*"

They didn't have a car. They had a car-shaped horse.

Leo had never appreciated magic more than he did in this exact moment. A tired grin fought its way onto his face. "This is a million times cooler than the Camaro I wanted when I was a kid."

They salvaged what they could from the wreckage, hurrying as they became conscious of the sun climbing higher and higher. The first aid kit had been gnawed on, but its contents were mostly intact, so they rewrapped Tristan's wrist in fresh bandages. But before they could get in and go, Tristan said, "Wait!"

He jogged back to Leo's car, reached through the broken window, and pulled the keys out of the ignition, where Leo had left them last night.

"Something to remember her by," he said.

Tristan's fingertips grazed Leo's outstretched palm as he handed the keys over, and their eyes met briefly. Leo's heart pounded as the moment lingered. But then a shadow crossed Tristan's expression. And Leo knew he was thinking about the nymphs, and the bargain Leo had refused to tell him about.

Tristan opened his mouth, shut it again, and shook his head. "I'll drive," he said flatly.

He returned to the pooka, leaving Leo standing there feeling bereft, holding his now-useless car keys. Tristan grabbed the door handle—perhaps a little too harshly, because the pooka sprouted teeth and bit him—swore, and tried again, gently this time.

"You guys can't always be the ones bailing us out when we get in trouble," Leo told Aziza, defensively, dragging a hand through his hair. "It's fine. I know what I'm doing."

He headed for the passenger side. Before he could open the door, Aziza said, "I know what nymphs are like." He froze. "They wouldn't have accepted anything less than flesh and bone in exchange for a life."

His silence probably told her everything she needed to know.

CHAPTER 17

AZIZA

T HEY'D BEEN ON the road about an hour when the sprites returned to her. The pooka made a *whuff* sound, like a laugh through an exhaust pipe, as if it felt a tickle when they slipped inside through the wide-open window. Dion's voice said, *"What do you mean you won't go there at night? Do you have somewhere better to be? Wait, don't—Ouch!"*

"Is he all right?" Leo asked. Tristan said nothing, but he tilted his head toward her without taking his eyes off the road. Elphame's wilderness was webbed with dirt paths and occasional stretches of asphalt where abandoned human roads had been absorbed into fairyland. As for the pooka, it understood that the steering wheel was something like a set of reins and would tell it which direction to go, but it still responded like a horse, and a restless, easily distracted one. Tristan kept having to jerk at the wheel to stop it from veering off the path.

"He's fine," Aziza said. The sprites hadn't liked his tone, so he'd probably gotten another book chucked at his head. Now they did laps around the car, ruffling Tristan's hair but staying clear of Leo, who had the silver cloak folded in his lap, careful not to let it touch the pooka anywhere. "Please tell him: We're okay, but we have no idea what the hell we're going to do the next time we run into the Huntsman. We spent last night hiding, but if we want a chance at actually winning this thing, we're going to have to figure something else out."

The sprites blew away.

"How far do you think we are from the lake?" Tristan asked. "Beor's ahead of us now. We'll have to find a way to catch up and go around him."

"I'm pretty sure if we drive through the night, we could get there by sundown tomorrow," Leo said.

But when the sprites returned some time later, Dion put an end to the idea of *going around* the Huntsman.

"*I did some research last night. And I talked to Anne, in the vaguest terms possible. She doesn't know about you or what you're doing,*" he was quick to assure her, though she didn't find it very reassuring at all. "*The Huntsman has existed in one form or another for centuries. The current Huntsman, Beor, inherited the gift of necromancy from a distant witch ancestor. According to legend, he can outrace anyone, and he goes out of his way to cut down his competitors. I don't know what his weaknesses are, other than silver, and he has a low level of resistance to its effects, since he's part human. I don't recommend engaging him in combat. Not even with a gun.*"

"Darn," Leo said. "Guess I packed those silver bullets for nothing."

"*Do you have any binding or concealment spells? That's your best chance of getting through this,*" Dion finished.

Aziza felt an irrational surge of embarrassment as she replied, "I don't know any spells."

"If Beor doesn't move during the day, then we'll end up ahead of him before sundown most likely," Leo said, as the sprites left. "But he's going to come after us again tonight. So we hide."

"Not if it means asking the nymphs again," Tristan said.

"We'll find another way," Aziza agreed. "But there's still the question of what happens when we get to the lake. Beor will probably beat us there. Right?"

"Right," Leo said. "Which means a showdown with him if we want to take it."

Or they could turn back. But that wasn't really an option, not when it meant consigning Leo to a life of servitude at the Summer Court. And if they turned back now, then whatever deal Leo had made with the nymphs last night would've been for nothing.

Leo had saved them. Now they'd make sure he won.

They drove west, chased by the sun. By late morning they were well into the mountains they had seen from a distance yesterday. The road narrowed until it was thin as a fishing line cast into a rocky sea. It curved around cliffs, took them over ridges and past canyons, ever deeper into jagged foothills that knifed across the landscape like the dorsal fin of a great leviathan.

At noon, dark coils of smoke bloomed from the woods and surrounded the pooka, blocking out the sunlight. Long, hungry faces yawned out of the darkness, gaping mouths and gaunt eyes. The pooka launched forward, blowing through the wall of smoke—the *wraiths*, said a pixie's voice in her memory. Hunger spirits that preyed on travelers; the natural enemies of pookas. Tendrils of smoke clawed at the pooka as it fled, wriggling wormlike over the windows, so close Aziza shuddered, as if they'd brushed her cheek. It took a long time for Leo to get control of the wheel again, even after the wraiths were gone, and by the time he did, they'd gone way off course.

As they climbed, the temperature dropped, the shadows grew infested with shades, which nipped at the pooka's tires as it passed; the scare almost sent it, and all of them, hurtling off the side of a cliff.

In the high places lurked hill wights. These were undead beings in a state of perpetual, rapid decomposition, which survived by constantly repairing their festering bodies using parts stolen from travelers—fae and human alike. An old wight was a terrifying rag-doll creature with mismatched limbs and a decaying face, smart enough to set traps and lure them off course, but desperate enough to charge them head-on if its other tactics failed. Leo kept running them over; the pooka hated it.

Aziza had to pour her magical energy into keeping the pooka calm. The added benefit was that, as she and the pooka found a kind of communication—a knowledge exchange with no images and no words—it became more car-like, learning from her. This was a relief. Earlier, the pooka had grown an eye in the middle of the steering wheel the first time someone other than Tristan had touched it; it had studied Leo in fascination for an hour. And then it had grown more eyes across the dashboard and on the ceiling, like a slow-spreading rash. So Leo almost cried with happiness when he took the wheel again later in the day and found pedals under his feet. Soon they even had a gearshift, rearview mirrors, window glass, seat belts—and the eyes had blinked themselves out of existence.

"Why does this car smell like lemon?" Leo said, as if he'd been stewing on it for miles.

"I had to pick something or it would've kept smelling like horse," Aziza said.

"What's wrong with how *my* car smells?"

"Nothing! It smells like gasoline and whatever lunch you took home from your job. Usually mac and cheese. Sorry if that wasn't the first scent that sprang to my mind."

"That's how a car is supposed to smell."

Out of sympathy and respect for his grief, she chose not to argue with this.

"But the pooka smells *clean*," she said instead.

"It smells like *cleaning product*. That doesn't mean—hey! My car is clean!" He paused and then corrected himself, mournfully. "*Was. Was* clean. *Super* clean."

"I didn't say it wasn't."

"Tris, back me up."

"Don't drag me into this."

When the sun sank behind the tops of the mountains, a false twilight descended over the world. Aziza thought they'd have until midnight before the Huntsman caught up with them. She was wrong. By her estimation, it was barely a quarter past eight when Tristan said, "They're close."

The pooka made a noise underneath them, a long, low groan like an engine struggling through a deep pool of water, or an animal in fear.

"We'll be harder to find on foot," Leo said. "If we go off the path, uphill—"

Uphill where the wights lay in wait.

But it was their best option. They had the pooka stop and climbed out; their supplies were dumped unceremoniously on the ground as it transformed into something small and furry again. It was a cat long enough to leap into Aziza's arms, and then a dormouse as it scurried up her shoulder and nestled under her hair, between the back of her jacket and the nape of her neck. They took only their backpacks and the silver cloak.

"This way," she whispered, and led them up over the rocky terrain. Tiny stones dislodged under their feet, so they almost slipped, and the way forward was at times barred by boulders or ledges they had to climb. She had her eye on a sparsely wooded area above them, a patch of green clinging to the mountain like moss on a stone. She cast her magic out ahead of them, searchingly, and winced when she found it—a painful, festering energy, like a sore. The wight felt her, too, but it couldn't tell exactly where she was. Most travelers stayed on the path below, and so that was where it would search.

The baying of the hounds had started up again. She looked back, but night had fallen in earnest, and Beor evidently had no need of lanterns or flashlights; the hunting party closed in through total darkness. Tristan was just behind her, startlingly pale in the gloom. He shook his head minutely, his mouth a thin line, confirming what she'd guessed: They weren't moving fast enough.

"I'll try another diversion," Tristan said.

"No," Leo said. "It's too dangerous for you."

"We can't outrun him if he comes this way."

"There's a hill wight," she said. "It's waiting in that grove up there. It thinks we're on the road, so it's planning to—"

That was enough; they understood without her having to waste her breath spelling it out. They picked up their pace, scrambling over the remaining ledges, which cut into their hands and left scrapes on their arms and knees. Leo pulled Aziza up or gave her a boost where it got too steep for her to climb one-handed. They didn't dare turn on their flashlights, but the moon and stars were brighter than Aziza had ever seen them. The pooka's tiny, warm body trembled against her skin.

Just as they had reached level ground and the grove of scraggly fir trees, a shock wave ran through the hills. With it came a rumble that snuck into the air, so low at first it was inaudible, but then it swelled into a roar that drowned out the howls of Beor's pack. The three of them huddled close together under the trees as fir needles shook loose and fell into their hair.

It was the wight. With its stone magic and its gift for taking things apart, it had set off a landslide. A few of the earlier wights had tried the same tactic on them, never fast enough to catch the pooka. It probably hadn't touched Beor, either, and it wouldn't be enough to stop him, but maybe it would buy them time to put some distance between them and the hunting party.

If they could make it past the wight.

It heard them breathing, or maybe it sensed the warmth of their living bodies. Deep within the hilltop grove, something limped toward them.

This one had stolen a single wing from a fairy that must have been very old or sick to have been overtaken by a wight; it trailed on the ground, its iridescent sheen dulled by a layer of dirt. It had a scaly arm tipped with claws, outstretched toward them; its torso and legs were flesh of unidentifiable origin, black and purple with decay under shreds of rags, with skin sloughing off in places to reveal bone. Its face was human, though, a man's face, features drooping because the wight didn't know what to do with them.

Tristan drew his silver knife, but Aziza said, "Leo, the cloak!"

As the wight limped into the moonlight, which brought its wrecked features into ghastly clarity, Leo unclasped the cloak and flung it out in one smooth motion to cover the wight.

Its shriek of pain was thin and ragged; its stolen throat was not, after all, properly connected to the rest of it, so the noises it made were desperate, animal cries, pitiful but not loud enough to give them away.

"Run!" she told them, and they did, skirting around the thrashing wight. When she stopped to take back the cloak, it had fallen apart into a pile of limbs and stone, as the silver had negated its magic. The flesh parts of it were burned and twitching grotesquely. It would put itself back together, but that would take a while. She went after the boys, ears straining for the sounds of the hunting party. But there was only a dazed silence in the wake of the landslide.

Beyond the grove, the land lurched upward again, cliffs jutting out like an immense stairway to the mountaintops. She left the trees and followed the base of the cliff, and just as she was wondering where the hell they had disappeared to, Tristan's hand shot out and caught her by the arm, drawing her into a crack in the rock wall that she could've sworn hadn't been there a second ago. Leo was farther inside, whispering to a stranger.

The fae being that had led them into the crevice was a good eight feet tall and looked like it was made of volcanic rock, its features dark gray and craggy. In its weathered face she made out a heavy brow, shadowed obsidian eyes, and a jaw as square and solid as granite.

"He said he'll help us," Leo said, turning back to her.

The gargoyle inclined his head. "This is one of the hidden entrances to the Winter Court. Beor will not dare follow you here, even if he could find it."

His voice was low and harsh, but not unkind.

"What's your price?" she said.

"No price," the gargoyle said. "Queen Ceresia will be pleased to make Beor work for his victory this season."

The pixies had always said gargoyles were honorable and just; they mingled with fairy courts but did not play fairy games. They were more like selkies, and maybe it was because of that, because of this faint, echoing reminder of Meryl and Marinus, that Aziza nodded, and they followed the gargoyle deeper into the crevice, which widened into a cave. The cave turned into a downward-sloping tunnel, but he stopped them there, before they could descend.

"This is far enough. To bring you into the Winter Court itself would be more harm than help, I fear," the gargoyle said. "Rest, and leave at sunrise. The light will not reach you here, but your pooka companion will know when it is time."

They sat shoulder to shoulder in the dark, listening and waiting, not unlike the way they'd spent last night. The pooka turned into a snake and curled against her rapid heartbeat. Soon, though, the tension broke—there was only so long you could be afraid before exhaustion took over, and you just became numb.

Against all odds, she fell asleep.

SHE STOOD IN the cave over her own sleeping body, which was slumped against Tristan's shoulder. Leo was on his other side; he had thrown the silver cloak over all three of them before he'd passed out. A lock of hair that had fallen over her other self's face stirred as she exhaled, which was how Aziza knew she wasn't dead; still, it was one of the most unnerving things she'd ever experienced.

A dream, she thought. But she'd never had a dream like this before.

Across from where her body slept, there was a door set into the wall, which she was certain had not been there before—a mahogany door with a brass handle, which looked like it belonged inside a government building, not a cave in Elphame.

She opened it, of course.

The dream shifted smoothly into another one, and she was in someone's study. It was a wood-paneled space lit by the warm yellow light of a shaded desk lamp, lavish in an understated sort of way—the walls lined in bookcases filled with glossy leather tomes, the bay window overlooking a picturesque, moonlit countryside, the ornate twin-pedestal desk. Behind the desk, Dion Legrand sat in a tall wingback chair, leafing through a book with pages that, at least from her vantage point, were blank. His head was bent, and his eyes flicked from left to right, as if reading, but his expression was vacant.

Uneasily, she approached. She was reluctant to call attention to herself; it felt wrong, as if she were waking a sleepwalker. But he looked up at her then of his own accord, and it was like someone had breathed life into a statue; the fog cleared out of his eyes and was replaced with a familiar look of faint amusement.

"If you're my dream girl, then this must be a nightmare," he said by way of greeting.

"Stick to the books, Dion. Jokes aren't your thing."

She ignored the two chairs and perched on the corner of the desk instead, sensing that this would annoy even an imaginary version of Dion, and was gratified by the slight, almost imperceptible narrowing of his eyes, which told her she was right.

"Weirdly realistic for a dream," he drawled.

"If anyone here is dreaming, it's me. I'm just trying to figure out if my coven ran afoul of a sandman while we were on the road."

A tiny furrow appeared between Dion's eyebrows, as if he'd walked into a room and then forgotten the reason why. "Did you by chance happen to go through a door?"

"Yes?"

He sat bolt upright. "That's right—I remember now. We're not dreaming; we're astral projecting. I just needed you to be indoors so that I could find you."

"Wait, slow down. You did this? How?"

· 184 ·

"A spell. My craft can't get me to Elphame, but traveling through dreams is another matter. Astral projections are delicate, though. We may not have much time."

She had so many questions, chief among them being, "But . . . why?"

"Exchanging a few words every couple of hours while we wait for the wind sprites to go back and forth has been . . . inefficient. I thought if we could talk face-to-face, we could come up with a better plan. And, yes, I know how dangerous it can be to astral project without taking steps to mitigate the risks," he added, sounding defensive and stubborn in equal measures, "and that you didn't have a chance to meditate or do any of the necessary breathing exercises, but I assure you I wouldn't have let any harm—"

Astral projection was a skill compatible with many different kinds of witchcraft, but, according to Jiddo, it was *notoriously* difficult. It wasn't even that it required a lot of power. What it took was study, practice, and perseverance. Dion had not only accomplished it, but had brought another person, entirely unprepared, *with* him. Yes, it was risky. Jiddo would never have approved. But also, it was *infuriatingly* cool.

"Dion," she said, cutting him off. "This is *amazing*."

A pause as he processed the fact that he was not receiving the dressing-down he'd anticipated.

"Well, yes," he replied, visibly pleased with himself now. "That goes without saying. But do feel free to say it again."

"Shut up." Then she remembered that the last time she'd seen Dion, she had lied her way into a bargain, and that was the only reason he had gone to all the trouble of performing a spell powerful enough to *pull her consciousness from her body* so that they could meet in the realm of dreams.

"So you brought us to . . . what is this place?" she asked, to cover her discomfort.

"Emil's office. I've spent a lot of time here since he . . ." Dion trailed off, subdued, and Aziza examined her surroundings again with renewed interest, taking note of details she'd missed before. The photographs on the shelves, including a few with a solemn, dark-haired child that had to be Dion. A framed degree from a university, where Emil had gotten a doctorate in something called *thanatology*.

"It's a field of study on death and bereavement," Dion said, following her gaze. "He's a psychologist. He is, literally, an expert on the subject of loss and coping with it. If he were here, I know exactly what he'd say to me—how he'd want me to handle the possibility that he's not coming back—but I . . ."

As he trailed off, the study . . . deteriorated around them. A thick layer of dust settled over the leather-bound books. Shadows gaped in the corners, reaching for their circle of lamplight. The desk creaked under her, and when she looked down, she found it wasn't a sturdy antique anymore, but a scorched, blackened shell of what it had been before, practically falling apart. Hastily, she jumped off, not trusting it to carry her weight.

"Catch me up," Dion said. "If you're asleep, then you must be safe from the Huntsman."

It was like he hadn't noticed the way the room had changed. She decided not to call attention to it. Dion listened attentively while she recounted the last couple of days, and it was shockingly easy to tell him everything—a relief to do so, knowing he would take it all in stride.

When she was finished, she said, "Have you found anything we can use to fight Beor?"

"No, I haven't learned anything new." He settled back into the chair, elbows propped on the arms. "Tell me about your spells—that would be a good place to start."

"I already told you I don't have any."

"I thought you only meant you don't have any spells that you could use against Beor," Dion said. "You don't have *any* spells . . . at all? But then how do you get by?"

"I just . . . focus really hard, and my magic usually does what I want it to," she said. "What kind of spells am I supposed to have?"

"You really don't know anything," Dion said, with a kind of rising horror as the gravity of Aziza's predicament sank in.

"Oh, fuck off. If you can't help, I can go," she said, gesturing behind her at the door—and then she did a double take as she realized that there *was* no door, only a giant hole in the wall, the edges blackened. A long, dark hallway stretched away from the opening. Emil was at the end of it, unmistakable with his red hair, sitting with one leg crossed over the other and watching them in silence.

"I didn't mean it like that," Dion huffed.

She'd let the thing with the desk pass without comment—it was still charred, and creaked worryingly when Dion put a hand on it, not that he seemed to notice—but *this* she could not ignore.

"Are you seeing that?" She pointed at Emil.

Dion looked over her shoulder, squinting.

"Ah, yes," he said, after a moment. "The manifestation of my guilt at not having found him yet. Visions of Emil wander in and out of my dreams, but mostly it's just me in this study, trapped in a perpetual cycle of research that gets me nowhere. It should remain docile as long as we ignore it." He waved a hand in a dismissive gesture. "I'm not a hedgewitch, but I can still help. I once saw Anne Sterling make a knife out of resin from a nymph's veins, sea salt from a selkie's tears, and obsidian carved from a mountain by a goblin. I saw her rein in a kelpie using hemp twine and a rhyme she made up on the spot. I was with her when she redrew an entire city's boundary with Elphame—it took so much energy she couldn't cast another spell for a month, but she did it."

Aziza had leaned toward him unconsciously, hanging on his every word.

"Are you saying you can teach me her spells?" she asked.

Although there was a basic structure that all spells adhered to—a three-part formula consisting of language, offering, and a witch's innate magic—a spell could be made of almost *anything*. It could be spoken, written, signed, sung; it might require herbs or crystals, or water or fire, or blood or death. Tiny details like the difference of a single syllable in the words you used, your inflection if you spoke aloud, what offering you chose and how much of it—all of that could affect how the spell turned out. And if you didn't know what you were doing, the spell could go catastrophically wrong.

This was why Jiddo had never been able to teach her hedgewitch spells. But it was more than just not knowing the formulas: Jiddo didn't *understand* hedgecraft. He didn't know how the fae thought or what Elphame's magic felt like; he couldn't help her guide her intentions, and intent was an essential component in the casting of a spell. Witches like him—ward-keepers, and others with an affinity for protective magics—had a more rigid sort of craft, and hedgecraft was anything *but* rigid.

But if Dion had grown up around an experienced hedgewitch and her stories, then—

"I *might* be able to help you work out one of her basic spells. I've studied spell theory, and I can tell you a bit about the core principles," he said, getting up to search for something on the shelves. Absently, he wiped the dust off the books with his sleeve and scanned the titles. "A witch makes her own spells. But there are materials and techniques that respond semi-consistently to certain crafts, and these are universal. I'll give you the basics, and you'll go from there." He chose a few of the books and brought them back to the desk. Their pages were blank to her, but she supposed it didn't matter, if Dion remembered enough to explain it all.

"You have one day, so we'll focus on one spell," he said. "Think you can manage it?"

Her first spell. She couldn't help it; she practically beamed at him, and she must have looked a little manic, because his eyes went wide and he busied himself with the books again.

"I'm ready," she said, and Dion flipped the first book open so that they could begin.

CHAPTER 18

TRISTAN

IN THE MORNING, Aziza said, "I have a plan. Kind of."

"You came up with something in your sleep?" Leo said, with no sarcasm. He wouldn't have been surprised at all to learn that she had. He stretched his arms over his head, wincing, and Tristan was reminded that no matter what state he found himself in—wounded, sleep-deprived, in danger of imminent death—he would never not be transfixed by the sight of Leo Merritt's shirt riding up to reveal the trail of hair disappearing into his waistband.

God help me, he thought, and then, inconsolably: *Not even God can help me.*

He forced himself to look away as Aziza filled them in on her impromptu magic lesson with Dion Legrand. They were trudging down the side of the mountain, the pooka darting ahead of them in the shape of a magpie, occasionally swooping down to hunt spiders and millipedes. They'd have to find the road again before it could change back into a car; he tried not to think about how much time they were losing as the sun climbed higher into the sky.

"So he didn't teach you a spell," Tristan recapped. "He taught you about the ingredients that *might* work in a spell, and you still have to figure out the words yourself."

"He taught me a preschooler's version of spell theory, yeah," she said grimly. "But he thinks I can use one of Anne Sterling's spells instead of making up my own, and if our magic is similar enough, it should work. Hedgewitches don't tend toward as much variety as, say, oracles or ward-keepers, since we all have the same affinity for Elphame's magic. The problem is the language. He said hedgewitch spells require stories."

"Like, fairytales?" Leo said, grinning. "Literally?"

"See, you're joking, but yes. He said—and I still don't know if he was fucking with me or not—he said '*the Brothers Grimm were some of the greatest hedgewitches who ever lived.*'"

"How are you going to have the time to recite a story?" Tristan asked, over Leo's strangled laughter.

"I don't know! I told him that I usually just focus on one-word commands—*open* or *hold*—and he said words that simple will give you a shapeless spell, and shapeless spells are for children." She rolled her eyes. "So I'm borrowing a story Anne uses about a bird in a cage, but I have to fill in the details myself because Dion could only summarize it. He doesn't remember the exact words. I'll have to keep telling the story until the spell takes."

It was half a plan at best, and it would require the three of them to get much closer to Beor than they wanted to, but they had nothing else. By day, the threat of the Hunt felt far away, blunted; they found time for gallows humor as they drove onward, making brief detours to gather the things Aziza would need for the spell. Anne's story would provide the language; Aziza's own magic would power it. The only thing left was the offering. They collected water from a freshwater spring and a few strips of rowan that Aziza would have to braid. Dion had said both braids and knots held magical significance, but a braid would be easier for a first spell.

They wouldn't have time for a trial run. So they helped Aziza learn the story she would tell instead, making up details where she drew a blank and insisting she recite it to them until she had it memorized. Tristan had his doubts that a crowdsourced spell would be sufficient defense against Beor, but he didn't have any better ideas. There was also the question of the springtide lord, but they wouldn't even have a chance to worry about that if they couldn't get past Beor.

"If you can distract him, I might have time to cast the spell," Aziza said. "I'll keep him trapped while you and Leo finish the Hunt."

"Distract him," he repeated incredulously. "Sure! Why didn't I think of that?"

"Sorry, did you think this was going to be easy?"

"I didn't think I'd be *bait*."

"You're only bait if you get caught."

"No one's getting caught," Leo said.

"Tristan," she said. "I wouldn't ask if I didn't *know* you could do this."

There was doubt coming from her end of the bond. He opened his mouth to call her out on it, but then he met her eyes and understood. It wasn't him she doubted. It was herself.

But Leo's faith in them was, as ever, unwavering. Tristan was inclined to agree with him. They weren't going to die today. Couldn't. Because there were too many things Tristan hadn't said to Leo. Too much left unresolved between them.

The other night, when Leo had come to talk to him, he'd said it could be now or never. And what had Tristan done? He'd suggested that they could fool around and it didn't have to mean anything.

· 192 ·

His entire *soul* cringed when he thought back on that conversation. *What* had possessed him to do that? He should have been grateful that Leo hadn't laughed at him outright. But instead of backing off, he kept pressing his luck. He'd used their close quarters during this trip to observe how Leo responded to him, experimenting with touch and proximity and shared glances during quiet moments. He found excuses to get closer, leaning in to show Leo something on the map when they were parked at the gas station, wrapping the cloak around his shoulders before they hiked to the spring and letting his fingers brush against Leo's neck as he fixed the clasp for him. The look on Leo's face when Tristan tested his limits was fast becoming Tristan's new obsession; he needed to see it again and again before he could believe it was real. And it was nothing new. Leo had *always* looked at him like that, before the curse. But he was only now starting to understand that it wasn't a friendly look. It was a look that said if Tristan got any closer, Leo might forget how to breathe. It was *desire.*

Tristan wasn't playing fair. Leo wasn't aware of how well Tristan knew him—that Tristan knew exactly what he wanted and how he wanted it. But if he could make Leo want him again, maybe he could make Leo fall in love with him again, too. Somehow. Even though he didn't know how he'd done it the first time around. Because this . . . wasn't enough. Attraction wasn't enough. Breaking the curse wasn't enough, *true love* wasn't enough, as selfish as it felt to even think that. He didn't want Leo to love him again just because he'd loved him before, to pick him back up like a habit.

I want you to love me the way I am now, he thought. *Even if it's harder. Even if I don't deserve it.*

The clouds won their battle for the skies and obscured the setting sun from their view. The mountains bore down on them, cinching together until they were coasting into a long, icy valley bisected by a river.

"That's the tail," Leo said, and then shook his head as if to clear away a mental fog. "Uh. I don't even know what I mean by that. It's something I got from the map."

"The tail, huh?" Aziza said. "Then it must be connected to a body."

Leo shrugged helplessly. The map's insights ended there.

The slopes on either side of the river piled up into towering bluffs, glossed with ice toward the peaks. The light through the clouds set the valley aflame with sunset colors, so that it was as if they traveled through a frozen inferno, a surreal, dreamy landscape that could have existed nowhere else but in fairyland.

Ahead of them, maybe half a mile away, the valley tapered off. A natural granite arch marked the opening of a tight channel between a set of cliffs, barely wide enough for the river. Beyond that, the glint of water in a lake so still it was like a picture in one of Bishop Library's stained glass windows, framed within the archway.

The light faded as twilight fell. All at once, the valley was plunged into darkness.

The scarred hound sent a warning through their bond, and then Tristan saw movement in the rearview mirror. There was no time to react. One of Beor's hounds rose out of the shadows, directly beside the pooka. Tristan only caught a glimpse of it, it was moving so fast. It was a streak of black fur, wiry muscles stretching, mouth foaming, and it opened its jaws wide so Tristan could see into its throat, red and bloody, as it snapped at the pooka's back tire—

The pooka swerved out of control. Leo shouted, swore, fought with the wheel, and Tristan shielded his face with an arm as he slammed against the window. The slopes rushed toward them, and the pooka was transforming. Suddenly there were no doors, no windows, no seat underneath him—just empty air—and he was flung to the ground, the momentum sending him skidding and rolling—sky and earth and sky and earth revolved dizzyingly around him, and by the time he came to a halt, he was breathless, aching with fresh bruises, and completely disoriented. The smell of river water mingled with the sickening sweetness of the air; he took great gasps of it, and it made him sick, his lungs burning.

"Tris!"

That was Leo, sounding frantic. He dragged himself to his hands and knees, looking around until he found Leo a few yards away. Their supplies were scattered across the ground. No sign of their pooka; it was long gone. No sign of Aziza, either. He could only guess she'd followed the pooka.

"They're leaving us," Leo said, pulling Tristan to his feet.

The hunting party stuck close to the banks of the river, and seeing it with his own eyes was worse than he could have anticipated. The difference between the beasts Beor commanded and Tristan's hounds was vast—like the difference between the kind of darkness that happened when you turned off the light in your bedroom and tucked yourself into bed, and the kind of darkness that happened when the streetlamp by your bus stop all of a sudden flickered and died. And with the hounds were the spirits—more wisps of air and light than anything resembling flesh, a ghostly mist woven through the pack. But when the moonlight hit them a certain way, their outlines shifted into focus. Gallowglass warriors with their twisted armor and translucent blades. Human hunters from another time, in wool caps and riding boots, carrying rifles. And in the middle of it all, Beor and his antlered helmet towered over them on a steed Aziza had said was probably an illusion made of rain and clover. He didn't even glance their way.

"Why aren't they . . ." Tristan began.

"They're going straight for the lake," Leo said blankly. "Whatever we're looking for, it's there. He's going to win."

"We still have a plan," Tristan said. He called the scarred hound back, guided it from the shadows deep in the slopes behind them until it came slinking up to him, its head low, its teeth bared, unhappy to be this close to the Huntsman. "Go around. Climb up past the arch and back down the slopes on the other side. I'll hold him off until Aziza gets her spell going, and you figure out how to finish this. Nothing's changed."

"Nothing's changed? We don't even know where Aziza *is*. Tris—"

"It's that or go back. Your call."

Leo looked at the granite arch and then at Tristan. And instead of the hurried goodbye Tristan had expected, Leo reached for him, a hand sliding over the back of his neck, drawing him close and pressing their foreheads together.

Tristan shut his eyes, committing his warmth to memory.

"Be. Careful. *Promise me*," Leo said.

He knew he shouldn't, but he did anyway. "I promise."

Leo was the one to step away first this time. With one more long look at him, he left, heading uphill. Tristan didn't watch him go. His eyes found the pack, the last of them flowing through the arch at the end of the valley.

The hounds Tristan had lost the other night were in there, too. Three of them in total—the one he'd used to get his first look at the Hunt and then two more he'd used as a diversion while they searched for a place to hide. And Tristan was a thief. The hounds weren't his; he'd stolen them from Emil. But, in that moment, he didn't care the slightest bit about whether or not he had a right to the hounds.

He thought, *I'm getting my fucking dogs back.*

Beside him, the scarred hound growled low in its throat, as if it agreed.

Every other time his mind slipped into the hound's, he was a passenger, a spy. This time, as he wove his fingers into its fur and let their thoughts mingle, he kept no barrier between their minds. He didn't pull back when the hound's thoughts and impulses started to feel like his own. He wasn't a passenger. He possessed the hound; he *became* the hound. There were two of him: the Tristan who stood upright, balancing carefully on the valley's lower slopes, and the Tristan with bristling fur, claws digging into the gravel, sharp eyes glaring down at the thin, pale, fragile mortal body before him. He stopped clinging to that other self, that human self. He stopped fearing what would happen if he entrusted himself fully to the hound's consciousness. Would he lose himself? Or would he multiply, becoming, forever, one being with two bodies?

Tristan-the-hound navigated the slopes with ease, with a freedom of movement he'd never before felt. His huge paws slid over the riverbank and propelled him forward, through the arch and into the narrow channel beyond. Tristan-the-summoner followed slowly, carefully, so as not to slip and fall into the river. He did and experienced both things at once, seamlessly. All those times he'd slipped in and out of the hounds' minds and had worried his lack of control spoke to some weakness of character—a sign that he was ill-suited for this borrowed craft—he had really been training himself for this moment. He wasn't overwhelmed by the intensity of his new senses or intimidated by the impossible power and grace of his new shadow-flesh body. He raced after Beor, and when the magic of the other hunting party brought the low background simmer of his killing instinct to a boil—when his muscles went tight and tense with the need to attack—these were not foreign impulses. They didn't make him forget who he was. The Huntsman couldn't take the hound from him this time, because Tristan and the hound were one and the same.

The channel through the arch was sheer rock, too steep to climb, but then the valley widened again into a gorge, like a chalice containing a crystal lake. The melting ice from the mountains fed into it, and the lake in turn fed the river. The water was deep, but so clear that he could see the bottom, where the lakebed was made of smooth white and gray stone. Things flickered in its depths, too fast to make out, even with the eyes of a hound. Beor stood with his boots at the edge of the water, his back to Tristan, flanked on both sides by his spirits. His hounds, meanwhile, dove into the lake. They flowed through it like globs of ink, swimming as smoothly as they ran, chasing something—a ripple of blue in the silvery water, like a snake, or a rope. One of his massive, gauntleted hands rested on the hilt of a sheathed sword. A silver flask swung from a cord he held in his other fist.

Tristan's summoner-body edged along the narrow bank where the river passed through the arch, droplets of frigid water spraying the hem of his jeans. As he entered the gorge, the spirits converged on him. They tugged at his fur and clothes, and howled in both sets of ears. The strongest ones *hurt*, pushing at and through him with such force he was sure he'd have bruises later, slashing with transparent weapons that left long wounds, so thin and shallow they were almost invisible, like paper cuts; he threw up an arm to protect his face. But worse was how their touch drained the energy from his summoner-body, his muscles going weak. His knees shook. If he had been carrying something, he would have dropped it. He felt frail, boneless, and if this went on, he was certain it wouldn't just be his strength they drained—it would be his life, too. Waves of fear crashed over him, rooting him to the spot. Even with the hag he'd never felt this afraid. He *wasn't* afraid, not of Beor, not even of dying, but the fear came anyway, with the inevitability of nightfall.

His hound-body, though, did not even know what fear was.

Beor turned to him, carelessly, his body still half-angled toward the water. He laughed, the scars on his face puckering, sharp teeth showing past his thin lips.

"Hello, little summoner," he said, in his rough voice. "I never thought you'd be foolish enough to face me in person."

Tristan's ears flattened, and his lips pulled back in a snarl. Beor had addressed Tristan's summoner-self only. When he turned to Tristan-the-hound, it was to beckon, a simple *come here* gesture with his fingers.

He didn't know what Tristan had done. He couldn't tell.

With vicious triumph, Tristan bounded to the Huntsman, as if eager to obey. At the last possible moment, he lashed out teeth-first at Beor's throat. He crashed into him, paws on his shoulders, fangs sinking into the fleshy part of his neck where it met his collar, until he tasted blood—and they fell backward and into the lake. It got deep fast, the shore dropping off sharply under the water. Both of them were fully submerged before Beor's back finally hit the lakebed. Tough leather shredded between Tristan's teeth. Beor's pulse throbbed between his jaws; the water was icy cold, his fur heavy, his muscles seizing up from the chill; blood clouded the water and made it impossible to see. Beor's hands came up, fighting, and Tristan held him down and down until his vision went black—

Tristan drowned.

As a hound, he would heal, but not fast enough. His summoner-self called on a new hound, ignoring the spirits that whirled around him. They were only noise, they were only wind and fear and haste, they were the tracks you had no time to cover and the panic that made you clumsy when you should have been swift—they were the Hunt, but he was not prey, not anymore. He was a hound again, racing to the water and leaping on Beor just as he shoved the first hound's body aside and surfaced.

Tristan didn't know how many times he died fighting Beor. He drowned more than once. He was stabbed. He had his throat slit one time, his neck broken another. One of Beor's hounds crashed into him, flinging him off Beor and tearing his stomach open with its claws. But Beor, spitting out water, barked, "Leave me! Don't let it escape!"

It? Tristan thought dimly, but then one of his dead hounds had woken up again. He left the disemboweled one and used the healed one to drag Beor back into the deep. His summoner-self was on his knees now, in agony; dying was painful, coming back to life even more so, and even the body that hadn't been physically harmed was feeling the effects of the ordeal.

And the next time he drowned, he had no energy left to replace his hound-self with another one. When the hound came back to life, it belonged to Beor; it swam away into the lake, joining the rest of the pack in pursuit of the prey hidden deep in the water. And Beor— weak as he was from the fight, from the water he'd inhaled, the cold and his wounds, the bite marks in his neck and shoulders, the claw marks shredding his armor down his torso—still had the strength to drag himself from the water, climb onto the bank, and advance on Tristan. And Tristan was only human again, small, singular, freezing from the assault of Beor's spirits.

Beor drew the sword from his scabbard—a hilt of braided wood, a blade of shining silver.

"Had you been properly trained, you would have known better

than to attempt that," he rasped. Under the antler helm, his eyes burned. Water sluiced off him in rivulets as he approached. "A reckless thing you did, near suicidal, and all for naught."

He was raising the sword to execute Tristan right there where he knelt, too feeble even to shuffle away on his knees. The spirits roared louder than ever, infecting him with their terror, with the desire to flee, but he couldn't have done that even if he'd wanted to. Not when Leo was nearby, counting on him to hold Beor off. And Beor's eyes flashed twice as bright now—

No, that light in his eyes was coming from somewhere else. An inferno blazing through the confused fog of spirits. Beor lifted his head, searching for the source, and then there was a roar like—like an engine.

Beor lunged out of the way as something that was *mostly* a car charged at the place where he'd been standing.

And the sword slipped out of his damp glove.

CHAPTER 19

LEO

By the time he made it into the gorge, half walking and half climbing over steep slopes and across ledges barely wide enough for him to stand on, Beor was moving toward Tristan with his sword drawn. Covered in bloody wounds and dripping wet, Beor looked like he'd been through hell—but Tristan was the one on his knees as if too weak to stand.

Leo forgot all about looking for the springtide lord and whatever prize it guarded. Beor's hounds were in the water and they'd surely beat him to it. He had to get to Tristan. He scraped his hands trying to slide down as fast as he could without falling or tripping himself on the heavy silver cloak he still wore. As he descended, the spirits whipped around him. They tugged at his clothes, pulled roughly at his hair, moaned plaintively in his ears. Milky, translucent hands left blue bruises on his wrists, his throat. Shimmering, edgeless blades pierced his chest. His heart missed a beat, and then another. Could a ghost's blade stop his heart? It didn't hurt, not really, but it was so *cold*. And he was in pieces. He was being dragged down into the dark place where he'd been trapped after the curse had set in, where everything was hopeless, and nothing he did mattered, and it wasn't possible he'd feel anything but hollow ever again. He should stop trying. He should lie down. He should go to sleep, and if he still felt this way when he woke up, he shouldn't wake up. They sapped his energy, infected him with fear and doubt.

But the only thing he was really afraid of, just then, was not reaching Tristan in time.

He staggered onto level ground, but Beor was standing over Tristan, and Leo was still too far away. Despair crashed over him, and the windlike howls of the spirits were so loud it felt as if they were coming from inside his own head. Beor was lifting the sword—

And then something that was almost, but not quite, a Chevy tried to run him over.

Beor dodged, barely, and the pooka made a hairpin turn just short of the water, changing as it did into something houndlike. It dropped Aziza in the process, who landed on her knees. She still had her backpack, which held the rowan braid and the bottled spring water. The pooka's attempt at replicating a hound was as rough as its first transformations into a car. It became a big, black, four-legged thing that was part wolf and part bear, with round equine eyes and shovel-like paws spraying dirt and gravel in every direction as it tore across the shoreline and leapt on Beor.

He grappled barehanded with the pooka, but each time he got a good grip on it, it transformed again. The pooka was a lion, clawing at Beor's armor. It was a python, pinning his arms to his sides. It was an elk, pounding at his ribs with its hooves.

Aziza skirted around the fight, drawing the rowan braid through the dirt in a rough circle and whispering something as she went—a story, he figured, about a caged bird. She went around again, pouring the spring water into the circle, and when the bottle was empty, sank to her knees and pressed her hand to the ground at her starting point as if to hold down the edge of a blanket.

Leo went around the scuffle. The spirits had dissipated, a sign that the fighting had taken a toll on Beor, and only a soft mist lingered on the shore of the lake. He found Tristan pushing himself shakily up on his knees. The wound on his wrist had bled through the bandages, and he was frighteningly pale, his lips blue. But when Leo reached to help him up, Tristan shook his head; he picked up the sword Beor had dropped and held it out for Leo to take.

"Go now," Tristan told him. "While you can."

Leo accepted the sword—blade gleaming, birch hilt warm even though it had been lying untouched for long enough that it should have grown cool. But the lake was teeming with Beor's hounds. They whipped the water into a froth. There was something in there with them, but it was impossible to make out what it was.

With a roar and a surge of desperate strength, Beor shoved at the pooka—a saltwater crocodile whose tail almost whacked Aziza in the head as it thrashed—and finally pushed himself upright. And it seemed the pooka had reached its limit, the end of its courage, and not even its loyalty to Aziza—or the persuasion of Aziza's magic— would make it stay any longer. It turned into a finch and darted into the air, high up out of Beor's reach. Beor climbed to his knees, his eyes finding Leo.

"What now, upstart brat?" Beor growled, ignoring Aziza, who still muttered her story-spell under her breath. "Will you keep hiding behind your companions?"

Leo could only stare at him. His antler helmet had been knocked askew, revealing lank brown hair. Blood and water dripped off him. Beor lurched to his feet, snarling, "*Well? Face me!*"

He stepped forward—and stopped.

He was at the edge of the circle. His hand came up and pressed flat, as if against an invisible wall. Aziza's spell was working. She'd bought him time. Leo summoned what was left of the map memories—surely there had to be a clue in there, something he'd missed. The hounds were breaching the surface of the water one by one, popping out sleek and dark as seals, and if they came to Beor's aid, Leo was done for—but they were occupied, their jaws clamped around something, each of them lifting part of it and dragging it to the top of the lake. There, it floated, almost impossible to see, a flash of blue on the colorless moonlit surface of the water.

Something gleamed at the water's edge—a silver flask that Beor must have dropped. Leo bent and picked it up. Behind him, Beor roared in fury. Aziza's muttering stopped, and she said—a hoarse, desperate last resort—"*Hold.*"

Leo looked back as Beor broke free, the spell collapsing under his strength.

"Zee, run!" Leo shouted. Beor turned to find him holding the silver flask. And Leo knew he'd had the right idea, that the flask was important, because Beor ignored Aziza and charged at him. He fumbled trying to get the sword up—he might not know how to fight, but he'd get in a swing or two before Beor throttled him—

Then something struck him in the back, between his shoulder blades, like a shove. He spun unsteadily, thinking a hound had leapt at him—but there was nothing there. The hounds were still in the water. At his feet lay an arrow with a silver tip.

He'd been shot. Almost.

The cloak must have shielded him, which meant the arrow was enchanted—

Something whistled through the air. There was a wet sound of impact, and when he looked up, Beor was clutching at his neck. An arrow just like the one that had almost hit Leo stuck out of it. Whoever had fired it had perfect aim, and the arrow had sank into the spot just behind Beor's jaw where it met his neck, under the helmet. Blood bubbled from his lips.

"Leo, over here!" That was Aziza, somewhere close by, out of sight—she'd grabbed Tristan, too, he couldn't see either of them—which hopefully meant they were both safe. "Get out of there!"

"Not yet," he muttered under his breath.

He pulled up the hood of the cloak. Left Beor to collapse on his side, choking on his own blood. When he turned to the lake, the hounds had vanished; Beor wasn't keeping them there anymore. A whistling noise as something sliced through the air again; an impact on his side, under his ribs, but again the cloak shielded him from harm. And he had to keep going.

He had a clear line of sight, now, to whatever it was the hounds had fished out of the lake. Tentatively, he stepped into the water. Maybe he could wade in far enough to catch the end of the blue thing, and figure out what to do from there.

Only, when he stepped into the water, the tip of the sword dipped into the lake.

And the lake roared, as if in pain.

The water pulled away from the blade, as if it had been blown apart, so that there was a semicircle of dry lakebed at Leo's feet. A single droplet of water balanced on the point of the sword, and from that connection, swirling tendrils of lake currents arced away, as though he were conducting them. Stunned, he took another step into the lakebed, pressing the sword further into the water, and again the water retreated. He kept going. With the sword, he drew a path into the lake, his sphere of dry land following him even as the water rushed back into place in his wake. It was like he walked in a bubble of air. Soon, he had gone so deep that water surrounded him on all sides. He reached the middle of the lake, its deepest point. All he could hear was the churning of the currents around him, and beyond that, the bass pulse of deep water, dense and shifting and unknowable. If Aziza called his name again, he didn't know; the lake insulated him, muffled all sound. The air was clammy, and he shivered under the cloak.

In the daytime, he wouldn't have been able to see what he was looking for. Now, though, the water was black with night and pale with moonlight, and when he reached the ripple of blue threaded through its depths, it was impossible to miss. It was so blue it didn't look real. Blue like paint, or sapphire, but more intense. It snaked all the way to the surface where the hounds had dragged it. He uncapped the flask with his teeth and dipped it into the blue. His fingertips brushed against it, and his mind swam with memories then: the time he helped Aziza rescue a lost soul from the wills-o'-the-wisp and she laughed in front of him for the first time ever and he knew they were going to be friends; the time when Hazel was little and she learned to walk and all she did was follow him around; the first time Tristan had come to his door when they both couldn't sleep and they'd stayed up all night watching some terrible movie with their shoulders brushing. It was every shade of blue of every beginning. It wiped away the exhaustion of the last few days. It filled him with renewed strength, with energy and clarity and calm. And once the flask was overflowing, he capped it again. The blue shifted, swaying with the motion of the water swirling away from the tip of his sword, and then it slithered sharply out of reach as though it had been yanked. In the depths of the lake, past the watery wall around his bubble of air, he thought he saw a face there in the darkest currents.

It was alive, he thought suddenly. The whole lake was some kind of immense, ancient fae being. *This* was the springtide lord; the map had shown him the truth all along. That was why the water shrank away from the silver sword.

"I'm hurting you," he realized. "I'm sorry."

And he withdrew the sword without really thinking about it. That was a mistake—the water should have come crashing down on him then—but it didn't. Maybe because he still carried the sword at his side, though its tip was now tucked close to his shoes where it wouldn't touch the water, and he was wearing the cloak. If the lake tried to drown him, it would only get hurt again. But he saw that face flickering in the currents that swirled around him, lingering, examining him with eyes of froth and foam, and his circle of dry land opened wider. The currents above him pulled away, layer by layer, until he was no longer in a sphere, but a tower—a vertical tunnel capped with a perfect circle of night sky, allowing fresh air to pour down on him. He breathed in deep.

"Are you a sprite?" he asked as he walked back toward the shore.

The blue ribbon floated before him, and something about its rippling was insistent. He reached for it with his fingertips again, and a word floated into his mind—*undine*, it said. A distant cousin to sprites. It said it was very old and had known many Huntsmen.

It asked the names of the people in his blue memories. It kept him company until, at last, he was climbing onto dry land.

Once he was back on shore, he glanced over his shoulder. The surface of the water was mirror-smooth again, with no sign that it had ever been disturbed.

THE NEXT FEW hours were a blur. They found a shallow cave in the cliffs around the gorge and sheltered there while Tristan and the pooka recovered. The pooka was too exhausted to begin the journey back just yet. And Tristan had pushed his necromancy far beyond anything he'd ever attempted before. He spent all night shivering, even though he was wrapped in the silver cloak with Aziza and Leo on either side of him and the pooka curled up in his lap in mink form.

But when dawn broke over the mountains, shedding golden light across the lake and into their tiny shelter, both he and the pooka were more than ready to get the hell out of there.

On impulse, they checked on the Huntsman and found—to their alarm—that he was alive, breathing shallowly, staring at the sky. The arrows were silver and had badly burned the flesh around the wounds, but Beor's human blood must have saved him from death. His eyes traveled over them, dazed and cloudy, as they argued about whether to bring him along.

Leo wanted to leave him. So did Aziza.

It was Tristan who argued in the Huntsman's favor. And since he was in the worst shape, his vote counted twice.

When they arrived at the Summer Court—Leo with the sword

and flask in hand, Aziza with the arrows they'd salvaged and a fox nestled in the crook of her arm, Tristan leading a hound with the Huntsman's limp form slung over its back—the look on Prince Tal's face was almost worth everything they'd been through to get there.

CHAPTER 20

AZIZA

SHE WASN'T SURPRISED to see the birch wood again. She should have been, maybe. But it was as if her return to this place had been foretold, an inescapable outcome. Even if she hadn't known it.

The wood must have grown in the last decade, and they were in a deeper part of it than the place where the fairy ring had dropped her all those years ago. The morning light made the birch trees glow, and the pillowy moss baked in the warmth. Before her encounter with the hornet knight, this wood had been the most wondrous place she had ever seen. Its magic was all-encompassing, flowing harmlessly through and around her, exhilarating and peaceful at the same time. Now she understood that it hadn't really been the wood she'd felt; it had been the Folk, their magic, drawn from Elphame and given back to Elphame. Despite everything, she couldn't suppress the tiny part of herself that was grateful to have been able to come back here.

The journey had taken about a day. They hadn't needed to detour through the borderlands, and Elphame was smaller than the human world. But they'd driven through the night and were exhausted.

In her arms, the pooka rumbled contentedly. It still smelled like the all-purpose cleaner in her kitchen cabinet, even in fox form. She focused on the feeling of its fur against her skin, and breathed.

This was where the encampment of the nomadic Summer Court had moved in preparation for the solstice. Silk canopies had been erected among the trees, blankets of fur and velvet tossed over beds of wildflowers, table settings of porcelain and bone laid out on stumps and fallen logs. The winged ones had fashioned hanging tents like great silk nests. Here the Fair Folk lounged, and took their wine and tea among the toadstools, and played betting games with colorful stones and glass coins. As she and her coven passed, escorted by two of the Gallowglass—the one with the spider-fang helmet and another with supple, fish-scale armor—the fairies glanced slyly up at them with eyes that had slitted, vertical pupils or no pupils at all, or leaned forward inquisitively with their wings spreading open behind them.

But then the castle was in view, looming over them through the trees. She couldn't see it clearly from this vantage point, only got an impression of spires and walls the color of clouds—not white, but pinkish-purple like dawn, and fiery orange-red like sunset, and gray in brief flashes like a short-lived summer storm.

"Is the rest of the Summer Court in there?" Aziza asked as they were ushered up a flight of stone steps to the ornately carved double doors. There were not nearly as many Folk in the encampment as there had been in Blackthorn for the Midsummer Revels.

"Most of us," the spider-fang warrior said curtly. "The servants will take you from here."

"Wait!" Leo said. "Where's Hazel? I need to see her."

"You may be the Huntsman, but it is still not your place to make demands of us," the knight hissed. "The Hunt is not over until the solstice. No matter your deal with Princess Narra, for now, the changeling girl is still ours."

The heavy doors were pulled open—scraping against the floor as they were dragged—and the servant who was to be responsible for them appeared in the entrance. Beside her, Leo drew in a sharp breath.

The maid was a human girl not much older than they were, in a modest dress with her hair in a sleek bun. She curtsied neatly to the Gallowglass and said, "Welcome. This way, please."

"Who are you?" Leo said, steadying Tristan with a hand on his arm as they climbed the steps.

The maid kept her eyes demurely lowered as she responded, "I'm a member of the king's retinue and the head of the royal staff. You can call me Sophia."

She was already walking away, and they followed hastily.

"But—how'd you end up here? Are you . . ." Leo dropped his voice to a whisper. "Are you all right? Are you, um, a prisoner? Do you want us to get you out?"

Aziza winced. As if they weren't already in deep enough trouble, now Leo wanted to add a jailbreak to the mix. But Sophia shook her head.

"I'm fine, thank you," she said coolly. "King Ilanthus treats us well. He is kind and gracious."

"But—" Leo began, and Aziza nudged him with her shoulder to get his attention. When she had it, she shook her head. He fell into a troubled silence.

Each corridor seemed to go on for ages. The walls were made of tightly woven rows of narrow tree trunks; on them hung millefleur tapestries dyed with rose madder and indigo, linseed oil paintings in gilt scrollwork frames depicting scenes of love and strife, of wild fae, and even, sometimes, of humans. The floors were stone, and orbs of light hovered over sconces in place of lanterns. They illuminated columns of tiger-striped jasper, or calcite, of white marble striated with blue and gray. Indoor streams fed little gardens, so that the burbling of water followed them as they sank ever deeper into the castle. Aziza's shoulders bunched with tension as Sophia led them up the stairs, through side passages, until they reached the corridor that housed the guest quarters.

Their rooms were next to each other, so they split up to get clean. To her immense relief, the chamber had a bathroom where someone—Sophia, she figured—had arranged for them to have full buckets of cold water and a tub to bathe in. She scrubbed off three days' worth of dirt and sweat as best she could, one-handed and shivering, and felt restored. The idea of squirming back into her filthy clothes was unbearable, but Sophia had thought of everything, and a clean outfit was laid out on the bed, a simple tunic and pants.

She dragged it on, sat on the edge of the bed, and allowed herself a moment of relief. Only a moment, though. The Hunt was over, but the danger wasn't. Far from it. The Folk couldn't be trusted; Prince Tal had never wanted them here in the first place. They were depending on Princess Narra's mercy now, and if that failed, Aziza didn't know how they were supposed to protect themselves.

A tap at the window made her jump. She hurried over and shoved it open. The wind sprites spilled into the chamber, carrying the scents of toothpaste and black coffee, and the sweet early-morning air they must have picked up in the birch wood. They inspected the chamber thoroughly, nudging the corners of the tapestries and the bed dressed in silk damask, picking up and then swiftly dropping the pile of clothes she'd discarded on the ground.

"I'm surprised Dion sent you back," she said, collapsing on the bed again while the sprites finished their exploration. "He definitely didn't think I was going to survive that. I'm pretty sure he was composing my eulogy in his head last time I saw him."

But the voice the wind sprites delivered to her wasn't Dion's.

"If you're listening to this, then you must be alive, and you can thank God or your ancestors or whatever you believe in for that, because you surely didn't do it without the aid of either luck or divine intervention," the woman said. The words were sour but her tone was matter-of-fact. Somehow, Aziza knew who she was before she even got around to introducing herself. *"My name is Anne Sterling. No, Dion didn't tell me about you. I intercepted your wind sprites, and they apprised me of your decision to join the Hunt. I understand there is no convincing you to return, so what I am going to do instead is tell you how to survive the Summer Court, and also, ideally, avoid causing a diplomatic disaster. I don't need the headache of making amends with King Ilanthus because a teenage witch and her ragtag coven caused offense."*

It was kind of uncomfortable to realize that she had actually been looking forward to hearing from Dion, and to be met with someone else's voice when she'd expected his was—disappointing, though she wouldn't have said so out loud on pain of death. But she had also never spoken to another hedgewitch before, so she hung on Anne's every word. And there were a *lot* of them; the wind sprites never got bored and cut her off midsentence the way they sometimes did with Dion and even Aziza. Anne went over fairy etiquette, the precautions Aziza must take, and what she must and mustn't do, and some of it was useful, but some of it she'd picked up years ago from the borderland fae, or otherwise was just plain common sense.

She bristled. Anne seemed to think she was *completely* useless.

When Anne's voice faded, one final wind sprite piped up, and this one *did* carry Dion's voice: "*Are you all right? Did the spell work? Listen, I'm going to keep these messages short. I think Anne suspects something. Let me know if you need anything.*"

The pooka, curled next to her as a Siamese cat, responded to this with a single, scathing meow. Aziza had to agree with the sentiment.

She slid off the bed and wandered around the chamber, formulating her response. The wind sprites circled her like a very gentle cyclone while she inspected a locked chest. Most of the furniture grew straight out of the wall. In the bookcase, webs of sproutlings had trapped the dusty books on their shelves. Atop a dresser, a half-formed row of drawers had grown off-center, thanks to a lump of thickened bark—covered in burls and lichen scabs—that marked the place where a jewelry box had been set down and forgotten. Aziza struck gold when she pried open the wardrobe and found a row of gowns; when she ran a hand along them, making the skirts rustle, they coughed out a handful of moths, dust that caught in her cyclone and shone in swirls when it passed before the sunlit window, and the lingering scents of old perfume.

"Okay," she told the sprites. "Please tell Anne . . . tell her . . ."

What did she want to say to the first hedgewitch she'd ever met?

"First of all, it's not a ragtag coven," she blurted. "Thanks for the advice, but you don't need to tell me to mind my manners. I wasn't exactly planning to spit in the king's face. Why didn't the trap spell work? It did at first, but he just pushed right through. Did I mess it up . . . ? Shit, wait, let me start over—"

But the sprites had already gone, through the open window and away, taking the musty smell of old silk and perfume. Aziza winced. As far as introductions went, that had not been her best work.

The last wind sprite nudged at her hand, as if to remind her it was there. She hadn't forgotten.

"Please tell Dion: Too late. Anne already knows. I'm not sure if she knows about your . . . project . . . but you probably shouldn't contact me again." She hesitated, and then went on. "The spell bought us time. The cloak, too—it saved Leo's life. Thank you . . . for everything. I'm sorry if I got you into trouble."

It was almost a relief to have something she could apologize for. The sprite departed with its message. She left the window cracked and went back out into the hall to knock on the neighboring door.

"Leo?" she said.

He shouted for her to come in. She opened the door and found the two of them sitting on the bed, each dressed in borrowed garments like hers. Tristan was propped up against a mound of pillows, still looking a little sallow and pained, like someone on the mend from the flu. Leo sat next to him with his backpack open, checking what was left of their food stash. She clambered onto the bed with them. The pooka, which had been draped around her neck in the form of a garter snake, slithered down her arm and disappeared into the blankets.

"Are you all right?" she asked Tristan.

"Fine. Better now that I'm clean."

"Can I propose an addition to the Coven Blackthorn code of

conduct?" Leo said, raising a hand like they were in class. "From now on, only one of us gets to do something stupid and reckless per quest. I already filled our quota when I volunteered us for the Hunt. No more hellhound possessions or one-on-one fights with scary magical Huntsmen until the equinox at least."

"Then *my* addition to the Coven Blackthorn code of conduct is, no secrets allowed," Tristan said. "Maybe I'll agree to no more possessions if *you* tell us about the deal you made with the nymphs."

"Those are terrible rules," Aziza informed them. "Coven Blackthorn can't stop being reckless or secretive any more than a pooka could stop shapeshifting. Let's not ask ourselves to do the impossible."

Leo laughed. "Thanks for the pep talk. Really lifted the team spirit there."

"Forget the pep talk. We need a game plan. Someone tried to kill you."

"*And* Beor. I don't think it was personal," he said brightly, as if being collateral damage to someone else's assassination was somehow better than being *personally* murdered.

"If they wanted to kill Beor, they could've done that anytime," Tristan pointed out. He pushed himself upright, his damp hair falling into his gaunt face. "They didn't have to wait for the Hunt. Unless sabotaging the Hunt was the point."

Aziza thought it over. If both Huntsmen had died, then there would have been no one to bring the heart of the springtide lord to the Summer Court—the elixir required to wake the king. If that had happened, the king would have been trapped in his enchanted sleep, missing the solstice ceremony and leaving his people vulnerable to the jade rot. But she didn't know what that meant, really, or who stood to benefit from something like that.

"All we have to do is survive the next couple of nights, and then we can take Hazel and get out of here," Leo said. "And . . ."

He faltered.

"What?" she said.

"That maid—the human," he said. "Are there others like her? What's she doing here?"

She shrugged uncomfortably. "There are probably others, yeah. Human servants in fairy courts are nothing new. Some people get tricked into it. Some of them come willingly. Some of them are under enchantments and don't even know what's happening to them, though I don't think that's the case with Sophia. She seems . . . lucid."

"What if . . ." He stopped, looking away as if he couldn't meet their eyes. "What if my true love is one of them?"

She didn't look at Tristan. "What do you mean?"

"The curse said my true love would be taken from me," Leo said, an urgency beginning to creep into his voice. "The enchantress was part of the Summer Court. So maybe the curse somehow . . . lured my true love here, and they're . . . trapped."

"That's a leap," she told him evenly. "I really don't think you have to worry about that."

"Why not?" he asked, wide-eyed and hopeful, like he was desperate for a good reason to believe his true love wasn't some fairy's pet human right now. But she couldn't give him one, because the only good reason was sitting next to him with a pale, tight-lipped expression, looking up at the ceiling like he was trying to unhear this conversation.

"I just know," Aziza said. "I can't tell you how, but I know for a fact that your true love is not in the Summer Court."

"Aziza," Tristan said, quietly.

"I don't want him putting himself in danger over something that's not even—"

Leo frowned at them both, puzzled. "You know . . . for a fact? But how could you . . ."

"She didn't mean it like that," Tristan said.

"How else could she have meant it?" Leo said, his hand rising to his skull, brow furrowing with pain as what she assumed was a splitting migraine began. "If you know *for a fact* that my true love isn't here . . . then you must know where they are, and *who* they are. So either someone told you, or it's someone who's still . . ."

His face went blank, and he was silent for a long moment. Aziza closed her eyes briefly against a wave of guilt.

"I'm sorry," Aziza said. "I thought I was being vague enough."

She wasn't sure which one of them she was talking to.

Tristan shook his head. "It's all right. I just hate watching this."

"Sorry, what were we talking about?" Leo said, shaking his head as if snapping out of a trance. He pressed the heel of his hand to his forehead and winced. "Oh, right. Zee, why is it a leap?"

"Because," she said, and hesitated for too long. His face fell. She changed tactics. "Dion's hedgewitch friend got in touch with me. I'll ask her if it's possible. But if they *were* here, would you even recognize them?"

"I would," Leo answered, staunchly.

"How?"

"I think I'd just know. Like I'd—I'd feel it."

"You think that's how it works?" Tristan asked, like he was just curious. "True love, I mean. That it's this instant connection, and you . . . *just know*?"

"Maybe that's the key to beating the curse. It took my memories away so that I wouldn't know who my true love is. In knowing them . . . I overcome the curse. Right? It's like that. Like a test," Leo said. "I don't know, but I have to believe something."

The ensuing pause felt like it lasted forever.

"You're right," Tristan said, eventually. "We should try and look for them. And if we find them, or . . . someone who feels like . . . the right person, then we'll save them. Right, Aziza?"

She nodded stiffly.

"Thank you," Leo told them both, his voice full of gratitude. She couldn't stand it, so it was a relief when he changed the subject. "So, uh. Tell us about this other hedgewitch?"

"Anne Sterling. Dion mentioned her a few times. She told me a little bit about the Summer Court—apparently the witch community has a *diplomatic relationship* with the king and we're supposed to not ruin it."

She paraphrased Anne's message, most of it as unsurprising to them as it was to her—not to eat fairy food or drink lily wine, not to accept any gifts, not to play any games or make any bets, not to enter into any promises or trades, even ones that seemed innocuous. The basic rules of etiquette by which they needed to abide. She had just about finished telling them everything she could remember when someone banged on the door. It opened a crack, and a silvery eye peeked inside.

Leo sat up, brightening instantly. "Hazel!"

She threw it open and flew across the room, dragonfly wings fluttering blurry-quick and braid whipping behind her. She landed on the bed and crashed into Leo, knocking him on his side. The Gallowglass who'd escorted her shut the door quietly, leaving the four of them alone.

"You did it! You won! I knew you would!" she shouted, almost right in Leo's ear. He winced but didn't complain, only pushed himself upright, bringing Hazel with him. Her overexcited wings lifted her off the bed even as she clung to his shoulders, so that she stayed attached to him like a sparkly green balloon.

"What, were you worried?" he said, grinning.

"No! I told them all you'd win. I'm just glad you didn't embarrass me."

He rolled his eyes. "Are you okay? What did you do for the last three days?"

"Lots of walking, mainly," she said, finally sitting properly on the bed, though it required her to arrange a pool of satiny, rose-colored skirts around herself first. "And parties, and magic lessons."

It was a relief to see her looking not just unhurt, but well taken care of—dressed nicely, with her hair neatly combed and braided. And she'd been allowed to come and see them. Being the prince's cousin must have made up for her being an outsider.

"That sounds . . . fun. Right?" Leo said, trying to sound encouraging and probe for more information at the same time.

"They think it's so weird that I grew up in the human world. They sneak over the boundary sometimes, but they're like tourists. They only see bits and pieces of it, and they don't really get it." She leaned in, as if to let them in on a secret. "They tell stories about us, like how we have stories about them. Fairytales. About heroes from old legends. They thought humans like that didn't exist anymore—that they're all weak, and boring, and cowardly now. But you three proved them wrong. They think you're so . . . *interesting*."

Aziza and Leo traded grim looks.

You never wanted to be interesting to the Fair Folk. *Interesting* meant it was not a question of *if* there would be trouble.

It was a question of how much and what kind.

It was a question of *when*.

CHAPTER 21

TRISTAN

THE DAY PASSED in a blur. Sophia returned three times, usually with a couple of other servants in tow. First she brought them food that was safe for human consumption—bread, cheese, fruit.

"How do we know it's not fairy food?" Aziza asked flatly.

"They wouldn't do that to us—I mean, why would they?" Leo's smile was warm and friendly, taking the edge off Aziza's comment. He reached out to take the tray from the servant that had come to assist Sophia—a boy that Tristan judged to be a little younger than her, though he couldn't be sure. Something about the slightly too-large ears, rumpled clothes, and tousled hair gave him a youthful look that might have been deceptive. He smiled tentatively back at Leo.

"*Princess Narra* would never do that," Sophia corrected, bristling. "Are you accusing your generous host of trickery?"

"Princess Narra isn't the one who's here," Aziza said.

Before Sophia could respond, the other servant, Evan, stepped forward.

"Here," he said, taking a piece of bread off the plate and biting into it. Tristan and Aziza watched a great deal more carefully than Leo, but nothing happened—his eyes remained alert and unclouded, he didn't succumb to any hidden enchantments that would've compelled him to gorge himself on the food until he got sick, and he had no trouble chewing or swallowing, which confirmed it was real food, nothing raw or rotten or still alive and just illusioned to look edible. "See? It's fine. You're right to be cautious, but everything we bring you will be safe. Ask me to test it anytime, and I will."

"You don't have to do that, but thanks," Leo said. "There's plenty of food here—do you wanna sit down?"

"Oh, we already ate, but that's very kind of—"

"We have work to do," Sophia snapped.

She dipped into a shallow curtsy and turned to go. Evan gave them all a sheepish grin and a bow before he followed her.

The second time they returned, it was to put them in nicer outfits for the Midsummer Revels; the three of them had to dress the part if they were going to attend. Aziza said it would be rude to refuse the invitation, so they had to go along with it. It was a whirlwind lesson in fairy fashion trends: glossy feather coats; backless garments that tied at the neck and waist to leave room for two, four, six wings; corsets and waistcoats that cinched impossibly thin, as if to emphasize figures with funhouse mirror proportions; gold lacework and silk trimming, and beading made from natural materials like stone and crystal and glass. Aziza ended up in the simplest dress she could find, dark green linen with minimal embellishments, and Tristan in a slightly fancier version of the pants and tunic getup he'd found on his bed earlier. For Leo, Sophia insisted on a complicated outfit consisting of a stiff jacket, a vest with two rows of tiny topaz buttons, and at least half his weight in embroidery. And the silver cloak that had saved his life, the flask tied to his belt, and the sword in its sheath strapped across his back. To Tristan, Leo always looked perfect, even in baggy gym shorts and Target T-shirts, but now he looked like he'd walked straight out of a fairytale.

The last time Sophia returned, it was to lead them outside. There was no ballroom in the castle; the fairies celebrated midsummer under the stars. A trail through the birch wood led to a place where the trees grew so tall and so close together that they were like walls. It wasn't a forest anymore, but a network of cavernous halls, separated by curtains of jasmine and lavender, and open to the sky. Streams dashed off low ridges, forming small waterfalls that fed into pools where sprites splashed at the feet of passing revelers.

There, Sophia split them up. Leo was to follow the Gallowglass by a side route to the far end of the ballrooms, where Princess Narra was waiting. Aziza and Tristan were to go through the crowds. She would hear no argument, and with the spider-fang knight waiting impatiently and Anne's warnings still fresh in their minds, there was nothing to be done.

If anything happened, Tristan would know; he had the hounds creeping through the tops of the trees, shifting in and out of the shadows to watch them from above. But as Leo disappeared into a side passage in the woods, escorted by a small contingent of Gallowglass, and Sophia led him and Aziza through the crowd, he hesitated. He tugged on the bond to Aziza, and she followed his cue, slowing down to put distance between them and Sophia.

"I'm going to go look around," he said under his breath. "Cover for me?"

They needed to find out who had tried to kill Leo yesterday, what they stood to gain from it, and whether they intended to try again. They needed to know if they'd *really* be allowed to walk away with Hazel when all of this was over, or if the Folk had something else in store for them. The answer to those questions wasn't here.

He slipped away, going back the way they'd come. When he used to have to make that terrible journey into the hag's territory, foxes would flee at the sound of his footsteps. Squirrels would race to their dens, and the birds would leap out of their nests. In almost two years he had not once been able to pass a dog on the street without it barking violently at him, or else freezing in such terror he'd seen confused owners have to pick them up off the ground to get them to move. Animals could smell the dark magic on him. The hag, then the hounds. The Fair Folk could sense it, too, though they didn't scare so easily. But there was always a beat of hesitation—a double take, a flinch, a leaning away. It didn't last long, but that moment of wariness allowed him to slip away from the strange boys with mountain laurel woven through their hair before they could extend their hands toward him, the opal-eyed girls before they could demand his name with their musical voices. He stayed clear of the Gallowglass—he saw one whose armor wrapped around her torso in plates like bark, and another whose gauntlets had spines that protruded past the knuckles, like stingers. The servants, too, he avoided, in case they were like Sophia, fanatically loyal to their fairy masters. Nearby, Evan was setting food and drink on a table alongside another servant, this one a woman in her twenties, with wavy brown hair, a small mole under the corner of her eye, and a thin, tired mouth.

And Leo thought his true love was one of these poor lost souls being kept by the fairies. Leo wanted to save them. Leo thought he'd look into someone's eyes and just *know*.

Tristan didn't even know if he was right or not. Maybe that really *was* how Leo had fallen in love with him the first time. Maybe it had been a flash of intuition, a *knowing*, instant and effortless. Tristan himself had always wondered what he'd done to win Leo's affection, and maybe the answer really was that he'd done nothing. That neither of them had. That it had been fate.

And Tristan was no longer the person he'd been back then, so maybe that meant he wasn't Leo's true love anymore, either. How would he know? Maybe Leo would be happier with someone less damaged. Someone who hadn't done the things Tristan had done. Maybe he'd fall in love at first sight with someone here in Elphame, rescue them from the Fair Folk, and live happily ever after.

Tristan felt sick with jealousy. It was acid, dissolving him from the inside out. He was being beyond irrational. Jealous of someone who wasn't even *real*. And at the same time half hoping, miserably, that Leo really *did* have a different true love now and he would find that person here, because Leo deserved better than him. Always had.

He went over to the table where Evan had been; the crystal bottles had caught his eye. They contained the amethyst-colored liquid he'd seen swishing around in the glasses of passing fairies. Before he had a chance to think it through, he was swiping one of the bottles and heading back up the path to the castle, which was enhanced with so much illusion magic the hounds didn't like to stare at it for too long—it was too bright and hurt their eyes. Inside, he still felt like a hound himself—something animal and restless curled around a rigid, cold determination—as if the time he'd spent as one at the mountain lake had changed him indelibly.

Once he was back on the trail to the castle, and had checked that no one was around to see, he summoned the scarred hound. They shadow-traveled; it dropped him off in an unfamiliar wing of the castle, one where the woven walls were made up of gently curved stems of ash and the air was filled with their mild, medicinal aroma. The corridor contained only one door.

He knocked.

A gruff voice from within answered, "What is it now?"

The sound of it made him shiver. The taste of blood filled his mouth. Swallowing down the nausea, he opened the door and paused there at the threshold. Without the armor and the antler helmet, the figure lying in the bed was almost unrecognizable. But his eyes gave him away—that fiery red-gold stare. It was Beor, the former Huntsman.

Despite the sputtering candle on the bedside table and the moonlight streaming in through the window, darkness gathered around Beor where he leaned up against the headboard. His eyes were the brightest point in the room, so bright that when Tristan blinked, they left searing afterimages on the inside of his eyelids. Beor's hair was straggly and dull, and unlike the other fairies, his age showed in the lines around his mouth and the scars slashed over his face and shoulders—some long and straight, as though made by a blade, and others in the shape of fang and claw marks, much like the ones Tristan had under his shirt. He grimaced at the sight of Tristan, revealing stained, crooked teeth. But he made no move to sit up or call his hounds. This emboldened Tristan enough to step inside and shut the door.

"As if I haven't suffered enough humiliation," Beor said in a voice that, despite his weakened state, had all the coarseness and bristle of a boar's hide. "Now the summoner brat invites himself into my private quarters to demand an audience. If not for the princess, I would pay you back tenfold for your temerity before, and your insolence now."

Quickly, Tristan held up the bottle as though it were a shield.

"I brought a gift," he said.

After a terribly long pause, during which Tristan did not even dare breathe, Beor snorted. "What is this, a bargain? Learning from the Folk, are you?"

"Not a bargain. A *gift*," Tristan said again. He forced himself to approach with the bottle outstretched. Beor eyed it, glared up at him, and then snatched it from his hand.

"Making a gift of what's rightfully mine," he grumbled, uncorking it and taking a long swig. "Any other year, I'd have been down there myself, celebrating my victory."

"If someone else hadn't interfered in the Hunt," Tristan agreed, evenly. "That . . . assassin."

"Precisely." He drank again, deeply. "I thought that was your doing at first, but I should have known better. The way you flailed about with your magic. You could never have devised a plan that would actually best me."

"I didn't *flail*," Tristan said, stung. He'd worked hard to get the hounds under his control. Taking them over the way he had—that had been a kind of breakthrough for him. He'd put all of himself into that fight. It had been painful, but—and he hadn't fully realized it until this moment—he was sort of proud of it, too. "I almost beat you."

"You performed a possession on your own blækhounds," Beor snapped. "Have you any idea the danger you put yourself in?"

"I don't see how it could be any worse than the danger *you* put me in."

The more Beor drank, the louder he got. He jabbed the bottle in Tristan's general direction as he ranted. "When you have power over the boundary between life and death, you can't unravel yourself. You must remain grounded, and keep a tight hold on your humanity. Summoners who are careless with their magic go mad, soon enough, or worse."

Tristan wanted to argue—to say that Beor was just angry that Tristan had almost gotten the better of him. But . . . in the aftermath of that fight, when Tristan had spent the night drifting in and out of consciousness . . . he had dreamed. He'd been outside his body, watching himself sleep as Aziza and Leo found shelter and checked on him through the night. He'd heard some of what they'd said to him and to each other. He'd watched the pooka nestle in the crook of his arm, but hadn't felt the warmth of its coat.

He'd *thought* those had been dreams, anyway, mixed with the half-remembered impressions he absorbed during his bouts of wakefulness.

But maybe he hadn't dreamed at all. Maybe he really had come untethered from his body.

"If I hadn't done it, you would've taken the hounds from me," Tristan said. "I didn't have another option."

"The hounds have no loyalty to you," Beor said, scornfully. "That's why I was able to take them from you so easily."

"They can be loyal?"

"Of course."

His mind worked to assimilate this new piece of information into his limited bank of hound-related knowledge. Leo had used that word too, *loyalty*, and Tristan had dismissed it out of hand. Why was it so hard for him to believe it? Wasn't there at least one hound that had shown some sort of . . . attachment to him? Even if he wasn't ready to call it loyalty, it was undeniably different from the behavior he'd learned to expect from the hounds.

"But I thought," he said, "that the hounds only cared about power, and whoever had the most of it."

"Who on earth told you that?" Beor snapped.

Who indeed? Tristan opened his mouth. Shut it again. "Someone . . . I shouldn't have listened to."

He was more stunned by this than he had any right to be. It should have come as no surprise that his fundamental knowledge about the hounds was wrong. He'd learned it from the hag. Of *course* what he'd thought was normal actually . . . wasn't.

Beor's lip curled. "You haven't even named them."

"I should name them?"

"*Some* of them, at least," Beor said heatedly.

"So then," Tristan said, feeling deflated, "I'm nothing but a glorified dog trainer. It sounds like the only thing I can safely do is order the hounds around."

"Is that what you think I am?"

"No! I just meant—"

Beor made a noise in his throat that sounded like a growl. He threw the covers off and swung his legs over the side of the bed.

Tristan wheeled backward, certain that Beor had taken his comment as an insult and was dragging himself out of his sickbed to wring Tristan's neck. But, to his shock, Beor laughed—a sea god's laugh, resonant as the pulse of deep ocean currents.

"I'll tell you what I am, boy. I am death itself. For what is death but a tireless hunter?"

That's what I want, Tristan thought.

He wanted to be able to speak about his abilities with that sense of ownership he heard in Beor's voice. He wanted to think of his . . . his *craft* not just as something he had, something he was borrowing from a better necromancer, but something that he *was*. Like how Aziza didn't just perform witchcraft; she *was* a witch. He wanted to be something, too. Even death itself.

Beor groaned as he got to his feet. One hand rested on the edge of the bedside table; the other held on to the bottle, and he swayed on his feet as he lifted it to his lips again, draining the last of it. "Come with me."

"Come . . . where?" Tristan said.

"You'll see."

He limped past Tristan. Wordlessly, Tristan called back the scarred hound, which crawled out from under the bed like a ghoul, claws clicking, its large black eyes shining wetly in the lamplight. At his nod, it sidled up to Beor.

Beor laid a hand on its flank to steady himself as he walked out the door, and Tristan followed.

CHAPTER 22

LEO

THE SPIDER-FANG WARRIOR was saying, "Speak to Princess Narra with utmost respect, and only when spoken to first. Bow when you see her. Do not leave until dismissed. Follow her instructions to the letter . . ."

As he droned on, Leo's mind wandered. He stole glances at the other Gallowglass, trying to see their faces under the helmets, and up at the sky, wondering if Elphame had different constellations or if those were another thing they shared with the human world. In the narrow passage, the sounds from the ballroom were muffled as if by enchantment, and the birches grew dense and close.

Before it could occur to Leo that maybe it would be a good idea to pay attention to what the spider-fang warrior had to say, in case he slipped something important in between all the condescension, the trail blew wide and light poured in, briefly blinding him. When his eyes adjusted, he was at the end of the ballroom, standing before a crowd. The dress code was a cross between the Met Gala and a royal wedding; in their gowns and suits and adornments, the Folk were dazzling, and Leo felt impossibly plain before them. Nearest to him was Princess Narra, who stood beside a casket. She turned as Leo emerged from the passage.

The spider-fang warrior bowed, and when Leo failed to follow suit quickly enough, he grabbed Leo by the back of his neck and forced him down. His grip was harsh, but Leo didn't resist. He only straightened when Narra said, "Hello, Huntsman. Come forward, please," and the Gallowglass released him.

Leo approached. The casket was sculpted out of tangled roots, stringy and dirt-clumped at the base, rising into intricate webs of mossy, leaf-speckled branches that framed panes of translucent resin. The shape inside the casket was a dark blur.

"Aren't you a delightful surprise?" Narra said. Her dress was a warm, shifting gold that reminded him of all the sweet things in nature, honey and cinnamon and syrup, a color he could almost taste. She wore a diadem with a topaz set into the front. Her hair was pinned up and collar cut low, leaving the scar on her neck exposed. "The last time anyone but Beor stood where you stand now, the elders were still calling me 'sproutling' and my brother didn't even have his antlers yet."

He focused on her so that he wouldn't have to pay attention to the crowd, though it was impossible to drown out their voices. He'd never thought of himself as the type to get stage fright, but those were a *lot* of eyes on him.

"Thanks for . . . all of this. The clothes, and the rooms," he said awkwardly, in an undertone that matched hers. He hesitated—this probably wasn't the best time to ask, but if he didn't do it now, he didn't know if or when he'd get a chance. "Look, did your brother tell you what happened to Beor? Someone tried to—"

"It's under control," she told him softly. Then, with a touch on his shoulder, she said, "Wait here," and moved around the casket to address the crowd. She had a whole speech. She told them he had earned the right to be called Huntsman, and something about her father's dedication to the Summer Court, and other things that were lost on him. The light came mostly from lesser fairies, so it was constantly moving, the way the firelight at St. Sithney's campgrounds had been, and it left him disoriented. He looked for Aziza, Tristan, and Hazel in the crowd, but couldn't find them.

"Our Huntsman," Narra was saying, "has brought us the heart of the springtide lord. It is the purest substance in Elphame, an elixir of new beginnings, a draught of renewal, and a magic so potent it can forge an unbreakable connection between a worthy monarch and the land over which they rule. With it, we begin the summer rites."

She beckoned him nearer. Obediently, he went up to the casket, and now he could clearly see the person asleep inside. It was hard to look at the Summer King directly. His face was like one of those optical illusions: a vase that was also a person's profile, a duck that was also a rabbit. He had strong, classically handsome features and smooth golden skin—but when the light caught him at a particular angle, Leo glimpsed deep lines and wrinkles, gone again the next moment. The tips of his pointed ears disappeared into hair that was curly and golden as a young man's but also, at once, utterly white with age. A set of antlers rose from his brow, wide and curving, bleached pale from years of sunlight. They were dotted with shining crystal bands, pale green and pink and blue. The intricate gold beading on his tunic and heavy, wintry mantle of pure white fur outshone even Narra's honey-gold gown.

Narra instructed him to pour a few drops over the casket, so he did, quickly capping it again before he could spill the whole thing. As Narra finished her speech—explaining that the sleeping enchantment would be washed away, and the king would wake tomorrow night and drink what was left of the elixir to complete the summer rites—he watched the water dissolve into the resin.

Inside, the king's eyes fluttered, and Leo jerked back. But he didn't wake. Not yet.

HE DIDN'T HAVE a chance to look for Aziza and Tristan. When the music started, a fairy girl caught his hand and pulled him into a dance. And then a boy with wine-colored skin and locust wings, who asked him if it was true he'd bested Beor in hand-to-hand combat. A pink-haired girl with vines tattooed up her arms and neck—sprouting tiny leaves in vibrant green ink even as he watched—wanted to know if he planned to stay very long with the Summer Court. When he admitted, apologetically, that he didn't, she smiled with pointed teeth and told him she was sure she could convince him to extend his visit.

The fairies didn't seem to mind how stiffly he moved, and they weren't intimidated by the cloak, though they were careful not to touch it. They asked him to bargain with them for tiny trinkets and favors and laughed delightedly at his polite refusals, as if he'd seen through a prank. They tried to impress him with minor, harmless illusions—ones that turned their faces into ghoulish masks or made the stars drop out of the sky to skitter up his arms like mosquitoes—and he forced a smile and made a show of being amazed. They offered him lily wine, and he refused, and kept refusing.

He had questions for them, too. *How do you break a curse? If a curse has a loophole, how do you find it? If the fairy who cast the curse is gone, how do you get around that?*

And they replied, coyly, *You don't. You don't. You don't.*

None of the Folk were interested in teaching him how to disman-
tle their own magic.

Every now and then, movement in the corner of his eye would
distract him—it was something with a different cadence from the
rest of the revel. Not the graceful dancing of the Fair Folk, but a
wind-struck swaying, like a tree branch.

But it was always gone by the time he turned around.

It's not them, he told himself. The nymphs would come for him
soon enough, but it wasn't time yet.

In Elphame, everything was magical, even the air. Warmth crept
through him as if summer were unfolding in the valley of his rib
cage, a slow crawl to the solstice tomorrow, and had he refused the
last time someone had held a glass of lily wine to his lips or had he
slipped up? Suddenly, he wasn't sure.

When the music changed, it was so subtle he almost missed it;
most of the time, his partner realized before he did, and handed
him off to another before the thought of excusing himself could
even cross his mind. The next girl, in a gray dress that felt so fine
and soft under his hands it might have been made of actual smoke,
leaned in conspiratorially and said, "Do you like being human? Be
honest."

He started to say, *Yeah, sure I do,* but then it struck him that the
words *be honest* might not be a throwaway remark but a command,
or a warning, even. Aziza had said fairies hated lies. They couldn't
lie, so it made them jealous when someone else did it.

"I don't really know," he said finally, the most truthful thing he
could think of. "I've never been anything else."

She smiled with small, sharp teeth, foxlike, but they didn't frighten him. He felt somehow certain she wasn't going to hurt him, and she was so pretty. He let her tug him closer.

"Just for tonight," she said, "I think you should be one of us."

Her cool fingers brushed his cheek, his brow, his lips. He flinched back then, thinking suddenly and with a rush of clarity of the last person who'd touched him like that—Tristan.

"Um," he said, eloquently. Aziza had told him about fairy charm, he remembered now—the quality of preternatural beauty and allure that clouded human minds and made them more susceptible to trickery. He hadn't had any wine. He was just in way over his head. His skin tingled everywhere the girl had touched him, not in a pleasant way, but like the sensation of pins and needles, or a healing wound.

"There," she said. She had golden eyes with no pupils, and he started to feel the warm summer clouds taking him over when he looked at them too long. "What do you think?"

"Of what?" he said blankly.

Another fairy looked over with brows raised over his catlike eyes, his smile wide and predatory. Leo was passed over to him seamlessly, still spinning in the same dance. The boy said, "She did a good job. No one would recognize you if you didn't want them to. You could disappear here. So many of your kind do."

And finally, finally, after he'd lost count of how many people he'd danced with, he managed to slip away, extracting himself from the crowd before another pair of hands could take his. He retreated to the shadows under the birch trees and paused there to breathe, resting a hand on one of their smooth trunks.

That was when he realized something was wrong. The hand didn't look like his, even though it was attached to his body. It was longer, narrower, and completely unmarked, not by freckles or the tiny scar he'd gotten from falling off his bike as a kid. He flexed it experimentally and with a sinking feeling—nope, that was definitely his hand—and then touched his face carefully, following the path the fairy girl had taken earlier, over his cheekbones, his brow. His face had new angles and planes, heavily pronounced, and ears that were as pointy as Hazel's. Higher, his fingers made contact with something hard and ridged. Something bony. *Horns.* Ram's horns, he thought, half-hysterical. They curved back into a dramatic loop and tapered to sharp points. Couldn't be real—they were weightless—but they felt solid to the touch. His fingers brushed over the place where they met his scalp, his curls parting around them.

He was starting to feel like he was dreaming. Nothing made sense. His mind was clear enough still to think, *I'm fucked, aren't I?*

Everything they'd set out to do tonight—stick together, get information if they could, stay out of trouble—was pretty much out the window.

There was one good thing about being illusioned to resemble the Fair Folk, and it was that no one was looking at him anymore. No one knew who he was. He took the silver cloak off hurriedly, folded it up, and shoved it into the back of his clothes, tucking it under his jacket and the waistband of his pants. It was fine enough that it probably wouldn't show through the stiff material of his jacket. It would be a lot easier to make his way through the crowd this time, with less attention on him. He could probably avoid getting dragged into the dancing again. He could find the others. He could . . .

Again: a stirring in his peripheral vision. This time he was sure something reached for him through a gap in the throng, something with a scratching splinter grip that made him recoil, already imagining he could feel it scraping his skin—he flinched away from—

Nothing. There was nothing.

He put a hand on the warm hilt of the sword. The polished wood under his fingers was oddly comforting.

Nearby, two servants were refilling wineglasses on a table; one of them was Evan. Leo almost went up to talk to them, only then he remembered he was supposed to be undercover right now. Still, when they left the table, carrying their empty trays at their sides, Leo followed. If there was a chance his true love was among the servants at the castle, then Leo had to talk to them. He had to know more about them, what their lives were like and what was keeping them here. He had to see if anyone among them was . . . familiar.

They left the ballroom and went up the path to the house, Leo slipping into the trees when he could and speeding up so that he could get close enough to hear what they were saying without being seen. At a fork in the trail, they stopped. One way led up to the castle, but the other path branched off in the direction of the encampment. The woman that Evan was with started to go that way, but he caught her arm, stopping her.

"What are you doing?" he said.

"It's Viren," she mumbled, looking at the ground. "He asked for me."

"*Again?*" Evan sounded outraged. She nodded wordlessly, trying to pull away, but he held on. "I'll go."

This made her head snap up, her eyes wide with disbelief.

"You can't," she said, voice wobbling a little. "Anyway, you're not the one he asked for."

"He doesn't really care which of us goes, we're all the same to him. Anyway, I haven't in a while, so—"

She laughed, a choked, painful sound. "We're not taking turns—"

"I'll go, May." He passed her his tray and gave her a gentle nudge in the direction of the castle. "Go back now. I'll see you later."

Head down, shamefaced, she did. Leo hesitated for a split second before he decided to keep following Evan. Maybe he could pull him aside and talk to him alone, without Sophia interrupting; anyway, he wanted to know what the two of them had been talking about just now. The woods weren't dense enough here to hide in, so he came out onto the trail, hanging back as far as he could without losing Evan. It was quiet down in the encampment, since most of the Folk were off at the revel or staying in the castle, but a few lounged here and there, in pairs or small groups, talking quietly over drinks. They paid Evan no mind, but some of them glanced at Leo. Either his costume wasn't as foolproof as he'd hoped, or he was just naturally conspicuous. He wished he'd thought to bring a glass of wine, just to hold; maybe then he'd look more like he was taking a casual stroll and less like he was lost.

Evan disappeared into one of the tents. That was what Leo was calling it in his head, anyway, a tent—but it was actually a large, drapey construction of pale blue silk with an opening flap like a curtain, tall enough for Evan to enter without having to bend over. Leo walked past it slowly, listening for voices, but he didn't catch anything.

A short way past it, he turned off into the woods and found a small creek. From there, he was mostly out of sight from anyone who might wander past, but near enough to the path that he'd see Evan once he emerged from the blue tent.

He knelt by the creek. Its banks were low and ferny, the water black as mud, but it felt cool and clean when he dipped his abnormally long fingers into it. They looked like they'd been pulled out of shape like sticks of taffy. He grimaced. It was too dark to see his reflection in the water, even when a trio of lesser fairies came over to investigate, flitting between him and the creek as if wondering what was so interesting about it.

"Can you tell I'm a fraud?" he asked them lightly.

They said something to him in the squeaky, incomprehensible language of lesser fairies. If Aziza were here, she'd know what they were saying—not because she understood their words, but because she could feel their intentions with her magic. Leo, though, must have seemed to them like a clueless, lumbering giant. They wandered away again, twirling around each other and diving into playful loops.

If the nymphs wanted to come for him, now would be the perfect time. But they hadn't. And if they weren't going to do it now, then it wasn't happening tonight.

He sat back on his heels, one hand rising to the horns again. God, that was weird.

What would you say if you knew what I was doing right now? he thought, and he closed his eyes and held the scraps of his mostly forgotten dreams in his mind like a candle flame he had to shield from the winds of the curse. He had tried to sound confident when he'd told his friends that he'd recognize his true love, but he wasn't even sure if his true love would recognize *him* in the state he was in right now. Or after the nymphs were done with him.

Footsteps made him look up. He didn't know how long it had been—twenty, thirty minutes, maybe? But Evan had emerged from the tent and was heading back. Leo followed, returning to the path and quietly closing the distance between them. Once Evan had reached the junction in the trail where he could've turned back either to the revel or the castle, Leo made his move, darting forward to catch him by the wrist and pull him into the woods.

Evan twisted to get away, but Leo said, "Shh, wait, it's me! Uh,

Leo. The . . . Huntsman. The fairies put this . . ." He released Evan's hand and made a vague gesture at his own face. "They put an illusion on me. Or something. Sorry I scared you."

Evan's hand rose to cover a shy smile. He had disarming green eyes that were a little too close together and a gap between his front teeth, and it was such a relief to see another human with comforting human flaws.

"Wow. That's pretty convincing," Evan said, looking him up and down. "I think they meant it as a compliment. Ah . . . did you need something, sir?"

"You don't have to call me *sir*," Leo said, embarrassed. *Sir*. Hazel would've laughed herself into tears if she'd heard that. "But yeah, I . . . have questions. Like, so many questions. I don't know who else to ask."

Evan shifted uncomfortably, breaking eye contact. "I can't be long. If I'm late getting back, Sophia will notice."

"I'll walk with you."

Reluctantly, Evan nodded, and they headed uphill, all the while staying off the path. People passed them by, coming to or from the ballroom, too loud and drunk to notice them in the dark, but the two of them kept their voices hushed out of an abundance of caution. Leo just didn't want to be interrupted. As for Evan, Leo didn't know if he'd get in trouble for talking to Leo one-on-one like this, but he seemed content to steer clear of the Folk, too.

"During the Hunt," Leo said in an undertone, "someone tried to kill me and Beor. Narra says it's under control, but I don't know what that means."

"She probably thinks one of the minor courts is responsible," Evan said. At Leo's blank look, he went on. "We're one half of the Court of the Seasons. The Summer and Winter Courts rule over Elphame.

But there are smaller courts that stand to gain a lot from potentially destabilizing us."

"Gain what?" Leo asked. Aziza had explained some of this already, but in the confusion of the Hunt, he'd forgotten all about it.

Evan shrugged. "Territory and power. Most of the land belongs to King Ilanthus and the Winter Queen, Ceresia. The other courts live at their mercy. But if any of them grew powerful enough, they could overthrow the current Summer Court and take its place."

This was just great. Fairyland politics. As if learning how the electoral college worked hadn't been bad enough.

"Does that seem, uh . . . likely?" Leo asked.

"King Ilanthus wouldn't let that happen. And we'd know—the servants, I mean. We'd know if the Folk were expecting trouble," Evan said. "Some of them confide in us, and we all talk to each other. But the Summer Court has had a long, stable reign, from what I've heard. Especially since Prince Talarix took over command of the Gallowglass. He's almost as ruthless as Queen Ceresia."

"So you're saying it has nothing to do with me, and as long as I keep my head down and get through tomorrow, I can leave and forget all about this."

Evan hesitated. "I'm just guessing here. You should probably be careful either way."

"Planning on it," Leo said. "Say something *does* happen to the Summer Court. Will you be okay? And the other servants. Is there anything I can do to help you get out of here?"

"I'm not a prisoner. I could walk away if I wanted," Evan said, and laughed at Leo's skeptical look. "I only have to finish out the year. Then I've got a choice. I go back to the human world, or I stay another four seasons. And it's not a bad gig. Most of the time, they're traveling. When they're here, I do some chores and serve some drinks and entertain them, and they pay me in magical gifts. When they're not, the servants rest in an enchanted sleep. Well, it's more like being in stasis. We don't age, and we don't need to eat or anything. I've been here four years, but I've aged less than one, because the Folk are only here a few weeks every year."

"Then when you leave . . ."

"It'll feel like I time-traveled."

They were coming up on the castle, and had to pause as another pair of servants passed. When they'd gone, Evan led him around, bypassing the path to the front door and going for a side entrance.

"And you're okay with that?" Leo said. "Your family, your friends . . ."

Evan was about a half step ahead of him, so Leo couldn't see much of his expression, but there was a defensive tightness to his shoulders now. "This year, I'll earn enough gold to buy the apartment my family's been renting and an enchantment that'll give me perfect skin for life. Next year, if I stay on, they said they'll fix my teeth and make me better at games of chance. Beats dental work, doesn't it? When I finally go back to the human world, I'll be rich, naturally lucky, and good-looking. Seems like a better way to give myself a leg up than getting a shitty job in retail and going to college."

Leo swallowed. "And is that . . . all of you? You're all here willingly?"

"No. Some of us got tricked into it, and they've got longer terms, like . . . May agreed to seven years. She's got three left. And I can't leave without her, so . . ."

"She's a friend of yours?"

"I think so."

"What do you mean you think?"

Evan stopped at the edge of the clearing. Up the slope, servants entered and exited from a side door in the castle, partly hidden by a curtain of ivy so that Leo wouldn't have noticed it if he hadn't been watching.

"They dull our memories so we don't get homesick," Evan said, distractedly. "In a way, it's a blessing, because it makes it easier to serve. Less painful to be away from your old life. But it also makes you not want to leave. The Summer Court begins to feel like home, and everything before it feels like a dream."

And now Leo had something else to be afraid of: that he had been forgotten, too. He stared at Evan, his throat too tight to speak. But Evan had been here four years, he'd said. The timing was all wrong; he couldn't be Leo's true love. That didn't rule out the others, though.

"So how do you know you're choosing to stay because you want to, and not because they're making you want it?" he asked roughly.

"If it feels the same either way, then does it matter?" Evan glanced around. No one was in sight; if he wanted to slip back into the castle unnoticed, now was the time.

"Wait. About two years ago, I—lost someone," Leo said hurriedly. "I think they might be here. Did anyone new show up a couple years back? Do you remember?"

"We get new people every year," Evan said. "It's possible. But even if you find them, they'll be stuck. The Folk would notice if you tried to break someone's contract. And when they're gone on their caravan route, we'll be asleep."

"In the castle?" Leo said.

"Well, yeah."

"So do they put you in—in glass coffins, like the king?"

Evan laughed. "No, of course not. We just go to sleep in the servants' quarters like always, and they wake us up a few months later."

Right now, Leo had to focus on getting Hazel out of here. But, later—once the Summer Court moved on and left the castle mostly empty—he could come back. The idea settled heavily inside him, hopeful and terrible in equal measures. That he could be *so close* and have to walk away. Because he *knew* that his true love was here. Same way he knew that his dreams carried pieces of reality in disguise. Instinct. His heart telling him what his mind couldn't.

The familiar old pain sharpened inside him like a needle, whetting itself against bone. It never really went away, he just got better at functioning around it. But his grief was in proportion to his love, and he wouldn't trade that love for anything.

He had always thought that true love must be a kind of destiny; it was a fate that bound him to someone else, a connection the enchantress had tried to sever. He had to trust the same force that connected them would also help them find each other again. Curse or no curse.

I'm sorry, he thought. *I just need you to wait a little longer.*

"I have to get back to work," Evan said. "Think you can find your way back all right?"

"Just one more thing," Leo said. "Earlier, I saw you when . . . you told May you'd go instead of her. What . . ."

He stopped because of the stricken look on Evan's face.

"It's just Viren. He's one of the Gallowglass, Prince Tal's second-in-command. He . . ."

Only then did Leo notice how red and swollen his mouth looked, the bruises on his neck, the fact that some of the obsidian buttons in his shirt were undone when they hadn't been before, one of them missing altogether, leaving loose threads.

"Don't," Evan snapped, his kind green eyes going hard and furious. "Don't judge me. You have no idea—"

"I'm not!" Leo said. He felt sick. "How can you stay?"

"That sounds pretty judgey to me."

"Sorry. You're right."

"They're not all—" Evan did up his buttons, as if he'd just realized they were open. "Most of them are fine. The Folk, I mean. There are good ones and bad ones, and some that are both. Just like humans. Their agreements aren't always fair, but they honor them to the letter. I don't have any regrets."

The silence was thick. Evan was going to leave any second now, and Leo couldn't let him go without trying to smooth things over first. "You really helped me out here, so if you need anything . . . if I can pay you back somehow, just tell me. Okay?"

Evan nodded, softening just a little, and left. Leo might've stayed there for the rest of the night, only it hit him that he'd left Aziza and Tristan back at the revel. Though he knew both of them could take care of themselves, all he could think about was Evan's defiant insistence he was fine and May's beaten-down exhaustion, and he needed to find his friends, right now. But the ballroom was vast, and when he looked at the dancing for too long or paid too much attention to the music, his senses got fuzzy again.

Someone caught his wrist, and he figured he was about to be pulled back into the dancing himself. But when he swung around, he came face-to-face with the Gallowglass in the spider-fang helmet.

"And who might you be?" the Gallowglass said. Up close, through the opening in the front of the helmet, Leo could see that the Gallowglass had purplish skin, a frostbitten color, and a double set of black eyes, two on each side.

Leo tried to tug his wrist free, but the Gallowglass held on.

"I'm no one," Leo said automatically, trying to shut down the conversation. His grip on Leo was iron, but his posture was languid; anyone watching might have mistaken it for a casual, even flirtatious hold. His other hand fidgeted with something between his long fingers, which he glanced at now, as if mulling over what Leo had said.

"You can't be one of us," the Gallowglass said. "Are you?"

"What makes you say that?" Leo said.

"I've been following you for a time, and you've talked to no one, only wandered around searching for something. You came from the direction of the castle; if you're a visitor, you have no reason to be there alone. If you're a spy," and here the Gallowglass leaned in close, until Leo could smell the wine on his breath, "and if our enemies think that now, while our king rests, is the time for devious tricks, I shall make you regret every decision you ever made that brought you here."

"I'm not a spy," Leo said. The Gallowglass was tossing the object in his other hand up and down. It was in his peripheral vision, maddening, the visual equivalent of an incessant tapping.

"Then to which court do you pledge your loyalty?"

"None," Leo said, pulling again. And then his eyes slid to the thing that the Gallowglass was toying with, tossing and catching: a tiny obsidian button. Before he could think twice, he was blurting out, "It's you. You're Viren."

"Oh? Was it me you were looking for?"

Leo's free hand whipped out and caught the button on the next toss. His thoughts had gone blank with rage, and it must have shown on his face; Viren's grip on Leo's wrist constricted until Leo could practically feel his bones grinding. He held the button so tightly he wouldn't have been surprised if it left a permanent imprint in his palm. Viren was a trained fighter, and stronger and faster than any human, and could kick Leo's ass without breaking a sweat, and Leo didn't even care. He wanted to pull the silver cloak out and smother him with it. Wanted to yank the sword out of its sheath and cut him in half.

But before either of them could do or say anything else, a new voice cut in.

"Viren, I see you've found my guest."

"*Your* guest?" Viren said, in disbelief.

"That's right."

It was Narra. Viren released him, and Leo turned, rubbing at his wrist.

"Mind your pets, Princess," Viren said, with a short bow. "No telling what might happen to them if they wander where they shouldn't."

"You're always looking out for me," she said dryly.

She held out a hand to Leo, and he took it automatically. Then he was right back where he'd started, being led through a dance and hardly knowing what had hit him. The rage from earlier subsided, and now he just felt wrung out.

"This is quite good," she said, releasing his hand briefly to gesture at his face, the horns and everything. "Who put the enchantment on you? I admire the handiwork."

"How'd you know it was me?"

Narra guided him through the dance while he focused on trying not to step on her skirt. She was so light he felt like she could float away any second, wingless though she was.

"I am the Summer Court's princess. I know what my people's magic looks like."

"Thanks for the save," he said, sheepishly. "I guess I could've just told him who I was. But . . ."

She took the hand that Leo had on her waist. It had been resting there loosely, closed, knuckles against her hip. She opened it—he didn't resist—to reveal the tiny black button, and brushed her fingers over it.

"I see," Narra said. She must have recognized it. "Yes, Viren is cruel. Loyal, but cruel. I can't blame you for wishing not to speak with him."

"Couldn't you—" he began, and stopped.

She laughed, not unkindly. "What, let them go, when most of them don't want to? Forbid my people from doing what they wish with them? I am the heir, but I am not yet queen."

"And if you were?"

She shrugged. "And then, I suppose, many things would be possible."

"Are you really going to let me and Hazel go tomorrow?"

"Was that not our agreement? Fairies can't lie, you know."

"But . . . Hazel can lie."

It had just occurred to him. Hazel lied all the time, just innocent little-kid lies. Like the time she dropped Dad's laptop and blamed Spot. Or when she told Leah she was too sick to go to her birthday party, but really she was just having a fight with Jacqueline and she didn't want to see her.

"Changelings can lie," Narra said. "When a fairy child is placed in the human world for long enough, their connection to the Court of their birth is severed. Their very nature changes. After the solstice, as long as she's here among her people, the Summer Court's magic will recognize her and take her back. But she'll always be able to lie. I imagine that was why Lady Thula did it, though she probably never intended for anyone else to know."

"You think she wanted Hazel to be able to lie? And she wanted it so badly she was willing to leave her in the human realm?" Leo said. He was distantly curious about her—Hazel's mother and the person responsible for his curse. "Why?"

"I can only speculate," she murmured. "I told you she had enemies."

"Because people thought she was in league with her sister." The sister who had killed Narra's mother and tried to secure the crown for herself, only to be caught and executed. "I gotta say, I don't think an innocent person would've cared so much about making sure her daughter could lie."

"Perhaps," Narra said. "Or perhaps Lady Thula knew that the truth isn't always enough to change a mind that's already made up."

"How can you . . ." Too late, he stopped himself. But Narra smiled knowingly.

"How can I have sympathy for someone who may have aided my mother's murderer?" Narra shrugged. "I don't know for sure if she had anything to do with it, but I do know what it's like to feel trapped."

He thought back to what she'd said about how Tal got to go wherever he pleased—got to travel and fight battles and forge alliances on the Summer Court's behalf—but Narra had to stay safe at home. How she got all of the responsibility and none of the freedom.

"So you've never left the Summer Court?" he asked. "You said something about distant friends, one time."

When he'd caught her outside the revel in the woods by St. Sithney's, she'd been whispering to those tiny, luminous birds. She'd said they were messengers.

"We do receive visitors from other courts, and our caravan route takes us to them in turn. But I've never been allowed to go anywhere on my own." Narra's hand tightened on his, but her voice remained serene as she said, "I . . . had a rebellious phase, when I was younger. I snuck away to the human world. I'd go in the night and come back before dawn, but . . . the Gallowglass eventually caught me. Father and Talarix were . . . upset."

"Upset," he repeated.

She touched the pinkish scar at the base of her throat. "But my punishment only lasted a year, and then I was forgiven."

Leo looked more closely at the mark. At last, he recognized it for what it was: a burn scar. The same one that the pooka had, from a silver collar.

He stumbled over his own feet, but she didn't miss a beat, steadying him through the next steps.

"You're better at this than I expected," she said.

He forced a laugh. "Then your expectations must have been on the ground."

"I can at least say, with total honesty, that you are a better dancer than Beor."

"Let me guess—because Beor doesn't dance." He managed a real smile this time. "I think I'm getting better at reading between the lines."

The Folk thought Hazel belonged with the Summer Court—belonged *to* the Summer Court. Prince Talarix would have had no qualms about killing Leo for the crime of trying to take her back home. So Narra had given Leo and Hazel an out, and done it without raising any objections, not even from her brother. She'd turned it into a game.

All he'd wanted was a chance, and she'd given him that.

CHAPTER 23

AZIZA

SHE NEVER GOT close enough to the front of the crowd to see Leo or Princess Narra. Still, she heard Narra's voice as if it spoke directly into her ear, carried to her by some enchantment. Aziza was so intent on listening in case she said something important that she missed the musicians' cue. The rapt audience dissolved into noise and motion, and Aziza was pulled into a dance. The fairies didn't mind her broken hand, but they did offer to use their illusions to temporarily erase her scars, and seemed perplexed by her polite refusal. They wanted to tell her riddles. They had heard from the borderland fae how she and her coven had slain a hag, and asked her to tell the story. They said they'd never spoken to a gatewalker so young before, that only elder hedgewitches were permitted to associate with the Court of the Seasons, and that Anne Sterling never came to their parties no matter how many lavish invitations they sent, and how had Aziza convinced them to let her come here?

From the bond, she knew Tristan was safe; that left her to find Leo. But it was Hazel she spotted first, over someone's shoulder:

a slight, green figure in a dress made of about a thousand layers of chiffon, her braid dotted with forget-me-nots, following her friends into a side passage. Through gaps in the trees, Aziza glimpsed the fairy children climbing up what must have been a hidden staircase, swiftly disappearing into shadow and out of her sight.

She had to wait until the end of the song before she could slip away and follow them. The forest walls had been sculpted in overlapping layers, like flower petals, and the openings into the side passages were hidden between them. Where Hazel had vanished, she found a staircase made of braided roots and branches. The uneven steps pressed into the soles of her feet through the flimsy cloth slippers she'd been given to replace her muddy sneakers. Her good hand ran along smooth columns of birch, and she inhaled their sweet, green scent. It was easier to think here, in the cool quiet, where the music and voices were muffled. Soon, voices drifted to her from up above, distorted slightly by running water.

The stairs opened onto a balcony that had been hidden among the tops of the trees, a ridge with a flat top where a waterfall from an enchanted pool dove over the far side of the bluff. Hazel sat there with her friends, legs dangling over the edge, under the light of the moon and a small swarm of lesser fairies.

Aziza hung back in the staircase, hidden from view, not wanting to interrupt. Hazel liked her, but there probably wasn't anything more embarrassing than your big brother's best friend turning up to check on you when you were trying to hang out with people your own age.

One of the children was saying, "Honestly, it's like you've never even taken lessons."

Tristan had described the fairy children he'd seen with Hazel before. That was Vetiver, based on the haughty voice and the little antlers. They were with the blue fairy, Ephira, and the one with black-and-red wings, Glora.

"I haven't," Hazel said.

Ephira made a noise that was somewhere between shocked and appalled. "Humans don't take dance lessons?" she asked. She was shoulder to shoulder with Hazel, their wings brushing when they fluttered.

"Some of them do," Hazel said, awkwardly. "I didn't."

"Mother will fix that," Ephira said, in soothing tones.

Hazel shrugged. "The . . . the princess said if my brother won the Hunt, I could go back to the human realm. I probably won't have time for lessons."

"She said you could *choose*," Vetiver said. "Why would you choose that?"

"It's my home. My family's there."

"You have family here," Vetiver said. "Like Prince Talarix."

"You mustn't rush back just because you know nothing else," Ephira agreed.

"It's not because of that," Hazel said, hotly.

Vetiver opened his mouth to respond with something snide, from the irritated look on his face, but Glora beat him to it, interjecting in her slow, thoughtful way.

"Why would they let you go?" she asked.

"What do you mean?" Hazel said.

"Fairy courts are locked in an endless chain of minor wars and territorial disputes," Glora said, sounding unconcerned. "The borderlands shift as the human world does, so we're constantly redrawing our territories. An enchantress like your mother, like you could be if you take after her . . . why would they let you leave?"

Hazel shook her head. "But Princess Narra said . . ."

"It doesn't matter," Vetiver said. "Prince Talarix is the true heir, everyone knows that."

Ephira gasped. "Vetiver, that's treasonous! *Hush.*"

"And the prince," Vetiver continued, ignoring her, "is opposed to giving up any of our people, even lost changelings, unless we have something to gain in return."

"Well, it's not *up* to the prince," Ephira said huffily. "Don't listen to him, Hazel. Prince Tal is Captain of the Gallowglass, and Vetiver wants to be a knight, so he thinks he has to start sucking up right now."

"You'll see," Vetiver said. "When the king wakes up tomorrow, he'll side with Prince Tal."

"It doesn't matter, because King Ilanthus left Princess Narra in charge, and she gave her word on behalf of the Summer Court," Ephira reminded him. "There are no sides to be chosen, it's done."

Hazel was very quiet. Aziza couldn't tell if she was hanging on every word or trying to tune the conversation out.

Vetiver shrugged, as if he'd already lost interest in the argument.

"I'm bored," he announced. "Let's go back downstairs."

Before Aziza could retreat, thinking she was on the verge of being caught, new footsteps came—from the other side of the balcony. There must have been a second staircase down. The children looked over, and then Vetiver shot to his feet, overjoyed.

"Prince Tal!" he said, launching himself into Tal's arms. Aziza withdrew into the cover of the shadows, but not before she saw Tal lift his wineglass out of the way and accept the hug, ruffling Vetiver's hair with his free hand.

"I was wondering where my favorite troublemakers had disappeared to," he said, his voice fond. "Have you been looking after Hazel?"

A chorus of agreement from the children. Only Hazel's voice was absent.

"Hello," Tal said softly. When Aziza inched forward to take another look, he'd knelt in front of Hazel, setting his glass on the floor and offering her his hand. She took it, and he folded his other hand over hers. "I meant to find you sooner. Did the others tell you that you and I are cousins? Lady Thula was my mother's sister."

"Yeah," Hazel said, more timid than Aziza had heard her sound in months. She was forcefully reminded of the first time she'd met her—after the holiday fair at St. Sithney's, the same night she'd met Leo. Hazel had been almost too shy to speak; Leo had later said she was always like that with strangers. It felt so long ago, Aziza had forgotten.

She should have gone back downstairs. But she couldn't let Hazel out of her sight, not when the prince was there.

"I loved Aunt Thula," he said. "After my mother . . . after she passed, Aunt Thula was always there to look after me. Father, too, of course. But Aunt Thula and I were very close. She taught me enchantments and illusion-weaving herself instead of leaving it to the tutors. She crafted my first sword, from obsidian and chimera bone—charmed so that it would burn the hand of anyone who tried to take it from me. I could tell you about her, another time. If you would like that."

Hazel was very still; Aziza couldn't be sure she was even breathing. At last, she said, "I would . . . like that."

Tal gave her hand an affectionate pat and stood. "If you need anything, or if anyone bothers you, come to me straightaway. I will take care of it."

She stuttered out a thank-you. The other children bowed—Ephira tugged on Hazel's hand, reminding her to curtsy—and Tal sent them off, back down the stairs he'd come from and into the revel.

Aziza had waited too long to make her escape. She had taken only a couple of silent steps back when Tal said, "Running away again, gatewalker?"

That *had* been the plan, but it would be unforgivably rude for her to ignore him when he'd addressed her directly. She took a steadying breath and stepped out onto the balcony. To Aziza's right, the edge of the bluff overlooked the woods, which rose into the hills that ringed the valley. The lesser fairies landed briefly on her shoulders before darting away, skittish as mice, casting splotches of reflected gold light over the enchanted pool.

Prince Tal had gone without his armor for the night and was resplendent in violet brocade. His antlers were adorned with rings of shining onyx and ruby, connected by chains of gold. Unlike the princess, whose eyes spoke of wisdom and humor, the prince's carried a wickedness that sharpened his slender, graceful features like a whetstone did a blade. He picked up his glass and approached, smiling down at her. It was a decidedly different smile from the one he'd shown the children.

"Are you enjoying the festivities?" he asked, and held out the glass. "Please, take this."

It wasn't optional. She took it.

"Thank you," she said, backing away. "Excuse me."

"Aren't you going to try it? I brought it here especially for you." He didn't move; he didn't need to chase her, and he knew it. "Consider it a peace offering. I frightened you, didn't I? That day."

"A little," she said, not raising the glass. "I'd never met a fairy before."

"Was I really your first?" he said, his dark eyes glittering. "I'm honored. Pity I made such a poor impression. Allow me the chance to make it right."

As a child, Aziza hadn't known why Prince Tal had scared her. He'd had an intimidating air of power to him, but Aziza had always been more fascinated by powerful things than frightened of them. With the benefit of age and many conversations with the borderland fae over the years, she knew now exactly what happened to humans who served the Folk, all the myriad torments they faced, from minor humiliations to outright abuse. The slow loss of their free will, so that they thought they could leave anytime but gradually forgot why they ever wanted to. She knew what she had to fear if she drank lily wine, lost her senses, and left herself vulnerable and alone with Prince Tal.

Anne Sterling would have had no trouble getting rid of him, Aziza thought, bitterly. A trained hedgewitch would know what to do in this situation. Maybe she'd have a spell that would protect her from the effects of lily wine, or distract Tal long enough for her to slip away.

She looked down at the glass, and then up at Tal. "I can't drink lily wine," she said. "But I thank you for your hospitality."

AZIZA

"You would scorn this token of friendship?" he asked lightly, but he didn't sound scorned; if anything, his smile had grown wider. His head tilted just slightly, light blinking off the rings adorning his antlers.

"You mean, if I accept this drink," Aziza said slowly, "that makes me your friend?"

"Certainly." He drifted closer. "I'd like to think we're already friends. We have known each other for rather a long time, by human standards."

"True friendship is reciprocal," she said, and he laughed.

"And how shall I prove my friendship, then?" he said.

"I would never presume to tell a Prince of Summer what to do," she demurred.

"Oh, but please do. I am desperately curious to know what you want. Your Huntsman is an easy one—he's here for glory."

"He's here for his sister."

"His *sister*, of course." He pronounced that word, *sister*, skeptically, like the name of a city in a strange land. "That's what he says. But is it the truth? For you, though, there is no glory. No title or reward. So you must have another reason. Another desire."

"I don't want anything."

"Impossible. Everyone wants something." There was no obvious change to his expression, but it brightened somehow, like a sunrise at sea, from an elusive glimmer to a blinding radiance. "I could grant you the deepest, most secret, most unlikely wishes of your heart. A rare opportunity, isn't it?"

"I guess it is," she said, lifting the glass tentatively, as if she was thinking about taking that drink after all. "Is it really okay if I ask you for something?"

"More than okay," Prince Tal said, his voice soft and indulgent now that she'd signaled her willingness to acquiesce. "Drink the wine, and I'll grant you your request."

Her mind raced; she needed to choose just the right words. Abruptly, she thought of Dion, as if a wind sprite had carried the scent of matches to her. She thought of the silver cloak.

"You will?" she asked innocently. "Right away?"

"Right away. As soon as you drink. I imagine you'll be shocked by how quickly I'm able to give you exactly what you want," he said, in a tone of voice that made her want to gag.

That was the opening she'd been waiting for; quickly, before he had time to realize the error he'd made, she said, "Show me a fairy who can hold silver in his bare hands. That's my request."

The smile slid off his face. "What are you talking about?"

"Just what I said." She raised the glass and tipped it back carefully, just letting the liquid inside touch her lips before she lowered it. Barely a drop made contact with her skin, but the taste of it still flooded her mouth. The world grew hazy. Tal was a bronze, glittering blur in her spinning vision. When she spoke next, the words may have run together; she couldn't tell. "Your turn. You said . . . right away."

Fairies couldn't lie. And their words carried power, over themselves and others. He had said he would grant her request right away, so he had to do it right away. Had to find her a fairy who could touch pure silver, which of course was something that didn't exist. Even Beor, whose moderate resistance to silver had probably saved his life from those arrows, had still been burned where it had touched him. If Tal couldn't do what he'd promised, then he would be lying, and his own magic wouldn't allow that.

He said something, but everything had gone slow and fuzzy, and she didn't understand. He moved, and it was like the sun had gotten up and walked away, sending the whole world careening through outer space.

The last thing she remembered, later, was a cool hand touching her shoulder.

CHAPTER 24

TRISTAN

THERE WAS A place in the birch wood away from the path but near enough to the revel for them to hear the music, where the forest was young. Saplings dotted the grove, and the older trees were barely half the height of the ballroom's walls. The lesser fairies hadn't followed them here. The only light came from drifting wills-o'-the-wisp and the lantern Beor had taken from the castle. The walk had left Beor winded, despite the hound's support.

"This," he huffed, catching his breath, "is where we lay our dead to rest."

Tristan scanned the area again with sharper eyes, looking for gravestones. His attention kept wandering back to the saplings, the youngest one in sight maybe five feet tall, the base embedded in a small pile of moss-covered stones. Or . . . what he'd *thought* were stones. Now he picked out strands of white hair, the curve of a cheek and a pointed ear—it was a body, and the sapling's trunk burst from its chest. Everywhere he looked, he found more bodies in various states of decay, intertwined with tree roots and the lush undergrowth of the forest.

"What . . . is this?" Tristan asked, though that wasn't precisely the right question; the right questions were all *why*, not *what*.

"When a fairy dies, their magic, dispersing into Elphame, brings forth new life," Beor said. "It is a form of immortality, and one the Summer Court reveres."

"And is the entire forest . . ."

"Not all of it, nowhere near that. But there are many of our ancestors scattered through the birch wood, certainly."

Once, Tristan had wished this same fate for himself. He'd wanted to lie down and give himself over to the woods; he'd thought it would be peaceful. But there was nothing peaceful about the way coiling roots had pulled rib cages open like wishbones; the way thorns had gouged through burial garments and made tally marks on bloodless skin; the way tiny green seedlings had annexed the dark, warm cavities of mouths and eye sockets. Fairy skeletons didn't look human—the skulls were shaped wrong, there were joints where there shouldn't be—but under the cover of moss and shadow, they were close enough. Tristan's stomach lurched.

"Don't tell me the little necromancer is afraid of the dead," Beor said, mockingly.

"I'm not," Tristan snapped. "So what now?"

"Think of the Hunt," Beor said. He dropped his empty wine bottle on the ground. It rolled away. "What did you observe?"

Observe was such a clinical word for what he'd experienced. There had been Beor's pack—countless hounds, overtaking the mountain paths like the army Tristan had once envisioned making for Hazel, diving into the lake water all slick and amorphous in the billow of their fur. There had been the smell of blood, sulfur, smoke; fish and algae in the river, snow melt from the mountains. There had been all that noise—the baying of the hounds, the rumble of a distant landslide, the howling of the winds—

Not the winds, but the phantom horsemen on steeds made of mist.

"The ghosts," Tristan said abruptly.

"Spirits." Beor walked onward, taking them deeper into the grave-yard. "When something dies, it leaves behind an energy. Most of it clings to the body or whatever is left of the body; some of it remains in objects or places of significance to the deceased. This energy is called anima. Over time, most of it is reabsorbed into the world—people, plants, animals. Have you ever tried to raise the dead?"

Tristan hadn't been to school in almost two years, but he still knew what a teacher sounded like, and Beor was, amazingly, trying to teach him.

"Yes," Tristan said. "Once I tried to . . . bring someone back to life. It didn't work, it . . . He was all wrong, like a monster. Another time, I just woke up the bodies so we could talk to them."

Beor nodded. "A resurrection is extremely difficult—it requires a ritual, or what a human witch might call a spell. It is also more likely to work on a subject who has died very recently, and whose anima has not yet faded much or at all. When you spoke to the dead, that was what you called on, knowingly or not—their lingering anima, which contains a small piece of their soul's essence. Not enough for true life, but enough to communicate, a semblance of the person they once were. If you attempt a resurrection without the proper spell to reunify the soul with the body, then you will end up with something hollow, something that instinctively seeks to fill itself up by drawing in anima from other beings. A black hole disguised as a person. There are also, however, uses for anima that do not require the involvement of the body at all; anima with form and purpose but no body becomes what you would know as a *ghost* or a *spirit*."

"I thought spirits were like . . ." Like the Ash Witch, he wanted to say, but Beor wouldn't know who that was.

He must have understood what Tristan was getting at, though, because he said, "There is a natural process by which anima, if strengthened by a powerful force of personality or emotion, can accumulate energy over time rather than dissipating. A new body, a new form, is created from that energy. This powerful anima becomes a force of nature, then, like the wind—sometimes vanishing, but never truly gone. This, too, is a kind of spirit, but one that would be difficult for a summoner to control. You've met a spirit like this, I gather." When Tristan nodded, he said, "This spirit would have elicited a strong emotion from you. Correct?"

The question triggered a vivid memory—how the Ash Witch had called him *guilty*, and he'd known he was.

"Remorse," he told Beor quietly.

"Yes," Beor said, and Tristan was absurdly pleased. God, how desperate was he for approval that even one syllable of it from someone like Beor felt like a hard-won victory? "More than any-thing else, spirits are emotion given physical form—emotions so potent they can infect anyone who encounters these spirits. You felt remorse not because of the spirit, but because that remorse lived inside of *you*. The spirit drew it out of you. Thus do spirits of the dead inspire the dread and terror that most mortals feel toward death."

"The spirits in your hunting party," Tristan said. "They didn't just *upset* me. I'm covered in bruises."

"A powerful enough spirit commanded by a skilled summoner can do real harm, yes," Beor said, unapologetic. "It can push against the veil of death and touch the mortal realm."

The graveyard smelled earthy and clean, and only sometimes did he catch a whiff of the dank, musty reek of death. If not for the way his bond to the hounds had sharpened his sense of smell, he'd never have detected it at all.

"Are you going to teach me a spell?" Tristan asked, and Beor laughed.

"I may be a summoner, but I do not practice in the way a human witch does. You might, one day, but it is not a path I can lead you down. I shall teach you my way." He stopped before a body that rested beneath one of the tallest birch trees. There was no flesh left to the remains; even the bones had mostly disintegrated. Beor reached down and broke off a piece of something, and held it out to Tristan, who took it gingerly.

He scraped the moss off and revealed something pointed, slightly curved, and bony—the tip of an antler.

Reflexively, he dropped it.

"A summoner cannot be squeamish," Beor said. "It won't do."

"I'm not squeamish," Tristan said, which was a lie. "You could've warned me."

"What did you think we came here to do? Pray?" He laughed, a full-on belly laugh like Tristan was the best entertainment he'd had in ages.

Scowling, Tristan picked up the antler and pretended it didn't make his skin crawl. "Isn't this . . . disrespectful?"

"No. As far as the Folk are concerned, this man is here." Beor laid his hand flat on the birch tree. "Alive and well."

Remains held anima. Mostly, the anima of these dead fairies had gone into feeding the forest, but a few scraps lingered in their bodies, including in the antler Tristan held. Beor instructed him to call on the anima, infuse it with his own magic, and give it form so that it could materialize.

All he could produce, at first, were milky pale wisps of energy. A spirit was the opposite of shadow; it was a kind of light.

"Again," Beor said. "Spirits are forces of emotion, I told you. So *feel* something. Give the spirit something that will make it pay attention."

"Feel *what*?"

"Anger. Fear. Grief. These are forceful emotions to which spirits readily respond. Think of a memory, if you must. You won't always need to use them as a crutch, but memories can be useful tools at this stage."

Tristan wasn't quick to anger; it required a fire he didn't have. He was intimately familiar with fear, but he'd never choose to feel that way, hated how it turned him into someone he didn't recognize. But grief—that was a feeling he knew all too well.

When he thought of grief, he thought firstly of losing Leo. Of being forgotten. But that grief stemmed from love, and there was no separating one from the other. Then he thought of his parents. There was plenty of grief in the memory of their last fight, how he'd been turned out on the street with a backpack and a promise that he could come back if he swore to never, ever, speak of what he'd told them again. But he wasn't letting his parents be a part of this—part of the thing that gave him power. They weren't in his life anymore, and he was keeping it that way.

Then he settled on last winter. He was in Elphame, burying people the hounds had killed. The handle of the shovel was warm from his grip, his palms stung with bright spots of pain that would soon turn into blisters, and the trees were laden with frost, his breath visible when he panted. He'd had to push down what he felt so that he could do what needed to be done.

There had been countless other victims. Countless homes the hag had invaded with his help. He had mourned, quietly, for each of them. Only he'd thought he didn't have the right to mourn. Not when their deaths were his fault. And so what he'd mostly felt, what he'd allowed himself to feel, had been guilt and shame. Those feelings were still there, but now he let himself have the grief, too. And what he had was an endless supply of it.

The wispy presence before him resolved into a silhouette, tall and imposing, and magnificently antlered. The leaves of the birch tree rustled; the ferny undergrowth stirred.

"Good," Beor rasped, quietly, as if not to break Tristan's concentration. "Now reach out to the others."

To the hag, a bondservant who never learned to harden his heart was all but useless, barely able to complete the work she required. A failure. But here was something his useless heart could do. The wild-eyed rage he forbade the hounds—took from them and bundled up like wrapping a butcher's knife in cloth so it couldn't hurt anyone— he used it now. The nightmares. The self-loathing. The secret desire for vengeance against a tormentor who had died *too quickly* when she'd deserved to suffer. The bitterness at all the people who'd . . . failed him. He'd never thought of it that way, that it wasn't just *him* who'd failed, that there were people—his teachers, his parents, the people he used to call his friends, even Greg and Maria—who could've reached out to him and hadn't. And here he was being *mentored*, for the first time ever, by someone who should've been an enemy. No one else had ever bothered to say, *Here, this is what you should do,* but why hadn't they? He knew that wasn't fair, that he pushed people away too, that *he* didn't reach out either, but the bitterness was there anyway, and maybe it wasn't rational, but at least he could use it.

The stirring around him picked up. He'd mistaken it for wind before, but it didn't move in predictable currents, and it wasn't aware or intentional like a sprite; it was just energy, chaotic, waiting to be tamed and given purpose. It blew the hound's fur and Beor's hair into disarray; it set the trees rustling, their fragile leaves whipping around. The temperature dropped to wintry levels, and then the spirits began to *howl,* deafening and agonized and—he thought with a surge of pride—utterly chilling.

The antlered spirit reached for Tristan's neck with a ghostly hand, but he stood his ground, and it faltered short of touching him. He had done this before, with the dead, holding them in line with will-power and magic—and, if all else failed, a shovel—and it struck him now how similar it was to the way Aziza dealt with fae. You had to be more stubborn than they were. The spirit went formless like the others then, dissolving, flashing back into existence first beside him, then in front again, as if awaiting a command.

"Stronger!" Beor said. "Give shape to the others, too. Anchor them in the land of the living."

His teeth were bared in a grimace as the spirits buffeted him, eyes wide with vicious satisfaction, goading Tristan on. Was he so unaffected by this display, that he still had the breath to demand more? Tristan remembered the way Beor's spirits had overwhelmed his thoughts and senses at the mountain lake. That was his goal, then. No bystander should be able to speak, should be able to *think* in Tristan's presence.

This was why he'd taken the necromancy gift back instead of letting it die with the hag: so that he'd never have to be powerless again. But he hadn't felt truly empowered until this moment. Until he'd turned his weak heart into a weapon.

"*Stronger!*" Beor commanded, and his terrible voice didn't make Tristan flinch this time. He could be terrible, too. He poured magic into the spirits, and they roared like a hurricane, all ice and anguish, and the trees bowed for him, and the lantern went out, and—

And then—

He stopped. Everything.

The spirits fell silent, and the whipping branches settled down. The first flush of warmth began to creep back into the forest. His attention had turned to a corner of his mind that was carefully blocked off—not like a wall, impenetrable, but more like a curtain. A curtain that now was fluttering. It was his bond to Aziza. A curious mix of sensations drifted through it—not particularly strong, easy enough for him to block out, but so *unusual* coming from Aziza, who hardly ever let him feel anything from her end. Confusion, queasiness, fear. An inquisitive tug, not as if to get his attention, but as if she'd forgotten what the bond was for and had decided to investigate.

"What? Done already?" Beor said.

"I have to go," he told Beor. "I'm sorry. My coven needs me."

"Very well. Don't come back without another bottle." And then, as Tristan bent to put the antler tip back, Beor said sharply, "No, keep that. You'll find such mementos and keepsakes necessary as you're starting out."

"All right," Tristan said, pocketing it. He didn't want to offend Beor after he'd taught him so well. He turned away, hesitated, and stopped, finally remembering why he'd wanted to talk to Beor in the first place. "Who shot you? Do you know?"

"If I did, do you think that person would still be alive?"

"Right. Okay. Thank you for—" He cut himself off, feeling oddly embarrassed. Beor made a dismissive noise that Tristan took to mean he did not want gratitude and that in fact he'd feel better about this whole thing if they didn't call undue attention to how generous he'd been. So Tristan said, instead, "I'll call another hound to stay with you. Until you want to go back."

Beor's eyebrows lifted as he glanced from Tristan to the scarred hound, which had sat patiently through Tristan's impromptu necromancy lesson.

"Another one? Is it important that *this* one goes with you?"

"It usually does."

"And what is its name?"

"I . . . haven't decided. But I think it's been waiting, so I will. Soon."

Beor didn't smile, but Tristan could see that he approved.

THE HOUND DEPOSITED him in a secluded staircase where light from the ballroom shone through the gaps between woven shoots of birch. The music and chatter were muffled. A few steps up, on a balcony, Aziza sat alone against the wall, eyes half-lidded. He scanned her for injuries, but found none—no blood, or tears in her clothing, or anything broken, at least at a glance. She just looked drowsy, as if she'd decided to take a nap.

He knelt next to her and touched her shoulder lightly. "Aziza? What happened?"

Her head tilted toward him. She blinked, as if puzzled, either by his question or by his existence.

"He can't use his gloves," she slurred. "It would be a lie."

"Are you drunk?" he whispered incredulously. He looked around again, over the balcony with its pool of crystal water, back down the staircase speckled with light. After all her warnings not to drink lily wine, he couldn't imagine she'd have done it of her own accord— but if someone else had compelled her, they were nowhere to be found.

Her head fell back against the wall with a thunk.

"Okay. That's enough reveling for us, I think," he said. Then, to the hound: "Wait here with her."

He stood to go, but the hound stood, too.

"*No.* You're not going to act like a rebellious mutt right now," he told it, in his most severe tone of voice. "You'll get your name later. It's not that easy to name something. You're not a *pet.* What am I supposed to do, stick a collar on you and call you Lucky?"

Its ears perked with unmistakable interest.

"No! I'm not calling you that," he snapped. "Don't even think about it."

But it lay down at Aziza's side, docile. Aziza rested her arm on it, her scarred hand mussing its fur.

"Good dog," she mumbled.

The hound grinned at him with its inches-long white teeth and its reflective eyes, as if to say, *See? I can be a pet if I want.*

He left them and hurried downstairs to find Leo. After the time he'd spent in the solemn tranquility of the graveyard, the revel was overwhelming—the sheer volume of light, color, smells, noise. But he was a ghost; he was a haunting. Traces of spiritual energy still lingered on him, and the hound's scent, too, and maybe a little of the ferocity that had swept through him when he'd performed his first proper summoning of spirits—a wild abandon not unlike what he'd sensed from Beor's hunting party that first night. The Folk gave him a berth, knowingly or not, some of them flinching as he passed behind them even though they couldn't have seen him there; others extended a hand as if to invite him to dance, only to hesitate, which gave him time to walk away as if he hadn't noticed. No one touched him.

He found Leo on the sidelines, watching the crowd like he was steeling himself to dive back in. As soon as he caught sight of Tristan, he brightened.

"Tris!" he said. "I was looking for you. Uh, it's me, by the way, I know I look like—"

"I know it's you," Tristan replied, amused.

"You do?" Leo's hand flew up to one of his horns, as if to check that it was still there. "How'd you know?"

Because he'd know Leo anywhere.

But he couldn't say that to someone he was supposed to just be friends with.

"I think there's a gap in the enchantment," he said. "I caught a glimpse. That's what it is, right? An enchantment?"

"I guess so." He held his arms out at his sides and looked down at himself critically. "This girl touched my face like she was putting something on me. I didn't feel anything, but then I . . . looked like this."

"Where?" Tristan said, frowning. Leo wore a stranger's fine, delicate features, with strikingly high cheekbones and desert-colored eyes that had ovoid, horizontal pupils. Not even a speck of dust marred his flawless complexion.

Tristan found this a little offensive. Whoever thought getting rid of Leo's freckles was an improvement?

"Here, I think," Leo said, pointing vaguely at his cheek.

Tristan's hands moved before he could think twice about it, holding Leo steady with a light touch to his jaw while his fingers swiped carefully over the place Leo had indicated. All he felt at first was unnaturally smooth flesh, cool and perfect as glass. Another brush, and something gave way; he found Leo's skin under the illusion, warmer than the magic was. It must have been a simple, fragile enchantment, not something designed to last. He wiped it away, and the illusion sloughed off—half of it, at least. And there he was. One wide brown eye, a dusting of summer freckles, faintly chapped lips parted in surprise.

"Found you," Tristan said, unable to hold back a small, victorious smile.

Then he realized that their noses were inches apart, and Leo was staring at him.

"Sure did," Leo said, sounding as breathless as he had when Tristan had kissed him.

Tristan's heartbeat sped up, stuttering in his chest, a desperately hopeful, faltering rhythm. He couldn't come up with a response. It had been a long time since he could be this close to Leo and just— look at him. When they were younger, they used to fall asleep together, wake up together, and Tristan had had all the time in the world to trace Leo's features with his eyes and his hands. He didn't have the right to do that anymore. Belatedly, he pulled his fingertips away from where they still rested lightly on Leo's cheek, terribly close to his mouth. Leo's eyes widened, and he inhaled audibly, as if, until just then, he had been holding his breath. Then he reddened and looked away. Days ago, Tristan might've taken that as a rejection and been crushed by it. But nothing now could fool him into believing that Leo didn't want him anymore. He was insecure, but he wasn't *completely* oblivious.

You're mine, Tristan thought. He knew it wasn't right. Leo didn't belong to anyone, least of all Tristan, who had debased himself in the hag's service. Twisted himself into someone, *something* that was, frankly, beneath Leo's affection. But he didn't care anymore. What was right and wrong to death itself?

You're mine. You're mine. You're so fucking mine.

Being selfish was what Tristan was good at; it was only natural that he was too selfish to give up on Leo. Even if Leo *could* find someone better. Tristan was a total fucking nightmare, and he wanted Leo to love him for his awful, nightmarish self. And if Leo couldn't, then Tristan would have to live with that, but he wasn't going to give up without a fight.

"We should go," Leo said, hoarsely. And the moment was over.

Leo scrubbed off the rest of the illusion, and they went back to the balcony to collect Aziza. Hazel found them along the way. It was late enough in the night that the revel was winding down; the Folk were drunk and absorbed in one another, and paid the little knot of humans no attention. Slowly, they made their way back up the path and into the castle.

CHAPTER 25

LEO

THE BED WAS the softest thing he'd ever touched, like lying in a mountain of down feathers and dandelions, but he woke up aching all over, his head pounding. It must've been morning, because the chamber was awash in pale sunlight. To his right, Aziza had her arms thrown over her face, as if to defend herself from it. To his left, Tristan lay on his side facing Leo, hands loosely curled before him, the old scars on his palms faintly visible.

The three of them had collapsed in the same room last night mostly by accident. They'd set Aziza down, and then Leo had flopped onto the bed next to her to rest for what he'd thought would just be a minute, and then Tristan had said he'd walk Hazel back to where she was sleeping in the encampment. Leo had asked her if she wanted to stay over with them—she could share with Aziza, or Leo could sleep on the chaise in his room and she could take the bed—but she had said that Ephira would wonder where she'd gone.

Leo had wanted to say, *So what? Let Ephira wonder.*

But his head was already on the pillow, and he must have

passed out right around then. He didn't remember Tristan coming back.

In this light, Tristan was the same shade of gold as a languid summer morning. He wanted to touch him. He wanted to bury his face in Tristan's neck and see if he smelled like summer, too, like citrus, sweat, and fresh air. He wanted him in this excruciating all-over way that defied reason, like his body had rewired itself so that even the parts of him that weren't capable of want had learned to feel its ache. Like even his bones wanted Tristan. Even his blood wanted Tristan. The places Tristan had brushed his fingers over when he'd wiped away the illusion yesterday *especially* wanted Tristan, his cheekbone and just next to the corner of his mouth, his skin tingling with remembered warmth.

But Tristan wasn't his. Leo had forgotten a lot of things, but he couldn't let himself forget that. Sometimes, in his weakest moments, he'd think, *My true love is gone, and I should accept that.* Sometimes he'd think, *I wish it was you,* and feel terrible, because that wasn't fair to anyone, including himself. Whoever he was looking for, it wasn't Tristan. Tristan didn't feel like the presence from his dreams, and the dreams were the only clue he had. It was like when you had a word on the tip of your tongue, and you knew when you'd finally come up with the right one. And . . . you knew when you hadn't.

There was no way he was going back to sleep, so he crawled off the foot of the bed and went into the room next door to wash up without waking the others. He couldn't remember which room had been his, and which ones had been Aziza's and Tristan's, but the clothes laid out on the bed looked like they were meant for him, another fancy outfit like the one they'd given him yesterday.

Probably Sophia's doing. His stomach turned, again, at the thought of Evan's bruises and the way he and May had debated which of them would be going to the blue tent that night. He still had the black button in his pocket. He took it out, looked at it for a moment, and stashed it in the pocket of his new outfit so that he could return it to Evan later.

They had survived their first night in the Summer Court. No one had tried to kill him again, or if they had, he hadn't noticed. He was hours away from finishing what he'd come here to do and taking Hazel home.

But he didn't feel like he was winning. He felt like a plastic toy being batted around between a cat's paws.

The halls were deserted; the tents in the encampment had been drawn tightly closed. The makeshift tables, cushions, empty bottles of wine lay strewn beside them. The Fair Folk, it seemed, would sleep most of the day away in preparation for their last night of reveling. But Hazel had gone to bed earlier than the rest, and she didn't like sleeping in, anyway. He was hoping he'd find her awake. And he did. She was by the creek he'd stumbled across last night, whispering to a water sprite, a lesser fairy perched on her shoulder. She still had last night's dress on, but her braid had come undone. At the sound of his footsteps, she looked up.

"You're awake!" she said, bouncing into the air—literally, a hop to her feet and then off the ground as her wings fluttered to life, bringing her to hover at eye level with him. "Is Aziza okay?"

"Fine, I think. She's still asleep. So's Tris." He glanced in the direction of the tents, a short ways behind them in the main path. "So you've been staying with Ephira?"

LEO

"And her mom," Hazel said. "She's nice. She was friends with my . . . with Lady Thula. When they were kids."

She'd stopped herself from calling Lady Thula her mother, but Leo heard it anyway. It shouldn't have stung, but it did. Because if Hazel stopped thinking of his mom as *her* mom, too, then did that mean she'd stop thinking of Leo as her brother?

"Here," he said, digging something out of his backpack and handing it to her. "I meant to give it to you yesterday, but I forgot I had it."

It was her copy of *The Complete Sherlock Holmes*, a brick-sized leather-bound tome that was only a little worse for wear after having been stashed in the back of his car with their food and supplies, dumped on the forest floor, rescued and transferred to the pooka, dropped on the side of a mountain when the pooka had fled from the Hunt, rescued again and then lugged around in his backpack.

She flipped through it reverently, her long green fingers riffling the pages and holding the spine in the same way she'd always held it, pressed at the same spots that were worn dull from dozens of rereads. Then she hugged it to her chest, blinking the brightness from her eyes. "Thanks," she said quietly.

"I only brought it in case . . ." He shrugged. "If something happened to me, and I couldn't bring you home, I wanted to make sure you had it."

"And you think something could happen tonight," she said. "Is that why you're giving it to me now?"

In the creek, the water sprite played with a gaggle of tadpoles. Patches of sunlight lay over its banks like a cobblestone road, going nowhere but in circles. He wanted to tell Hazel there was no reason to think anything bad was going to happen. Everyone he'd asked had assured him the danger he'd faced in the Hunt had passed. Beor was injured and hadn't even bothered showing his face at the revel last night. Tristan's hounds had caught no more assassins lying in wait. He had already given the first drop of the elixir of renewal to King Ilanthus.

But a reassuring lie, if she saw through it, would scare her a lot more than honest uncertainty.

"Maybe. It's not over till it's over, right?" He attempted a smile, but it came out like a grimace. "But we got this far. The Hunt was the hard part. All we have to do is get through the ceremony tonight, and then we can go back home. Try and stay close to us until we can leave, all right? We don't want to stick around longer than we have to."

Her fingers traced the design on the spine of the book. "But when I go back . . . I'll still look like this."

"Mom and Dad won't care. I promise."

"I care. If . . . if I stay here, I can learn magic," she said, slowly at first and then all in a rush. "And illusions. I can make myself look like a human again. And then I can go wherever I want. I won't have to hide in my room because I'm afraid of people thinking I'm a freak. My . . . Lady Thula was really, really good at magic, really strong, and everyone thinks I could be, too. So maybe . . . I shouldn't go yet."

She watched nervously for his reaction, as if she expected him to be upset. And, sure, he wasn't thrilled to hear it. But he wasn't surprised, either. Part of him had known this was coming. Anyone would be tempted to stay in a place as beautiful as this one, with the promise of a magical inheritance in their near future. Anyone could be tricked.

"You remember how me, Tris, and Aziza had to fight a monster in the woods a few months ago? The thing that . . . talked in your mind and convinced you to do things?"

She nodded, a frown pulling at the corner of her mouth. "And it tried to bury us."

"Yeah. And you remember what we told you about it later? How it feeds on people. How it can make you think it's another person, someone who wants to help you, but it's not a person. It's just . . . a void that takes and takes, and all it cares about is surviving."

"Why are you talking about this?" Hazel said, her voice shaky and small. She hadn't come down into the hag's den under the gateway tree, hadn't seen the full horrifying truth of what they'd been up against, but she—like Leo—had felt the hag's inexorable power in her mind, and it had stayed with her. It wasn't the sort of thing you forgot easily.

And it was the only thing he could think of that might help her understand.

"Back then, we talked about finding the Fair Folk and asking for their help with the hag. Tristan said fairies were the only thing that made the hag nervous," Leo said. "Only Aziza shut it down hard every time. She said it would make things worse if we got fairies involved. I didn't get it back then, because what could be worse than the hag? But now I do. Fairies can control people, too, like the hag did, just . . . different."

"*I'm* a fairy," she said. "Maybe I belong with other fairies. Even if you do think they're monsters."

"I didn't say that."

"You compared them to the hag!"

Her voice was climbing. He kept his low, conscious of the tents nearby. "I'm saying that they're manipulating you. And you don't have to stay here just because you're a fairy."

"If I go back home and Mom can't even look at me, these people are going to be all I have left," Hazel said, her hands clutching the book so tightly they shook.

"That's not true. You'll always have me, and Aziza and Tris—"

"*That's* not true!" Hazel shouted. "I won't always have you. Humans don't live as long as fairies. Even if you lived to be one hundred, I won't even be middle-aged yet when you die. And then what do I do?"

Tears streamed down her face, with that odd, pearly quality that fairy tears had, and the clouded sunlight made them look opaque and milky.

"You have time," Leo said, pleading with her to understand. "I'm not going anywhere yet. You don't need them, you don't have to be so desperate for—"

"Now I'm desperate? *You* try finding out you're a whole different species! Try finding out you're an alien and you have to live on another planet with no mom and dad, or school, or bikes, or pumpkin spice lattes or Benedict Cumberbatch or—"

"That's not what—I just mean you have choices!" He could feel himself losing his temper, but couldn't stop it from happening. It was like the rational part of him was locked up in a box inside his head, cringing and ashamed, while the rest of him raised his voice to match Hazel's. "Don't you get that the whole reason they let me be part of the Hunt is that they thought I'd die, and they got a kick out of it? Isn't that kind of messed up?"

"But you *didn't* die and you didn't have to say yes—"

"If they cared about what was best for you, they'd teach you magic without forcing you to leave your family!"

"You just want to keep pretending that nothing's changed and I can go back to my old life, but I *can't*."

"If they were allowed, your new best friends would get me drunk on lily wine and trick me into signing years of my life away so I could serve them drinks and do god knows what else for them. They'd mess with my memories so I wouldn't even want to go home. They wouldn't think twice about it," he said, remembering the button in his pocket, the blue tent just a stone's throw away, feeling sick to his stomach. "That the kind of magic you want to learn?"

"SHUT UP!" she screamed in his face, which was his second least favorite of her numerous strategies for winning arguments.

"Why can't you listen to me for once?" he said, completely at the end of his rope. If he'd had any doubt Hazel was his sister, it was gone now; she still knew exactly how to push his buttons in the way that only a little sister could.

"If you think fairies are monsters, then that means I am, too," Hazel said, voice hitching as she began to cry, which *was* his least favorite of her strategies for winning arguments.

"I don't think that. That's not what I meant."

He would've been lying if he'd said his voice wasn't a little choked, too. The Summer Court wasn't monstrous because they were fairies; they were monstrous for sending him and his friends into mortal danger on a whim, for pretending they cared about Hazel when really they just felt *possessive* of her, for what they did to their human servants.

"You just want me to be like how I was before," she accused. "You don't care about Hazel-the-fairy, you only care about Hazel-the-fake-human."

"How can you say that? How the hell can you say I don't care?"

He felt like he was losing touch with reality the longer this conversation went on. How could her read on this whole situation be so different from his? Had he stepped into an alternate universe where up was down and left was right? Was he the one who'd lost it?

He couldn't tell if he was more mad or hurt. Everything he'd done for her. Days of nonstop driving. Trying to sleep through the echoes that had mimicked her voice. His deal with the nymphs. The nightmares he'd doubtless be having for a very long time about nearly being run down by Beor's hunting party. Aziza and Tristan—two people he'd give up anything for, do anything to protect, who had already had more than their fair share of near-death experiences, and he'd dragged them into danger for Hazel. And Hazel could accuse him—could even let the thought cross her mind—that he was deliberately trying to hurt her? That he didn't care? How could she say that to him? Had he failed that badly as a brother? Did he suck that much at it?

Sibling fights were like nothing else. You could be raging at each other one minute, shouting at the top of your lungs, and then a few hours later everything was back to normal. Hazel could throw a fit because he'd knocked over her bike or eaten the last waffle and then an hour later fling his door open without knocking, sprawl on his bed, and chatter away at him like nothing had happened. No apologies needed. No point; being siblings pretty much meant you were stuck together. Did that still apply to adopted siblings? He had no clue. He thought it did, probably, but Hazel had a whole other family now, a whole other home, if she wanted it, and maybe she'd never come to him for anything ever again now that she didn't need to.

He wished Mom and Dad were here. Maybe they'd know what to say to her.

"Just go away!" Hazel said.

Numbly, he did.

CHAPTER 26

AZIZA

ON THE ONE-MONTH anniversary of the hag's demise, Leo had insisted on a celebration. He got one of his older coworkers to help him buy beer and vodka; brought home a mountain of individually wrapped cookies from work, a day past their sell-by date and destined for the trash bin if Leo hadn't rescued them; and snuck Aziza into his house after midnight. The three of them had sat in his room, lit some candles, and practically made themselves sick on stale cookies and lukewarm beer and made up drinking games until they were laughing too hard to speak.

She'd never had anything stronger to drink than that. She'd never blacked out. But the morning after the penultimate night of the Midsummer Revels, she had a splitting headache, her mouth tasted sour, her stomach was staging a full-fledged mutiny—she rolled out of bed and stumbled to the bathroom to throw up—and she couldn't remember a damn thing after she took that sip of lily wine.

She washed out her mouth in the basin using the fresh water Sophia must have supplied. Then she took stock of herself. She'd slept on top of the covers. Her clothes were intact. Nothing hurt, and she wasn't bleeding . . . anywhere. Most likely, Tristan had figured out something was wrong through the bond and gotten to her before anything could happen. But it was unsettling not to know for sure.

So this was how Leo felt *all* the time.

She found him and Tristan next door, with trays of human food like the ones Sophia had procured for them yesterday. To Leo's credit, he asked if she was okay at least three times before the loving mockery began.

"I just never thought out of all of us you'd be the first one to get completely wasted," he said, through a grin. "I'm scandalized."

"Please. You've got me beaten in the scandal department. I lost count of all the boys and girls you had hanging off you. You must have broken about a dozen hearts." She picked up a piece of bread, since she didn't think her stomach would tolerate much else, and sat leaning back against the bed. "What did I miss?"

They swapped stories from last night, pooling what they'd learned. It turned out that while Aziza and Leo had been courting scandal, Tristan was the one who'd managed to have the most interesting night out of all of them. They listened in growing horror as he recounted a series of events which began and ended with his usual blatant disregard for his own life and well-being.

"We can't all get our magic lessons from handsome librarians," Tristan said airily.

"You haven't even met him, how do you know if he's *handsome* or not?" she said, pronouncing the word *handsome* like it was the foulest profanity, almost unable to bring herself to repeat it. "And he's not a librarian."

"I know because I have the hounds watch him sometimes," he said.

"What, really? Why?"

"What do you mean *why*? You said he was suspicious."

"He *was*. You put the hounds on him just because I said that?"

"Of course," Tristan said, as if he was confused about why *she* was confused.

She found this admission so moving she could not produce a response. Leo passed her a slice of an orange he'd peeled using Tristan's silver knife—which was fairly disgusting, considering its grisly history, but also not the first time they'd misused it in this way.

"He's derailing us on purpose, and you're falling for it," Leo said, which she already knew, but chose not to say so because such an admission did her no credit. "Tris, I'm still not getting why you thought it was a good idea to go and talk to Beor alone."

"There was no harm done," Tristan insisted. "He's . . . by the book. The Hunt was over, so we weren't enemies anymore. I wasn't in any danger."

But they were all in danger, every second they stayed there. When Sophia had dropped off the food earlier, she'd informed them that Princess Narra hadn't made their precise location in the castle public knowledge, and that they had better stay put and avoid letting any of the Folk stumble upon them alone in some corridor. If someone dragged them into a game with lethally high stakes or tricked them into making a bargain they shouldn't have made, it would be too late for the princess to do anything about it after the fact. They were prisoners in the most lavish of cages, just waiting for sundown.

Maybe an hour after she woke up, Aziza heard something fall over next door, in her room. When she checked, she found the wind sprites; they had tugged open the wardrobe and knocked the heavy gowns off the hangers, as if they thought she might be hiding in there. They carried another message from Anne Sterling.

"*The trap spell didn't work because it was your first try. You were up against an incredibly powerful opponent, and you were using a borrowed story,*" she said. "*To make a trap circle with the strength to subdue someone like the Huntsman, you have to move beyond basic spellwork, and make it your own. The easiest way to do that is to come up with a story yourself, one that's specific to the task at hand.*"

Was this why Meryl had always listened so attentively to Aziza's stories of her encounters with Blackthorn's fae, even sometimes requesting her favorites, in the days when she had pretended to be an ordinary human librarian who didn't believe in magic? Had she, like the pixies, been training Aziza as a hedgewitch, in her own way? Her heart gave a pang at the memory. But Aziza had no gift for storytelling. She was not a talkative person or a particularly imaginative one. Magic, to her, was a tool. A skill. She loved it, but not because it . . . inspired her creatively.

She returned to the other room, the wind sprites following her.

"*Once you escape the Summer Court, come to me straightaway. You need to be trained—you are so far behind where you should be for a hedgewitch your age, just thinking about it gives me a migraine. And one final word of warning. I'm trying to come and get you myself, but I need their permission if I want to do it without insulting King Ilanthus and making the situation worse. The Folk aren't responding to me, which doesn't bode well. Be careful.*"

Leo winced. "As if we needed any more bad news."

Before she could respond, the wind sprites began another message, just like they had last time.

"*I should have known she'd figure it out,*" Dion said. "*I've never been able to get anything past her. I'm not in trouble, so don't worry about that. But if the Hunt is over, does that mean you're on your way back?"* After a pause, he added, with some exasperation, *"And the cloak was for you."*

The sprites often picked up some of the ambient noise, when they captured these messages, so she could tell from the acoustics of Dion's voice that he was in the library, and that he wasn't alone.

She would've told Dion, *Saving Leo is the same thing as saving me,* but firstly, she wasn't going to say that out loud with Leo in the room—he was sentimental on the best of days, and those misty-eyed looks he gave her when she even implied that she cared about him made her feel like she was going to break out in hives—and secondly, if she didn't know who Dion was with, she wasn't going to talk about things that were important to her.

"The cloak did exactly what I needed it to do," she said instead. "No, we're not going back yet. There's a ceremony tonight we have to get through first. What were those voices? The library's never that busy."

The wind sprites took her message and the scent of crushed grapes and slipped away. And then all she could do was wait.

It had been late morning when the boys woke, and afternoon when Aziza joined them, so they had hours to fill. Tristan practiced summoning the spirit he'd manifested yesterday using the antler tip he'd taken from the graveyard. Leo tested out the sword, swinging at air, just to get accustomed to the weight and feel of it; he was no master swordsman, and he was realistic about his dismal chances of successfully defending himself against an actual opponent if it came to that, but at least he wouldn't poke out his own eye with it.

"Maybe we can bribe Beor for sword lessons, too," Aziza said, only half joking.

Leo laughed. "Sure, that'll work. *Hey, sorry I stole your weapon and your title and almost left you in the middle of nowhere to die. Mind giving me a few pointers now?"*

"We'll need all the wine we can carry," Tristan said.

When a *whoosh* of air signaled that they were in the company of the wind sprites again, all conversation ceased; Tristan banished his spirit and Leo lowered the sword.

Dion's voice slipped into the room: *"It's not busy. A friend of mine is here. And . . . Anne, too. I'm glad the cloak came in handy, though I'm surprised to hear you mention your covenmates. It occurs to me that you've said almost nothing about them."*

A sense of unease stirred in her.

She could picture the look on his face when he said, *"It occurs to me . . ."* in that stilted way of his. Until the night before last, when he had arranged a lesson in witchcraft for her, she had not paid any particular attention to what Dion looked like, no matter what Tristan thought. They'd known each other for a few months, but she'd never spent more than ten or fifteen minutes at a time with him, and when she did, the thing she noticed most about his appearance was the arrogant lift of his chin and the superior smirk he wore when he got a rise out of her.

She had been blissfully unaware of the fact that, when he was working through a problem or racking his brain for a half-remembered scrap of information, he'd raise a hand as if to run it through his hair, and then stop, not wanting to mess it up even in his sleep. And when he was talking about something that interested him, he'd pick up a pen just to keep his hands occupied, tapping at the page when he wanted to draw her attention to a particular line—forgetting that, in the dream, she couldn't see the words—and otherwise twirling it expertly between his fingers. She'd watched avidly, waiting for him to drop it, and he never had. She'd told herself that because it was a dream, ballpoint pen physics abided by his rules. And if you talked to him while he was reading, he'd start to respond before he looked up from the page, and eye contact would come a few beats later. Despite herself, when she was supposed to be studying spellwork, she had studied Dion, too, and had learned more than she had bargained for.

It was only against her will that she knew that when Dion's voice sounded like this, it meant his eyes had gone their coldest shade of gray, and he was holding something back.

"There's not much to say. I guess I've been a little too distracted for introductions," she said, as if she hadn't noticed anything was wrong. "What's Anne doing there?"

After the pains Dion had taken to keep his presence in Blackthorn a secret—and the fact he'd bribed his way into a job that wasn't his— he was being shockingly cavalier about the fact that his plans had gone up in smoke. Maybe he didn't want her to feel guilty about her role in that. Or maybe he no longer needed secrecy because he had the answers he had been looking for.

She could hardly sit still waiting for the sprites to return; their exchanges were quicker now that she was back on the East Coast, but it still took anywhere from thirty minutes to two hours.

"As soon as she learned there was an untrained hedgewitch here, she wanted to check over your handiwork. She said your work on the boundaries is surprisingly tight, and that the local fae are loyal to you, in their own way. She had to pay three times her usual bargaining rates to get anything out of them, and even then they talked her in circles half the time. I haven't seen her this aggravated in a while. But they said something strange to her, the fae. They called your coven hag-slayers. Aziza, what does that mean?"

Arguments were meant to be fast—they were meant to have a

momentum that left no room for agonizing over your words until after all was said and done. The ensuing argument between her and Dion stretched over hours, maddening, her teeth on edge the whole time, unable to eat when Sophia came in again to bring them the last meal they'd have before their final night of reveling, unable to face Leo's and Tristan's worried gazes as they reluctantly bore witness to this slow-motion disaster.

"There was a hag in the woods near St. Sithney's," she told Dion. "We killed it. The borderland fae were grateful. What does that have to do with anything?"

"*It has everything to do with everything, and I suspect you know that,*" he said, and now he sounded bitter. "*Why would you . . . What are you hiding? Who are you protecting?*"

She was cornered. In concealing the fact that there had been a hag in Blackthorn during the same period of time Emil had disappeared, she had given herself away. Dion knew that she knew Emil had met his demise in the hag's clearing.

It was only a few hours until sunset. They wouldn't have time for many more exchanges before she had to leave for the revel.

"If Emil ran into the hag, then he's gone. I'm trying to protect the living," she said, and, too late, heard how harsh it sounded. "I'm sorry. I never met him myself. I never saw him. I . . . I was hoping it wasn't true."

"*Tell me about your covenmates.*"

"Tell me why it matters," she snapped.

"*Because you knew from the start! Emil is dead, and I don't even have a body to bury. You let me go on looking. You made a deal with me on false pretenses to save your own skin. Don't pretend it doesn't matter!*"

"I told you I'm sorry," she said. "I have nothing else to say."

"*I do, though. Emil's blækhounds are still in Blackthorn even though he* and the hag are both dead, which means they must belong to someone else now. If what I suspect is true, you and your coven have been dabbling in black magic of the worst kind. And should the necromancers who considered Emil a trusted colleague catch wind of it? They're an old guard, and they won't let this slide. There will be consequences for what you've done. They'll make sure of it."

She had never heard Dion sound so furious. Nothing like the person who had taught her spells in a dream the other night; not even like the aloof librarian she'd met three months ago. She had wanted to get under his skin, and it looked like she'd finally succeeded. It was not as satisfying as she'd once thought it would be. Anger rose in her to match his, and she let it, comforting in its familiarity.

"Is that supposed to be a threat?" she said. "Be mad at me—fine, I've earned that. No one else has."

"Obviously I'm mad! You lied to my face so I wouldn't find out that the man who raised me was brutally murdered. God, why am I arguing with you? Maybe I should wash my hands of this. Let someone else deal with you."

"Do it, then!" she snarled.

As the wind sprites soared away, they left behind a ringing silence. She glared at the wall, her mind blank, and probably could've sat there for hours just fuming to herself if Leo hadn't come over to put an arm around her shoulders.

"You okay?" he asked.

"Yes."

"I don't think he meant that."

"Who cares if he meant it? Who cares what Dion thinks?"

Tristan gave her a look that said, very plainly, *You and I both know who cares.*

"No one cares! Fuck him!" Leo said, loyally.

She sighed. "This is my fault. I never should have talked to him."

"Nah. We wouldn't have gotten through the Hunt without his help."

"I can still tell him the truth," Tristan offered.

"Why bother? Since he thinks he's got it all figured out already."

"Forget it," Leo said. "Both of you. Let's get through tonight first, and then we'll worry about Dion."

She nodded. Tonight first, and then they would deal with whatever waited for them back home.

CHAPTER 27

LEO

By the time the last night of the Midsummer Revels began, King Ilanthus was awake. He had risen from the casket sometime during the day, the resin surface dissolving and the sleeping enchantment with it; then the casket had reshaped itself into a throne of woven birch and briar vines. His advisors fluttered around him, updating him on what he had missed in his seven-month absence. Sophia led a battalion of servants in the charge to comb and braid his hair, bring him water, replace his outer robe and mantle with a new one in a cobalt blue that shone almost metallic when its folds caught the light. The Gallowglass stood watch over him as he recovered his strength; Viren knelt to deliver a report on their behalf, which—Leo gathered, based on the comments he overheard—would have been Prince Tal's job, only Prince Tal hadn't been seen since last night. What seemed the entire Summer Court took turns going up to the king, wishing him well, giving thanks, and kissing his hands.

From across the room, the king met Leo's gaze, as if he'd felt it. His eyes were like Narra's and Tal's—long lashed and dark and somber, with a smear of topaz in their depths.

The elixir of renewal had to be consumed after midnight and before sunrise; Leo wouldn't speak to the king until then. In the meantime, the Summer Court indulged in a final night of dancing and drinking. The moon was degrees away from being full, drooping heavily in the sky, large and close. The lesser fairies got into the wine, tipping over bottles and lapping up what they spilled like butterflies sipping nectar, or landing on the rims of people's glasses and stealing a few drops until they were shooed away. Something was being smoked—he didn't know what, but it tasted like pepper and cloves on the air; he stayed away from places where the smoke was thickest, wary of the glint of eyes half-obscured by tendrils of spiced haze.

Tristan had promised to stay close this time, but the crowd had pulled them apart in seconds. Aziza was gathering intel from the wild fae. And Leo—

"Am I boring you, Huntsman?" his dance partner said, sounding more amused than offended.

"N-no," Leo stuttered. "I'm sorry, I . . ."

The boy smiled, as if Leo was more pleasing to him this way, absentminded and clumsy, than if he'd been better able to live up to his questionably won title. He had lapis lazuli eyes and translucent, fan-shaped insect wings that he kept folded down his back like an iridescent cape.

"There is no shortage of distraction here," the boy said agreeably, as if to give Leo an out. "Though I must admit I was led to believe your disposition was a little more . . . steadfast. You danced with my cousin yesterday, you know. She wears a necklace made of human wishes. Give her your wish, be her lover for three years, then take the wish back, and it is certain to come true. But she couldn't even persuade you to tell her how you took your tea, let alone what you wished for. She spent the rest of the night pouting."

"Why do they want to . . ." Leo said. "I mean, why do any of them care if I drink their wine or . . . Why are any of them interested in me? Don't know if you noticed, but there's nothing special about me. I'm here pretty much by accident. Compared to all of you, I'm boring. What am I missing?"

"Does a human need a reason to be interested in a sparrow?" the boy said. "It's enough for a creature to be charming, to sing prettily, and to look good in a cage."

Leo didn't know what he'd expected. Of course he was nothing but a pet to them, a bit of entertainment.

Why had he agreed to all this in the first place? Was it only for Hazel's sake?

Or was it that he thought he had something to prove?

He'd needed to make up for the fact that it was, at least in part, *his* fault that Hazel was in this situation; he was the reason she'd been discovered after all these years. Unconsciously, maybe he had been trying to redeem himself as much as he'd been trying to protect her. He had needed to believe that he could stand up to the forces that were responsible for his curse—even if the enchantress herself was long gone. He had already lost so much to the Fair Folk; if he lost Hazel, too, then how could he ever hope to beat the curse? And he wanted to be able to measure up to his powerful, magical friends. To prove he wasn't the weakest link. Maybe he'd been insecure, desperate to do something, to fight back, to show that he wasn't helpless.

Maybe Hazel had just been his excuse. But was he saving Hazel, or just making things worse for her?

Shame made him cold and hot at the same time, ice in his chest and a dizzy flush on his skin that he hoped his dance partner read as a sign of exertion. He didn't want him to know how—how vulnerable and weak he felt.

Pull it together, he told himself.

The boy gave Leo a parting kiss on the cheek before they changed partners; the next was a Gallowglass, her armor waxy-smooth to the touch. Under her helmet—which was sculpted carefully close to her skull, its plates cupping the nape of her neck and wrapping around her jaw—her lips were a vampiric red that appeared to be their natural color.

"Off duty?" Leo asked her.

"Not quite," she said. "But we believe duty and pleasure are not mutually exclusive. Viren asked us to keep an eye on you, and it's my turn. Lucky me."

"Viren, huh?" he said. "So he's in charge tonight? Where's the prince?"

"They say he's caught in an impossible task, but I have my doubts. He's clever enough to have worked his way out of that snare by now. Perhaps he is otherwise indisposed." There was something suggestive in how she said that. He ignored it. With every spin, he caught sight of the king like a monument in his throne; it was as if, in waking, he had reoriented the gravity of the ballroom, and everything in it had a subtle pull to him.

"And what about Princess Narra?" he asked. "I haven't seen her around, either."

It was important that he speak to Narra before it was time for him to meet King Ilanthus. He needed to know what would happen if the king didn't want to honor the agreement she had made with him, or . . . if Hazel chose to stay.

Because maybe what mattered most wasn't saving Hazel or bringing her home. Maybe it was about making sure she had a place to
belong.

With or without him.

But the Gallowglass said, "Princess Narra's whereabouts are
hardly your business. Already she has indulged you with far more
of her attention than you deserve."

He pushed, but she sidestepped his questions easily, and he gave
up. But, the more he looked around, the more uneasy he felt. He
really couldn't see Narra anywhere, even when he began to search
for her in earnest. None of his dance partners had seen her. He
crashed into Aziza once—both of them frazzled and winded and
utterly relieved to see each other. They spun unsteadily in place,
less dancing and more trying not to collide with the people around
them. She hadn't seen Narra, either, and she'd gotten nothing of
use from the pixies, only a confirmation that there was no one
here from the Winter Court that wasn't already accounted for as
a political representative or an invited guest, plus a few ambassadors and allies from other courts. When the song changed, instead
of accepting new partners, they both fought through the crowd and
made it to the edge of the ballroom. She went to talk to the water
sprites in the creek, and he zeroed in on the servants. He went to
Sophia first, but she brushed him off before he could say more than
a couple of words to her. Then he caught sight of another familiar
face—the girl from yesterday that he'd seen with Evan. Her brown
hair was slipping out of its loose ponytail, her cheeks flushed as if
she'd been running around. He tapped her on the shoulder, and
she startled.

"Hi," he said. "Are you May?"

She looked nervous. "Y-yes. How did you know?"

"I met Evan and he mentioned you," Leo said, giving her his most reassuring smile. "I was wondering if you've seen Princess Narra around?"

She shook her head. "No one has. Sophia is . . ." Then she stopped. "Sorry, I shouldn't—"

"It's okay," Leo said. He inched closer, dropping his voice. "It's just, I'm supposed to be doing this . . . ceremony later, and I don't even know . . . what to do, where to stand, what to say. Narra helped me out yesterday, so I was hoping she'd tell me what to expect today, too. Before I embarrass myself in front of the king."

May smiled back, a little tremulous. "Well . . . Sophia's been on a warpath because no one can find the royal siblings. So I can't help you."

"Oh." That made Leo uneasy. "Listen, if you see Evan . . . stick with him, okay? I've got a bad feeling something's going to happen tonight."

She nodded slowly. "I will."

Movement to his right caught his eye—someone with a familiar gait, passing by—and he instinctively stepped in front of May to block her from view. It was Viren. Leo kept his eyes on him as he walked away.

"Thank you," May said under her breath. "He . . . he has been very intense lately. More so than usual. It's . . . frightening."

"He has?" Leo said.

"He's been—rough with us. When he asks for company, he doesn't usually leave any bruises, but lately it's like—he's been—restless, tense, and he's taking it out on us."

"And you're sure he's not just an asshole?" Leo asked.

She nodded. "There are things you can only tell from touch."

"I guess so," he said. "Hey, if you want, you could go back up to the castle and take a breather. Use me as an excuse if you need to. Tell Sophia I asked you to get something for me, or whatever. I'll back up anything you say. I'm your get-out-of-jail-free card tonight."

She laughed. "I might take you up on that. Thank you."

As soon as he left her, he went after Viren.

It was getting late by now, maybe an hour to midnight. Viren had been moving with purpose; maybe he was finally going to find Tal, and if he wasn't, then Leo wanted to see what he was up to. He had disappeared into a passage in the trees, which turned out to contain a staircase. Leo didn't think he was that far behind, but he couldn't see him anymore, or hear his footsteps. Light seeped in through the cracks in the lacework of the walls, so that it was as if he walked through webs of shadow. When he got to the top, Viren was nowhere to be found.

There was a balcony; unlike the one they'd found Aziza on yesterday, which had faced the woods, this one overlooked the ballroom and had a view of the castle. If he looked at it too long, it gave him that wobbly, unfocused feeling he'd had at the bonfire party when he hadn't been sure of what he was seeing. He stared at it hard, its spires, the way the moonlight almost overpowered it, as if its light were cumbersome and the castle something delicate, gossamer or dew. But Leo couldn't see through its illusions. He looked down at the ballroom instead, his eyes drawn to the king, and his heart skipped a beat when he saw that Ephira and Vetiver had brought Hazel up to him. She gave an awkward curtsy.

The sense of foreboding he'd been fighting all night congealed into something hard and immobilizing. If he couldn't find Narra, Tal, or

Viren, then he needed to round up Aziza and Tristan and Hazel. They had to stick together. As he turned to go, the archway over the staircase rippled, and a face surfaced in the grain of the wood, watching him.

"It's not time yet," he said, touching the flask tied to his belt.

"No," the nymph agreed. "But it will be, soon. You must cooperate when we come for you. Fighting us will make it worse. I warn you as a courtesy."

The fae didn't do courtesy calls. What did she really want?

"I won't fight," he said. "Thank you for the warning."

He stepped under the arch and made his way down the stairs, feeling her tree-sap eyes on his back as he retreated. He didn't have time to worry about the nymphs right now. In the ballroom, though, the revel swallowed him again; fighting through the crowd to reach the throne was just about impossible.

Someone stumbled into him. His body knew it was Tristan before his mind did, and he caught him by the shoulders, relief sweeping through him.

"Sorry," Tristan said breathlessly. "I was trying to get to Hazel, but you looked a little lost, and—"

He shook his head, amused. "I was looking for you."

Someone knocked into Tristan from behind, and Tristan pitched into him. He threw an arm over Leo's shoulder for balance, his fingers glancing off the back of Leo's neck, and that minuscule touch felt like a live wire pumping pure electricity into his veins. It seemed impossible that it wouldn't leave a mark; he expected to pull his collar down and find a brand there later. Leo's arm went around him instinctively, steadying him, so that they must have looked like any other pair of dancers. Tristan's other hand slipped into his—scar tissue and calluses. The night they'd hidden in the hollow tree flashed through his mind, and how badly he'd wanted to slide his hand over Tristan's again this morning; to have that touch given to him so easily now made him feel as drunk as if he'd downed a whole bottle of lily wine.

"When the song ends, we should . . ." Leo looked up, through a gap in the crowd. Hazel was still at the throne, and the king had taken one of her hands in both of his. He was saying something to her that Leo had no hope of hearing from this distance. But his expression was fond and indulgent. For the first time since Leo had caught that glimpse of him in the casket, King Ilanthus just looked like a person, and not like some sort of untouchable deity. Then the crowd shifted, and he couldn't see her anymore.

"She's all right," Tristan said. "The hounds are keeping an eye on her."

Leo would've responded, but he made the mistake of looking back at Tristan and promptly forgot what he meant to say. Tristan had this one smile that started in his eyes, like a light had come on, but it didn't touch his lips unless you coaxed it out. Sometimes it would sit there for an entire morning, just out of reach. Leo took it as a personal challenge; he'd say whatever he needed to say or do whatever he needed to do for a glimpse of it. If all else failed, it responded to touch nine times out of ten. Leo would nudge his shoulder on his way past him in the kitchen or lean in close to show him something on his phone, and then he'd look over and it would be there, slight and secretive at the corner of Tristan's mouth, gone again in a flash. Every time, Leo had to fight the urge to chase after it, press his mouth against Tristan's, as if to say *come back here* or *don't go*. And he knew he was in trouble now, because those translucent green eyes had gone bright and clear in the way that meant that elusive, favorite smile of his was close. Without thinking, Leo ran his palm down Tristan's spine, and Tristan shivered, a full-body shiver that Leo felt everywhere.

They were, at this point, barely moving. Surrounded by people, knowing full well how he stood out in his cloak and his ridiculous getup, he still felt anonymous, like he could do anything and get away with it. A dangerous, unrestrained feeling. He was intensely aware of all the places where they were connected—their joined hands, their chests flush, their knees knocking together—and aware of how fast his heart was beating. Everything that wasn't Tristan blurred to insignificance around him. They were much closer than they needed to be, even closer than demanded by the claustrophobic crowd, and Leo was pretty sure he was the one who had pulled Tristan in. Tristan had relaxed into his arms, waiting for Leo to close the distance or widen it. Demanding nothing. Giving over control to Leo. But Leo didn't feel in control at all as he tipped closer to Tristan, felt Tristan exhale, his breath ghosting over Leo's mouth.

And then—and this almost convinced him that he was asleep, the abruptness with which a dream mutated into a nightmare—someone screamed.

Heartrending, grief-stricken screams. Wailing. The crowd juddered as if the earth had trembled underfoot; he and Tristan looked at each other, immobilized with shock, and then they were turning with the rest to try and find the source of the disturbance. More screams—some were running away, others were pressing nearer. Tristan took his hand and tugged him through the crowd, with that way he had of sliding shadowlike through spaces where he should not have been able to fit. The screaming had started at the far end of the ballroom, near the throne, where he'd last seen Hazel. He couldn't see her anymore; he didn't even know where to start looking through all the chaos.

The crowd shifted, and Leo glimpsed the epicenter of the disaster, the place where the nightmare began. A body on the floor, lying in a slowly spreading pool of blood, three silver-tipped arrows sticking out of his torso.

King Ilanthus was dead.

CHAPTER 28

TRISTAN

He had the benefit of extra eyes and ears as he and Leo were caught in what was fast becoming a stampede. The hounds climbed the highest branches of the forest canopy. Through them, he saw, too late, a balcony above the throne concealed by a curtain of jasmine, where the Gallowglass with the spider-fang helmet was slinging a bow over his shoulders, hefting a quiver of arrows, and hurrying away down a passage.

The hound chased him, but there must have been a hidden exit somewhere. He was gone in the instant it took the hound to slide through the shadows to the place where he'd been.

"Tris!" Leo said, practically shouting to be heard over the din. The crowd jostled them. Even the winged fairies, attempting to take flight, collided and quickly touched down again, causing a ripple effect of people stumbling and shoving into each other. "Can you see anything?"

"Viren did this," Tristan said.

"What? You're sure?"

From a lower vantage point, another hound watched Hazel. She was frozen in terror. The king's blood stained her dainty white slippers. A Gallowglass with a collar like a spiny frill knocked her aside to get to the body; she almost fell, but her wings saved her, lifting her into the air. But some of the Gallowglass were in the air, too, racing to the king's side, and Hazel dodged them clumsily, like a dragonfly being buffeted by a flock of ravens.

Last, from high up and far away, he saw himself and Leo. Leo had hooked his arm around Tristan's as he fought to get to Hazel. When the Folk made contact with the silver cloak on the bare skin of their hands or arms, they leapt back, shouting in pain, causing shockwaves of disturbance around them, but as soon as one person moved away, there was someone else to take their place.

He extracted himself from the hounds' minds, and it was like surfacing from deep water; the noise of the crowd dialed up to one hundred. The iron tang of blood overpowered the scents he'd grown to expect from the revel—perfume, alcohol, the cloying sweetness of fae magic. He dug in his heels, bringing himself and Leo to a halt.

"We need to find Aziza and get out of here," he said.

"But Hazel—"

"I'll get her."

When he called the scarred hound, it climbed out from his shadow, forcing people to spring away and clearing a space around them. It was shapeless at first, a rising tide of darkness with the beginnings of a snout and the gleam of wolfish eyes, until at full height it towered over them like a reaper, reeking of sulfur and emitting its hellish heat. Tristan took its snout in a firm grip and looked it in the eye.

"Get Leo through this," he told it, "and maybe I really will call you Lucky."

There was no time for a goodbye; it was like they were being ripped apart by storm-tossed seas. And while his every instinct told him to stay with Leo, there were certain facts that trumped his instincts. Facts like how Hazel needed him more than Leo did right now. And how he could be certain that Leo wanted Hazel to be safe more than he wanted absolutely anything else. And how Tristan had gained enough of the hounds' agility and quickness that he could slip through gaps in the crowd in ways that Leo could not. And how, when he shouted Hazel's name and held out his hand—like he had once before, in the woods at St. Sithney's—this time, Hazel would take it without question. Because whatever had happened between her and Leo earlier, and whatever she did or didn't want to do after all this was over, she still trusted Leo and the people closest to him to take care of her when it counted.

She practically fell out of the air and into his arms. He carried her to the edge of the ballroom—her arms in a stranglehold around his neck, her face wet against his collar—and only released her once they'd escaped into the cool, dark peace of the birch wood.

"Are you hurt?" he asked.

She shook her head, unable to speak through her tears.

The crowd had flowed in the direction of the castle, so he took Hazel the other way, deeper into the woods. The hound would help Leo find Aziza, and then lead them both back to Tristan. In the meantime, Tristan needed to find a safe place for them to meet. He didn't know what was going on, but common sense said that Viren wasn't acting alone.

He took Hazel's hand. Her slim green fingers curled weakly around his, her footsteps stumbling and hesitant as she sniffled quietly. Half his attention was on the-hound-that-wasn't-Lucky-yet, as it guided Leo through the crowd, matching his slow human pace, impatient but knowing its summoner would be livid if it left Leo's side. It nudged Leo in the direction where—because of Tristan's bond to Aziza—it knew they'd find her.

There was going to be bloodshed. Whatever happened next, they needed to be out of the way.

With no time to dawdle, he made a split-second decision. They'd go to the graveyard. Even to him, an outsider, it had felt like a sacred place. The Folk would leave it alone. He hoped. He hesitated to take Hazel there, but she had seen death already tonight. There was no shielding her from it. He had to trust that she could handle this, too.

Hazel spoke then, as if she'd heard her name in his thoughts.

"Where's Leo?" she asked. Her wings were folded flat against her back. She wasn't crying anymore, but her eyes were still shiny and swollen.

"Meeting up with Aziza," he said. "I told him I'd look out for you until they got here."

Every other time disaster had struck, he had run *toward* Leo, and that had always been the easy choice even when it was also the most dangerous one. This time, he was fleeing to safety, and it was unbearable. All he wanted was to undo it. Retrace his steps. Take Leo's hand back. But he couldn't, because *this* was what Leo needed from him right now.

Hazel's lip trembled. "We had a fight this morning. I yelled at him."

"I know. It's all right."

"No," Hazel said, and she rubbed furiously at her eyes with the hand that wasn't clinging to Tristan's, as if to hold back a fresh wave of tears. "He wanted me to go back home, and I want to, but I also don't want to? I feel like I belong here more than I ever did in the human world. But I keep saying the wrong thing and sometimes I can't even tell if my friends like me or not, and then the king was so nice to me but someone killed him? Why would they do that? And . . . what if something happens to Leo now? And I don't get to talk to him again?"

Her hair had come loose from the complicated knot someone had done for her, so that glossy green-black strands of it stuck to her wet face and tangled around the points of her ears.

"Siblings fight. Leo knows you didn't mean it. I promise he didn't mean to hurt your feelings, either." He almost said, *Don't worry about Leo*, but it would've made him a hypocrite. Tentatively, he asked, "Did the king say anything to you?"

It was a long shot, but she was the last person he'd ever talked to. Maybe he'd told her something useful.

"He said I look like my mom," she said morosely. "Lady Thula, I mean. Everyone says that."

Moonlight flooded the grove of the dead. Primroses dotted its beds of clover, joyful and irreverent where they crowned the resting bones with color. There was a macabre beauty to this place that struck him as almost mocking now.

He took Hazel far from the path, to where the grove was older and the remains almost undetectable.

"Hide up there, in the branches," he said.

"What about you?" she asked.

"I'm going to keep watch. I'll send a hound to keep you company."

He gave her a parting hug, and she sniffled against his collar. Although she could've crushed him with that fairy strength of hers, she felt tiny and delicate in his arms, her wings fluttering so lightly it was as if they were made of glitter. She released him and darted into the air, disappearing into the canopy.

He summoned another hound and held its jaw in both hands, looking it in the eye, like he'd done with the other. He couldn't risk any disobedience tonight.

"Your name is Lupa," he said.

It understood; he barely even had to think his next command. It loped up the side of the tree—its paws were wider than the trunk, but it moved with the liquid lightness all the hounds shared, and soon he couldn't see it anymore. Then Hazel's green fairy scent was in its nose, and it was half shadow where it melted into papery peeling bark and half flesh where Hazel's fingers clutched at its fur. The leaves enveloped them completely, murmuring into the hound's pricked ears.

Satisfied that Hazel was as safe as she could be, he withdrew from Lupa's mind. At his feet lay a skull and two fan-shaped patches of moss that might have been wings once. Something shiny was nestled between them. He scooped it up; it was a necklace of glass beads crusted with dirt. The spirit attached to it felt so close that if Tristan had closed his eyes, he could've believed they were here, standing over his shoulder. This necklace had meant something to the person it had belonged to. He hesitated only briefly before he tucked it into his pocket, with a silent promise to take good care of it until he could bring it back.

Methodically, he retraced his steps, weaving his way through the graveyard and picking up pieces as he went. A finger bone here, a scrap of wing there. The tip of a horn or antler, a handful of grave dirt where an organ or a muscle had dissolved into the earth.

It was just in case. That was what he told himself. He wanted to be ready for anything.

Tris, Leo said.

Tristan ripped his hand out of someone's rib cage and was on his feet, searching for a familiar mop of curls, almost before he understood what he was reacting to. But he was alone.

Of course. Leo wasn't here—he was speaking to the hound. He stood beside the darkly glinting waters of a creek, the silver cloak radiant in the moonlight, Aziza visible over his shoulder a few feet away. He had this look of stubborn, determined hope that put an answering glow in Tristan's chest—though he knew, with a sinking certainty, that he was not going to like what Leo had to say.

And he didn't.

They weren't coming to meet up with him after all, Leo said. At least not yet. True to form, he and Aziza had elected to walk *into* danger, not away from it.

Part of him had expected this. There was nothing else for it; he would have to go after them while Lupa stayed with Hazel. But before he could make another move, the soft padding sound of footsteps made him freeze. That hadn't come from the hound's end of the bond. Someone was here, coming off the narrow, overgrown path that led up to the castle, into the moonlight where Tristan could see him. Fire-fleck eyes and broad shoulders clad in furs and leather; a pair of hounds that weren't Tristan's. It was Beor.

Tristan's breath escaped him in a hard, relieved exhale.

"What are you doing here?" Tristan asked. "Can you tell me what's going on?"

Beor drew nearer, his expression inscrutable. "I cannot."

And Tristan had a bad feeling that the Beor who had taught him about drawing out spirits and naming hounds was gone, and this Beor was the Huntsman, and they were again, somehow, on opposite sides.

CHAPTER 29

AZIZA

SHE STAYED AT the revel long enough to steal a couple of bottles of lily wine, figuring Tristan had had the right idea yesterday, and then she went in search of the creek Leo had told her about. The creek flowed into a pond, its banks lush with emerald ferns and clusters of purple flowers. A band of nixies lounged there, two of them in the water with their hair floating on the surface among the water lilies, two more of them on land, playing their own instruments in harmony with the music from the revel.

"Have you seen Prince Talarix tonight?" she asked warily, once they'd accepted the wine. She had little experience with nixies. They didn't tend to turn up around Blackthorn, steering clear of coastal towns on account of a long-standing feud with the sirens, their mortal enemies. Some kind of musical rivalry, apparently.

"No, but he was in a rage, we heard," one of them said. She was nude, though her long blue-black hair protected her modesty, cascading down her body and trailing into the water. Her delicate fingers strummed at a string instrument that could have been a distant cousin of the violin. "Something to do with a *brazen little witch who has no idea what's coming for her*—what on earth did you do to him?"

"He did it to himself," Aziza said, to peals of melodious laughter.

"Poor thing," said one of them, taking a drink and then passing the bottle to the nixie boy with long white hair submerged up to his eyes in the pond. "Perhaps he'll let us comfort him."

"Sure, poor Prince Talarix," Aziza said, unable to help herself. "He has it so rough, being royalty and wanting for nothing."

They burst into giggles. Air bubbles floated up around the nixie boy's head.

"Of course you wouldn't understand," one of them said.

"No one understands him like we do," said another.

"He used to come to us all the time, but we never see him now that he's Captain," the first one said, pouting. "I suppose he doesn't need us anymore."

"Maybe the Gallowglass comfort him."

"Maybe the servants do."

"Help me understand, then," Aziza said.

"They say he has three mothers," the first nixie said. "The mother who birthed him, the aunt who raised him, and Lady Death, who watches over him."

"Death stole away his other mothers so that she might have him to herself," another of the nixies chimed in. "She follows him into battle and shields him from his enemies. But she always calls her favored children home too soon."

"How soon?" Aziza said. "I think someone has plans to interfere with the solstice ceremony, and no one's seen either Talarix or Narra in hours. Are they in danger?"

"If there are plans, they're well hidden."

"And no one would tell us, anyway."

"Tell the prince to pay us a visit, would you?"

"Sure, if I could find him." Aziza was reconsidering her decision to pay them in wine after all. The bottles were nearly empty already and they were falling over themselves drunk. "Which, like I said, I can't."

"Oh, but you'll see him soon, I think," the first nixie said, smiling wide behind her curtain of wet, dark hair. "Shouldn't have made him angry. He takes after his mother. You can never hide from him."

Aziza didn't have time to dwell on superstitions or dire warnings. The pixies and water sprites had nothing useful to tell her, either. She wished she could say that she asked the right questions, but it felt like she was trying to solve a puzzle with the pieces facedown. Her mind strayed back to Dion, who probably *could* have solved a puzzle without looking. He'd sit there painstakingly sorting through every piece until he'd come up with the solution, his skilled, careful fingers feeling out the edges, his brow furrowed in concentration, endlessly patient and determined.

Was he, too, a favored child of Lady Death?

He'd lost his family and then he'd lost Emil. Emil, who had been her parents' covenmate. Who had stayed with Aziza when they'd gone to fight the hag. Who would've taken her in if Jiddo hadn't come back. Emil had almost been her *father*. It was bizarre to think about that—she hated to even imagine a version of her life without Jiddo there—but the fact remained that Emil had been willing, and Leila had trusted him. And Aziza had shown no regard for his memory.

She wanted to see Meryl, whose presence was cool water on a sweltering day, an instant dose of clarity and calm. Aziza missed her more sharply than ever now. She wanted to go back in time and stop herself from ever speaking to Dion. She wanted to have meant it when she'd said, *Do it, then*, so coldly, as if nothing he did or said mattered to her.

She stayed kneeling in the mud in her too-long borrowed dress after the sprites had wandered away, scrubbing her good hand over her face in mounting frustration.

Think, she told herself. *What are you missing?*

That was when the screaming began.

"You don't want to leave yet," she said. In the half hour since the Midsummer Revels had dissolved into chaos, she'd found Leo, gotten caught up on what she'd missed, started following the hound back to Tristan, realized Leo was dragging his feet, and stopped them again. She knew what he was thinking the moment she saw the look on his face. "You want to take the elixir to Narra."

"The Hunt's technically not over until I do," he said. "And the servants are stuck here—we can't leave without making sure they're going to be all right."

They had stayed off the path as they'd ventured back in the direction of the ballroom, letting the woods conceal them. Judging by the urgent pitch of the voices coming from the encampment, the Summer Court was preparing to either fight or flee. They were completely out of their depth here, and as much as she wanted to help, staying in Elphame any longer was not a decision she could justify, rationalize, or defend to anyone with half an ounce of common sense. She opened her mouth to tell Leo exactly that.

Leo gave her a look that was equal parts guilty and hopeful. Her resolve crumbled like stale bread.

"We won't be able to find her," she said, which sounded like an argument but wasn't one.

"Sophia will know. All we have to do is find one of the servants,"

Leo said, which sounded like a counterargument, but was actually a thank-you.

"All right," she said. "I guess this means we have to get back into the castle."

The ensuing silence was oddly heavy. Leo rested a hand on the hound's neck, absently, and its fur made a soft *shush* sound as his fingers mussed it. It had been so easy to read him just a minute ago, but he suddenly couldn't meet her eyes, and she didn't have a clue as to why.

"Zee, I know we said no apologies," he began, "but I—"

"Don't even," she said.

"I know, I know, it's just—"

"I don't want to hear it."

The noise he made couldn't be called a laugh; it was strained and unhappy, almost painful to hear. "I just don't want to be the weak link."

"The . . . what?" she said.

"The—the token civilian friend with no magic powers who doesn't do anything but get in the way!" he said, running a hand through his hair to push his tangled curls out of his face, to little effect. "You and Tristan walked into the hag's territory to save me. Months later, you're still dealing with my problems. I don't want to be someone who makes things worse for you."

She was speechless. Tristan would know what to say right now, and it would probably be more tactful than, *That's the most ridiculous thing that's ever come out of your mouth, which is really saying something.* But he wasn't here, so Aziza was going to have to rise to the occasion.

"You think that's what we think?" she managed.

"No, but . . . maybe you should," he said. "I wanted to be better than that, for you and Tris. I don't want to be someone that other people can use against you. Again."

"Leo," she said, choosing her words carefully. This was difficult. Back on the road, Tristan had said, *I don't have anything but the two of you,* and she had just barely managed to return the sentiment because Tristan had already done the hard work of putting it into words. To do it herself was a feat she wasn't sure she was capable of; she floundered, and what came out of her mouth in the end was, "I'm . . . really angry with Dion."

"Um—what?" he said, bewildered, as if he had braced himself for any number of responses, but had failed to anticipate this one.

"Because of you."

"*What?*"

"I mean," she said, warming to this line of reasoning, "I did a good job of being an antisocial recluse who didn't even know the names of my classmates until I met you. Now here I am, giving a damn about the opinions of people who are practically strangers, and it never would have happened if I didn't start by giving a damn about you. It's annoying, but also an improvement, I think, even if it doesn't always feel like it."

Leo's nose scrunched a little as he translated that. And then a slow smile spread over his face. "You're saying I'm your best friend, and you love me, and you've learned how to let other people in because of me? I'm gonna cry."

She didn't know if he meant that literally, because she was no longer making eye contact with him.

"If you ever say you think you make things worse for us," she said, "I'm telling Tristan. Just imagine the look on his face."

"Point taken," he said. "Okay. Speaking of Tristan—" He turned to the hound, letting the conversation end there, which was proof he really *was* her best friend. "Hey, can you get his attention? He needs to hear this."

The hound made a faintly derisive *whuff* noise. But it bent its head obligingly so that Leo could look into its eyes.

"Tris," he said. "Listen, I know we were supposed to find each other and get away from here. But we can't do that until I've given the elixir of renewal to Narra. Otherwise the entire Summer Court goes down in flames. So . . . we're going to look for Sophia, and hopefully she can tell us where Narra is. Can you stay with Hazel? And, uh . . . be careful." He swallowed hard, as if he wanted to say something else, but thought better of it. Instead, he turned to Aziza. "Ready?"

"Since when do you have to ask?" she said.

Together, they set off in the direction of the castle, the hound at their side and the rising moon lighting their way.

CHAPTER 30

LEO

H E WOULDN'T HAVE known he was looking at the castle if Aziza hadn't confirmed it. The structure that loomed over them through a net of silver-green boughs no longer resembled something out of a fairytale; it was a derelict Victorian-style home with a gabled roof and weather-worn walls. Something that had clearly been made by human hands. It must have been built in a borderland place—somewhere close to a boundary, where the human world and Elphame overlapped—and once it had been abandoned by its original owners, Elphame had swallowed it. Had repurposed it.

The magnificent double doors where Sophia had met them on their arrival were gone. Instead, there was a porch streaked in grime and wrapped in a torn screen. They went around to the back, which should have taken a few seconds, but halfway through they were in the shadow of the castle again. He stopped—he was absolutely positive those spires and battlements hadn't been there a second ago—but Aziza tugged him onward.

"The castle's only an illusion," she told him. "It's rooted in the Summer Court's magic; without a monarch, it's unraveling."

They found a back door and slipped inside. The illusions weren't exactly *unraveling*, because that implied a one-way change, a falling-apart. It was more of a waffling back and forth, as if the building couldn't decide between being what it really was or what the Fair Folk had wanted it to be. The inside was as vast as it had ever been, the corridors stretching so long at times he couldn't see where they stopped, but then they'd turn a corner and run into a dead end, sickly black growths like scabs webbing the walls together. They'd double back and find the halls had rearranged themselves, and a fork that had been there before was missing now. At one point, they stumbled into a gutted kitchen, the floor going abruptly from stone to peeling linoleum; there was a fridge with a missing door and a sink mottled with soap scum.

"If this whole place is really just a run-down old house," he said, "how does everything . . . fit? The halls, the rooms . . ."

"It's part of the enchantment," she explained. "It's not that the castle is *inside* the house—it's more like the house is a foundation that the illusion was built on."

Things rotted in real time—paintings faded, tapestries grew shredded and moth-eaten, and cracks spread over the pillars as if an invisible artist was sketching them in as he watched. The dreamy, floating orbs of light were going out, one by one, some of them dimming moodily while others flickered like electric lamps in a storm. The two of them clung to the wall, listening for the stomp of boots—loud and fast and tumbling into each other, so that he couldn't have said how many there were—and going the other way when they came too close for comfort. These footsteps were too heavy to be the human servants in their soft shoes; it had to be the Gallowglass, with the whirring of their wings, the clink of their armor, their low voices made harsh by anger and fear.

They ran into trouble when a corridor decided it didn't want to end in a staircase but would in fact prefer to take them in a loop, like a lazy river from hell. When they found the turnoff that would get them back out of it, they swung around the corner—forgetting to stop and listen first—and came face-to-face with a pair of Gallowglass in thorned armor.

Leo's heart hammered. The sword was in its scabbard, and he wasn't going to be fast enough to draw it.

The Gallowglass recovered quickly, lifting their spears. But it was the hound that reacted first, striking out of the shadows and knocking one of the Gallowglass to the ground. She landed hard on her back, and something cracked under the hound's weight, but she had to be alive, based on how energetically she was swearing. Luckily for her, the hound had a long-standing no-kill order from Tristan.

The other Gallowglass had lunged at Leo; he faltered when his companion went down, but he had too much momentum to stop, and that gave Leo time to dodge, Aziza time to duck around and jab her silver pocketknife into the gap under the knight's arm, where the shoulder of his armor met the chest plates. The Gallowglass howled in pain. Leo yanked the spear from his boneless grip, tugged the helmet off, and pointed the tip of his own weapon at his throat.

Beside him, Aziza drew in a sharp breath, dismayed. The spear shook in Leo's grip, just for a second, until he forced himself to steady it.

Under the helmet, brown spots of decay were spreading over the fairy's grayish-blue skin like a pox. His veins showed up green, down his neck and in his bloodshot eyes. He was breathing heavily, skin beaded with sweat, as if feverish. With the solstice ceremony incomplete and midnight fast approaching, the magic that allowed the Summer Court to rule Elphame was draining from the Folk, the jade rot taking root in its place.

"Where are the other humans?" Leo said.

"Huntsman you may be, but you are still an outsider," he rasped. "I'll tell you nothing."

"Who gave you your orders?" Aziza asked.

He only bared his teeth, his eyes rolling a little as they found her. "I need no orders. I know my duty."

They gave up and left the two Gallowglass there, bleeding but alive, too weak to call for help.

It soon became apparent that the illusions weren't just wearing off; they were corrupted, sick, like the Gallowglass had been. Broken glass, the musty-damp smell of mold, the squirm of infestation in the forest-lace walls. More of the lights died out second by second, almost as if responding to their footsteps. The shadows rose around them like lake water, and they waded in until they were submerged—only they weren't heading down, they were heading up. Aziza turned on her phone for the flashlight and hid it against her bodice, letting out only enough light so that they didn't trip over jagged chunks of broken flagstone or slip in the murky puddles that hid dips in the floor. They'd yet to see another human.

Finally, they found the guest quarters. They grabbed one of their backpacks, quickly consolidating their most important supplies into the same bag in case they didn't have a chance to return for the others. The pooka had taken the form of a hedgehog, trembling violently with all its quills pointed out, and had to be coaxed from under the bed.

They'd left the door cracked so they'd hear if any Gallowglass approached, and none had. But then a voice from *inside* the room said, "Leo?"

Aziza shot to her feet and pointed her flashlight up. The voice had come from the far side of the room, in the corner where the shadows were opaque. When Leo saw who it was stepping into the light, his shoulders slumped with relief.

"Evan!" he said. "What are you doing here?"

"I was hoping you'd show up," Evan said, hoarsely. His clothes were rumpled and muddy, as if he'd fallen over outside, and there was a smear of blood on his cheek. It wasn't coming from a cut, though; more likely he'd scraped his hands and then touched his face, not realizing. "I didn't know who else to ask for help."

"Where are the others?" Leo asked.

"In the servants' dorms downstairs. It's actually a basement, I think." He shook his head helplessly. "I don't know what's going to happen to us."

"Can't you leave?"

"Some of us can. The ones whose contracts would've been up after this season . . . A few of them already ran away. But some of us can't. They're bound to the castle."

Which was exactly what Leo had been hoping he wouldn't say.

"We need to find Princess Narra so we can help her finish the solstice ceremony," he said. "But we don't know where she is. No one's seen her for hours, and this place is a maze."

Before Evan could reply, the door swung open behind them, its rusty hinges creaking.

"I know where she is," Sophia said. White-faced, lip trembling, sweaty hair falling out of her bun, she was unraveling as swiftly as the castle.

"Sophia!" Evan said. "Where have you been?"

"Pleading with the Gallowglass to release the princess, of course, but they're all—they won't *listen*—" Her voice was full of unshed tears. "That—that awful man—"

"Viren?" Leo said.

"Viren can barely dress himself without checking with Prince Tal first," Sophia snapped, so vehemently it took him aback. "I know this is his fault. I don't care what he does to me—if you want to find the princess, I can take you."

Leo had figured that all of this was a play by one of the lesser courts to overthrow King Ilanthus and ascend to the Court of the Seasons. But Tal, too, had something to gain; if he wanted the throne, he had to take it by force, since he wasn't the first in line. And the king had killed Tal's mother. The nixies that Aziza talked to had made it sound like Tal was still stuck on the impossible task she'd given him, but maybe he'd only been using it as a cover.

While they spoke, Aziza had set the flashlight down on the bed and knelt again. Now, she stood with the pooka in her arms. "Let's go, then. We don't have time to waste."

Leo hesitated, fishing around in his pocket and turning to Evan.

"Here," he said, holding out his hand, the obsidian button cupped in his palm. "I meant to give this back to you."

Evan closed Leo's fingers around it. "Keep it for luck."

In the hall, they went in opposite directions, Evan heading back downstairs to let the rest of the servants know what was happening while Leo, Aziza, and Sophia went up.

"She's in the east tower," Sophia said. "Or . . . what used to be the east tower."

The hound stopped them before they had gone very far, surging ahead with its ears flat and teeth bared. They retreated and hid behind the corner, listening, until he caught it—uneven, limping footsteps. Ragged breathing. A low, agitated muttering, like someone talking to himself.

Sophia's eyes went wide with fear. Her hand clutched at Leo's sleeve.

"*The prince,*" she hissed.

"You keep going," Aziza told them. "I'll stay and hold him off. Sophia—there has to be another route, right?"

"What?" he whispered. "Why?"

"He's coming after you," Aziza said under her breath. "If I don't distract him, he could catch us before we get to Narra. And I have help." She touched her collar, where a garter snake was poking its head out from under her hair. "*Go.*"

And before he could argue, she was walking away.

"Go with her!" he whispered to the hound, but it looked at him blankly and didn't move. Tristan had told it to stay with Leo, so it was staying with Leo. The fact that Tristan hadn't noticed what was happening here made him uneasy—in fact, Tristan not being here himself made Leo uneasy. Leo had asked him to stay with Hazel, but he knew Tristan; he wasn't going to sit back and wait when Leo and Aziza were in trouble. He had probably planned to find Hazel a good hiding spot and then come after the two of them the second he could. But he hadn't yet.

It hasn't been that long, Leo told himself. *He's fine. Aziza would've felt it if he wasn't.*

Reluctantly, he followed Sophia. She led the way in stony silence, like she didn't want to be here with him any more than he wanted to be here with her. The castle expanded and contracted around them, at times unfurling its decadent corridors, and at times dusty and claustrophobic as a shack. A haunted one. They zigzagged drunkenly to avoid tumbling through gaping holes in the floor or walking under sagging parts of the ceiling that looked like they were going to cave in.

There wasn't a single moment, during that mind-bending journey, where he didn't question if he'd done the right thing. Maybe he should've stayed with Aziza. Maybe he should've waited for Tristan. Getting to Narra was urgent, but if he'd insisted on sticking together, maybe he'd feel less like he was going in the wrong direction.

The hound stopped walking. Leo stopped, too, alert for signs of approaching Gallowglass. It wasn't growling this time, though. It tilted its head; its tail swished once, and it huffed out a breath through its nose. With a fluid turn, it circled in on itself as if to curl up and go to sleep, and vanished. It had . . . left.

"What is it?" Sophia said impatiently. "Where did it go?"

"It . . . went back to its summoner," he said, unable to move. Either the hound had gone of its own accord, disobeying a direct order from Tristan, or Tristan had called it back. Both scenarios could only mean something was horribly wrong. Tristan wouldn't have left him and Aziza on their own otherwise. He wouldn't have left him. He just *wouldn't*.

It was one thing to know, in an abstract way, that they could die in Elphame, and another to be standing there, in that corridor, in that moment, and confront the fact that Tristan might not be coming back. He couldn't even imagine it. Tristan, who fell asleep listening to music with Leo in the early morning. Tristan, who made that improbably charming expression of disgust when the hounds ate something that shouldn't have been edible. Tristan, who had kissed him with such easy conviction, and who had recognized Leo through an illusion when Leo probably wouldn't have recognized himself.

"We can't stay here," Sophia said. "Come on."

Shakily, he touched the flask at his belt, trying to remind himself that he had something important to do. His breathing came too fast. He always did better when he was holding it together for someone else.

Sophia shook his arm. "Listen. Finding the princess is the *only* useful thing you can do right now. Come on."

Even if he dropped everything and went after Tristan, what then? He wouldn't even be able to *find* Tristan without the hound. The sooner he ended this, the sooner he could get back to his friends and Hazel. Their only chance of getting out of here safely was with Narra's help.

"Okay," he said. He breathed in. If anything, he should feel *better* now that Tristan's most loyal hound had gone back to him. It would look out for him. If Leo had heard right, earlier, Tristan had even said it was *lucky*. And Leo had some luck of his own. His fingers found the obsidian button in his pocket, a reminder of how much was at stake here.

He nodded once at Sophia, and they went on.

CHAPTER 31

TRISTAN

"Why can't you tell me?" Tristan said. "I don't understand."

"I saw you leave with the girl." Beor moved closer, his hounds circling around the two of them. "Where is she?"

"The girl?" The only girl he had been with was . . .

"The changeling girl," Beor said. "You took her. Tell me where she is."

Without another word, Tristan fled. But he only got a few yards away before one of the hounds was in front of him, cutting him off; he skidded to a halt and almost lost his balance. The other hound was on his heels.

"You cannot outrun a shadow," Beor said, sounding bored. "Enough of this."

He'd only named two hounds of his own. Both of them were presently elsewhere, carrying out tasks too important for him to summon them back. If he called the others, the nameless ones, Beor would take them from him again. He couldn't risk possession when it would leave his body vulnerable; with no Hunt to occupy them, Beor's hounds would rip him apart.

Hand in his pocket, glass beads sliding between his fingers, warm as flesh, as if the owner of the necklace had been waiting beside the veil between life and death for his summons. It responded to the heartbeat pulse of his urgency and produced a winged spirit that swept over his head and down, into the hound as if to knock it away—and it couldn't do that, but the hound backpedaled at its icy touch, baying wildly. Tristan sprinted in another direction, already reaching for the next keepsake.

The finger bone belonged to a Gallowglass—responding well to Tristan's defiance—and he wielded a phantom sword, hazy around the edges. When he brought it down on the next hound's skull, the hound released a noise that was half whine and half snarl, and Tristan shuddered; he'd felt that noise inside him, scratching at his bones as if to say, *Let me in.*

The birches gleamed as silver as a witch's cloak; the howling of the dead blended into the baying of the hounds. He'd lost track of Beor, who was letting his hounds do all the chasing for him. The spirits whipped at the hounds' fur only to collapse under their teeth, dissipating like wintertime illusions made of ice and vapor. But Tristan restored them—or maybe they restored themselves—with despair, as potent as the taste of coffee in a paper cup, bought with change left for him overnight by strangers, or the sting of frostbite blisters on his fingers, or the sound of wooden wind chimes knocking together outside a house that would be empty by morning.

For every spirit Tristan called, a new hound sprang up, overwhelming his small army of ghosts. Beor's pack was as endless as the night, and Tristan had only as many spirits as mementos he'd collected. The next time he thrust his hand into his pocket, he came up empty; he fell to his knees and scrabbled at the base of the nearest tree for another. But as his handful of grave dirt crumbled between his fingers, a new hound crashed into him from behind, and he was on the ground with teeth on his neck, not biting into him yet, just resting there in a silent threat.

The tips of Beor's boots entered his line of sight, and then Beor knelt.

"Come, now," Beor said, his voice a soft growl. "It will be easier for both of us if you tell me where she is. I could kill you, but searching for her will take time, especially if she runs, and time is of the essence tonight."

Beor grabbed Tristan's collar and dragged him upright, the hound moving back to let him up. Tristan found the silver knife he kept in his boot, ripped it out and stabbed wildly at Beor, who disarmed him easily, one-handed, and tossed his weapon aside.

"I thought," Tristan wheezed, "we were past this."

"What?" Beor said, scowling.

"The whole . . . strangling and slamming me into things," Tristan said, with a choked laugh. Calling all those spirits had drained him; he wasn't used to it yet. Beor gave him a shake using his grip on Tristan's collar, and Tristan went light-headed. He shut his eyes, nausea rising in him.

He never found out what scornful response Beor would have given him because, just when Tristan began to fear he would actually black out, a new hound launched itself from the shadows and slammed into Beor. *Tristan's* hound. The one that was supposed to be with Leo right now, but which had, inexplicably, come for Tristan when Tristan hadn't even thought to call it here. The impact made Beor drop him, and he scrambled away on his hands and knees as Beor wrestled with the hound, holding its snapping jaws away from his face with his bare hands. The hound that had pinned Tristan before leapt into the fray, and then the two were ripping into each other. Tristan snatched up his discarded knife just as Beor caught him by the ankle and dragged him in. Letting himself be pulled, Tristan spun, slashing, getting Beor across the cheek and nose, a deep slice that poured blood and would doubtless add another scar to his collection. Beor's face contorted in pain, and a strangled noise burst out of him. He caught Tristan's wrist in a grip tight enough to pop the joints, and for the second time, Tristan's knife was plucked from his grasp and thrown out of reach.

"I have no reason to harm you, foolish boy," Beor gasped. Blood had seeped between his lips, into his teeth. "But I will do what I must for the Summer Court."

"Who sent you after us?" Tristan said.

"*No one*. But I see only one way forward."

"Why—her?" Tristan asked, desperate.

"I owe you no explanations," Beor snarled.

The other hound was a better fighter, but Lucky was scrappy and vicious and had all of Tristan's insolence. Its opponent bit down on Lucky's shoulder, and Lucky twisted away, not caring that it made the bite tear open even wider. It sank into the shadows at Tristan's silent call, and when it reappeared, it was asserting itself into the space between his and Beor's bodies. Before Beor could move, both Lucky and Tristan had vanished, *literally* slipping through his fingers. The smothering cold of the shadow plane was almost comforting, like when you pressed down on your temples to soothe away a tension headache. When they reappeared, Lucky had taken them outside the tangle of hounds and spirits, nearer to the path. Beor was on his feet, panting, blood dripping down his neck and into his collar.

"Maybe I'd tell you where she was if I understood why it mattered," Tristan said.

"You're a poor liar," Beor said, "and a coward of a summoner. Enough running. Stand and fight!"

Tristan and his hound descended into the shadows, and emerged far across the grove. Beor's hound chased him out of the same shadow, but then Tristan was stepping into another and back into the constricting darkness. He kept Beor spinning to track him. Beor's hounds couldn't predict where he'd go next, so they stayed one step behind him. He retrieved the knife, darting out of the shadows and then retreating before Beor could catch him—"Next time I take that from you, I'll sheathe it in your heart," Beor promised, but Tristan was already gone, and barely heard him. He stepped back into existence behind Beor and buried the knife in his back, to the hilt. It came back out with a gush of blood, and he disappeared again before Beor could finish turning, with a roar of pain and anger, to swipe at him.

Tristan knew he couldn't go on like this all night. But he had hoped he'd last longer than he did, in the end.

The sensation of shadow-traveling into a shadow that was already occupied was jarring, a shock like getting into a car crash with your eyes closed. He had no words to describe what he felt because he didn't technically have a body when it happened, didn't technically have senses; all he knew was that the familiar presence of his own hound, the familiar bounds of his own consciousness, were assaulted by something foreign and unforgiving, something that even in a toothless form found a way to bite into him, and he was dragged unceremoniously into the physical plane. His arm was clamped between the hound's jaws, and he was trailing blood. Lucky lunged at the hound, but it didn't matter, because Beor had him again. He pulled Tristan up, Tristan choking out a pathetic, agonized noise as Beor squeezed his wounded arm.

His strength was waning. He was bleeding—he might actually bleed to death, and wouldn't that be an astonishingly mundane way to die after everything he'd been through? He laughed, delirious, as

Beor shook him. Through the bond, he felt the pain of Lucky's injuries as it struggled with not one, but two, three of Beor's hounds; he felt Lupa practically vibrating with the desire to come fight, and he put more energy than he really had to spare into a command to *stay with Hazel*; he felt, from Aziza, a frantic emotion he couldn't interpret, but it frightened him, and there was absolutely nothing he could do because Beor slammed his back against one of the trees and he lost his concentration.

"I am giving you one more chance to talk," Beor said. "Cooperate, or I will put you down."

Tristan blinked the spots out of his eyes. His head lolled, and he looked down. If spirits and hounds weren't enough to defend him, then there was at least one more thing he knew he could do.

His last resort.

CHAPTER 32

AZIZA

"There you are," Tal said.

The prince was still dressed in the same outfit he'd worn yesterday. He was limping, his hair disheveled, his eyes puffy as if he hadn't slept since the last time she'd seen him. In one hand, he held a bottle of lily wine, open and half-empty; in the other, a crystal dagger.

"Were you looking for me?" she asked.

"Of course I was. I have something to show you." He tipped forward precariously as he set the bottle down and sheathed the knife. Making a cup of his hands, he scooped up some water from a puddle under the broken window and held it under the moonlight. "I've brought you a fairy who can hold silver in his bare hands."

It did indeed look as if he held molten silver.

"That's not what I meant," she said, with little conviction. Something stung the back of her ankle, like a scratch. Without thinking much of it, she inched forward, instinctively avoiding the tiny spot of pain.

"No? Then you should have been clearer. Have you ever seen a purer silver than this?"

He let the water fall through his fingers, dripping to the floor, and then shook the moisture off with an elegant flick of his hands.

"Fine. You win," she said. "Will you at least tell me why you did all this?"

Something snagged at the hem of her skirt, another faint, minor annoyance she barely noticed. Tal was picking up the bottle, advancing on her. As he did, the castle was briefly returned to its full glory; the floating lights popped back into being, the puddle became a gently babbling fountain under a hanging garden, the rickety floorboards turned to polished flagstone. It was like the magic that the Summer Court had poured into the castle was gathering around him, the way rain made a kind of halo when it struck something unyielding, almost sizzling off it; it marked him as royalty more effectively than any crown could.

"Did what?"

His voice had lost its false charm; it was low and raspy.

"Your father, you . . ." She took a step back but could go no further; her heel bumped into something prickly. She didn't dare take her eyes off Tal to see what it was.

"What about my father?"

He was sick like the others, she realized. A faint sheen of sweat clung to his skin. His antlers were pocked with hollow spots as if something had started to eat away at the bone.

"Okay, fine. If you won't tell me about that, then what do you want from me?"

"Nothing at all," he said, and held out the bottle. "Only to offer you a drink. No games this time. No more of your petty tricks. Refuse me, and I will shove it down your throat."

She backed away reflexively, and something pierced her ankle, drawing blood.

Creeping toward her from the corners, slowly snaking around her feet, was a sea of thorns. Holly with its blood-drop berries and prickly leaves. Stinging nettle fanning open, deceptively soft. Spiny blackberry tendrils stretching out, tangling together. Starburst-shaped clusters of honey locust spikes, the smallest ones the length of her finger. And cream-colored flowers on dusky barbed branches—blackthorn.

In a less dire situation, she would've laughed.

They cinched closed around her ankles, their thorns just barely pricking her skin. If she moved, they'd flay her open. And still they grew, higher and higher, quickly reaching her knees. It was like being in the center of a dry, bloodthirsty whirlpool.

"Beg for my forgiveness," Tal said, "and I will consider letting you go."

It was vindicating to see this side of Tal. No more pretenses. Here it was, the violence she'd always known he was capable of, from the moment she'd first seen him.

She held her hand to her collar, and the pooka slithered into it.

"Just distract him," she whispered. "Don't fight. I just need a little time."

It turned into a finch, took flight, and changed into a mountain lion in midair to pounce on Tal. He dodged easily, lashing out with his crystal dagger, but the pooka was fast, and it didn't hold the same shape for more than two or three seconds at a time. It favored lithe, muscular forms with teeth and claws; when it tried something heavier, an elephant, a rhino, the floor groaned underneath it, threatening to give way. It took Tal in circles, giving Aziza time to hack at the thorny vines with her pocketknife, which was barely up to the task; it worked, but it took forever. She kept nicking her fingers on the thorns. In her boots, she'd have climbed over them. But the silken slippers the fairies had given her offered little protection, and if she tore up her feet getting out of this trap, she wouldn't be able to run.

And she really wanted to be able to run.

The innermost ring of thorns had gotten tall enough to graze against her upper thigh before the pooka had stolen Tal's attention. She cut a section of it down to about knee height—impulsively tucking a length of blackthorn under her arm—and scraped the thorns off a thick bough at the top, giving herself a place she could step. A tiny one she'd missed pricked the arch of her foot, but didn't pierce her skin, even when she put down more of her weight. Balancing carefully, she picked a path through the sea of thorns, until the spaces in between the vines grew big enough that she could plant her feet on the ground again.

She had to choose between holding the blackthorn switch and holding the pocketknife. With only a half-formed idea of what she was going to do, she tucked away the knife. Her grip on the branch was slick with sweat and blood.

Tal looked away from the pooka then and made a furious noise through gritted teeth as he caught on to her escape attempt. A wave of his hand, and thorny growths snaked down from the ceiling, reaching for her, catching at her arms; they tore through the sleeves of the dress and left gashes beneath as she wrenched free. The pooka was a gray wolf when it pounced on him next, paws on his back and teeth going for his neck. Tal stabbed backward, nicking it across the flank, and the pooka whimpered as it retreated into the air. But the cut showed up on its left wing; it wobbled and then touched down again in cougar form, body low to the ground and teeth bared.

The sight of the pooka's wound made a wave of anger surge through her.

"I can't believe that at a time like this," she said, in the most derisive tone of voice she could muster, "you're bothering with *me*. Did I hurt your pride that badly, Your Highness?"

"It's not a matter of pride," Tal said. "Someone has to teach you your place."

"And where is that?" She moved slowly, circling around Tal as she made her way to the pooka. The blackthorn switch was limp in her hand, dragging through the blood, water, and lily wine that had spilled when the pooka's fight with Tal had knocked it over, leaving a wet streak in her wake.

It wasn't exactly braided rowan and freshwater, but Anne had said to make the spell her own. She hadn't practiced it. She didn't know if it would work any better this time. But it was all she had.

"I think it would be better to show you," Tal said, and lunged at her blade-first. The pooka leapt at him, but he caught its teeth on his forearm—he winced, bleeding—and threw it away so that it slammed into the wall. It yowled as thorny vines sprang from the cracks in the wall, growing around the pooka and pinning it in place.

She dodged Tal's next slash, swinging around him until she was nearly back where she'd started, completing the circle—or, well, it was more of a blob than a circle, but who said it had to be perfect? Her craft had never been perfect. But it had always sufficed. Maybe this would suffice, too.

The pooka had wriggled out of the trap in snake form, dropped to the ground, and landed on all fours in its preferred fox shape.

"Stay back!" Aziza called, but the pooka came at Tal again, this time in its not-quite-right imitation of a blækhound. If not for the still-healing welts around its neck, she'd never have guessed this was the same pooka they'd rescued from the Midsummer Revels a few days ago, fearless as it was now, throwing itself at Tal again, being knocked away. He was quick and agile, a skilled fighter even in his drunken, sick, exhausted state—he was Captain of the Gallowglass for a reason, and it wasn't just because he was the king's son. But if this kept going, he'd leave the circle she'd drawn, and she couldn't let that happen.

Tal batted away the pooka's next attack and came after her again, slashing at her neck; she flung herself to the side, and his blade gouged the wall where she'd been standing. She dropped the blackthorn branch—she didn't need it anymore—and opened her pocketknife in time to stab him in the side while he yanked his dagger out of the wall. It was a shallow blow, unlikely to do more than annoy him, and it did just that; he whirled on her, following her to the middle of the circle, swinging again with the dagger.

She dodged, but a vine wrapped around her leg and yanked, sending her sprawling. His cruel laugh rang out through the corridor as she struggled to kick it away. He stabbed the crystal dagger into the ground, pinning her skirt, and took his time retrieving the wine bottle from where it had been knocked over.

Frantically, she ripped free, leaving the hem of her skirt in tatters. But the second she was on her feet, his hand clamped around her throat and pinned her to the wall. It knocked the wind out of her, and the knife slipped out of her grasp. She clawed at his arm, his face, but he leaned away without loosening his grip on her, a malicious smile tugging at the corners of his mouth.

Where the pooka had fallen last, a cage of thorns had sprung up around it, woven so tightly that it couldn't find an opening to squirm out of even in garter snake form. It tried transforming into something large enough to break free, but as soon as the thorns sank into its flesh, it shrank again.

"You are a waste of fine drink," Tal said, and smashed the bottle against the wall. Shattered glass rained down on them. She struck at him again and caught him in the nose almost by accident; something cracked, blood dripped out, and she managed to shove him away at last. He grabbed her arm, but her momentum brought them both to the ground.

When he stabbed at her with the broken bottle, there was nowhere for her to dodge this time, and it pierced her thigh deep. She screamed, scratched him across the face, going for his broken nose again. He swore, and they were grappling, and all she felt was rage, pure and blinding rage. All this power, and all he wanted to do with it was control other people. She thought of Meryl; if Aziza didn't get out of here, get back home, there was no one else in the world who would look for her. Marinus had given up; Dion had no reason to care anymore.

Aziza's left hand flung out as he pinned her, and she grabbed a fistful of some thorny plant—not caring that it made her hand bleed, not even feeling it—and raked it over his eyes. A mangled shout of pained fury escaped him. She took the opportunity to roll them over—she'd never have managed it if he'd been at full strength—and knelt on his chest, smashing her fist into his face, not even frightened anymore, thinking only of some stranger hoarding Meryl's seal-skin like a trophy.

The pooka had gnawed through its cage. As Tal pushed her off him, it cantered over to them—as a horse, it was scruffy and wild, but still about a million times more beautiful than the sunlight-and-pollen illusion she had once seen Tal ride. It reared up and pounded its hooves into Tal's chest, and something snapped, and he stayed down.

Aziza staggered outside of her trap circle and fell to her knees, utterly drained.

"Prince Tal," she said. "Listen."

He swore at her, blinking through the blood, one eye swollen shut. Brown spots like they'd seen on the Gallowglass earlier had ruined his perfect complexion. His hands pressed over his chest, gingerly feeling at the damage, as she beckoned the pooka back to her. She wanted it outside the spell before she began.

The castle illusion failed again as whatever brief surge of energy Tal's presence had given it wore off. The hall was just a decayed husk again, dim and cramped. His thorn illusions withered and vanished.

Kneeling, she told him a story she knew well: the story of a shade and how a witch had made a prison in her hands to take it back to Elphame, but it had been imperfect, and the shade had gotten away from her. She told him the story of a pooka in a silver collar, and a Huntsman caged beside a mountain lake.

The magic took. She concentrated on the spell with all her might as Tal rolled over onto his side, pushed himself to his feet, and came unsteadily closer. His threats were lost on her; she'd tuned him out. And when he tried to step over the circle, he couldn't. He pushed at the air, but it was like he'd hit a glass wall. Her trap spell was holding.

Rage twisted his face, making him, for the first time, truly ugly. "What is this?"

"Just another one of my petty tricks," she said. "Now, we're going to talk."

CHAPTER 33

LEO

"THROUGH THERE," SOPHIA whispered. "And then up the stairs. That's where she is."

The door Sophia had indicated was around the next corner, guarded by a Gallowglass. The corridor where they hid was birch and flagstone still, except sometimes if he concentrated on his feet for too long, he saw moldering floorboards and dusty carpet.

"Okay, but how do we get in?" Leo asked under his breath.

"He'll back down when he sees the sword," she assured him. "It's silver, and everyone knows what a fearsome weapon it was in Beor's hands."

"I don't know how to use it," Leo said.

"He doesn't know that."

So he drew the sword from its scabbard, gripped the hilt with both hands, and stepped out of hiding.

The Gallowglass didn't back down. Light flashed off the curve of his scimitar as he swung it at Leo's throat.

After that, things got . . . fuzzy.

It didn't matter that his stance was probably all wrong, and that he didn't know if his hands were in the right place. The silver sword came up—so quickly it didn't even feel like Leo made the decision to do it, like some self-defense instinct had kicked in and jerked his hands into the right position, like the sword had moved on its own and taken Leo with it. He blocked expertly, though the force of their blades connecting, with a clang, sent pain ringing up Leo's arms.

It wasn't instinct that had saved him, or even luck. Those were momentary miracles, and this—whatever was happening now— it just kept going. An energy washed over him, like he'd chugged a hot drink and he could feel it moving down his throat, sending warmth through his chest. It flowed into his muscles, and instead of dropping the sword when the next blow came—under the helmet, his opponent's teeth were gritted, his breath escaping him in a grunt as he put all his strength into it—Leo blocked that one, too. It was more than energy, it was more than warmth, it was like fire blazed through him, searing his nerves, making him jittery with the need to let it out. He blocked another swing, and then he pushed back on their connected blades, shoving the Gallowglass back against the door he was meant to be guarding. With a twist of the sword—dimly, he wondered when and how he'd learned to be so dexterous—he'd disarmed his opponent. The scimitar clattered to the ground.

Leo opened his mouth to say something, to tell him to give up, but his body was still moving without his input. He drew back and shoved forward—there was resistance against the tip of the blade, and then it gave, with a smooth sliding-in and a wet sound, and his opponent's mouth dropped open in a silent gasp. Leo looked into his eyes—brown with concentric rings of topaz and black, like the cross section of a tree trunk. Impossible, inhuman eyes. But they were wide with a shock that Leo felt mirrored in his own. The blade disappeared into the man's chest plate, the silver nullifying whatever fortifying enchantments were on it. Blood welled up in the place where armor and blade connected. Leo had skewered him straight through the torso.

"I . . . I don't . . ." he heard himself say. He stepped back. The blade came out wet and black, and the Gallowglass slid to the ground, still with that frozen look of blank surprise on his face.

Leo tried to drop the sword. To kneel and remove the man's helmet. To yank the chest plate off and press his hands over the wound, try and stem the bleeding, say *I'm sorry, I'm sorry, I'm sorry* over and over. Maybe—maybe he wasn't dead, maybe something could still be done.

He *tried* to drop the sword. He really did. But he couldn't.

"It's all right," Sophia said. The tears and panic from before were gone. She took one of the man's arms and dragged him aside, huffing from the effort of it, but she managed, probably because the stone underneath his body was slick with his blood. "The door's unlocked. We have to keep going."

"Sophia," he said. "I don't know how I . . ."

He stared uncomprehendingly at his hand on the hilt, willing it to open.

"They probably heard us. No helping that now," she said. She pulled the door open, but stood aside so that he could go ahead of her. He felt like a sleepwalker. His footsteps made a quiet, damp noise as he stepped through the bloody streaks the body had left at the threshold. Behind the door was a spiral staircase. All he could see was the first ten, twenty or so steps, and then it curved away and up; it was crowded with what might have been every Gallowglass that remained in the castle.

It should have been terrifying. Part of him *was* terrified, but it was as if that part was locked in a glass box inside his head, watching the proceedings with crystal clarity but powerless to intervene. What felt like an endless stream of deadly weapons, ghoulish helmets, armor of thorn and scale and chitin molded into all of nature's fierceness rushed down to meet him. Someone shouted at him to turn back as he continued his mechanical journey forward, but he didn't—couldn't. He lifted his sword as if he meant to cut through the entire troop single-handedly.

And that was what he did.

The staircase was narrow, so the guards could only come at him one or two at a time; three, sometimes, if a slim enough one with wings managed to swoop in. He fought his way through them, slashing and jabbing with a sword he barely should've been able to hold, executing the smooth sidesteps and twists of a dancer as he dodged blows and then shoved his opponents down the stairs with a smack of the hilt against the backs of their helmets. He stabbed through wings, twisted antlers until necks snapped. They were taller, stronger, infinitely better fighters. But that strange blaze of energy propelled him forward.

By the time he reached the top, there was no one left to stop him. The staircase ended at a short landing, about the size of a closet, with another door, which was closed. He was shaking. And he felt nothing. Actually, he felt great, physically, like he'd won a race or finished a satisfying workout, his muscles aching, his heart pumping, sweat dripping down his skin under the formal attire he'd worn for the revel.

He had just killed people.

The *hound* hadn't even killed anyone today. And Leo had left a trail of bodies behind him.

"What—what did you do to me?" he said, rounding on Sophia, who was stepping over fallen Gallowglass as she joined him at the top of the stairs. The sword was heavy in his hands, so heavy it seemed to drag his entire body down, now that there were no more opponents for it to spring forward and sheath itself in. His shoulders sagged. The tip of the sword scraped the ground.

"I didn't do anything. I can't do magic," she said.

"Then—the sword? No," he said, his breath coming in short, quick gasps as he tried to talk through it, because if he wasn't speaking aloud then he would have to think instead. "No way Beor uses a sword that controls him."

"The sword doesn't control its wielder," Sophia said. "Open the door. You'll get your answers."

If it wasn't the sword, then what? The only other things he had on him that didn't belong to him were the clothes and . . .

He managed to peel a hand off the hilt, shove it into his pocket, and produce the obsidian button.

"Evan?" he asked.

Sophia snorted. "Don't be ridiculous."

Viren, then, or . . .

He remembered, suddenly, when he'd danced with Narra. How she'd opened his hand, found the button there, and brushed her fingers over it with that sweet, sympathetic look.

Aziza had always warned him about fairy tricks. And he had fallen for one. This was why you didn't eat fairy food, why you didn't accept fairy gifts, why you didn't bargain with them, no matter how harmless the exchange may seem. He tipped his hand over so that the button slid off and fell to the ground. Instantly, the all-consuming energy drained out of him. His whole body ached from the exertion, from pushing himself beyond his physical limitations. He was covered in other people's blood. He could hear the labored breathing, the whimpering, the occasional groan of those who were still alive; but many more were silent, tiny shoots of green beginning to spring from their bodies as they burst into bloom.

"What did I just do?" he whispered aloud, expecting no answer from Sophia.

But someone else replied, "The princess had you in her thrall."

It was one of the Gallowglass he'd dispatched near the bottom of the stairs, with a wound in her shoulder that had almost severed her arm from her body; it dangled grotesquely. Her helmet had fallen off, revealing a graceful sweep of purple-blue hair, like a color the ocean turned at dusk; her iridescent wings tried to flap, but they were crumpled, as if they'd been crushed when she'd fallen. Somehow, she had managed to climb to the top, and she was only a few steps away now.

"Stay back," Leo said hollowly, not bothering to lift the sword. Leo was vulnerable now. He didn't know how to fight.

"You fool," Sophia snapped. "The king is dead. You are Queen Narra's soldier now."

The Gallowglass wasn't armed. Her one working hand supported her weight against the wall. Still, she heaved herself up another step.

"I kneel for no king-killer. The princess and Viren are traitors; my loyalty is to Prince Talarix." The Gallowglass smiled at Leo, her eyes shot through with green from the jade rot. "I saw you dispose of her charm. Without it, you're just a boy. You can't hurt me."

The Gallowglass threw herself up the last two steps and practically fell into Leo, ramming him against the closed door. Leo struggled weakly, dropping the sword at last to shove her away. The enchantment was gone, but he still felt the threat of violence inside him, as if the act of killing had left a mark, even if it hadn't been his choice. But it *had* been his choice, in a way. He had come here voluntarily, to Elphame, to the Summer Court; he had come back to the castle when he could have run. A gauntleted hand was on his neck, squeezing so that tiny specks of color danced through Leo's vision, but he could still see the bodies over her shoulder, the trail of blood. He had let that happen.

What would Tris and Zee say if they knew? he thought, as his vision went dark around the edges. But then his mind produced the answer, the one he didn't deserve but that he knew to be true: They would tell him to come back home, no matter what.

He grabbed for a fistful of wing, found it, and tore. The Gallowglass gave a ragged scream of pain and released him.

"Stop," Leo said, stumbling to the sword again and picking it up. "I don't want to hurt you," he said, though it must have sounded empty to her.

"I can't leave you alive," the Gallowglass choked out. "I am taking back the elixir of renewal. For Prince Talarix. For the Summer Court."

She lunged, and Leo stumbled backward until he hit the wall, the sword hilt braced against his rib cage and pointed vaguely up. And the Gallowglass, weak with blood loss and the rot taking hold of her, lost her footing. She tried to dodge, but she slipped instead, and she fell, impaling herself on the sword. It slid through her cleanly.

Leo couldn't blame enchanted buttons or scheming princesses this time. This one was all him.

The weight of the body, as it fell, ripped the sword from his hands. Numbly, he grasped the hilt and took it back from the corpse. He couldn't bear to have his hands empty right now. It made another one of those nauseating, slick noises as he pulled it out.

"Come on, then," Sophia said, as if bored with the delay. She'd gotten a key off one of the bodies. Before he could say another word, she had unlocked the door.

It opened into a circular room with three arched windows and a vaulted ceiling like a chapel. It was the brightest place in the castle, brimming with moonlight, and Leo—who had been envisioning a musty keep—was briefly disoriented. It looked like a cross between a study and a storage room—there was a painted bureau, a bookcase, a little table with a tea set and a half-melted, unlit candle, but there were also cardboard boxes piled off to the side, dirt and leaves that looked as if they'd been blown in through an open window or a hole in the ceiling, old furniture with sheets tossed over them, a chest full of raggedy disused toys.

This was an attic, he realized. Some of those things were real. Illusion had blended into reality so seamlessly he couldn't tell them apart.

Princess Narra perched in an ornate chair by the window that faced east, looking out at the night. One of those tiny golden birds he'd seen her with in the woods by St. Sithney's flew circles around her, darting from her hand to her shoulder to the windowsill. She smiled warmly when she saw him.

"You came," she said. "I knew you would."

"Yeah." He leaned the sword against the wall so he could untie the flask from his belt. "I brought you the heart of the springtide lord."

He held it out to her, though he was too far away for her to reach. Sophia could take it to her, since Sophia had done such a good job of fetching everything else Narra wanted, including Leo.

"Just like that?" Narra said, eyebrows lifted.

"What else am I going to do with it? Give it to your brother? Like that would be any better." His eyes stung. He told himself it was the dust.

"Come here, then," she said.

He took a step forward, jerkily, as if his body still didn't belong to himself.

"Distant friends," he said, eyes drawn to the bird, which made no sound as it flew. "You said they send you messages. You're working with someone—someone outside the Summer Court. And Viren, I guess."

"And Sophia," Narra said, with an indulgent smile. Sophia's entire face glowed at Narra's attention, and she curtsied hastily before flouncing over to stand at Narra's side, bypassing Leo.

"So the Gallowglass locked you up. To try and stop you."

"Yes. But I knew it wouldn't matter. I only needed my Huntsman, and I could be sure you would come to me."

Because he was a gullible, easily manipulated fool.

"That's why you sent Viren after me and Beor," he guessed. "So he could finish the Hunt for you instead?"

She shrugged. "It was only important that Beor did not succeed." Her smile was slow and sweet, and still impossibly pretty. Abruptly, he decided he didn't care all that much about her plan or why she'd done any of what she'd done. She had what she wanted. He had made enough of a mess here. It was time for him to bow out.

"You'll keep your word, won't you?" he asked, knowing there was nothing he could do if she said no. "We had a deal."

"We did, and I am bound to it."

There was nothing else he could think to do except finish what he'd started. He held the flask by the base and let her take it by the leather cord, so that she couldn't touch him. He tried to see the evil in her, the magic that had made him do everything he'd just done, but there was no trace of it. None that was visible to him, anyway.

Her cheek dimpled when she smiled; she wore the red mantle she'd had on when he'd met her, and it was a little dirty around the hem, as if she'd been forcefully dragged up here.

He backed away, waiting. Around him, the attic creaked. One of the windows in the tower room had vanished, and now there was just a wall, the paneling torn off in places so he could see the foam insulation. When nothing happened after several seconds, he said, "Aren't you going to drink it?"

"No," she said. Something cracked, loud, like burning firewood, so he almost didn't hear her. Almost.

He stared at her. "Then what . . . what was . . . all of this for?"

She laughed lightly, like he'd told a joke and she was being polite. "I don't want the crown. I want my freedom. There's just one more person we have to wait for."

"What?" Leo said, feeling slow and hazy, like a sleepwalker. "Who? Your brother?"

Narra started to reply, and then stopped, frowning, as the attic creaked again, louder this time. She got to her feet and backed away as the window next to her was pushed open by a wooden tendril, curled like a finger.

Something climbed onto the sill, letting itself into the room. It was a woman with tree-sap eyes and skin made of bark. She grinned wickedly at Leo, her mane of pine-needle hair falling around her shoulders. Another nymph followed her; more peeled themselves out of the walls. He could hear the others lurking in the tower staircase and listening in from outside the window, perched on the roof. The ones in the room turned to Narra and bowed to her.

"Your Highness," the first one murmured. "Forgive us our intrusion."

Understanding dawned on Narra's face. She stepped aside and swept a hand toward Leo. "Go on, then."

Now that he had given Narra the flask, the Hunt was truly over.

Come closer, then, contender, they had said, the other night. And he had. They had discussed the transaction in whispers, back and forth, too quietly for Tristan to hear. In exchange for a hiding place that would keep them safe from Beor, the nymphs had wanted his eye, his ear, and his tongue. Three of his senses, or a portion of them, for each life the nymphs were saving.

He had almost refused outright. Forget it—they'd run away instead. He wasn't going to sit there and let himself be mutilated. But then he'd looked back at Tristan, waiting for him, and then Aziza had returned and practically *begged* the nymphs to switch places with him. And he'd been reminded of how much he wanted to be able to claim even a fraction of the courage and resilience they had. How grateful he was to have them, not only then, during the Hunt, but always.

If you take one of my ears, he'd told the nymphs, *then I've paid you three times already.*

The nymphs had laughed, delighted rather than offended by this attempt at bartering. *Oh? How does that work out?* they'd wanted to know.

First, it's half my sense of hearing. Second, it's flesh, blood, skin, cartilage, he'd said. That was what they had meant: They wouldn't only cut off the outer part of his ear, but would also take, magically, from his ability to hear. The nymphs had spoken ambiguously on purpose; it tended to work in their favor. *Third, if something in the borderlands sneaks up on me because I didn't hear it coming, then that's time off my life span, too. I'll be more vulnerable than I am now. I don't know what it'll cost me yet, but it'll cost me something.*

He had reasoned his way through cutting himself into pieces, and he hadn't even felt afraid, once he'd gotten going. It was like putting together a puzzle, or solving a riddle, or turning over the words of a curse in search of a loophole.

You bargain like the fae, one of the nymphs had said, amused. *We'll take the eye. You can keep the rest.*

Not the ear? he'd tried.

The eye. Do we have a deal?

He had agreed on the condition that they wait until he'd won. And here he was, a victor, just like he'd promised them he would be. As disgraceful a victor as there had ever been.

"I'm ready," he said. Narra watched the proceedings with keen interest, whispering to the golden bird she now held cupped in her hands. And then the nymphs closed in.

When they crowded around him, it was like being back in the woods, the smell of resin and earth everywhere. The one with pine-needle hair pushed him down on his knees. Her coarse hands tilted his jaw up. The shape of them vaguely suggested palms and fingers, but they didn't move like limbs made of flesh and bone. They molded around his face like branches cradling his skull. Would it be ridiculous if he asked them to be gentle? Was there such a thing as magical anesthetic?

A tendril of wood stroked the corner of his left eye. He shuddered and closed them.

"Our visit to the Summer Court has been illuminating," the nymph said. "A change in power is at hand, and such times of transition bring revelations. You failed to tell us something of great importance. We did not know that we bargained with a Prince of the Seasons."

Leo's eyes opened into wary slits, squinting up at the nymph through the screen of his own eyelashes. "What are you talking about?"

"We will collect our payment as agreed, but we will repay you a portion, what we can," the nymph said, her breath cool as a zephyr when she bent over him. "The eye of a prince is worth far more, after all, than the eye of a Huntsman. We will not be accused of cheating the Summer Court."

He heard Narra laugh, but he couldn't see her past the nymphs.

"I'm not a . . . I'm not a Prince of the Seasons," he said. "I'm not even one of the Folk."

"The brother of a princess is a prince," the nymph said.

He thought the princess they meant was Narra, and that maybe, somehow, in defiance of all reason, they had mistaken him for Tal. No—he *wanted* to think they meant Narra. The part of his brain that understood what they were really saying was already denying it, repressing it, not wanting to look. And then he couldn't think at all, because the nymphs were holding his left eye open with their rough hands, like wooden hooks in his skin, and they were—and everything was white-hot pain—he was screaming, inhuman screams that fled from his throat like they didn't want to be in his body right now either—he thrashed, unable to stop himself, and the nymphs held him, his arms pinned, his knees bound to the floor—

There was a point where he went numb, but his body still understood that something terrible was happening, and the screaming and thrashing continued, and he had no idea how long it went on—

When it was done, he'd expected the side of his face to feel empty, but, horribly, it didn't. Only his eyelid felt a little strange, felt like a limp, dead flap of skin. His right eye was still tightly shut. His throat was hoarse, his mouth still open to scream, but all that was coming out was a choked, animal noise, a gasp, and then just his breathing, too loud.

"Last, our gift to you. Our repayment," the nymph murmured, calm as a surgeon.

His face was wet, a combination of blood and tears. His left eye, or the place where his left eye had been, ached like there was a knife embedded in it. The nymph touched the corner of the socket again, and he flinched, shaking all over. But then the pain was replaced by a soothing warmth. He waited for the pain to come back, his whole body tensed in anticipation, but it didn't. It felt like another trick; he almost could've believed that the last few minutes hadn't happened. That his eye had been put back. That there was . . . something . . . under the eyelid again, something that rolled and moved just like his remaining eye did.

"There," the nymph said. "It is all right. Look at me."

He looked.

His field of vision had been cut in half, just as if he had a patch over his left eye. But . . . with no effort, he could now see the room for what it really was. No vaulted ceiling. No ornate bureaus or old books. No silk or brocade. No mosaic tiles running into the old floorboards. It was just a derelict old attic. He could bring the illusions into focus, the pretty tower room, without losing sight of what was underneath.

"What is this?" he asked the pine nymph. One of the others held up a mirror they must have taken from somewhere in the attic, oval-shaped with a chipped gilt frame. He wiped the dust off with his sleeve.

His own face looked back at him. He mopped up the blood

automatically, even as his eyes—both eyes—went wide at what he saw. His left eye socket had been slashed open. It was healing over faster than it should, and was no longer bleeding, but it would almost certainly scar. The socket was not empty. Where his eye used to be, now there was something the color of sunlight through tree sap, reddish-gold and glinting in the dim light.

"Amber," the nymph told him. "It will give you truesight. You will see through every illusion. Fairy charms and compulsions will not work on you."

"They can't control me?" he said. "Even if I take something from them, like—like a token?"

"Even if you take their gifts. Even if you ate fairy food or drank their wine. You will always see clearly," the pine nymph said.

"Thank you," he breathed, covered in his own blood and half-blind, and meant it.

They bowed to Narra again before retreating the way they'd come, back out through the window or into the walls of the house that he would never mistake for a castle again.

"Wait!" he said, as the pine nymph climbed onto the sill. "I still don't understand. About—about being a Prince of the Seasons. Tell me what you mean."

He couldn't bear guessing. He needed it spelled out for him.

The nymph said, "What is there to explain? The fact that you are your sister's brother?"

"He thinks it's a mistake," Narra said. "Go on. I'll help him understand." She looked at him pityingly. "Truesight, hmm? How unfortunate. Illusions are like dreams; they make life worth living."

"Hazel," he said. "King Ilanthus was her father. And you want *her* to be queen."

And he had just enough time to think, *Good thing Tris got her out of here,* when he heard a new sound from the window the nymphs had left open. Dragonfly wings, fluttering rapidly. Coming near.

CHAPTER 34

TRISTAN

L AST DECEMBER, TRISTAN had tried to bring a dead man back to life.

He hadn't known how to perform a proper resurrection, or if such a thing was even possible, and it hadn't worked. The corpse had turned into a grasping monster whose touch would've sapped the life from him if Tristan hadn't knocked it out and pushed it back into its grave. But a monster was just what Tristan needed right now.

Beor's eyes narrowed. "What are you doing?"

His breath smelled so strongly of lily wine that it almost made Tristan dizzy. Or maybe he could attribute that to the hand slowly compressing his throat, forcing the air out of him. Tristan shut his eyes as the world tilted. He couldn't pay attention to Beor. He cast his magic out into the woods, like a net, finding the bodies resting unburied beside their grave markers. He ignored the spirit energy clinging to them; it was the physical remains he wanted this time, the empty vessels. The emptiness was what made them monstrous.

Live, he thought, which wasn't a spell, but it sufficed.

An ominous cracking resounded through the grove of the dead.

Beor dropped him, looking for the source of the noise. Tristan slid down the tree until his feet touched the ground; his knees were weak, but he managed to stay upright with his back braced against the trunk.

Decayed wings gave their first, unsteady flutters after many years of rest. Stiff bones disentangled themselves from vines. Half-disintegrated gowns whispered their relief as leaves and dirt fell away. Some of the bodies broke their own ribs freeing themselves from roots that wound through them. Others carried blooms that had grown wrapped around their spines and between their arm bones, into empty eye sockets and pockets where flesh and muscle had fallen in, like some kind of unsettling avant-garde art piece. Many were largely intact, and could have been mistaken for the living if not for the gray tinge to their skin, the small tooth-marked injuries where animals had started to eat away at them.

Beor spun back to him. "What are you doing?"

A laugh bubbled out of him; it sounded unhinged even to himself. "I guess you're too good to resort to something like this. But I'm not."

Every dead fairy in the birch wood limped, shuffled, and dragged their way toward the Huntsman. Something moved under Tristan's feet, and he stepped aside obligingly so that the woman could tug her skirt free. Whatever it had looked like before, now it was mostly the color of the earth she'd lain in. She had retained a lot of her skin and hair, but her rib cage was exposed where some of the flesh had rotted away, plus her jawbone and one eye socket. She made a motion like she wanted to tuck her long hair behind her pointed ear, only the ear was missing, so it fell back down into her face. The moonlight washed her out, but he thought her hair was gold; he thought in life she must have been almost as beautiful as Princess Narra. In a way, she still was.

Beor took a step back, his teeth bared in a grimace of utmost disgust. Tristan touched her shoulder, where the dress was intact, not daring to make contact with her skin.

"Thank you," he whispered to her. "He's all yours."

She wandered forward, the train of her dress hissing over the ground. Beor produced a dagger from god knew where and stabbed her, but this did nothing except get him close enough for her to reach out and stroke his cheek. He caught his breath in what was *almost* a gasp, only he swallowed it, dug his heels in, and shoved her away so forcefully she slammed into a tree and almost shattered into pieces right there. A bit of her might have actually fallen off—her other ear, that was unfortunate. But she picked herself back up and swayed in Beor's direction as if inviting him to dance.

"Do you know," Beor growled, "how difficult it is to make these things stay down once you've made them get up?"

"You should've thought of that before," Tristan said. His voice was hoarse, too, but it didn't make him sound growly. It made him sound like he had laryngitis.

He still had a loose grip on his small army of spirits, so he brought them back now. They were barely silhouettes at this point, unrecognizable as people, but they distracted Beor's hounds with their cold, dragging touches. It was a weak distraction, maybe, but it worked on at least some of the hounds. The vessels didn't bother with the hounds at all; the hounds weren't really alive, so they had nothing the vessels wanted. The hounds that tried to attack the vessels had no better luck killing them than Beor had. The vessels would lose limbs and just keep going. Others flew right over the hounds, their wings still working even with holes in them.

It was those, the winged ones, who were the first to reach Beor. One—two—three of them fell upon him. The touch of a vessel was an agonizing, leeching cold, a sense of something being pulled out of you; when Tristan had felt it, it had come from a single gray hand on his wrist, and even that much had been unbearable. The vessels had their hands all over Beor, grasping his face, his neck, pushing up his sleeves to find his skin. He roared with pain.

With the loss of Beor's concentration went the hounds' discipline. Some of them fled the graveyard; others went feral, attacking each other when the vessels slipped out of their jaws. A fourth, fifth vessel made it to Beor and took hold of him when he successfully flung the first wave off. A sixth, seventh . . .

Beor was borne down to his knees, no longer visible through the bodies crowding him. Only his shouts of rage and pain made it out of the crush. He'd get free, though. Eventually.

But Tristan would be long gone by then.

He stumbled away. Lucky was at his side, its own wounds healing up far more rapidly than his. He leaned against it gratefully.

"You were supposed to stay with Leo," he said, and Lucky made a scornful noise through its bloody teeth. They went back to where he'd left Hazel and Lupa. She could sneak away now, when Beor wasn't looking, and Tristan would be free to catch up with Leo and Aziza.

"Hazel!" he hissed.

There was no response.

He peered into Lupa's senses and swore aloud when it confirmed what he'd guessed—they were no longer in their hiding place. Lupa

was racing through the woods, making a circuit around the graveyard and past the ballroom, which was abandoned but for a handful of Gallowglass. Its eyes were fixed upward, in pursuit of a slim
green shape that fluttered her way through the canopy overhead,
going slow, and in starts and stops, to avoid detection.

Hazel was on her way to the castle. She was going after Leo.

CHAPTER 35

AZIZA

IN HER CLUMSY trap spell made of blood, rainwater, and blackthorn, Prince Tal was incandescent with rage. One hand pressed flat against the air, where her magic pushed back. The other arm was wrapped around his chest. Blood had dried under his nose, on his lips. The magical pox mottled his skin and antlers. If he'd been in better shape, she had no doubt he would've already pushed through her spell, the way Beor had. Would it hold long enough for her to catch up with Leo? She got to her feet, wincing at the stab wound in her thigh—she didn't think it was deep, but it hurt like hell. The pooka reclaimed its perch on her shoulder and slithered under her hair again, draping itself across the nape of her neck.

"Let me out," Tal demanded.

"What'll happen to me if I do that?"

"What will happen if you *don't*?" he hissed. "Raising your hand against me—setting your beast on me—you think you will leave the Summer Court alive after this? You should be begging me to ask my father to spare your life. My mercy is your only hope for salvation."

"Your father?" she repeated, unable to hide her revulsion. That he had the gall to invoke the king after what he'd done was shocking, even for one of the Folk. "Are you really that drunk or has the jade rot gotten to you? Your father's dead, Tal. You had him killed."

He stared at her, blank-faced. "To even suggest such a thing is treason."

"I'm not suggesting anything. Look around!" She gestured expansively at the cramped hallway with its peeling paint and torn paneling, which no longer bore any resemblance to the castle it had been.

Tal did as he was told and looked around, squinting, as if it hadn't occurred to him to do it before. The hand on his chest seized, clenching and unclenching.

"My father," he said, "is gone? No, you . . . you are mistaken."

Her heart sank. Fairies couldn't lie. If he said she'd made a mistake, then he honestly believed she had.

"He was shot at the revel earlier," she said. "We thought . . . you wanted to be king."

His hand lifted and came down hard, and she flinched back, forgetting he couldn't strike her. His arm jolted when his palm connected with the boundary line of the trap spell, though it made no sound.

"Let me out," he rasped. "I'll cut her throat for this."

Before she could respond, someone stepped into view from around the corner. Tal turned around, following her gaze. It was one of the Gallowglass, but his distinctive helmet was missing, so she didn't recognize him right away. He had two eyes on each side of his face, black and glistening. Tal's shoulders stiffened. He whirled around to face her again.

"Let me *out*," he said, his voice shaking with an emotion she slowly identified as fear.

It was the spider-fang warrior. Viren. Tal's second-in-command, who should have been here to help him, but then why did Tal seem so desperate to get away? Viren nocked an arrow, drew it back, aimed—Aziza reacted instinctively, sweeping the edge of the circle with her foot and breaking the trap spell—but it was too late. The twang of a bowstring, the whistle of the arrow in flight, and then a soft sound of impact as the arrow struck Tal in the back. He looked down at where it poked through his chest, touched it and the wound softly, in confusion. His fingers came away red.

Viren didn't even spare her a glance before he made an about-face and left.

The prince sank to his knees.

"No—" she said, following him to the ground. "Hold on!"

But he couldn't hold on; he didn't have Beor's resistance to silver-tipped arrows, which had saved him from the instant death the king had suffered. The bolt had pierced clean through Tal's body, corroding his flesh and leaving a wound that bled heavily. Bled all over her, as he sagged against her, still surrounded by the broken trap spell.

His mouth moved around words he no longer had the breath to speak. He listed sideways, fell on his shoulder with a final wheezing exhale, and was still.

She sat motionless, staring at him, trying to breathe. She had never killed one of the fae before. Not even a kelpie. Maybe she hadn't dealt the finishing blow, but it was her fault that he had been unable to fight back or run away.

Viren had killed two members of the royal family. If Tal wasn't pulling the strings, that left two options: someone outside the Summer Court, or . . .

She followed Viren, limping around Tal's body, and had made it about halfway down the next hall when she felt a tug on the bond. Relief came in a flood. She hadn't realized how worried she'd been about him, even when she wasn't actively thinking about it; she hadn't realized how numb and empty she had started to feel, the image of Tal's lifeless body tattooed on the inside of her eyelids, until Tristan walked out of the shadows with a hound at his side.

Tristan opened his mouth, got a good look at her, and stopped.

"You're bleeding," he said. "Are you—"

"*You're* bleeding. Is that a bite mark?"

They fell into step; he offered her a supporting arm, and she leaned on it. And if they were both quietly grateful for an excuse to hold on to each other for a little while, no one else ever had to know about that.

"Yeah," he said, "but this time it's not from one of *my* hounds, which is a nice change of pace. Where's Leo?"

"Went to find Narra." Uneasily, she added, "Didn't you send a hound with him?"

"*This* hound," he said, jerking his head at the hound in question, "made an executive decision without my input and came to get me out of a bind. It can't track by scent as easily in Elphame, so if we want to find him, we're going to have to do it the old-fashioned way."

She nodded grimly. "We're looking for an east tower. I think we got everything wrong."

They moved as quickly as they could, but she knew in her heart that they were already too late.

CHAPTER 36

LEO

Footsteps banged up the stairs, which were far narrower now, and just a rickety ten steps up to the tower room—the attic. Viren appeared in the doorway at almost the exact same time Hazel alighted clumsily on the windowsill, spilling into the room.

Princess Narra took her hand gently and helped her to her feet.

"Th-thank you," she stuttered, gazing up at her with starry eyes. Viren made a beeline to the princess, and then Hazel looked past him and saw Leo. The horror on her face made his heart sink. She tried to run to him, but Narra's grip on her hand was like a tether, tugging her back. She barely seemed to notice. Tears streamed down her face. "What happened to you?" she said, voice wobbly.

"It's okay!" He managed a smile—it felt as cracked and disused as the mirror the nymphs had left him with, but it was there. If anything, that made Hazel cry harder, so he abandoned smiling as a lost cause for now—maybe it would go over better if he put on an eye patch first—and casually picked up the sword from where he'd dropped it. "I'm fine! *Totally* fine!"

"But your face is—"

"I know, but it's okay. I swear. How did you know I was here?"

"The . . . the wind sprites," she said, hiccupping. "They told me where you were."

"Yes, I sent them to fetch you," Narra said. "I knew you'd want to see your brother. And I have something important to tell you. About your mother. And your father."

"My father?" Hazel said, sniffling. She wiped her nose on the back of her free hand, and then looked embarrassed about it. Narra held her hand palm up in Sophia's general direction. Sophia placed a handkerchief in it, and Narra gave the handkerchief to Hazel so that she could mop herself up.

"Let her go," Leo said. "Hazel, come here. Don't listen to her."

He started toward them, but Viren angled himself so that he was standing just the slightest bit in front of Narra, who had taken Hazel's shoulders in both hands.

"Your mother was the Summer Court's foremost enchantress. Many of the illusions on the castle were first created by her, did you know that?" Narra said brightly. When Hazel shook her head, Narra went on, "It's true. And she and my father were . . . quite close. So close, in fact, that once I heard you existed, I knew that you had to be my sister."

Hazel's mouth fell open. She looked at Leo, as if for confirmation. He couldn't bring himself to respond. And his silence was all the answer she needed.

"But," Hazel said. "Then why . . ."

"Why did she take you to the human world?" Narra finished. "I imagine she meant to conceal the truth about who your father was. To protect you, she wanted you to be able to lie. Princesses tend to get themselves into all kinds of trouble. It's much more dangerous nowadays to make the switch with a human child, of course, but

Lady Thula felt it was worth the risk. She didn't tell Father. He would never have allowed it."

"So the king was my dad, and he's . . . gone," Hazel said, in a small voice.

"She's leaving out the part where she's the one who killed him," Leo snapped. "Her and Viren."

Hazel jerked away from Narra, backing up, but she bumped into Sophia, whose hands clamped down on Hazel's arms. Narra looked at her with all the sympathy she'd have shown a squeaking mouse. "I had to."

"Why?" Leo asked, to get Narra's attention back on him.

"He wouldn't let me go," Narra said. She stood with the flask, holding it wrapped in a cloth so she wouldn't touch the silver part. "With my father or brother as king, even if I tried to leave, I would have been hunted down. But I *must* leave. A greater destiny awaits me."

"So leave," Leo said.

"Without a monarch to complete the summer rites, the jade rot will destroy me. Do you see my predicament? As queen, I am trapped. As a subject of my father or brother, I am trapped. The only way out is to give the crown to someone who will not keep me here. If you drink this," she said, turning to Hazel and lifting the flask, "you'll be queen. You'll have anything you want for the rest of your life, and people to take care of you, and everyone will want to be your friend. You can even go and see your brother in the human realm if you want, sometimes. Take it, and this will all be over."

And suddenly every eye in the room was trained on Hazel, all four-foot-nine of her in her poofy cake-topper dress and her hair in desperate need of a brush and that one particular pout of hers that signaled an impending tantrum.

His baby sister. Queen of summertime.

"Do you want to be queen?" Leo said quietly. It was the first time he'd really asked her what she wanted. He had been so sure he knew what was best for her. He had thrown himself into all of this because he was convinced she still needed him—no, because *he* had needed her to need him. He couldn't save her, though, and he couldn't make her come home. He couldn't give her old life back to her.

But he could make sure she had a choice. Maybe that was the most important thing.

Hazel looked at all of them watching her expectantly. She took a deep, shuddering breath. And then, voice breaking, tears welling up in her eyes, she said, in practically a wail: "*No!*"

He had to fight a laugh. "Okay," he said. "You heard her."

"It's not up for discussion," Narra said pleasantly. "She can take the elixir, or I can force-feed it to her."

"Try it," Leo said.

The next few moments felt like they lasted forever.

Sophia kept Hazel in place; Hazel struggled ineffectually; Narra uncapped the flask. Viren nocked an arrow, and Leo lifted the sword. His only hope was that Viren's first shot would miss, and then he wouldn't have time for another.

But the amber eye showed him everything. Trails of magic wrapped around Viren's gauntlets, his bow and arrow, the quiver on his back—ropes of grainy luminosity like tiny radioactive mites—enchantments to help Viren aim. He didn't know how he knew that, but he did, and he also knew just from looking at the tip of the arrow where Viren meant it to go.

Viren took his shot, and Leo sidestepped, letting it glance off his shoulder, still protected by the silver cloak. When Viren fired the next one, Leo was crossing the attic with the sword raised; over Viren's shoulder, Hazel writhed in Sophia's grasp and Narra gripped her jaw, prying it open. Leo dodged a third arrow and brought the blade down in a powerful swing. In an expert move, Viren flipped the bow horizontal and caught the edge of the blade on it. The sword almost cut the bow in half, but it held on. But Leo kept going, bearing down, throwing all his weight against the place where their weapons connected and into Viren's chest. He knocked Viren back, and Viren practically fell into Narra, who stumbled—and the flask slid out of her hand and spilled its contents onto the grimy floorboards.

For one long second, everything stopped.

Then Hazel elbowed Sophia in the gut and ran behind Leo, who backed away from Viren with the sword held up defensively. Sophia was frozen with her hands over her mouth. Viren straightened and turned to Leo with murder in his eyes.

"You've doomed the Summer Court and everyone in it," Narra said, with a sort of detached surprise, like he was a dog that had done a trick she didn't remember teaching him.

"I'll kill you," Viren snarled, but Narra flung out her hand in a quelling gesture.

"We're going," she said. "Now."

Downstairs, rapid footsteps neared the attic. If Narra had called for reinforcements, Leo was finished.

"The . . . the jade rot," Sophia said.

Narra took a deep breath. "Thorne will help us."

Leo filed that away—*thorn*, like a plant, or . . . like a person?

Narra's hands moved as if to draw the shape of something in the air, but loosely, in broad strokes. A winged horse shimmered into view. It looked real to his human sight, its nostrils flaring as it snorted, and its muscles flexed as it stomped restlessly. But his truesight told him it was just an illusion made out of moonlight and dust.

Only, something was wrong with it.

"Sophia," he said. "Back away. *Slowly.*"

In the magic that had stitched a semblance of life into the winged steed, black spots showed up like poison eating away at it. Narra didn't look sick yet, but her magic was sick. Her illusion had sharp teeth, awkward in its mouth, poorly shaped and sticking out past its lips. Narra wasn't paying attention; Viren was giving her a boost onto its back. But its rolling eyes found Sophia, who was white-faced and immobilized with fear. Before Leo could say another word, it lashed out and bit Sophia in the juncture between neck and shoulder. Blood sprayed from the wound, and Sophia screamed, a horrible, wrenching scream that Leo felt as if it had come from his own lungs.

"Don't look," he told Hazel, shielding her from the sight. She threw her arms around him, burying her face in his shoulder and sobbing.

The footsteps were on the stairs now. There were voices—

"Leave her," Narra said, and Viren swung onto the horse behind her without a backward glance at Sophia. They leapt out the window as Sophia slid to the ground, gasping, her hands covered in blood where they touched the wound in shock. It had taken a chunk of flesh out of her. She wasn't going to make it. Already her eyes were going glassy.

The first one to burst into the room was the hound, and Leo's heart lifted. It was Aziza and Tristan. But he avoided their eyes, so that he wouldn't have to see the looks on their faces when they caught sight of him. The hound rushed to the window, baying furiously, but Narra and Viren were gone.

IT WAS EASIER to get out of the house than it had been to get in. The Gallowglass that Leo had cut down earlier lay in the stairs and down on the landing. The other fairies had fled to some sheltered recess of the castle. They couldn't find the way to the basement; he prayed Evan had gotten the servants out, and that they'd run into each other outside.

But the only person waiting for them was Beor. He looked like someone had driven a tractor over him and then reversed two or three times. Hazel inched closer to Leo.

"You made it out," Tristan said, sounding a little—embarrassed?

"Of course I did." His voice was a wreck, too, like he'd swallowed a mouthful of coal. "Your childish outburst did nothing but give me a mess to clean up."

"Were you working with Narra the whole time?" Tristan asked.

"No," Leo said. "He wasn't. Narra told me so."

"I would never have betrayed the king," Beor confirmed, bitterly. "But once he was gone and I realized what the princess intended to do, there was no choice but to let her follow through with it. But of course you wouldn't cooperate, and now the Summer Court is ruined. Look at what has become of it."

Hazel turned while the rest of them hesitated. When she gasped, Leo's curiosity got the better of him.

The house was gone. There was nothing there but empty space.

"What . . ." he said.

"It came untethered," Beor said. "The house and its illusions were connected to the Summer Court. It will wander Elphame, spreading its corruption. The Folk will be pulled along with it, growing more and more sick by the day. The lower courts will war for the chance to become the new Summer Court. And without the Court of the

Seasons in balance, summer will never come to Elphame. Soon even the human realm will feel the consequences."

"All right. How do we fix it?" Leo said, though he felt dead on his feet and didn't think himself capable of fixing anything at all.

"You can't. But *she* can." He addressed Hazel. "Because the solstice ceremony remains incomplete, you never became a part of the Summer Court, and the jade rot will not grow within you. Like a fairy of the lower courts, you cannot catch it unless it enters your bloodstream. If we go to Queen Ceresia, she can aid us. But *you* are the heir; you are the one with the best chance of setting things right."

"No," Leo said. "Hazel's not the heir anymore. She refused."

"I . . . I want to go."

"But you said—"

"I *don't* want to be queen, but I want to save the Summer Court," she said. "And learn magic. Maybe someone else can be king or queen. Right?" she asked Beor.

Beor remained impassive. "It will be up to you and Queen Ceresia to make that decision."

"My friends are in there," Hazel said.

And the servants, Leo realized, his heart sinking. He'd hoped Evan, May, and the others had gotten out, but since they weren't here, they must not have had a chance to escape before the castle had vanished. If his true love really was among them, like he suspected, then that meant they were trapped with the rest. But sending Hazel to the Winter Court with Beor was not a solution he was okay with.

"But—aren't you sick, too?" he asked Beor.

"Because of my human blood and my summoning gift, the disease will move through me more slowly," Beor said. "I have more time than the others before I succumb."

Leo wanted so badly to refuse. But he had just promised himself that he would let Hazel make her own choices.

Don't you dare cry in front of her, he told himself sternly.

"You sure you can live without pumpkin spice lattes and Benedict Cumberbatch?" he asked skeptically, and grinned when she made a face at him.

"Shut up. Next time you see me, I'll be able to make illusions and you'll still be studying for math finals," she said. The way the two of them pretended at each other that everything was fine, with about equivalent levels of success, no one could say they weren't family. It struck him then: According to whatever laws governed Elphame, they *were* siblings. The nymphs considered him a Prince of the Seasons. Magic didn't care about blood; he was, and always would be, Hazel's brother, no matter where she went.

"If you need something, send a wind sprite," he told her. "We'll be there."

"Or use the hound to get my attention," Tristan added. It appeared at Hazel's side, on cue. "Lupa will look out for you."

Hazel took a shaky breath and curled her fingers into Lupa's fur.

They didn't hang around long after that; Beor couldn't afford to waste time, and none of them wanted to linger in the birch wood, which now felt eerie and desolate. Leo unstrapped the scabbard that held the silver sword, lifted it over his shoulder, and passed it to Beor. He was glad to be rid of it.

Hazel hesitated before following the Huntsman into the woods. She took a few steps, turned back, and flung herself into Leo's arms, sniffling.

He couldn't stop himself from saying, "Are you *sure*?"

"Just because I'm crying doesn't mean I can't do it," she said huffily, getting snot all over his shirt.

"Okay, okay."

"Will you . . . tell Mom and Dad, uh, that I . . ." She faltered, blinking out a few more tears. "I don't know. Tell them whatever will make them feel better."

What about, 'I miss you'? he wanted to ask. *Or, 'I love you, and I'll see you soon.'*

But one of those things would make them feel worse. One of them they'd prefer to hear from Hazel. And one of them might be a lie.

"Don't worry," he said. "I'll think of something."

He didn't move until Hazel had disappeared from view, and maybe a little while after that, and Aziza and Tristan didn't make him.

THE POOKA GOT them to the nearest boundary and through a fairy door, which put them in Vermont. It was dawn by then. They couldn't take a sentient shapeshifting car into traffic, so they were stuck using public transportation from there.

It was lucky he and Aziza had grabbed their stuff earlier; they had money for tickets and a vending machine breakfast. Leo tied a strip of cloth around his head to cover the amber eye, but that did nothing to make them less conspicuous; they looked like they'd just come out of a brawl at a Renaissance Faire. People gave them *looks*. Aziza glared at them as if daring them to open their mouths. They tried not to get blood on the seats.

On the bus to the nearest Amtrak station—a few hours away—they sat side by side on the bench in the back. At one point, Aziza fell asleep on his shoulder. Later, Tristan did. At the train station, waiting for the next trip to Boston, they washed most of the blood off in the bathroom, but it was still a miracle no one called the cops on them. Tristan said he hadn't looked this homeless even when he was actually homeless. Aziza was apparently too tired to summon the energy to talk. She kept having to remind the pooka to hide in the backpack because mice, raccoons, snakes, cats, crows, foxes, and—*yes, that too*—were not allowed on trains.

Then it was something like a ten-hour train ride, and from there they'd have to take another bus to get to Blackthorn. Aziza and Tristan managed to get some more sleep. Tristan said that Leo should try and rest, too. So he tried, for Tristan. He might've even managed to pretend convincingly. But he was wide awake the whole time.

CHAPTER 37

TRISTAN

THE WAY IT worked out, it was evening when they finally made it back home. Leo thought he should talk to his parents alone, so Tristan went upstairs and took a much-needed shower, and was ashamed at how thankful he was that the running water meant he couldn't hear Maria or Greg cry. When he came out, the whole house was deathly quiet. He waited another hour before he ventured downstairs to the kitchen for a glass of water, and by the time he realized Maria was there at the table, it was too late; she'd seen him. Her hands were cupped around a coffee mug, and her eyes were dry.

"Hello," he signed awkwardly, and then wanted to stick his head into the nearest cabinet and slam the door. Her daughter wasn't coming back and her son had lost an eye, and the best he could come up with was *hello*?

Maria could hear him—he could have just spoken aloud. But Leo and Hazel usually signed with her, and Tristan had picked up the habit from them years ago. He'd needed the practice, anyway, since he had been learning at an older age than they had.

A few days after Tristan had moved into the Merritt household, he had automatically signed back to Maria, and Leo—who had been the one to teach him in the first place—had excitedly asked him where he'd learned. Tristan had had to come up with a stammering excuse on the spot. Of all the lies he'd told Leo because of the curse, that one had been among the most difficult to force out.

"Sit," Maria signed, and got up to pour him a mug of chai. He hesitated—they hadn't talked one-on-one since he'd moved in—but could he really refuse her anything, right now? He sat, accepting the mug, and stared at it as she took her seat again. But then it occurred to him that he was being rude—not looking at someone who signed was like giving her the cold shoulder, wasn't it? He glanced up to find her looking at him with a warmth that surprised him.

"You're so tall now," she signed, her hand going above her head as if measuring him.

He nodded, unsure how to respond to that, and finally ended up saying what he'd been holding back for months: "I'm sorry."

The windows were black. The only sound was the AC switching on.

"What for?" she signed, and he didn't know what. Everything. He was sorry that Hazel wasn't here, and that he hadn't been able to help Leo get her back, and also that he hadn't stopped Leo from trying in the first place. He was sorry for leaving, a week ago and also two years ago, or maybe sorry for daring to come back. He wasn't sorry he was Leo's true love, but he *was* sorry he had anything to do with the curse, with the headaches Leo got when he thought too hard about it, and with his eyes glazing over when something reminded him. He was sorry for the things he'd done for the hag, though Maria didn't know about that and never would, because he didn't think he'd ever be able to speak of it to anyone but Leo and Aziza.

Finally, he shrugged and signed, "I'm sorry we made you worry." Right hand tapping against his left palm. "Again."

She touched the back of his hand briefly. "I don't want to lose any more children."

"I know," he signed. He didn't want to think about how she and Greg must have felt all week, with both their children gone and no way of knowing if they'd come back. But since now seemed like a good time for apologies in general, he continued: "And I'm sorry for imposing. I promise I'll move out as soon as I can."

Promise was made with the sign for *one*, starting with a touch at his chin and then brought down flat against his other fist. It was one of the signs Leo had taught him personally when Tristan had first started learning, not one he'd picked up elsewhere later, so it came with a memory of a thirteen-year-old Leo beaming at him as they sat on his bedroom floor, trading it back and forth: *I promise. I promise. I promise.*

Maria sighed, and for a half second he thought she was going to set a deadline, tell him when she expected him gone. He was already mentally calculating whether he had enough money for a deposit and a month or two of rent, and wondering how much time she'd give him to leave—so he almost missed what she said next.

"I just told you I don't want to lose any more children." She waited until she was sure he had understood. He could only gape at her. "Stay as long as you want to. You are not imposing. Ever."

"But . . ." he said, aloud.

"Is that why you told Greg you don't want to go to college?" she asked, her hands flying through the signs as worry made her impatient. "You think you need to save up and leave?"

"I mean, I—partly, I guess," he said. "I don't know what I'd even study. Or if it's worth it when I could just work."

"You don't have to worry about money as long as we're around. If you want to go to college, we will help you," she signed, fist against her palm, resolute.

This conversation was starting to feel surreal. Everything about today felt surreal.

"I'll think about it," he said, switching back to ASL.

"I saved some of your things," she signed. He frowned, wondering what that could mean—had he left some textbooks or a change of clothes at their place? And she'd bothered to keep them all this time? "I was waiting for the right time to give them to you, but you've been so quiet. I don't know what you went through. I thought you didn't want to talk."

He swallowed hard. "I thought you'd be angry with me because of . . ."

He couldn't say *because of me and Leo*. Part of him still felt, nonsensically, that maybe she somehow didn't *know* about him and Leo, and that was the only reason he was still allowed in her house.

After a moment's hesitation, she stood. "Wait here."

He waited as she left and came back downstairs with a cardboard box, which she deposited on the table beside him.

Opening it, he inhaled sharply. All of his old sketchbooks going back to middle school were in there. He'd always assumed they'd been thrown away. It was the only material possession he'd truly regretted losing when his parents had kicked him out. He picked up the one on the top of the stack and flipped open the cover, needing to check. Definitely his. This one was from sophomore year—the most recent, and not even half full.

"Where did you find these?" he asked aloud, and it was only then that he realized how tight his throat had gotten.

"Broke into your locker," Maria signed, unabashed. "After hours, when the school was closed. Terrible security. I should have complained."

When she grinned like that, the resemblance between her and Leo was painfully clear.

"But," he said. "Why?"

There were many different questions contained in that *why*, and Maria heard at least a few of them. Her smile faded.

"You stopped coming over," she signed. "After Leo's birthday."

Tristan's heart gave a jerk, like it had seized, as terror shot through him. It was irrational, but he couldn't help it.

She had started to sign something else, saw the look on his face, and stopped. Her fingers brushed the back of his hand, where he still held the sketchbook so tightly the edge was starting to bend.

"What?" she signed, palms open in front of her, head tilted in confusion.

He took a breath, reminded himself that Maria was *not* his mother, and that this was a good thing, and shook his head.

"When did you figure it out?" He expected her to say she'd asked after him, and when Leo didn't remember who he was, that was what had tipped her off. He used to lose sleep imagining how they must have reacted, how upset they must have been, how—

"We always knew it was you," she signed. *Always* was a wide circle drawn in the air, decisive, unhesitating. "From the first time Leo brought you over. You were so cute—so quiet and polite, all skinny with those big green eyes. My poor son didn't know what to do with himself."

Tristan was speechless for a long moment. *He* certainly didn't remember it like that.

"You knew the entire time we were together?" he asked finally, mortified, and in disbelief. All those times they'd let him stay the night, had him over for dinner, gave him a hug and said to be careful biking home . . . when Greg had told him how proud he was after Tristan had aced his finals, and Maria had fussily straightened his collar and stroked his hair out of his eyes before he and Leo left for school in the morning . . . every single time, they'd known?

"We didn't know everything, but we knew how Leo felt. You two thought you were so sneaky." Her lips twitched with clear amusement. "He might as well have put it on a billboard. We couldn't have missed it if we'd tried."

His face felt so hot it was a miracle steam wasn't coming off him.

"So I stopped coming over, and then?" he asked, hurriedly moving on from the subject of their sneakiness or lack thereof.

Slowly at first, and then more assuredly, she signed, "We thought you needed time, and that eventually you would come back on your own. After a couple of weeks, we tried to call. You never picked up, so we knew something was wrong."

He had taken his phone with him when he'd left his parents' house for the last time, but since he'd had no one he needed to call anymore, he'd sold it on the street.

"We learned you had dropped out," Maria was saying. "We watched your parents' house until we were sure you didn't live there anymore. We reported them, but nothing happened, and you never came back."

His parents were very good at getting their way. They had probably had a story prepared for that exact situation. Idly, he wondered what it was. That they'd sent him to stay with distant relatives? That he'd run away? Maybe they'd even reported him missing themselves. His mother could've wept about it to her book club friends and been the center of attention for days, maybe even *weeks*.

"We drove around looking for you. But it was like you'd disappeared. We should have called sooner. We thought you wouldn't want to hear from us, that it would be painful." She made a closed fist and rotated it in a circle over her chest, the sign for *regret* or *sorry*, which was another surprise in a conversation full of them, because he didn't think a parent had ever apologized to him in his life, for anything. There was a faint, uncertain quiver in her hands as she added, "We missed you. The next time something happens, you come straight home. Okay?"

He put down the sketchbook and lifted his hands to say *thank you* or maybe *I don't deserve this* or maybe even *I missed you too*, but he couldn't make himself form the right signs. Finally, he said, "Okay."

They finished their chai in silence. He rinsed off both their mugs and put them in the dishwasher. Then he said good night and picked up the box.

"Good night," Maria signed, and then pointed at the wounds on his arms, the one from Beor's hound and the other from when his own hound had bitten him during the Hunt, both of which he'd bandaged earlier. "Take the painkillers from the kitchen drawer if you need them."

He was all the way upstairs, setting the box of sketchbooks down on the dresser in the guest room, before he realized how much lighter he felt.

The bottle of painkillers rattled as he turned it over in his hand. Leo was alone right now, but Tristan knew very well that Leo was not the kind of person who liked to be alone when something was wrong. If there was ever a time when he needed Tristan more than Tristan needed him, it was now.

He slipped out into the hall. The last time he had showed up at Leo's door, it had been for himself. Because *he* wanted Leo back. Because he wanted the way they used to be. This time, he was here for Leo, and if all Leo wanted from him was the painkillers and a "good night," then that was fine.

He rapped on the door with his knuckles, lightly, so that Leo could sleep through it—or pretend he had. But the door swung open. Leo's hair was damp from his shower, and he'd changed into a sweater it was nowhere near cold enough to be wearing, which was what he did when he needed to be touched but didn't want to ask for it. Tristan's chest hurt.

"Hey," Leo said, with an empty smile. "I was about to text you. How's your arm?"

"Fine." He passed over the painkillers. "I brought you these. Just in case."

"Thanks. Maybe they'll knock me out."

It wasn't lost on him that Leo had kept his face angled slightly away from Tristan, and wasn't quite meeting his eyes. It was so staggeringly wrong for Leo to think he needed to hide anything about himself from Tristan that—instead of giving in to his most cowardly impulses and retreating—he said, "Are you actually going to take them, or are you just saying that? Like when you said you'd sleep on the train?"

Leo's tight smile relaxed into something more genuine.

"Tris, please," he said, flinging a hand over his heart as if mortally wounded. "No calling me out on my bullshit for three business days per traumatic event."

Tristan looked up contemplatively. "Is that in the Coven Black-thorn code of conduct?"

"It will be if I can sneak it past Aziza. Otherwise it's going in the roommate agreement."

"Are we roommates if we're not sharing a room?" Tristan asked, very innocently and not at all as if he wanted Leo to picture him making himself at home in Leo's bedroom.

"Uh . . . housemates?" Leo corrected himself, voice failing, turning it into a question.

Because Tristan was an opportunistic piece of shit—and if he'd ever had any shame to begin with, he'd taken it into a back alley and shot it a long time ago—he took a step closer. Tristan had maybe a few centimeters on Leo in height; it usually didn't matter, because Leo was broader and had an athlete's build and the kind of magnetic presence that made everyone in a given room want to look at him, where Tristan was adept at fading into the background. But every now and then, it made all the difference in the world.

"What else should I do?" Tristan said. "To be a good roommate?"

Leo must have forgotten that he was self-conscious about the amber eye, because he had turned the full, considerable force of his gaze on Tristan, who felt a little like he was staring down a wight, if an earth-shatteringly attractive one, something that wanted to take him apart piece by piece and had the means to do it.

But then he laughed—a warm, quiet sound that made Tristan want to crawl inside it and curl up like an affection-starved cat—and said, "You're perfect, Tris. You don't have to do anything."

This was how it always was—Leo disarming him with a word,

or a look, so thoroughly it was as if Tristan had never had any defenses at all.

"Forget the painkillers," Tristan said, spurred into honesty. "I just wanted an excuse to come see you."

That was the right thing to say, he thought, because Leo looked pleased about it.

"Earlier, I wanted to thank you," Leo said. "For taking Hazel someplace safe. Fighting Beor, again, to protect her. We couldn't have gotten through this without you."

"Don't thank me. Just tell me what you need right now," Tristan said. "Do you want me to leave you alone? Because I don't think you do."

He knew he was crossing a line, and that if Leo slammed the door in his face, it would be no less than what he deserved. He also knew that Leo *wouldn't*.

Leo started to say something and faltered. His curls fell into his face, not quite long enough to conceal the amber eye. The light from his room lovingly traced the line of his jaw, his neck, his shoulders. He looked every bit a prince of summer itself, striking and brilliant.

"I can't . . ." he tried, and then, as if he was convincing himself at the same time, "I can't ask you to—"

"You can ask me for whatever you want," Tristan said, and there it was, the savage truth concealed within their friendship like an animal in a cage in a safe under a trap door, dragged out into the light for Leo to see in all its terrible ferocity.

"I don't want to lose you," Leo said. A confession.

"You won't," Tristan told him. "You couldn't. I promise."

He looked away, hiding the amber eye again, and Tristan couldn't tolerate that any longer. He took Leo's face in his hands so that their eyes met squarely. The scarring looked old, healed up, as if it had happened months ago. Tristan touched it gently, just with his finger-tips, and Leo flinched. "Does it hurt?"

"No, it's just . . . kind of gruesome?" Leo said, with a false laugh.

"It's not. Is it insensitive if I say it's kind of beautiful?"

Leo went red, down into his collar and probably on the back of his neck, too. His gaze turned intent as he studied Tristan in return.

"Fairy magic is all . . . restless and bright, like sparks. Yours is more like a glow," he said. "*You're* beautiful, Tris."

His hands had come up to cover Tristan's, lacing their fingers together; now it felt less like he was holding Leo in place and more like the other way around.

"Ask me," Tristan said.

"I . . . I fucked up, and I can't stop thinking about it," Leo said. "I don't think I could sleep if I tried. I'm afraid to lie down in the dark and just be—be alone with it all."

"Then let me help," Tristan said.

With this final push, something in Leo snapped, and then he was dragging Tristan into a harsh kiss. It was fast and desperate from the get-go, openmouthed and clinging, a kiss that Tristan felt through his whole body, in every nerve ending, a kiss that was a question and an answer. With his eyes closed, Tristan could shut out every-thing in the world that wasn't Leo's heartbeat against his chest, Leo's skin fever-hot under his hands, Leo's restless grip sliding from his hair to the back of his neck to his waist, anything to get closer. He thought he tasted blood, like one of them had nicked his lip on the other's teeth, but he couldn't have said who and didn't care. This time, it was Leo who walked them into his room, and when they were over the threshold pulled away from him with a gasp, a filthy wet sound as their mouths broke apart—"Please stay," Leo said, as if the space between them was a well where he could drown his secrets.

Tristan dragged the door shut behind them, locking it.

They didn't have to talk about it. It didn't have to mean anything. All that mattered to Tristan was making sure Leo didn't have time to think about anything tonight aside from him.

CHAPTER 38

AZIZA

SNEAKING INTO THE house was out of the question. Her bedroom window was on the second floor, and there were no decent footholds, so even with two working hands and no busted leg, she wouldn't have been able to make the climb. It wasn't late enough for Jiddo to be asleep. Still, she had expected to return to a house as silent as the one she'd left. Maybe the sound of news on the TV, no lights on except the one table lamp in the living room.

But when she opened the door, the hall light was on; so was the kitchen light, spilling into the entryway. The voices in the living room weren't coming from the TV—there was someone there, with Jiddo. He *never* had people over.

She froze, but it was too late. The voices had cut off abruptly when she'd shut the door behind her, though she'd tried her best to do it without making a sound. And then Jiddo called, with painful hope, "Aziza? Is that you?"

"Yes," she said, hoarsely. There was nothing for it. She set her backpack down and walked into the living room as if to the gallows. Silences came in many varieties, and the silence that ensued when she made her entrance had a distinct undercurrent of horror. She looked like if you said her name three times in a mirror, she'd pop out from behind your shower curtain to scare the crap out of you, in her tattered, bloodstained dress, with a dormouse huddled on her shoulder where its tiny face peeked out through her tangles of filthy hair, and her eyes puffy from sleeping in fits and starts on trains and buses.

Jiddo shot to his feet, got across the room faster than she had ever seen him move, and gathered her up in his arms, squeezing her tightly. He smelled like herbal tea and aftershave. She wanted to fall asleep right there, standing up with her face pressed against his shoulder.

Someone gave a long, low whistle, as if surveying the wreckage in the aftermath of an earthquake. But the only magnitude-level-nine disaster in this room was Aziza.

She pulled away. The person who'd whistled was a college-aged girl, slouched in the seat nearest to the entrance. An older woman had claimed the chair next to Jiddo's. Not slouching. She carried herself with a prima ballerina's combination of elegance and authority. Tall, with perfect posture, dark brown skin, and gray hair scraped back from a severe face. Her shrewd, assessing eyes surveyed Aziza as if comparing the real thing to a picture she'd seen once.

Before she even opened her mouth, Aziza knew who she was.

"I'm pleased to finally meet you," Anne Sterling said. "I know you're tired, but this can't wait. Please, sit down."

Jiddo was already pulling out one of the chairs from the table and moving it closer to the others. He guided her to it, and she sat down automatically.

"How did you get through the wards?" she asked, mostly stalling. Aziza's mind was not working the way she wanted it to work.

What was the last thing she had said to Anne? How much had Dion told her?

"They didn't. I let them in," Jiddo said.

"*You?* But you never talk to other witches."

"Ms. Sterling told me she knew where you were."

"*I* told you where I was going," she said, affronted.

"You left a note and said you'd be in Elphame!" He rubbed a hand over his eyes, as if he had completely failed to appreciate the fact that the note had represented significant forward progress in Aziza's communication skills. But she suspected that saying, *Fine! I won't leave a note next time!* would not go well for her, so she kept her mouth shut. "I can't keep doing this," Jiddo said. "Watching you run off, praying you come back home, never knowing if you will. So I'm trying something new."

She would have asked him to elaborate, but she was still adjusting to the alternate reality she'd stumbled into wherein her curmudgeonly grandfather entertained such notions as *trying new things* and allowing not one but *two* strange witches into their home. The younger one had long hair dyed a reddish color with its natural brown showing at the roots, and was wearing bulky headphones. She scooted forward, so that she was perched on the edge of the cushion, and held out a water bottle.

"You look like you need it," she said, with a sympathetic smile.

"I'm not thirsty."

Her smile bypassed sympathetic and landed squarely on mischievous. "It's not water."

"Nelle, enough," Anne said, in tones that suggested this was a frequent refrain.

"Nelle? You're Dion's—" Aziza stopped, remembering that she didn't want to talk about Dion; realized it was too late, and that cutting herself off just made her sound suspicious; and then finished, stiffly, "Dion's oracle friend."

"Yup," Nelle said. "He told us you killed the thing that got Emil."

Aziza schooled her expression into careful neutrality. Had he really said that? Was that *all* he'd said? There wasn't a safe way to respond. Even a simple nod could invite questions she had no intention of answering. Instead, she turned back to Anne. "Thank you for the trap spell. It worked better the second time I tried it. But what are you doing here?"

"I'm here because the Summer Court collapsed last night," Anne said. "And I need to know why. I am also here because *you* need training. Khaled agrees."

"You do?" she said, in disbelief.

"You haven't left me much of a choice," he said, grouchily.

"Do I get a say in this?"

His eyebrows went up. "You . . . *don't* want to learn spells?"

Of course she did, and Jiddo knew it. She had no good reason to refuse. None that she wanted to share, anyway.

"Okay. Why is Nelle here?" Then, before she could stop herself, not knowing *why* she couldn't stop herself, she asked, "And where's Dion?"

"He said that something urgent came up," Nelle said, dropping against the back of the couch, slouching so low in her seat she was practically lying down. "Kind of shady, but when's he not."

"You lied about his whereabouts for months. *You're* shady," Anne told her flatly.

"He was upset about something yesterday," Nelle said, uncapping the not-water bottle and taking the drink Aziza had refused. "But I couldn't get him to talk."

Every eye in the room turned on Aziza, as if waiting for her to volunteer her thoughts on Dion's emotional well-being, which she wouldn't do if they held her at knifepoint.

But it was fast becoming apparent to her that Dion hadn't told them the whole truth about Emil, or his suspicions about what Aziza had been hiding from him. He hadn't told them that Aziza had deceived and used him, and that she couldn't be trusted. Shame, guilt, and gratitude burned in the back of her throat. She got to her feet, suddenly needing to be alone more than she had ever needed anything else. "I'll tell you about the Summer Court, but this conversation isn't happening before I take a shower."

"Your grandfather told us that he gave you a picture," Anne said.

Aziza stopped in her tracks, only a few steps short of the doorway and her escape. "What picture?"

"Leila's coven," he said, gruffly and without meeting her eyes.

"Would you bring it here?" Anne asked, phrasing it as a polite request, though Aziza couldn't have refused without looking and feeling like a petulant child. Besides—if Anne could answer the questions Aziza had about that photo, then . . .

Without a word, she retrieved her backpack from the hall. Actually, it wasn't her backpack; it was the one they'd picked up at random during their flight through the castle. Tristan's, it turned out. She just happened to be the one carrying it when they'd arrived in Blackthorn. It contained all of their wallets and keys, a roll of bandages, a refillable water bottle they'd all shared on the journey back, the receipts from their train tickets, a couple of uneaten energy bars they'd gotten from a vending machine earlier, and the photo.

She brought it back to Anne, who leaned forward in her seat to study it.

"You were right," Anne said, quietly, to Jiddo. "That's Thorne. Right there."

Aziza's stomach lurched. Hadn't Leo said that Narra had been counting on help from "thorn"? She was sure he had.

"Who?" she asked.

"Castor Thorne." Anne tapped the image of the man who'd been captured mid-conversation with Leila. "If you answer our questions, I'll answer yours."

Aziza hesitated, and then, instead of leaving the room, she changed course and went to the kitchen. "The shower can wait. Coffee can't."

It was going to be a long night. But, under the exhaustion and the unease, a drop of excitement swelled uncertainly in her chest. Everything she had ever wanted to know about magic was here in this room. All she had to do was let herself be led into their world. And— though there was a suspicious quality to the silence on Tristan's end of the bond that told her it was best not to disturb him right now— she was certain she wouldn't be taking those first steps alone.

Methodically, she got the coffee brewing and finger-combed her hair into something approaching presentable while she waited for it to finish. When she turned to face the other witches, and their stories and their questions, and whatever revelations they had in store for her, she would be ready.

ACKNOWLEDGMENTS

I WOULD LIKE to thank my editor, Mekisha Telfer—this book has come a long way over the past couple of years, and her feedback and enthusiasm for the story have made all the difference in the world. I'm also grateful to my agent, Erica Bauman, for her continued support and guidance through all parts of the publishing process.

Endless gratitude to the amazing team at Roaring Brook Press/ Macmillan—Kathy Wielgosz, Ana Deboo, Sara Elroubi, Leigh Ann Higgins, Jennifer Healey, Nicole Wayland, Katy Miller, Celeste Cass, Raymond Ernesto Colón, Molly Ellis, Mariel Dawson, Gretchen Fredericksen, Taylor Armstrong, Jennifer Edwards, Beth Clark, Mallory Griggs, Jordan Winch, Kristin Dulaney—for turning the Word document on my computer into a real book and putting it into readers' hands. A huge thank-you in particular to designer Samira Iravani and illustrator Helen Mask for working their magic on the cover.

I am incredibly thankful for my friends in the writing community— especially Meg Long, who read the earliest coherent version of this book, not to mention countless rambling DMs about life, the universe, and everything; and my Slacker fam, who have kept me company through many hours of drafting, revising, and brainstorming approximately one billion titles (only to watch me give in and pick the first one I came up with). I'm grateful to my family for their love and support, and to my friends, both in and out of the publishing world, for saving me from being a complete shut-in.

Finally, thank you to everyone who supported *The Buried and the Bound*—all my gratitude to the booksellers, librarians, and educators; the book boxes and their subscribers; every reader who spent a moment of their time with it, and especially those of you who have returned for the sequel. I hope it takes you away, at least for a little while.